Praise for
The Worst Day of My Life, So Far

"M.A. Harper's new novel . . . hooks the reader right from the beginning. . . . It is to Harper's immense credit that she lightens the graphic and painful reality of living with a loved one with Alzheimer's with her acerbic humor. Readers who think this book will be depressing (and who wouldn't from the title?) will find themselves laughing out loud, and moved to tears. . . . *The Worst Day of My Life, So Far* only confirms Harper's immense and original talent."
—*The Times-Picayune* (New Orleans)

"A fascinating and moving piece of literature which provides an intimate portrait of a mother and a daughter, touching upon sacrifice, forgiveness, frustration, alienation, and understanding."
—*The Advocate* (Baton Rouge)

"M.A. Harper's spirited novel . . . tackles a difficult subject with wit and candor. . . . Funny, sharp and tough-minded, this will appeal especially to relatives of Alzheimer's sufferers, but deserves to be noticed by general readers as well." —*Publishers Weekly*

"[Harper] unfolds a modern-day domestic nightmare in this account of a mother's slow submersion beneath the murky waters of Alzheimer's. . . . Sentimental but not overly so: a story of real grace and power." —*Kirkus Reviews*

The
Worst
Day
of
My
Life,
So
Far

M. A. Harper

The Worst Day of My Life, So Far

my mother,
alzheimer's,
and me

a novel

A Harvest Book · Harcourt, Inc.
San Diego   New York   London

www.HarcourtBooks.com

First published by Hill Street Press in 2001

Library of Congress Cataloging-in-Publication Data
Harper, M. A., 1949–
The worst day of my life, so far: my mother,
Alzheimer's and me/M. A. Harper.
p. cm.
ISBN 0-15-600718-5
1. Alzheimer's disease—Patients—Fiction.
2. Mothers and daughters—Fiction. 3. Southern States—Fiction.
I. Title.
PS3558.A6247937 W6 2002
813'.54—dc21   2001051825

Text set in ACaslon
Designed by Anne Richmond Boston

Printed in the United States of America

First Harvest edition 2002
A C E G I K J H F D B

For the Caregivers

Contents

The
Worst
Day
of
My
Life,
So
Far

chapter 1

Auletta

First of all, let me say that I am not now, nor have I ever been, a voodoo practitioner. That allegation was one of the less attractive charges made by my ex-husband during a past custody skirmish. It is true that I did read a few palms in college, along with about two million other fellow-traveler hippies. So?

Maybe sometimes, during those later difficult years I spent caring for my mother down in Auletta, I looked the part. When I'd glimpse my reflection in the glass of my mother's garage window when I took out the garbage, I saw the face of a disgruntled crone. I'd smile at myself until the illusion went away, because it certainly was not fair that I should appear so used up from the front. After all, I had lost a lot of weight, and male drivers would honk their horns at me from the rear whenever I found enough time to walk up the highway in my cutoffs. And me in my forties.

Actually, there were no men in Auletta except the married, the stupid, and the dead. In Auletta this worked out to be basically the same thing. Old widowers in the back woods of the north shore got frog marched down the chapel aisle by the first of the women quick enough to make eye contact with one of them over potato salad at a dead wife's wake. The decent men were minimally-divorced Baptist Sunday school teachers, used car dealers, gas station owners, or high school coaches with wedding ring grooves worn into their beefy pink fingers. The indecent drank beer and ran around on their wives, although I could not imagine with whom. Big beer stomachs, tattoos, and bumper stickers reading *God, Guns, and Guts Made This Country Great* just did not attract me. A man's IQ and the number of individual gun racks in his pickup truck seemed inversely proportional. Why some fat yahoo might suppose I'd go right into heat at the sight of armpit hair sprouting between sweaty layers of adipose tissue was a mystery. I say, if you don't have actual well-defined biceps, it ought to be against the law to wear a muscle shirt.

"Hey, sweet thang," I'd hear at the bait shop when I'd stop for gas, my mother in the front seat with me complaining about the heat and wanting to know who I was talking to. "Nobody," I would say, and mean it.

Fat girls with too many curls and too few teeth snagged these princes, and acted like they'd won the lottery. Aulettans enthusiastically paired up, even though the mutual attraction seemed mysterious to a witch like me. Fat and stupid children got happily born.

We had absolutely no common ground, Auletta and I. The town had none of the sense of place and rural hospitality of nearby Pearl River, and it was smaller, uglier, and less diverse than Slidell. I saw no black people in Auletta. The jobs or amenities that might have made it worthwhile to African Americans to tolerate Auletta's ingrained KKK mentality were absent. In fact, nobody lived here voluntarily, except my mother. Aulettans proper just got born here, grew up here, dropped out of high school and got married here, and were too incurious to travel and discover just what a hell-hole this place really was.

You'd never know there was a gigantic perpetual party—the city of New Orleans—going on just south of the lake, because Auletta was a constant Fundamentalist funeral. That's all they discussed, those neighbors of my mother's: who had died; who was just about to drop dead; who was getting married to whom, so that they could have a miserable life together and then die.

No wonder I had these bags under my eyes like an old hag.

I would lie awake during those hot nights that first summer back home, trying to reason with myself and talk myself out of such energetic hostility towards my fellow man. I wasn't proud of my excessive contempt for all things Aulettan. I'd try to think things through. I'd attempt to pat myself on the back for having done The Right Thing in relocating to this pus pit. The choices I had made in regard to my parents were noble ones, I told myself. Voluntary ones. I should be proud of myself. As a matter of fact, my own sainthood should just be knocking me out in breathless admiration for myself, every day in every way. Whatta gal.

"Every day in every way, I'm getting better and better," I'd repeat that shopworn old affirmation to myself each morning before my mother could awaken and instigate the daily chaos. However, what I'd notice in the mirror as I brushed my teeth was that what I was really getting was older.

Every morning that I woke up in Auletta and realized that I had not yet poisoned her, nor put my head in the oven, I figured that I was doing okay.

That was the summer that I picked up the scissors and cut all of my hair off. It was ninety-seven degrees outside, and close to that inside my mother's humid laundry room. There were no men around worth attracting, anyway, so I might as well make myself as ugly as I felt. Lighten my load. Get rid of this blanket of heat that grew from my scalp and weighed me down. There was too much gray in it. It took me too long to get it shampooed these days, with my mother banging on the outside of the sliding glass shower door like this and calling, "Where are you? Where is everybody?"

My mother had always hated my hair.

chapter 2

The
Beautiful
Velma

I was born with my father's red hair, thick and rusty and as multi-layered as corrosion. Daddy kept his under control with Brylcreem. The waves of mine, however, knew no control. My mother said I looked like I was being perpetually electrocuted.

She spent an entire afternoon giving me a Tonette home permanent the summer I turned six. "Just hold still, and it won't get into your eyes again," she said, pouring neutralizer over my bristling tight curlers in our steamy New Orleans back yard. Chemicals were running down both sides of my face, dripping off my chin, and plopping like acid rain onto the clover between my bare toes. My eyes still stung. I closed them and cried like I was being murdered.

"Hold *still!*" my beautiful mother said as she anointed me. "I hate stinging you, punkin, I wouldn't deliberately sting you for a million dollars! But don't you want to see how pretty this is going to make your hair, Jeanne? Aren't we going to be excited over your pretty hair?"

I contemplated the outcome in the mirror that night. I had become Little Orphan Annie, except for the eyeballs. I still miraculously had some.

So my hair was not mine to style. It belonged to my mother. Hair grew out of my head, and became my mother's problem. I cared nothing about it.

But Mama more-or-less surrendered on the beauty front when the school nurse discovered that I needed glasses. My mother threw up her hands. I was seven years old, and my permanent teeth were beginning to come in—very large and very crooked. There was a big gap between my two upper incisors.

"I swear!" my mother would grab my wrists in frustration. "If I could just keep you from chewing on those fingernails, Jeanne, maybe the teeth would have some kind of chance!"

"You look real grown up in glasses," my father optimistically offered. "Real adult, Jay-jay."

Yeah, I thought. Like a midget old maid.

Nobody else in my second grade class wore glasses. Danny Ducote started calling me Four Eyes at recess, until Sister Mary Anne made him stop.

My face was filling up with freckles, too. If they had just run together, I would have had one hell of a tan. My dad's faded freckles had blended into the ruddy farm boy bloom of his face, and he was good looking. His eyes appeared attractively green by contrast. Nobody could say exactly what color my own eyes were. Nobody could really see them now, behind these thick lenses.

My mama did her best. She chose eyeglass frames for me in the latest style, shaped like a cat's eyes, in a pearl white to brighten my scleras and my teeth. Shiny silver flecks of glitter were embedded in their plastic. The heavy weight of my new glasses sank into the tender skin of my nose, and their silver flecks reinforced my zillion freckles. I was as thoroughly speckled now as the egg of some wild but unattractive bird.

"So whaddaya think?" My mother's face appeared alongside mine in the optometrist's mirror. She put an arm around my shoulders.

I think I am stunned, I realized, dazed by my misfortune. Kids like Danny Ducote were waiting for me.

But on the plus side, I could read my library books now with astonishing clarity. Their pages contained a new sharpness that began to go beyond the shapes of printed letters and on down into the melancholy depths of their texts. My favorites were classic fairy tales, like *Cinderella* and *The Ugly Duckling*. I began to really understand them.

"You might be reading a little too much these days, punkin," my mama observed. All she ever read was beauty magazines and *Better Homes And Gardens*. "Your eyes might get all squinted up, if we don't watch out."

So? I thought, discovering a sullen component to my personality.

Heredity was betraying me. I looked nothing like my beautiful mother, and I knew that nothing that she or I could ever do would change that. My little brother Rocky looked more like her than I did, but nobody expected him to be a fairy princess. Nobody cared whether or not he bit his fingernails, or had gapped teeth.

I still had reasonable hopes, though, of developing some of Mama's dash. She was heroine material. I would ponder mental images of her at her most fascinating, the way she tossed back her long pale hair to laugh, and the attentive motions of her leaning into the lighter flame held out by some gentleman to get her cigarette lit. The cigarette was a spike of glamour between the red jewels of her nails, her hair curtaining her cheeks like a movie star's. She'd let the tiny fire create a grotto of beauty in the shelter of her hair, her red lips illumined, until something the gentleman said would send the head and hair back into a laughing shiver of brilliant blonde light. The cigarette hand never moved, but would remain in place with its blue votive smoke until the lovely face rose upright again to claim it with controlled and lacquered lips. Mama listened to gentlemen like they were all presidents of the United States. Gentlemen loved Mama.

And she wasn't as hated by their wives as she might have been, because it was clear to everybody that she had eyes only for her tall redheaded husband. My mother was always luminous, but she radiated megawatts whenever my daddy came into the room. They'd make goo-goo eyes at one another. Hold hands. It would've been embarrassing, but they were so classy about it, like a couple of screen stars. Like, say, Jimmy Stewart co-starring with Barbara Stanwyck in some romantic comedy.

I practiced tossing my own hair, holding candy cigarettes in an unmoving hand between bitten fingernails. My perm would not toss. It was a single kinky mass, like a big tumor.

I pondered my memories of Mama's gallantry during our last hurricane—the cinematic way she had jollied up my little brother and me once the lights had gone out. We had been too young to be frightened but not too young to be bored by the enforced early darkness, and she had kept us entertained with ghost stories and marshmallows toasted over sterno. She had shaken out her glorious hair in the light of candles, and she had shot cap pistols with us, over the roar of the wind and rain. The storm made alarming noises, but our beautiful mother had made alarming noise right back at it with Rocky's six-shooter as she shot at the ceiling, yelling "Take that! And *that!*" in a growly voice that caused us giggle fits.

"For God's sake, Velma!" Daddy had complained over the bangs and laughter, yet smiled, as Mama shot the hell out of the hurricane for her little kids.

"I'm Annie Oakley!" she had shouted, whirling the cap pistol around one red nail. "I'm Calamity Jane! They don't make 'em like me anymore!"

No wonder Daddy loves her, I thought, remembering. No wonder he paints her toenails red for her, and lights her cigarettes for her. Mama is a heroine. She always knows what to do. She's very dashing. Very competent. Very brave, actually.

Maybe I can become competent. Or even brave.

But the April that Rocky drank the poison, I flunked both competence and bravery. I washed out.

I couldn't manage bravery. I was scared that Rocky was going to die. I was afraid that I was going to get hit by a car.

"Come *on*, for crying out loud!" was what Mama, carrying Rocky, was screaming back at me as we crossed Claiborne Avenue on foot. "Look where you're going! *Look where you're going,* Jeanne, you're gonna get hit by a car!"

And I had not been competent. Rocky was only six, two years my junior, and he had swallowed poison practically in my presence.

"Jeanne!"

I pattered after Mama in my saddle oxfords across endless asphalt, with traffic honking and swishing behind me, Claiborne Avenue becoming the widest street in the world. My mother flew ahead, sprinting in high heels and seamed nylons, my little brother in her arms in his cowboy suit, crying and maybe dying.

I cried, too, but it merited no attention. I understood that nothing I could do now, short of getting run over, would merit attention.

We had been playing cowboys again, Rocky and I. We had played cowboys together hundreds of times without mishap. Most days, between the time when we got home from school and Daddy got home from work, we played cowboys. Rocky had no friends who lived close by, and my best friend Margaret from next door wasn't always in the mood to play with dolls.

I had a ballerina doll named Nina, whose limbs I arranged in the graceful poses I knew I would never manage, since Mama had nixed any ballet lessons that might make my calf muscles too large and unfeminine.

Nina possessed marvelously jointed hips, knees, and ankles. There was nothing remotely unfeminine about her calves. She wore opaque pink tights over the long and shapely legs of an adult dancer. I dreamed of developing Nina's legs.

But the body above the doll's tutu was the flat-chested torso of a child. Nina was a toddler from the waist up, with chipmunk cheeks, stubby sausage arms, and blunt and dimpled baby hands.

I couldn't figure it out. Even the bride dolls owned by Margaret were the grotesque effigies of children—tykes in wedding veils.

I pretended that Nina was going through puberty. Maybe she would eventually develop a ballerina's thin, articulate arms and hands. Maybe she would win a swan neck and a dancer's small breasts and narrow waist, so that her upper body would finally match her lower. Maybe puberty was all that was wrong with Nina. She was going through a phase, which would pass.

Center stage awaited her at the Bolshoi. All it would take would be time.

So maybe I'm going through a phase myself, I thought, which will pass. When my body will catch up with my brain, which tries real hard to be pretty. I'm consumed by the desire to look passable.

My brother was consumed by the desire to be a cowpoke. He had a six-shooter cap pistol, a red cowboy hat, and a fringed outfit that our mother had sewn for him last Mardi Gras. We had to wear uniforms to Our Lady of Lourdes School, but that cowboy suit was what Rocky wanted to wear most of the rest of the time. Mama kept it washed and ready, and tried to mend its split seams, muttering, "Rocky, you could play Tarzan in an old pair of underpants."

He'd gotten a wooden rocking horse from Santa Claus the same Christmas I got my Nina, and it hung from springs in a metal frame. The toy gave him his nickname, because he was always chanting, "Rocky, rocky, rocky," at age two, as he rode it gently, his legs too short for his feet to reach the stirrups. But by the time he was six, he was big enough to bounce up and down on it with such ferocity that the metal frame itself began leaping into the air on each upswing. The crashes as it fell back to earth were fearful. Rocky's horse left permanent dents in the linoleum of the kitchen floor. His horsemanship drove our dad out onto the front porch on these warm spring evenings, beer in hand, radio at his elbow, and radiant wife Velma coming out to join him after the supper dishes were done. We could hear them out there talking and softly laughing. Sometimes they danced to radio music, and I was left to my books and Rocky to his horse.

I didn't mind playing with Rocky all that much, when you got right down to it. He never called me Four Eyes. He was imaginative for a little kid, and I liked him. He was all right.

He woke up every Saturday morning before eight to watch his cowboy shows. We had only two television stations on the air in New Orleans, and if you didn't like old Tex Ritter movies, *The Lone Ranger, Hopalong Cassidy,* or *Roy Rogers,* you were pretty much out of luck on Saturday mornings that year. Rocky wore his cowboy hat and kept the volume turned low, but I'd hear him, and I'd get up to watch TV with him. Cowboys were better than nothing. They had adventures. They were brave and competent. Their girlfriends got thrown by horses, captured by Indians, terrified by rattlesnakes, and generally could always be depended on to act like whining morons. Characters like Dale Evans and Annie Oakley did display some moxie, but it was always the dance hall girls who looked the most glamorous and got the best lines. I wondered why none of the cowboy heroes ever married the saloon girls. The hero always rode off into the sunset with the whiny rancher's daughter who had twisted her ankle and gotten kidnapped by Apaches twenty commercials ago.

There's some saloon girl in Mama, I decided.

When she wasn't around, like for instance when she'd be fixing her makeup and hair in the bathroom mirror every day before Daddy got home from work, was when we played "Cowboys At The Saloon." We were very literal. Rocky would belly up to Mama's oak dresser in the master bedroom like John Wayne, plop his elbows on top of it, and say, "I've just rode in from the Oregon Trail and I'm powerful thirsty."

"What'll it be, pardner?" was my customary line, delivered off-screen from the bed, where I could play with my doll Nina and try to point my toes the way she could.

"The usual," Rocky would say.

"Here ya go," I'd answer, not actually having to move a muscle. All I had to do was speak the line. I encouraged my brother to play Saloon, because it required little effort or imagination from me, and I was free to obsess about my doll while he did all the work. It was Rocky himself who would reach across the dresser top for a little bottle of Mama's perfume, unscrew the cap, and then knock back a double shot of *My Sin*.

We did have high production values, Rocky downing his drink in the mirror of the bar while I made my doll Nina do the cancan in the reflected background like a dance hall girl.

Rocky eventually added details, moving the wooden horse in its metal frame so that he could see it through the doorway, hitched up to the doorknob. I presented Nina with two plumes for her hair, plucked from a Mardi Gras mask that my friend Margaret's mother kept in a closet.

"Jeanne!" Mama would sniff the air and start in on me, whenever her smoker's poor olfactory sense finally kicked in. "You been in my perfume?"

"No ma'am."

"I smell it! How come I can smell it?"

And Daddy began to wonder out loud why Rocky sometimes smelled so downright *sissy*, and he'd hustle him out into the back yard for a sudden desperate game of catch.

"I'm not going to play in their bedroom anymore, Rocky," I finally put my foot down to my brother. "You're getting me in trouble, playing in there."

"But that's where the saloon is!"

"Yeah, and Mama blames *me* whenever her perfume bottles look empty! You want me to tell her it's you?"

"No!"

"Okay, then. We can still do 'Indian Attack.' We can do that in the living room, and we can pretend the sofa is our fort, and we won't get into any trouble if we don't get any of the cushions dirty. Okay? Okay?"

But it wasn't really okay with him, because televised cowboys did work up mighty thirsts after a tussle with Apaches, even if Tex or Hopalong never ordered any drink stronger than sarsaparilla. So we played "Indian Attack" in the living room for several days, while Rocky's nonstop imagination secretly worked at new saloon locations.

"Okay: Ask me, 'What'll it be?'" he ordered me one afternoon, dismounting his horse in the kitchen, pushing up the brim of his hat with the barrel of his revolver. "I'm powerful thirsty."

I pointed at the refrigerator. "Kool-Aid."

"They did *not* have Kool-Aid back then!"

"You drink any more perfume and I'll kill ya."

"You're not playing the game right, you big stupid cuckoo! Jeez!" He stomped across the kitchen floor in his little boots.

"All I know is, you drink any more perfume, and I'll tell."

"Come onnnn! I'm not going into the bedroom! Do I look like I'm going into the bedroom? Jeezum!"

"You're such a little creep," I pushed my glasses higher onto my nose, "I can't tell what you look like you're about to do. So, what'll it be, creepface? You new in these parts?"

His face was like a large tomato. I laughed at his anger.

"You're a big jerk, Jeanne," he said. "You're not playing the game right, and you're calling me bad names, and I'm gonna go tell!"

I still laughed, but I spoke my line. "What'll it be?"

"'Pardner.'"

"What'll it be, *pardner*?" I had to shout it from the hall as I went to fetch Nina, the dance hall girl, from my toy stash. I stopped to stick feathers into Nina's hair with a bobby pin. "What'll it be, pard-ner, you little creep? The usual, *pardner?*"

"Yep!"

So Rocky had the usual, somewhere off camera, as I fixed my doll's hair. He was still in the kitchen when I finally made my bored way back. I saw that he had pulled a lot of jugs and bottles out from under the sink.

I didn't stay in character. "That's floor wax, Rocky. That's Clorox."

"So?"

"You didn't actually drink anything, did you?"

"Well, we're not supposed to drink real beer! It'll make you drunk!"

"Rocky, you didn't touch any of this stuff, did you? Mama says never ever to touch any of this stuff! Drāno will kill you! I'm not kid-ding!"

"I know better than to drink *Drāno,* stupid!" But his mouth was all bowed in its middle now, like he was about to cry.

"Floor wax will kill a person, Rocky!"

Yeah, he had removed the tops from a whole bunch of bottles. Bleach, turpentine, dishwashing liquid. Pine cleaner.

"*Mama!*" I screeched, suddenly sure.

Rocky began to sob. His face reddened to a deep purple.

My hair stood up on the back of my neck. I started to jump up and down without meaning to, holding my doll by one of its legs, screaming, "*Mama! Mama!*"

I took off towards the forbidden bedroom and its adjacent bath, its beauty products, mirror, and hairbrushes, where our mother made her daily transformation from mommy to wife before Daddy got home. My upper arms pimply with the gooseflesh of certainty that Rocky was dying, I saw that there was no light shining beneath the bathroom door before I wrenched it open. The bathroom was dark, but scented.

"Mama?" I retreated. "Where are you? *Mama?*"

Where had she gone? Where did she go every day after she'd pret-tied herself up, while Rocky and I roamed the Wild West of our imag-inations? I'd never given the matter much thought. I paid little attention to her routine, the dull duties she performed. I took for granted the laundered and ironed clothes she provided for all of us, the dishes washed, shelves dusted, floors cleaned, groceries bought, meals prepared and served. When something like red kidney beans appeared like magic to bubble fragrantly among sausage and bayleaves in a pot on the stove, as if they could do that by themselves, I took it as no more than our due. Crisp, starched, white school blouses chronically materialized in my closets. I never thought of my mother as working hard at any of that, because she made it all look so easy. I never saw her as working, really, at anything.

What she's supposed to be doing is watching us! I thought now in panic as I galloped from room to room. She's not supposed to disappear, she's supposed to be looking out for us!

But I ought to have known. Even over the roar of the washing machine downstairs in the ground floor storage room that we low-lying New Orleanians called a basement—where she had just put in a big load of sheets and towels and white cotton underwear—she had automatically been monitoring our high chatter and our light footsteps on the ceiling above her head. Listening out for us, as always. Rocky's mishap had made no unusual noise and had caused her no alarm, but my subsequent squalls were something that even neighbors had probably heard.

I was sucking in a deep breath to holler again when I heard her footfalls.

She beat me to the kitchen, charging up the back stairs, dressed for Daddy, but with little white specks of laundry soap stuck to her wet hands.

Rocky sobbed and reached for her.

"Rocky's drank poison, Mama!"

She never looked at me. She crouched on the linoleum with the hiccupping Rocky, her brows registering comprehension, all those open bottles and jugs in a semicircle around her high heeled shoes. I could feel her blood pressure shoot up like a distress flare.

"I don't know what he drank, Mama!" I said. "He drank something bad!"

She lifted Rocky with a straining of her young knees, held him close in her arms, and fled through the empty rooms while I held onto her hem and still tried to explain.

Rocky's little red cowboy hat fell off. I picked it up.

Daddy had the car, off at work. I was thinking out loud about cars and neighbors and ambulances and taxis, voice soupy with tears, unable to stop speaking.

"*Hush up*, for Chrissake!" She kicked open the front door. "Just hush up, *hush up*, shut your yap, I can't think! It's faster on foot. Hush up and come on."

Our house was on Napoleon Avenue in a nice neighborhood, with a nice small front yard that Mama tried to make look like something out of *Better Homes And Gardens,* only five blocks from Southern Baptist Hospital. Mama headed that way now, never slowing, galloping in her high heeled shoes. They made loud staccato clicks on the concrete. The big oak trees cast dark shade, black lace pools that she moved through.

"What'd you drink, Rock?" was what she muttered as she pounded ahead of me, out of breath, her voice gappy with pauses and gasps. "I'm not gonna spank you, Rocky. Tell me what you drank, baby."

But he cried and cried.

"I'm not gonna spank you, baby. Please tell me."

Neighbors watched from their porches, old folks and young housewives. Rocky sounded like some part of him was being amputated.

"Dear sweet Jesus!" Mama's back and shoulders bunched up.

And here I came, bringing up the rear, stumbling along in my school uniform blouse and plaid skirt, trying to keep up, my glasses sliding down my teary nose. Rocky's red cowboy hat was still in my hand.

Old Mr. DiBenedetto down at the corner of Claiborne heard our approach. I saw him drop the paint brush he had been using to touch up the blue robe of the Blessed Virgin who stood in plaster form among the blooming impatiens of his small front yard. Blue paint made freckles on the magenta flowers. He began an old man's sprint as my mother drew even with his front gate, and he swung into step right beside her now. "Velma? Whassamatta, dawlin'? Velma?"

But the beautiful Velma was younger and faster and more upset than Mr. DiBenedetto, and she would not slow down. "Rocky's drank poison!" she shouted over her shoulder as she outdistanced him. "Call C. Ray! Please call C. Ray! Tell him to meet us at the emergency room at Baptist!"

C. Ray Buchanan was our father, and everybody he knew in this city called him "See-Ray" for some reason. His folks back in South Carolina preferred his first name, Calvin, and so we could tell when we answered the phone if it was his relatives calling long distance. They had real drawly voices and spoke with iron-hard R's like Texans. Rocky and I saw little of our Buchanan grandparents, although they sent us birthday presents. I wondered sometimes if Mama was the reason the Buchanans rarely visited us, since she didn't seem to like them very much. Maybe her glamour was intimidating.

They were Presbyterian tee-totalers, thin and dried-up farmers, Scots, taciturn. Their humor was quiet and dry. Neither of them tossed their heads to laugh. Neither laughed loudly.

My father C. Ray had met and married Velma Connolly in 1946, immediately after the war, and had never gone back home to live. He had found a job with the Falstaff Brewery right after his discharge from the navy, and had centered his happy life around Velma and beer from then on. He did love beer. He brewed it, he studied it, he drank it, and he lived with a wife who appreciated it. His dream was to someday take her to Munich for Oktoberfest, although Mama wasn't too keen on either foreigners or distant travel. All of our neighbors knew where C. Ray Buchanan worked. C. Ray provided kegs for neighborhood crawfish boils, weddings, wakes, and Mardi Gras, always at cost and always on time.

Mr. DiBenedetto collided with me as he skidded to a stop, and then he bounded off across his flower garden. The flat breasts of an old man flapped inside his white undershirt. He waved as he hurried up his porch steps, nodded, and shouted something about C. Ray that I couldn't make out. Traffic screeched and honked at the intersection. Rocky screamed.

We made it across Claiborne Avenue without getting run over. My mother stopped looking back at me. She stopped telling me to watch where I was going.

I toiled behind her, focusing on her seamed nylons as we went up the hospital steps, my eyes on a level with her biceps as we reached the top.

She knew exactly how to talk to the nurses and the doctor at the cool marbled emergency room desk, and I was thrilled by her poise. My pride in her drew me closer to her side. She was like a queen when she told a nurse, "I think it must've been the bleach," pointing to whitening spots on the front of Rocky's cowboy suit. "The dye is affected. And I believe that I can smell chlorine on him."

I stood under her elbow, lost in love and awe. The doctor explained what he planned to do. Her red lips pressed together. Her chin nodded at the medical terminology, bright hair spilling over the shoulders of her dress.

She pried Rocky's fingers off of her wrist and relinquished him to a nurse. Then I saw her notice me as Rocky began to howl. I prepared myself for a furious lecture now, or maybe even a spanking. I heard the rustling of her nylons as she stooped to my eye level. I lowered my head.

That was when I noticed that I no longer held Rocky's cowboy hat. I had dropped it somewhere. It was lost.

"I'm sorry, Mama." Tears began to splash onto the insides of my glasses lenses. "I didn't mean to, Mama. I didn't mean to let him drink Clorox. I didn't mean to lose his cowboy hat."

Mama was somebody who would not hesitate to spank us if she thought we'd earned it, but she didn't spank me. She crouched there for a while, right in front of me. She finally pushed my glasses back up onto my wet nose with a gentle finger. "Looks like you need some windshield wipers in there, punkin."

I nodded.

"Let's go get us some ice cream." She waited for me to stop sniffling. Or to look up. "Would you like that, punk? I bet they sell ice cream here at the coffee shop. 'Cause I know they have milk shakes." Her voice was very kind. "Wouldn't that be nice? Chocolate?"

"What about Rocky?"

"He'll be okay. They're pumping his stomach out, but he'll be fine."

I pondered this. Kids our age had all been terrorized at one time or another with the verbal threat of stomach pumps. Rocky was actually going to experience a real live stomach pump. It would make him famous in the first grade. "Will it hurt?"

"It'll keep him from drinking anything but *beverages* for the rest of his life, I imagine."

"But what about Daddy, Mama? What if we're off drinking milk shakes, and Daddy gets here?"

"That nice nurse back there'll tell Daddy where we are. Maybe Daddy'll want a milk shake himself. Whaddaya think?"

I hadn't really wanted a milk shake yet, because I didn't think that I ought to be enjoying one while my little brother was getting his stomach pumped. But my taste buds were beginning to be teased.

Mama took my hand. Her touch was warm and dry.

We stepped over to the wall and studied one of those *You Are Here* maps of the hospital layout. There were signs on the wall above it, painted arrows pointing off in all directions. Mama's index finger found the words "Coffee Shop." "Right down that hall, Jeanne. C'mon."

I tugged at the gathered skirt material below the waist of her dress.

"Don't do that, punk." She looked down. "Get it wrinkled."

I moved my hand away. The cotton of her dress was soft and flowered. "Your pocketbook. It's at home."

She punched her own hip finally with a small huff, wrinkles be damned.

"I don't need a milk shake," I said, watching.

"I sure could use a Lucky, though." She threw her weight onto one hip, swiveling to look at the hospital entrance behind us. "Long walk."

"Maybe that nurse has a cigarette."

"I'm sorry, Jeanne."

"Well, we can wait until Daddy gets here. Daddy'll have cigarettes. And money." I took off my glasses and wiped them with the hem of my plaid skirt. My mouth drooled for a chocolate milk shake now. The anticipation of it was almost pain.

"Yeah. Let me just go and see if that nurse has a cigarette, just in case."

I noticed a vinyl upholstered bench against the wall near the elevators, well out of the way of strangers and the scariness of the emergency room entrance. I didn't want to be near the places where the ambulance guys might bring in bleeding wreck victims on stretchers. Real blood might not be like TV blood, black and discreet.

Magazines littered the top of the distant bench. I pointed at it. "Can I go sit on that bench over there, Mama?"

"*May* I," she corrected me.

"May I go read those magazines while you go see the nurse?"

"I've never seen a girl so determined to squint up her eyes in all my life."

"Is it okay?"

"Watch where you sit." She started across the floor. "Don't sit in that shiny stuff. Looks like Coca-Cola."

There was movement in my peripheral vision, the stirring of blurred images in that gap of imperfection between the lens of my glasses and my temple. I kept walking.

"Here come the DiBenedettos," Mama called over her shoulder. "They'll have cigarettes."

Nothing was said about milk shakes yet. I sat down on the bench and swung my short legs as the elderly couple came on. I squirmed backwards until I could press my shoulders against the cool and hard wall. I felt my bones like birds' bones, thin, light. They crunched a little as I pushed them into the marble. My thick rusty hair cushioned the back of my head. I looked for fire and murder in *Life* magazine. I looked for children living through worse trials than myopia and Clorox.

"Don't bite your nails, Jeanne!"

I wasn't. But I put my hand down anyway, onto the slick paper of the magazine page where the greasy fingers of strangers had smeared the ink. Brown coffee stains ringed random photos of nuclear test sites, beauty queens, President Eisenhower and Elvis Presley.

I heard my mother's debriefing by the DiBenedettos. She sounded like a movie actress from this distance, low and mellow, no shrillness, speaking in the cultivated tones that she was trying to cultivate in me. Up close, though, her accent came through, that special New Orleans working class gumbo of Irish/Sicilian/Yiddish/African/Cajun intonations sounding like a Brooklynite on tranquilizers. Velma Connolly had reminded seaman Calvin Ray Buchanan of Brooklynite Barbara Stanwyck back in 1946. Velma supposed her accent was long gone now, eliminated by deliberate elocution, because she couldn't hear it. Her son Rocky couldn't hear it. I, her daughter, had not been able to hear it. Not yet.

Consider this: my name is Jeanne Girod Buchanan, and I am Irish on my mother's side and Scottish on my father's. My first name is pronounced "Zhonn" in the New Orleans manner, not "Gene," like in the rest of the USA. My middle name is also French. It is a family name, borne by the descendents of an early mayor of the city. But I am not kin to any of them. I would not be able to hear my mother's working class accent until the day I realized how phony and contrived my debutante Frenchified names were, not a leucocyte of French blood in any of us.

"Here comes Daddy!" my mother called back to me now.

Yeah, here came my daddy, loping in silhouette across the marble floors, long legged and very calm. His unconcern told me that he had already stopped by the nurse's station and knew for a fact that Rocky was going to be fine.

"Hey," he said to his neighbors, and put out a quick hand for Mr. DiBenedetto. He hugged little old Mrs. DiBenedetto like a fond nephew. "Thanks for calling me, y'all. Thanks for coming over and waiting with Velma. I can't thank y'all enough."

My mother shoved the neighbors apart, but gently, so that she could finally fall into her husband's embrace and give in to her nerves.

Mama never cries, I noticed, unless she's where Daddy can see her.

I sat on my bench and went back to my magazine, while my father produced a cigarette for my mother and lit it. I tapped the wall with the back of my head, feeling my hair like a pillow. My glasses bounced down my nose.

"We'll go get us that milkshake in a minute, punkin," my mother called over to me. I looked up again. Daddy's arm was looped around her waist, easy and lazy. Her own hand covered his, red fingernails the color of the shiny gorgeous red seeds of magnolias, the ones I'd tried to preserve in a cigar box once, and did. Except they lost their color and turned brown.

"Okay," I said, receiving no acknowledgment.

I knew now that none of them would move an inch, the Buchanans nor the DiBenedettos, until Rocky had been officially pronounced fine. I realized that they couldn't go anywhere until that happened, that they had to stay. It was like a formality that adults had to perform. So they'd stay nearby like this, smoking and laughing, until the doctor came out all smiles. Yes. And then Daddy would mention a celebratory round of beer. And off we would go to some neighborhood bar, where no milk shakes would be available and nobody but me would mind.

I felt my sinuses congest with mild emotion. I was extremely glad that Rocky would be okay. I was glad that my parents felt like laughing. But still.

I didn't even want a milk shake, I remembered, until Mama talked me into it. I didn't even think of wanting one until she made me.

chapter 3

Why
My
Teeth
Are
Crooked

O f course, my development into who I am today did not begin
and end with bad hair and a few disappointments in childhood. If I
could freeze myself at any stage of life, it would be at age nineteen. I
was at my best at nineteen, and things were very good for me that
year. But more on that later.

Middle age has taught me a lot that I would've rather not learned,
but I guess that's true of most people. I became an expert on depression, for instance, that first year I found myself stuck down in Auletta
alone with my mother, taking out the garbage and frightening myself
with my own reflection in the garage window, having no one to talk
to except my mother and the occasional bait shop casanova.

I saw myself turning into the clinical depression poster child, and
it gave me the willies. I've never liked feeling weak. But I also discovered that if I could get away from Mama long enough, a long, brisk
walk, with a John Philip Sousa tape in my walkman, could raise my
serotonin and endorphin levels and make me feel some better.

So would a stiff shot of bourbon.

Too, the customary bubblebath in scented bath oil could work
small miracles. Unless having no privacy or time for bathing was one
of the things you were depressed about.

Never look at your high school yearbook when you're depressed, I learned. Unless you know for a fact that the Homecoming Queen now weighs three-eighty. Or is dead.

Chocolate is a serotonin booster, cheaper than Prozac. As a matter of fact, chocolate and a couple of shots of bourbon and a yearbook full of fat dead people have been known to induce actual laughing fits.

Actually, my own yearbook had no homecoming queen, since we had had no homecoming. I had attended Ursuline Academy, an all-girl outfit. So whenever I wanted to look at a photo of Frank Campo when my mother was finally tucked away in bed and I had my bourbon at my elbow, I opened Rocky's yearbook. All boys.

That picture of myself at age fifteen, the year I fell in love with Frank Campo, was the one I really wanted to stay away from. I had been more nearsighted than ever, flatchested, my freckles and acne a challenge to the coverage of liquid makeup. I was five-foot-seven and still growing.

The bone-straight hairdos that had swept into vogue in the wake of the Beatles were something that my wild hair couldn't pull off. But long bangs had come into style, and I could cover up more of my face with them. They brushed the gold metal rims of my round eyeglasses. Green eyeliner made my eyes visible. I was just barely hanging on to self-respect.

"I'll kill myself," I told my mother the day she suggested braces for my teeth.

"Jeanne! I'd think any young lady with a less-than-perfect smile would be tickled to death for the chance to do something about it," said Mama. "That lady from New York I met last week at the beauty parlor, both her daughters have braces."

"Her gross hippo daughters. Combined weight of four hundred pounds, but at least their *mouths* will be glamorous."

"I don't like that tone of voice, young lady."

"I'm sorry." I wasn't.

"Kids up north, they all get braces, if they can afford them. It's a rite of passage."

"Look at a map, Mama."

"You smart-mouth me one more time, I'm gonna smack you!"

"I'm sorry," I said. I still wasn't.

"Your daddy offers to scrape together enough money to buy you braces, and this is how you act. Be ashamed."

"I said I'm sorry."

"Yeah," she said, "sorry's what you're going to be someday all right, when you look in the mirror and see all those crooked teeth!"

I wouldn't even spare her a sigh.

"Don't you care, punkin?" Her blue-eyed stare was as flat as a clear sky. "Don't you care just the tiniest little bit? We're trying to help you, is all. Just help you."

I care more than you can possibly imagine, Mary Velma Connolly, I thought, you with your natural beauty and perfect bleach job. Boys never called you Four Eyes and pizza face, and made puking noises when they passed you in the hall.

But I'm not getting any braces, that's for damned sure. I'll kill myself if I have to appear in public with a barbed wire mouth, on top of everything else. I can already hear Danny Ducote right now: How'd you get your face stuck in that rat trap, Four Eyes? How many radio stations can you pick up on that thing?

Hell, no, I'm not getting any braces. And I'll never be sorry.

But of course I became sorry, sometime later when I noticed how cute Frank Campo was becoming. When it had become too late to get braces and have them off by my real dating years.

I had had crushes on boys before, and had learned never to act upon them. I had limited the expression of my passions to "I love Jeff" or "I love Tony R.," penciled anonymously in tiny script on the walls of public places, usually over the water fountain in the school library, where I could never be connected with it. Where the pencil marks could easily be removed by cleaning personnel. I was not a vandal.

But I never confided in my girl friends anymore, not since making the grievous mistake of telling Margaret Bordelon, back in the seventh grade, that I had a secret crush on Joey Guidroz. In two hours, the news that Jeanne Buchanan loved Joey Guidroz was all over Lourdes School. Joey made loud barfing noises at recess to entertain his pals, until Sister Mary Clothilde declared he was ill and sent him to the school nurse.

"Daddy, I'm ugly," I grieved to my father that night.

"That ain't true. You're pretty now, and you're gonna get even prettier. Just give yourself some time, Jay."

"Boys think I'm ugly."

"Boys ain't got no sense. That's why we send boys out to fight the wars."

"Don't laugh at me, Daddy."

"I'm not laughing at you, baby. Dearest little Jay-jay. I think you hung the moon. Did you know that? Did you know that I think you hung the moon?"

"No." I was sniffling.

He handed me a kleenex from the box that Mama always kept beside the sofa in front of the TV set, where she could remove her makeup and watch *Doctor Kildare* at the same time. "Jay, you know what a pearl is, baby? A real one?"

"Yeah."

"How it's made, I mean,"

"I know how it's made," I said. "A grain of sand gets inside an oyster's shell."

"Don't you think that that oyster goes through all kinds of upsets and oyster what-all, trying to overcome that grain of sand that's making its life miserable?"

I wiped my eyes. "Am I an oyster?"

"Baby," he looked at me over the top of his evening paper, and maybe he would have gotten to his feet to come over and touch me, if we both had not known that I was a person who became even more upset when touched. His voice, however, was very kind. "See, you're the whole thing, Jay. Yeah, you're the oyster. You're the pearl. It's a process, creating that thing of beauty. It must take a heckuva long time for that oyster to get that sand covered up, layer by layer like that. But look at the outcome, Jay. That thing of beauty comes into being." Daddy sometimes sounded as if he read too much *National Geographic*.

"I'm a microcosm. Terrific."

"Outer beauty isn't built to last, baby, and it never does. Nobody can count on it forever. A day comes when it's gone, no matter who you are and what you looked like when you were young. I read somewhere that God sent us into this world with whatever looks we have, but we ourselves are responsible for how our faces look after age fifty. If you're full of meanness and you don't have any kindness in you, then you're gonna look ugly and mean at age fifty, no matter what kind of makeup you use. Kind thoughts make for a beautiful face. My mother has a beautiful face. That kind of beauty."

He sounded sententious, but my father knew no direct way to discuss these man/woman things. And I knew that he meant every word he was saying.

But I don't know if I can wait until age fifty to shed my ugliness, I thought, still blotting tears with the wad of tissue. I'll be an old maid by then. I'll be alone. It'll be too late.

"Don't hunch over like that!" my mother scolded me later as I sat on the front porch and tried to mentally secrete mother-of-pearl over the sand that was in me. "You'll get all round-shouldered, I swear!"

So there was no way that I was going to tell anybody at all about my crush on Frank Campo. Posture lectures and nature parables from my parents would've made me feel even more inadequate. I did not want my father feeling sorry for me, watching me moon over somebody who'd never give me the time of day. And I certainly didn't want to involve my mother and let myself in for more of her critiques.

So I began confiding in a diary. It was a place to write Frank's name.

There were also ways to bring up Frank's name in casual conversation with my brother. Frank Campo and Rocky were on the same football team that fall at Jesuit. In fact, Frank had been named the starting quarterback the previous year. So I began to develop an interest in the sport. I quizzed Rocky about coaching strategies, plays, and personnel.

"Frank's a turd," was Rocky's opinion.

Frank Campo was the best-looking boy I had ever seen in real life, not counting television. He had not been all that great looking growing up. He was the grandson of the DiBenedettos, down on the corner of Claiborne, and he used to spend a lot of time with them. His skin had once been terrible, the surface of Mars. He'd lived with his own parents somewhere off of Carrollton Avenue, I had not cared where. He had also been kind of fat, until the tenth grade.

"Well, he's mowing the grass for his grandparents," I answered Rocky's charge, "so he can't be all that bad."

"Mr. DiBenedetto *pays* him to mow the grass," said Rocky. "Don't worry, he ain't doing it for free."

I really liked watching Frank Campo mow the small front yard down on the corner, with his shirt off. He had smooth tanned skin. He smoked cigarettes while he mowed.

"He's an arrogant son of a bitch," said Rocky. "He gripes my ass. He thinks he's hot shit."

But how could a guy who had been fat and pimply only two years ago get up to speed so fast now? I wondered. Frank was decayed pastrami only two short years ago. Rocky has to be wrong, I thought, or envious. Or both. Even if I got a fairy godmother standard makeover tomorrow, and won Miss Universe tomorrow, I'd still be too insecure to be *secure,* let alone arrogant.

This cannot be.

Rocky's wrong. Or lying. Frank's a good football player, Daddy says he's good. Daddy says Frank is bound to get a full scholarship to just about anywhere he wants to go. He's big, he's tall, he has muscles, and he still has a neck. He's got a cute face. He's going out with Cathy Noel, and she's the prettiest and most popular senior at Ursuline. Frank's just too fine to be arrogant. But he does have a lot to be proud of.

Maybe he just didn't care all that much that he was fat and had killer acne, I thought, back in his fat days. Maybe boys don't care all that much. Maybe they don't see it as something that will absolutely ruin their lives—not being attractive. If a boy is good at something, like football or math, or fishing, or even collecting stamps or raising gerbils, maybe he doesn't care what he looks like. I can't figure it out.

This is giving me a headache.

"Don't frown that way!" said my mother. "You want to get crow's feet?"

I bought some paperback books in my desperation, on astrology, palmistry, and *The Secrets of The Tarot*, trying to work a little magic in my colorless world and make Frank notice me. I read up on love charms and astrological sign compatibilities. I cast spells and tried to think of a way to get my hands upon strands of Frank's hair or his fingernail parings.

Unless I came up with a way to strike Frank Campo absolutely blind, I realized after a while, my cause was hopeless. As long as he literally had eyesight, I was dogfood.

Mama tolerated my votive candles because she thought them evidence of religion. Since my father had not converted, my parents had never settled upon a church. Mama just sent us to parochial school and hoped for the best. She rarely went to Mass anymore, and didn't seem to miss it. C. Ray Buchanan had become her religion.

Just as Frank Campo was becoming mine.

What is it with us women? Is it our chromosomes that make us such nitwits?

I discovered J.R.R. Tolkien's *The Lord of The Rings* on the same paperback racks with the astrology books that fall. I let my hair grow long and tried to imagine myself as an Elvish maiden with otherworldly beauty and enchantment in my every gesture, but I knew that I was really one of Tolkien's Hobbits. A very tall one, yeah. But plain and big-footed and faintly ridiculous, altogether unworthy of a prince like Frank.

"Frank's a jerk," said Rocky.

"Then he certainly has Cathy Noel fooled," I said, "and she's in the National Honor Society, and she could have any boy she wanted. They're probably going to get married."

"Yeah, right. Frank sticks his fingers under your nose in the locker room, and says, 'smell my girlfriend,' and shit like that," said Rocky, fourteen years old. "He brags about fucking her. Fucking other girls, too. And he says that Mama dresses like a go-go girl. Right in front of me, he says it. Him and Danny Ducote."

"Well," I said, "she does. Those white boots and miniskirts. Open your eyes, Rock. Mama's too flashy sometimes. She cheapens herself."

"I think she looks *great*." He got all red underneath his freckles. He had thick sandy hair, his eyebrows so light that they were invisible from a distance. He was beginning to improvise daily workouts for himself, chinning himself on our old swing set in the back yard, readying his biceps for their big debut. There was nothing wrong now with the treble-voiced Rocky Buchanan that a big dose of the testosterone his body was producing would not eventually set to rights. "You're just jealous," he said, "'cause Mama's a cool chick."

Jesus, I thought, seeing how his red rage made his eyes look greener. Rocky's going to be *handsome*.

"They make me sick," he said. "Frank and Danny. Think they're hot shit. Think they're so funny. *You* make me sick. You oughta hear the things they say about you."

His deep set eyes were framed by sculptural brow ridges and cleanly planed cheekbones. His freckles were neither large nor dark. He was already tall, and he would grow taller. Buchanan men were all tall, Grandad Buchanan and Daddy and his brother, our Uncle Wallace.

I was sixteen, and I was still growing. Tall was great for a guy. Tall might not be so great for me. I might turn out to be the tallest Hobbit on the face of the earth.

And girls are going to think my brother is cute, I realized. Girls are going to want me to introduce them to my brother. He's got Mama's looks, plus the best of Daddy's. And he couldn't care less.

"You're just jealous of Mama," he accused me, and I knew it was true. And I felt a little bit of genuine witch begin to grow inside me, along with that grain of sand that Daddy had talked about. I wasn't proud of the witch part. It was the witch part of me that secretly rejoiced when Mama began to grow wider in the waistline at age forty-one, and I saw her struggling to zip up a skirt that had fit her okay the year before.

The witch loved it when Mama's dark hair roots began to display a glimmering of silver, those times when she couldn't make it to the beauty shop on time.

My beautiful mother discovered me at the bathroom mirror one night during my senior year at Ursuline Academy, when Frank

Campo and Cathy Noel were still going steady up at LSU. Mama caught me grinning at myself and then pouting at my reflection, trying to look seductive, kissing the air. Pulling back my lips in a benign snarl to finally examine my overbite. She said, "I told you you'd be sorry about those teeth."

chapter 4

Saint
Jeanne
of
Auletta

"How's poor Velma these days?" Mrs. Bordelon asked me over the telephone, early in my exile to Auletta, just after I had cut off all my hair but before anybody except Mama had seen me shorn this way.

I seem to mark epochs with hair. My memories sort themselves out in chronological order by how long my hair was, how red or how faded; how bald my father was; how blonde or brassy or thin or gray my mother's hair.

I picture myself on the phone with Dolores Bordelon, my hair butchered like my patron saint's, Joan's. Jeanne d'Arc, peculiar maiden, martyred for witchcraft. Had St. Joan been an ugly girl?

Mrs. Bordelon was Margaret's mother, Margaret who had been my best friend back on Napoleon Avenue when we were kids. I hadn't seen Margaret now in twenty years or so. I had heard that she'd married a chiropractor and moved to Houston, but I'd so completely lost touch with her that I was embarrassed now to ask Mrs. Bordelon about her.

Mrs. Bordelon did all the asking. "Tell me about poor Velma, Jeanne."

I turned to locate my mother, who sat in a flounced rocking chair, watching a soap opera on television. "I'm not sure how she is," I answered in a very low voice. "About the same, I guess. I can't tell if I'm seeing any changes."

"Aren't there some new drugs now that can help? I keep reading . . ."

"Tacrine isn't out yet, it's the one getting all the publicity buildup. But it probably won't help Mama much, the doctor says. You'll have to give 'em Tacrine in the earliest stages to see any positive effect, I understand. Yeah, I read up on this stuff, too, Mrs. Bordelon."

She sighed. "What would Velma do without you? You're a saint, Jeanne."

"No."

"Isn't it marvelous, Jeanne, when you think about it, how our Heavenly Father broke up your marriage so that you'd be free to come home and look after poor Velma now? The Heavenly Father does work in mysterious ways, dawlin'. He truly does."

What was marvelous was that Dolores Bordelon had the good luck to be living way across the lake in Orleans Parish, where she couldn't see my face and how badly I wanted to rip her old Godloving lips right off her face.

If God had really wanted to perform valuable work for the Buchanan family, I thought, he would have kept my husband from chasing younger women. He would have kept my daddy alive. My son close to me.

He would have kept my mother from losing her mind.

Breaking up a marriage? Doesn't take an act of God, you silly old woman. Divorce is no miracle, you ignorant old twat.

"Who's there?" Mama turned her head from the rocker.

"Nobody's here," I said. "I'm just on the phone."

She reached out a spotted hand with swollen knuckles and made a hesitant gesture at the television screen. "Who's this boy, then?"

I looked. Saw an automobile commercial. "That's a *commercial,* Mama. That's a man selling Nissans. We don't know him. Let me finish talking to Mrs. Bordelon."

"Who?"

"Mrs. *Bordelon,* Mama. From Napoleon Avenue. Dolores Bordelon. Next door."

"Where is she?"

I could feel the frustration popping out of my pores like toxic waste. I was decades too old now for acne. But I could actually feel it erupting sometimes, from stress and perimenopause. From the heat. From my perpetual frustration, as constant as the humid summer.

"Who's this boy here?" Mama demanded to know, waving at the television set.

I could hear the clothes dryer honking its final honk in the laundry room, shutting itself off with a clunk of tennis shoes settling to its bottom. "I'm going to have to call you back, Mrs. Bordelon. The dryer just quit. I've got to go take out all the good clothes and get them all hung up before they wrinkle."

I knew that she wanted to yak some more. I understood what a morbid fascination Alzheimer's disease held for older people. Just like imaginary monsters had once held for me and Rocky and Margaret, back when we thought that they might be real and hidden away in the deep lochs of Scotland or the Nepalese mountains or hometown cemeteries, regardless of what adults said or thought they knew. Monsters just might be real, and they might slip up on you and carry you off some bleak night, and there was nothing at all that you could do about escaping your fate.

But I did make it a point these days to never discuss Mama's condition over the phone in detail, not even if I knew for a fact that she was asleep. Because she might not be asleep, not really. She might be able to hear things in her sleep. Or she might be up and shuffling around, overhearing bad news, even in the middle of the night.

Alzheimer's disease had not affected her ability to hear. Mama's hearing was still very good. Alzheimer's prevented her from hearing things correctly, however, and making sense of what she heard. Her misinterpretation could lead to paranoia. And paranoia led to my being awakened at three o'clock in the morning by her uncertain approach, her dreaded quavering of "Jeanne? Is something wrong? Did somebody break into the house?"

I think that 3:00 a.m. or thereabouts must have been the time when Mama tried to think things through, prodded awake by her full bladder. Since she could no longer follow her own train of thought, though, she was forced at these times to come to my bedside to debrief me.

I tried to be pleasant about it. On those nights when I was able to figure out what she was upset about, I'd try to wake up, sit up, and explain things to her in simple and positive language. If I noticed that she had neglected to pull her pajama bottoms all the way back up after peeing, I'd yank them up for her and make sure that the absorbent panty liner was still in place. Mama no longer understood what toilet tissue was for. She had stopped using it.

One of these days, I realized, she's going to forget what the commode itself is for. And nobody will be able to explain it to her, ever again. She is unlearning things, in roughly the same order that she learned them as a toddler. *Unlearning.* Dolores Bordelon thinks that this is all about memory loss, and it's not. It's about personhood loss.

Mary Velma Connolly Buchanan is losing herself: She is eroding like a coastal sand dune, and there's nothing that anybody can do to stop the erosion or even slow it down.

I had been so proud of Mama, the day I finally got her to the neurologist right after my father had died. She had fought actual diagnosis for as long as she could, postponing the appointment until I literally had to lie about our destination in order to get her into the automobile. "Mrs. Buchanan," the doctor had leaned forward onto his desk, after asking her a barrage of what-month-is-this questions and giving her small wooden spatial puzzles to solve, "we're going to have to get a CAT-scan, and rule out a few vitamin deficiency problems. But I wouldn't be surprised if this turned out to be Alzheimer's."

Mama had faced the dreadful word without flinching, with a cordial smile on her face, and she put out a hand, like a queen, to clasp his and thank him. My knees gave out, at this news that I so much had not wanted to hear, but Mama's back was straight and her head high as we went down the silent hallway to the elevator.

Maybe she didn't understand him, I was thinking. Maybe her memory is so shot, she's already forgotten what he's told her.

But she spoke two words once the elevator door had shut us inside. "Oh, Lord," she said, and that was all that she said. No tears, no lamentation. I took her arm, and we stepped out into sunshine. My pride in her, my awe at her courage, would be cheapened by any words I might try to speak. So we didn't speak. I couldn't've spoken clearly, anyway, since the brightness of the day had melted into my eyes and was running through my tear ducts into my throat. So we had just held onto each other, but tightly, not like invalids but like comrades, and had walked to the car.

Mrs. Buchanan, you have Alzheimer's disease.

Mrs. Buchanan, you have just lost your beloved husband, and now you know that you will lose your mind. And for an extra added bonus attraction, you're also about to be moved to New York and lose your own home, unless your daughter Jeanne decides to give up her apartment, job, and friends, to relocate to Auletta and move in with you. Ha ha. Don't count on that.

Congratulations, Mrs. Buchanan, I imagined the neurologist saying. *Have a nice day.*

That had been nearly nine months ago. Nine more months of my mother has eroded forever, I thought now while I folded her laundered sheets.

She might be forgetting her married name, for all I know. Is she mostly pared down now to Velma Connolly? Someday, she will recognize and respond to only that single name, Velma, like an eighteen-month-old child.

When will that be? How long from now? Who is a person, when she no longer knows who she is? Will she care? Will her impaired mind let her care?

Will *I* care? Because I'm not sure that I'll be able to, by then. I'm not going to tell Mrs. Bordelon, and I'm not going to tell Rocky, because I don't know for sure, but some days I think that I have bitten off more here than I can chew. Some days, there is just too much laundry and too many incoherent conversations. Some days, Mama is too crazy and too hostile. I'm not afraid of her, but I'm afraid.

Wow, I'm tired, I realized that night, after getting my mother back to bed in the wake of the late hour's first debriefing. I'm tired clear through to my soul. Enough answerless questions for you, Jeanne, you bad-tempered witch. Go back to sleep while you still can.

Tomorrow will be here soon, and it's going to be just like today was, like something out of Lewis Carroll on crystal meth. Rest up.

Whenever my mother seemed uncertain about finding her own way back to bed on nights like tonight, I'd get up and take her by the hand and lead her to the master bedroom adjacent to my own, where her coverlets lay in tangles on the floor. I'd unscramble them and finally get her tucked back in, there among the late C. Ray Buchanan's dusty *National Geographics* and catalogs, the old radios in the room's corners, and his lithographs of Highlander warriors in frames on the walls. His weaponry was up there too, reproductions of Scottish daggers and dirks, hanging high and undisturbed.

But I had hidden his *claidheamh mor*, his great sword, an impressive reproduction of the two-handed broadsword that had been worn into battle tip-down on the backs of our belligerent Highland ancestors. Daddy's claymore was both authentic and expensive, something that he had been very proud of when he'd started collecting this stuff after his retirement. But Rocky's kids had tried to behead each other with it, sometime back in the autumn, and I had thought it prudent to take it down from the wall and shove the thing under the bed. It now lay hidden among Daddy's shoes and Mama's mothproof blanket storage boxes, under a thick fuzz of dust.

Mama never missed the claymore, once I put it away.

About the only reason a person could fail to notice the absence of a four-foot-long broadsword is Alzheimer's disease, I thought. Or maybe Jack Daniel's.

But I'm glad she hasn't missed it. I wonder how much she misses Daddy now. I wonder how much she is able to miss Daddy, since that involves a mental function that she may no longer thoroughly possess. Maybe it is a blessing, if Dolores Bordelon wants to look for blessings in this situation, that Velma isn't able to miss C. Ray as much as other widows might miss their husbands. As much as Dolores Bordelon probably misses hers.

When there was time for me to move things in the master bedroom without Mama knowing about it, I tried to cram stuff against the walls and throw the dustiest of the catalogs away. Mama could easily trip over something in here and break a hip. I wanted to get rid of all this dusty old clutter. The radios would not play. The daggers were dangerous. Yet Mama wouldn't hear of it.

"We can give it all to Rocky," I urged her. "That's not like really giving it away, Mama, if Rocky and Barbara just store it for us. It'd still be in the family. Maybe Rocky knows how to fix these old radios."

But she missed Daddy as much as she was able. She would stand there in front of me, shrunken and desolate, and her saggy eyes would water until I couldn't stand to look at them. "This is your daddy's stuff. I can't give away your daddy's stuff, punkin."

"But I'm tired of living in a pig sty, Mama! Look at all these old magazines and books, and everything. This stuff could spontaneously combust. We're living in a fire trap, Mama!"

"It's just too soon, Jeanne." She'd silently weep with only her eyes. And it might have gotten to me, her grief and pitifulness, and moved me, had I not been so tired. "Your daddy was my sweetheart. I've lost my sweetheart, and my heart is broken. It's too soon."

Like she was the only one who'd ever lost love.

If I had been a genuine sorceress, I would have cooked up a powerful spell to make myself invulnerable to grief, and resentment, and the undiminished ability of my mother to make me feel like an ungenerous and unnatural changeling: a cowbird hatched in the loving nest of the Connolly Buchanans.

"You don't have to be there, Jeanne, you know," was what my ex-mother-in-law kept reminding me. "You do have choices, dear. Empower yourself by remembering that. It's your own choice to be down there in that house, looking after your mother. You are not a victim."

Yeah, I thought. Like somebody really has a *choice* when her helpless mama needs her. What is even a mean old witch to say? *No?*

The threat of fire in Mama's Auletta house had been a very real one, not so long ago. She was still smoking cigarettes when Daddy died and I moved in with her, and one night she just tossed a lit butt into a pile of mail-order catalogs. Just like that. It had taken me a full hour and a couple of stiff drinks to calm down afterwards, once I had located the fire extinguisher and had made a soggy but safe mess of my father's paper pile.

I didn't purchase any more cigarettes, after that evening. I kept putting Mama off by telling her that I'd forgotten to buy any at the grocery store, until the inevitable day when she finally forgot to ask me for some.

"Well, I can't see why you don't just let her smoke, Jeanne," was Rocky's input. "It's not like we've got to worry about her getting heart disease or lung cancer. It's not like smoking is going to hurt her any."

"Fire will hurt her. Fire will kill us both, her and me."

"But if you're right there supervising her, what's the problem?" Rocky had grown up into a responsible and reasonable man, a veterinarian, a pragmatic person used to dealing with patients who couldn't talk and couldn't argue with his considerable logic. "What's Mama got to look forward to now, if you take away one of the few pleasures she has left? What enjoyment does she get out of life?"

Stung by guilt, I'd try to explain to him my reservations about being burned alive, but he just didn't get it. Well, to give Rocky his due here, I guess a person had to have been there that night, in order to get it. You had to be there. You had to witness Mama's utter unconcern, when she tossed that blazing butt across the room into two year's worth of dust bunnies. With no more thought than a little girl spitting watermelon seeds.

It gave me about seven thousand new gray hairs, and I wasn't all that redheaded to begin with.

Rocky, dearest brother, you had to *be there*. You had to be there in order to understand that it would definitely happen again. Maybe in the middle of the night, this time. Well, there was no way that I could be awake at all times to supervise. Mama was still able to open drawers and cabinets to search for matches or smokes. Mama was strong and implacable, no baby. Mama did things that made no sense. She would turn on the electric burners of the stove for no reason, until I purchased some of those childproofing gizmos that kept the knobs from engaging when twisted. Matches were another story, though, matches and lighters. Childproofing was not always Velmaproofing.

So I put my mother back to bed on these cigaretteless and paranoid nights, my contact lenses out and my vision blurred. I mean *seriously* blurred. I was so myopic now that I couldn't distinguish a lamp table from a German shepherd. So if Velma had peanut butter on her pajamas or fecal matter under her fingernails, I could not detect it. What Jeanne could not see would just have to wait until the morning, thank God.

"But it's dangerous, Jeanne, if you can't *see!*" Rocky told me. "Why don't you get yourself some glasses? To augment your contacts, is all I'm saying."

"Okay, but they'd have to be half-an-inch thick. My prescription is about off the charts now, and I still can't see well through glasses."

"Are we speaking of vanity, Jeanne?"

"Are we speaking of a guy who got all the decent genes in this family?"

"Seeing lousy through eyeglasses is probably a lot better than not seeing at all, for Chrissake! How can you dial 911? What if somebody tried to break in on you or something? I'm talking *crime,* Jeanne."

"I've already been there."

"So are you gonna put Mama through that? Your New York bout with crime?"

"Okay, I give up. You're absolutely right, Rocky. You can come out here and watch Mama while I go to the eye doctor for some glasses. So what day you wanna do that? When can I pencil you in?"

"Well," he'd huff, and consult his calendar. Rocky did indeed work hard, and I sometimes felt guilty for winning arguments this way. He took only Sundays off, and once in a while he worked Sundays, for the Animal Emergency Clinic. If his wife Barbara had had her way, Rocky would've worked twenty-five hours a day. Barbara had a weakness for expensive automobiles and flashy clothes.

So I'd climb into my lonely bed in Auletta, Louisiana, at one o'clock in the morning, after a considerable late supper of good bourbon, actually grateful for my physical blindness. I was in denial that the sun would soon rise again, and that I'd have to perform another day's stultifying nursing duties and housework. I'd punch up my pillow with vigor, pleasantly fuzzy, and visualize somebody bad and evil climbing into this house through a window, if they could find a way to get in past Daddy's industrial-strength burglar bars.

They're welcome to kill us all, I'd think, indifferent and beaten into sleep.

chapter 5

Just
Thinking

More things I realized while I was stuck in Auletta:

We women are programmed to be depressed. If "Don't suck your thumb, baby, it'll ruin the shape of your pretty lips!" are some of the first words you can remember hearing, you're always going to feel that you've fallen short of something.

Typical parental comment to a boy of eleven: "Finish your dinner, son, so you can grow up big and strong!"

Typical parental comment to a girl of eleven: "Should you be eating that second helping of mashed potatoes?"

Parental observation made to a boy of thirteen, like the ones I had once made to my own son: "Study harder and apply yourself, Rad, so that you can get a good job someday."

Parental observation to a girl of thirteen: "All those damned books are going to ruin your posture!"

I rest my case.

chapter 6

Back
to
Our
Story

I loved college. I was able to sort of start all over in college.

I had been dreading it, before I actually went. It all seemed so complicated, all the freshman orientation materials I got in the mail. Tulane was attended by all kinds of kids. Locals like me would be in the minority. I had already spent so many of my high school nights alone and alienated, listening to deejay Poppa Stoppa on Daddy's radio, wishing that some boy would take me to the F&M Patio sometime to dance. I could dance.

"You won't like it," said my mother, when I received my acceptance and my academic scholarship, "all those snotty sorority girls."

I loved it.

I remember hiking across the Quad on October days so sharp they cut, and my lungs just could not take in enough of the clean electric air, and my eyes could not register enough of the shadow-edged shapes of oaks and buildings, students and automobiles. The slanted autumn sun outlined every object with black shadow and I moved through a stained glass world, wholly holy.

Sororities might very well lurk at the edges, but they were totally irrelevant to the hopped-up-on-coffee intellectuals and rabid anti-war activists that I found myself among as an art history major.

I was majoring in art history because I liked to look at beautiful things, and thought that it might be very pleasant and easy to get good grades for doing it. I didn't know enough about the world to consider the job market. Neither, for that matter, did my advisors, C. Ray and Velma. All matters collegiate were foreign to them.

As for sororities, let me just say that I did visit three houses on Rush Sunday, and found out long before the afternoon was over that sorority life would not be for me. Quite apart from the likelihood that I would not have received a bid from any of them, I found them personally abhorrent. For an ugly girl, remember, embarrassment is always just around the corner. And as I watched sorority sisters file out of each house we visited, all *uniformed* in matching pastel jumpers and pins, and heard them alarmingly break into loud *song*, right there in public on Broadway, clapping their hands in rhythm like kindergartners to ditties about Winnie-The-Pooh and Zee-Tee-You, or whatever damn Greek name the club had, I felt my cheeks burn with shame at being present for such a silly and juvenile display. This was not my idea of sophistication.

I'd sooner strip to my underwear, I thought after the third such demonstration. And I went back home to Napoleon Avenue, relieved that nobody could make me join a sorority.

For some reason, I was considered a rather interesting person at Tulane. Cool, even. I behaved no differently from the way I had in high school. I read palms in the University Center for free, and was actually pretty good at it. I said exactly what I thought, and was frequently rewarded with wry laughter from onlookers. Boys no longer puked when I walked by. Boys wanted to converse with me.

So I decided to take up scuba diving, an interesting pastime for an interesting person, that second October at Tulane. I had noticed a flyer on a kiosk that advertised for members for a new diving club, and I went to the first meeting and passed the first swimming test in the University Center pool. But my eyesight finally stymied me. I was wearing contact lenses these days, and had not figured upon eyesight being a problem. I thought that a scuba face mask would serve me the same way it served the twenty-twenty types. Just slap it on over my face, over contact lenses and all, and that would be that.

"Water pressure," I said to Larry Roth after I got the bad news.

"They tell me that I can't dive in my contacts because of water pressure. It would do bad things to my eyes."

"Bummer."

"I could get a special mask made, I hear, with corrective lenses built right into the faceplate. I don't know how much that'd cost."

"Probably a lot."

"It'd have to be about an inch thick, I'm so nearsighted," I said. "It'd be like wearing a porthole. I'd look like a submarine."

We ambled across the Quad on our way to the University Center for coffee, and Larry stopped at the bulletin board outside. "Here's a notice for a skydiving club, Jeanne. Take up skydiving."

I laughed.

October was New Orleans' only decent month. October and maybe April. The rest were too hot and muggy, or too chilly and wet. I had always lived for my Octobers. They did make me feel adventurous, but perhaps my adventurism was really just high barometric pressure and low humidity.

"It's autumn. Lotta energy in the air," I said to Larry as we sat down on the browned grass outside the University Center and watched the bellbottoms of the jeans of passing students flap like flags. Red banners with white peace symbols flew from the windows of a passing van. The Beatles sang about revolution from the radio of a nearby Volkswagen beetle painted to look like the American flag. "No telling what I might do."

"Tolkien obviously loves autumn," Larry said. "He has his Hobbits all walking the Shire in autumn, singing their droll little Hobbit walking songs. Just what constitutes a walking song, anyway? Does our society have any?"

"I'm not singing in public for *anybody*," I said.

"You sang 'We Shall Overcome' last week."

"That was a demonstration, Larry. I can lose myself in a demonstration."

Larry Roth was an easy person to sit close to. He was one of the big pack of loose Reds I had fallen into. He hung around with the theatre department. He spoke of having come to Tulane originally for pre-med, but I was pretty certain that Larry wasn't studying any sciences now with enthusiasm. He had turned up once or twice onstage in campus theatrical productions, comedies. Whenever I observed that he'd make a good professional comic actor, he seemed humble but pleased.

"Well, if Tolkien had been a New Orleanian," I told him, "he'd have his autumn Hobbits drinking beer and rolling their car windows down, parking out by the Lakefront and hollering."

"Why?"

"You haven't spent a whole summer here yet, have you?"

"Not yet."

"Do it sometime," I said. "Kind of a preparation for Hell."

"You believe in Hell?"

"I should, I'm half-Catholic."

"I didn't know a person could be *half*-Catholic," he said.

"I'm talking ethnically. Like you being Jewish. Not what you believe about God and all. But where you come from. Family background."

The grass where we sat was spiky and turning brown. It had not been mowed the one final time that might have kept its blades exactly even, but mowing it this late would probably not be necessary. The dry weather was putting it to sleep. It was becoming dormant around my freckled fingers. Cool air blew over my multiple silver rings.

"You notice," Larry said, "how it's all different? The grass? It's not all the same kind of grass. Some of it is actually weeds."

"Yes."

"Clover. Dandelion. Whatever that whitish stuff is. It's the fact that it's all mowed to the same height that makes it quote-unquote *grass*. Mowing equals conformity."

"Yes," I said, terribly happy.

Deep thinkers like Larry took me seriously at this wonderful school. If I could have actually lived there on campus, instead of having to go home each night to Velma, C. Ray and Rocky, my happiness would have been complete. I was even becoming sort of famous at Tulane as the girl who read palms. I did not call myself a witch. Witchcraft was very much in vogue, and I had always shunned vogue. Witchcraft also meant joining a coven, and I was not a joiner. But I liked being known for my accurate palmistry. My wide reading had made me glib, I discovered, and I had begun to trust the stream-of-consciousness rap that came out of my mouth whenever I looked at someone's hand. Two-thirds of my magic was actually glibness.

And as for hair, it was a very good hair year. *Very* good. While I did not have the longest hair at school, nor the reddest, I did sport the longest red hair on campus. And certainly the thickest, hands down. My rough Buchanan hair hung in a plait to my waist, a braid with the diameter of a tugboat's hawser. My acne had cleared up. And I no longer had to struggle with makeup, since the natural look was the cool one now.

I had become my daddy's pearl, finally, and Tulane's Newcomb College was my oyster.

"Do you think that the Elves have pubic hair?" Larry asked me.

"What?"

He pulled at a blade of quote-unquote grass. "Tolkien's Elves."

This was a very Octobery question. It pleased me that Larry Roth would speak the words "pubic hair" like this, to me, so natural. The lungfuls of air I inhaled felt frisky. The brown grass I sat on was stiff, and prickled me through the seat of my bellbottoms. "Probably," I said. "But it would have to be very elegant. Like brocade."

"How about pit hair?"

"I don't know. Tarzan in the movies doesn't have armpit hair, for some reason. Isn't that kinda weird, when you think about it?"

"Body builders shave their whole bodies," said Larry.

"Tolkien writes his Elves as sort of tall and powerful demigods," I said, "not annoying little sprites. He makes a point of telling us how beautiful they are, physically."

"But they definitely aren't body builders."

"Nobody said they're body builders, Larry! Come on!"

He laughed. His laughter made me feel good.

"They seem to be kin to the *Tuatha De Danann* of Celtic mythology," I went on. "I'm a Celt, I know this shit. I'm also an art historian, and classical Greek statuary has pubic hair, and head hair, and occasionally facial hair. But no pit hair. The classical Western ideal of male beauty seems to make no special place for hairy pits."

"How about beards? The Elves have beards?"

"No."

"Wrong," he said. "Tolkien says explicitly that Cirdan has a beard."

"And he also says that Cirdan looks old. Maybe Cirdan is in a class by himself. None of the other Elves look old."

"Celeborn has silver hair."

"Yeah," I conceded, "but he doesn't look *old*. And he doesn't have a beard. Glorfindel doesn't have a beard. Legolas doesn't have a beard."

"How about Aragorn?"

"Aragorn's a *human*, Larry."

"My point exactly." He leaned in closer. I liked it when Larry and I went free-wheeling this way, off into trivial conjectures, shoulder to shoulder and knee to knee. "Aragorn's human. So we know for a fact that he is able to grow a beard. The Dwarves are heavily bearded. The Wizards are bearded. So what fashion trend does Aragorn follow?"

"Aragorn," I said, "shaves with his sword."

Larry was instantly inspired, and he had to act it out for me, a comic miming of an Old World warrior prince trying to shave his own face with a broadsword. Larry accentuated the difficulties. He pretended to accidentally remove his nose.

I fell back onto the grass in laughter, feeling light and yet grounded, like the Goodyear Blimp tied down securely in a high wind.

Sometimes the Goodyear Blimp passed over our Quad on Sundays, when the Saints played football in nearby Tulane Stadium. It could create very ominous shadows. I looked up at the sky now. No blimps in sight.

I am become my own blimp, I decided. Gassy and full of hot air.

"Dwarves are the real beard freaks," Larry went on. "Even their women are bearded, apparently. Elves detest Dwarves. So even if an Elf could grow a beard, he wouldn't. It's political. Like Army ROTC guys having long hair and beards. Identifies you with the wrong side."

"Dwarf women should definitely shave," I said.

"Would a shaven Dwarf woman be mistaken for an Elf? I think not. The best wax job in the world couldn't make a short female fire plug into a demigoddess."

I was comfortable discussing even ugly females with Larry Roth. "I'm not sure the word 'detest' is the correct one, Larry. Legolas likes Gimli, and Gimli's a Dwarf."

"Legolas is forced to *learn* to like Gimli," Larry objected. "It's not something he's planned on. It's probably only because he's so young that he's even open to it. His father couldn't hack it, in *The Hobbit*, you notice. Bare tolerance for Dwarves is about the best his father can manage."

"But Legolas isn't young."

"He's a *kid!* Read between the lines, Jeanne!"

"No, he's the oldest of the entire Fellowship, if you don't count Gandalf. He even says so."

"Well, if you're talking human years, yes, Legolas is maybe one or two thousand, who knows?" said Larry. "But we're talking Elf years. Remember what he says about memory? About the way Elves out-live everything and everybody else, and what a grief it is to them. Legolas is like a kid who's just realized that he's going to outlive his dog, you know what I mean? You remember what that felt like?"

"My mother wouldn't let us have any pets," I said.

"In Elf years, Legolas is maybe nineteen."

"We're nineteen," I said to Larry.

"He's never been away from his homeland before, he's never really associated with mortals before, and now he's thrown together with this Dwarf nobleman. All they have in common is the same enemy. Legolas is a king's son, remember, an honest-to-God royal prince. He outranks everyone else, except maybe Aragorn, but he's so naive that he never realizes it. His father the king has sent him off on a wartime mission. This kid may be a demigod, and is immune to sickness and exhaustion and old age, but he can get killed. A sword or an arrow will kill him just as dead as it will a Hobbit."

I thought about what Larry was saying as I watched a campus full of draft dodgers walk past me in their short jackets and tie-dye.

Bodies were absurdly soft and flimsy structures, when you thought about it.

"And Legolas takes orders so well," said Larry, "from Gandalf, from Aragorn, from the Rohirrim, from anybody who'll tell him what to do. And just about the time he begins to like Gimli, it dawns upon Legolas that he's going to outlive him. If they both make it alive through this war, Legolas is going to outlive his best friend. He hasn't even been in love yet. Or if he has, wartime circumstances keep him from acting upon it."

"Maybe he's gay."

"He's not gay, he's *young*, Jeanne."

"But do Elves really fall in love?" I looked up at the sky.

"God, Jeanne, the entire trilogy is littered with allusions to Elvish love affairs—Amroth drowning himself for Nimrodel, Luthien renouncing her immortality for Beren. Romantic love seems to be a very central and catastrophic item on the Elvish agenda."

"Elf women fall in love with human men," I said. "But you don't see any Elf men chasing human women, do you?"

"Well, no. Maybe it happened occasionally, in Tolkien's mind. Maybe he just didn't get around to writing about it."

"No," I said. "Males want their females young and pretty. A mortal woman isn't going to stay either one."

The sun had lowered itself behind the trees and buildings now. I felt chilled. There was a war on, here in this time, too.

It would soon be suppertime, and I'd have to head my old Chevy Impala off to the house on Napoleon Avenue, and listen to chatter about the price of hops and barley these days, and what the gals were saying down at the Hair Hut. Somebody, probably Rocky or my dad, might eventually get around to asking me about my classes, and what I was learning.

What *was* I learning these days? What were Larry and I really saying to each other, when we talked this Elf balderdash, when we discussed politics, when we made observations about men and women?

I still kept a diary, and I tried to puzzle all of this out on its pages. Larry's name began to appear in multiple places in each paragraph.

"Time is sad," I said to him now, as the sun went down.

"Yeah."

"I mean, the passage of time, and what it ultimately does."

"Well, we do know that academically, Jeanne. But actually, we haven't yet learned that from our own experience. We're both Legolas, remember."

"Uh-huh."

"I mean, it's kind of scary," he said, "anticipating loss this way. The end of childhood innocence. Everybody refers to the innocence of children as if it were sexual, exclusively. And it's not. What children are actually innocent of is the first-hand knowledge that everything dies. You end up losing everything."

"But I don't have anything to lose," I said, and thought that I meant it.

"Yeah, you do."

chapter 7

Aboard
the
Titanic

I'm not sure what I was learning then, back in my college days. But I can tell you a few things I picked up vicariously in Auletta in my middle age, watching my mother's fellow citizenesses leading their naive little lives. At least they had lives to lead. I could only watch, and wonder how I had gotten myself to this place.

Never go out with a man who wears a swastika is one of the lessons I learned from watching and reading the local paper. Never hitchhike in short shorts. You'd be amazed at the number of women who thought that either of these things might be a good idea.

Never get your hair done at a beauty college. Never name your kids after soap opera characters. This is what I learned, overhearing conversations in the supermarket.

Don't pencil in eyebrows either above or below whatever actual hairs you may have between your forehead and your eyelids.

Forget fake fingernails. Jackie Onassis did not wear fake fingernails. Sticking a big pink dirty claw back on with Crazy Glue in public does not say class.

Forget bleaching that hair on your upper lip, girls. If it's that thick, then *shave,* for God's sake.

And we're all too fat, most of us, because we eat crap. Crap is easy to microwave. I know.

None of us are Elf maidens. This is what I learned.

I also learned that there were adult daycare programs for senior citizens, but I didn't know how to take advantage of that knowledge. I had already cut my hair off. I was worried that that *meant* something.

"You might try daycare for Velma," my ex-mother-in-law suggested over the phone from New York. "They offer activities in most good daycare programs, I understand. Arts and crafts. Music therapy."

"I don't know, Nancy," I said. "Mama's never been the craftsy type. She's not musical. And she doesn't want to see anybody."

"But they wouldn't let her nap in daycare, so both of you might sleep better at night, don't you think?"

"I'll check it out. See what's available locally. Auletta isn't even a small town, understand."

"I hate to think of your getting so little uninterrupted sleep at night, Jeanne. Velma's not a little baby. This is only going to get worse, her wakefulness. Not better."

I had remained oddly close to Nancy Roth since my divorce, and I was grateful for her honest concern. It made me feel uncomfortable these days to hear anybody express any concern for me individually, since Mama was the sick one. I felt like I deserved no concern. I was younger and stronger than my mother, still had most of my marbles, and I felt a little guilty about it. Accepting queries about my own well-being made me feel undeserving. But I was still grateful that Nancy brought up the subject, these times when she called. Few people brought up the subject anymore.

"I'm fine! I'm fine!" I would wave my hand and brush off most folks. "Don't worry about *me*."

So could I blame them when they didn't? Even when I cut all my hair off, even though my hair was so short that people took me for a cancer survivor down at the supermarket, nobody asked me about my state of mind.

Nobody wants to know, I realized, looking at myself in the bathroom mirror. Nobody wants to know my exact state of mind, because it's too late now to do anything for me. I don't even know my exact state of mind. Maybe I'm okay. Anyway, it's all my fault, because I should've asked for help back when people could still give it. Mama and I, we have traveled now beyond the help that neighbors can reasonably offer—to have the oil changed in the car, to send over fried chicken and potato salad, and to buy and deliver our groceries. Just about the time I'm starting to reconsider these Aulettans, realizing how many really good people live in this hell hole—people caring enough to ask about us when I don't care enough to ask after them—I'm sailing right out of their reach. Just like the *Titanic*.

What they're able to do, I don't need. I need what nobody is able to do, and that's to send out a big lifeboat for me, with an outboard motor on it, and food and blankets and a tarpaulin and a map, so I can sail away from this iceberg and totally forget that I was ever here. I already crave freedom and amnesia, and I'm going to increasingly need both with each day that passes, and neither is possible. I don't see an end to the situation.

Coward. Wimp.

I'm afraid.

This iceberg has a name, and its name is Alzheimer's disease, and it has gashed a great big hole in my hull, and I don't know if I've got enough pumps to rescue myself.

"I'm fine," I told Nancy Roth. "Losing some weight, even. The Auletta diet, do laundry while you dine on a Slim Jim. Maybe I'll write a diet book."

I wanted to make her smile, and I thought I could hear her smiling now. I heard the creases forming under her eyes. I heard the movement of her curving, wrinkled lips. She had Rad's slow smile.

Rad was one of the reasons that Nancy and I had remained so close, certainly. My son had always been closer to his Roth grandparents than to Velma and C. Ray, and it wasn't all a matter of geography. Sid and Nancy had been frequent babysitters for Rad back in his toddler days, with both Larry and me working, and Nancy's other grandchildren out in California, too far away to dote on. Nancy had taken Rad to the zoo, and ice skating at Rockefeller Center, and to Jones Beach with Sid in the summertime, to swim and then catch the summer musical restagings of Broadway shows at nightfall. They had seen *The*

King And I this way, out of doors and under the stars, Rad and Nancy and Sidney. Rad tried to find Siam on a world map afterwards and would not let me explain about the name change. He had cried and screamed when I had tried to tell him that Siam had become Thailand. He was eight years old, and would not hear of it. Thailand, to me, meant the Vietnam War, and was also where really great dope came from. Rad wanted the kingdom of Siam, not the reality of Thailand.

My parents hadn't been able to visit us very often, and I did understand that airline tickets from Louisiana to New York were very expensive, and that Daddy's work schedule as brewmaster for Jax Beer now had priority. But when they did succeed in making the trip, Mama took every opportunity to complain about the noise, dirt, and congestion of Manhattan, as if it were her civic duty as a loyal New Orleanian Yat. Maybe she was just intimidated by the city, and this was her way of coping.

Still, I grew very tired of it. "We have prettier buildings back home," she'd comment. "Our streets are cleaner, on the whole."

"Not true," I'd mutter, remembering the stink of rotting crawfish parts in the gutters of the French Quarter on a sizzling summer day.

"They don't seem to be able to get their trees to really *grow* up here, either," she'd say.

"Not every city is lucky enough to be situated in a sweltering swamp, Mama."

"Where do all these people come from?" She'd look around herself in stagy wonderment. "And none of them are friendly!"

"Of course they are."

"Nobody up here would even *pee* on you," she'd maintain proudly, "to put out the fire if you were burning to death!"

What could I say?

"None of these girls know how to *dress*." This was the opinion of a woman in a frilly chiffon number, heels too high to allow her to comfortably sight-see with us out on the streets, blonde hairdo frozen in the bouffant bubble of ten years ago, red lipstick.

"Look at this picture Rad drew, Mama."

"You and Larry let Conrad cut up too much in public, and I was so embarrassed at his behavior at that restaurant last night that I woke up with heartburn at 3:00 A.M., and disturbed poor C. Ray. Your daddy needs his rest, punkin. This is supposed to be a vacation for him."

"I'm sorry about that, Mama, but look at how well Rad draws. He's only four."

"Honestly, if you or Rocky had ever behaved like that in a public place, I'd have turned you over my knee and spanked you right there!"

Nothing that Rad or Larry or I did was ever up to "Velma Standards". Our apartment wasn't clean enough. Our street was not well-lit nor safe enough. Our neighbors looked like thugs. Little Conrad, who had what I called an artistic temperament and what his Mam-maw Velma termed spoiled rottenness, was a source of alarm to Velma and C. Ray. I had elected not to subject him to the nineteen-fifties style of straitjacketed child-rearing that they had used on me and Rocky, and I was pleased by Rad's blossoming spirit and assertive creativity. Velma and C. Ray were convinced that he was destined, literally, for prison.

"And I just think that he should be baptized," my mother started in on me on one unfortunate occasion, "you know, just in case. You might be running a risk you can't even appreciate now, punkin."

"Risk of what?"

"Something could happen." She was quite serious. Her cigarette smoke ascended to the ceiling. "An accident, or an illness. He could die. His soul could be in danger."

"'Baptism' is not a word that we speak in this household, Mama." I popped the top off a bottle of beer for Larry, who was keeping Daddy quiet company out in our modest living room.

"So you're Jewish now."

"I'm nothing now."

"Am I going to die, Mommy?" Conrad pulled at my sleeve. "What is Mam-maw talking about?"

My mother rested her hand on the top of his head. "Everybody dies, Rad, sooner or later. But our Heavenly Father takes care of the good people, after they die. So you're going to have to ask your mommy and daddy to take you to church, so that your soul will have eternal life. And you're going to have to learn to be *good*. I'm tired of waking up at 3:00 A.M., worrying about the way you cut up. You're a sweet little boy, to be so bad."

"I don't want to die, Mommy!" Conrad began to beseech me. *"I'll be good!"*

"Don't upset the boy, Vel," called my father C. Ray from where he sat in the living room with a newspaper. "I don't believe he's old enough yet for theology, honey."

"I don't want to die, Mommy! I'll be good! You and Daddy's gotta take me to that Heavenly Father church *right now*, so I won't die! Right this very minute!"

I wasn't sure what to say, whether to promise him a trip to church or just try to distract him with something like ice cream. But distraction smacked of deception, of the less-than-direct ways in which my own mother had once dealt with me. I stood there in my tiny kitchen and strongly disapproved of distraction, while Conrad got himself really wound up and began to shriek and stomp the floor.

"Rad," I said.

"Now! Now! Now!" he demanded, his little face like a wet purplish blob. It was amazing that such a small mouth could emit such piercing, earsplitting howls. He threw himself down on the vinyl tile so that he could hammer it with both feet and fists. *"Now! Now!"*

I hated the way my mother refrained from rolling her eyes at the ceiling. I knew she wanted to. She folded her arms and would not look at me.

"Rad," I said evenly, "Time out. Go to your time out place, son."

There was no way he could hear me. None of us could hear anything at all but him.

Larry sat in a corner drinking a Heineken, and so it was me who crouched and lifted our screaming son and tucked his snotty face into my neck, under my chin. And I guess I had had too much beer myself to be nice now, because I was fed up with this tantrum and had not forgotten what had brought it on. "Mam-maw Velma's not right about everything, baby. She's not *always* right. She doesn't always know what she's talking about. You're not going to die, baby.

You're safe with us and in no danger, and if you stop crying, you can have some ice cream. Whatever you want. Come on now, booger baby, and stop crying."

"I don't know if you should pick them up, when they're like this," my mother nodded at the kicking toddler in my arms. "Rewarding them."

Rad's shrieks, right into my left ear, made me frantic. Holding onto him was like holding onto a rabid Sheltie.

"I see how well *time out* works," observed Mama, unable to let it alone.

"Sometimes," I yelled, "I think Mam-maw Velma shoots her mouth off before she knows what she's saying! Sometimes I think she's a crazy person!"

I said it to hurt my mother. I didn't think it was literally true. And the words did their job. They did hurt her. They gave her an opportunity to quietly dissolve into dignified outrage and then weep into the arms of her husband C. Ray. I felt like shit.

But the matter was resolved in the way most Buchanan family dramas were, with C. Ray soothing and smoothing, with more cold beer and good humor. My own tearful apology was lovingly waved away by my beautiful mother, while my father winked at Larry in a conspiratorial way meant to say: *Women!*, which Larry, blank, sat in his corner out of the way and did not get.

What I had said of my mother, I now think that maybe some of it had been true, my accusations of crazy talk. Maybe it had been in the process of becoming true, even back then.

How far back did her illness go? I wondered years later in Auletta. But remembering, too, the sane and tender way she would hold baby Conrad in her arms to burp him, bouncing his double chins over the towel on her left shoulder, the way she paced slowly up and down the floor and sang through smiles in her off-key contralto, "Pack up all my care and woe, here I go, singing low, bye-bye, blackbird . . ."

When did this illness begin to creep out of its potentiality in her genes, and start secretly to lay waste to her personality?

Is the Velma I remember the real and genuine Velma, or is she the damaged product of a terminal illness, and the genuine Mary Velma

Connolly an unrecoverable image in my childhood experience? How far back do I have to remember before I can be sure that I am remembering *her*, striking the true mother lode of her personality?

When does Alzheimer's disease begin?

Do I have it?

chapter 8

The
Diary

I dropped out of Tulane University in the middle of my junior year to marry Larry Roth. I ran off to New York City with him, and married him in a civil ceremony, just the two of us dressed in jeans, no family members present. It seemed like a good idea at the time.

Those are the words I want engraved upon my tombstone, a blanket explanation for all the *meshugas* I have caused myself in my life: "It Seemed Like A Good Idea At The Time."

"I just don't want my mother to mastermind this wedding, turn it into a Big Velma Production," I told Larry as I packed my books. "I don't need to begin this phase of my life, seeing myself through my mother's eyes. Because I'll come up short. My dress won't hang right. My veil will be lopsided."

"Okay."

"So screw the dress and the veil."

"Okay."

My mother had no idea that I was pregnant, but she probably would not have been surprised to hear it.

Mama had been reading my diaries for years, ever since the Frank Campo days, prowling their pages for evidence that I was about to run off the rails.

Because that was what homely girls often did, in her experience. Mama found indirect ways to tell me all about what homely girls might be capable of, just in case I had failed to notice that I was homely. Like I had grown up on the planet Neptune and hadn't received the message yet.

Here's how it went: Homely girls, starved for affection, became complete sluts if you turned your back on them for a second. Velma had known it to happen all the time, back in her own high school days. It had happened to her own sister, as a matter of fact, our Aunt Irene, who lived in Mississippi in a trailer park and whom we rarely saw. If a girl had neither the face and the figure nor the charm to keep a good catch hanging on the line, she could turn into either a wallflower or a tramp.

Ugly girls might get lots of guys this way, by "throwing their dresstails up over their heads," as Mama put it, but they couldn't keep the good ones this way. "Fella won't buy the cow if he's getting the milk for free," she warned me.

"You bet I kept my C. Ray on the line, dangling myself just out of his reach," she bragged to me in one of our mother-and-daughter chats, with mostly herself doing all the chatting. "And I reeled him in, finally. A good man. A *gentleman*, punkin, with good looks and lots of smarts and respect for me, too, you'd better believe. Not like some of those trashy boys I grew up around."

"Uh-huh," I said.

So I wasn't surprised when I began to suspect that she was snooping in my diaries, but I was hurt. No, I take that back. You have to be disappointed in somebody to get hurt, and Velma did not disappoint me. Reading my diary on the sly was completely in character for her. Velma was just being Velma.

The lingerie in the top drawer of my dresser wasn't always arranged the way I'd remembered arranging it. The diary sometimes lay face up underneath my half slips, when I could have sworn that I'd left it face down.

The day I set the trap for her, finally, with a single long red hair wrapped around the diary's brown leather circumference like in the movies, Mama had already started to get overconfident. Neglecting to remember just what position she had found the diary in. Forgetting that I never let any folded corners of my slips get tucked under.

Maybe she was already in the early stages of Alzheimer's then, but I doubt it. She was probably just frantic about this Larry, this Jewish boy, whom I never could shut up about. I couldn't stop talking about him. I gave myself away. It was Larry-Larry-Larry all the time with me now. "Larry says" this, "Larry thinks" that. What an idiot I was. But Mama was so proud of her C. Ray Buchanan, she bragged on her C. Ray all the time, never mind that they had been married nearly twenty-one years by this time. I guess I wanted to show her that I had somebody to talk about, too.

What'll I do, if Jeanne is sleeping with him? she perhaps wondered as she opened my diary and broke the red hair.

I doubt she noticed the hair. Even if she had seen it, she would have noticed only that I should keep my hairbrushes cleaner. She had a big thing about my hair and my nails. I didn't keep my nails polished. My cuticles were hopeless. I should be brushing my hair more often, one hundred strokes a night, to encourage luster and growth. As if my hair needed more body.

What'll I do, she might have thought, if Jeanne's run off the rails? I want so much for her. It's a tough world out there, and tough on women. No nice man'll marry a slut, my sister was a slut, look what happened to her. Living with a drunk in a trailer park in Mississippi, and he beats up on her. I don't want that for my Jeanne. My little punkin.

My Jeanne deserves better. My Jeanne deserves what help I can give her.

That's what I *hope* my mother was thinking about me as she opened my diary. I hope that she wasn't thinking about what Dolores Bordelon and the neighbors would think, if I was involved with a Yankee Jew. But I will give her the benefit of the doubt. In her own Velma way, she did love Rocky and me, I don't doubt that. Love and control were the same thing for her, and she controlled us with a passion. That's how I eventually got into the mess I later found myself in, in the Auletta of my nightmares. Like, how do you repay a mother's obsessive, controlling, but genuine love? Where is the borderline between repayment and martyrdom?

"She's in love with that Larry Roth," I overheard her telling my father on the night before she broke the hair, while she put her coiffure up in curlers and he lay reading in bed. "She's crazy about him."

I pressed my eye and then my ear to the keyhole in the closed door, my interest piqued by the mention of Larry's name as I passed down the short hallway to the kitchen.

Rocky was out on a date. There was nothing to stand between me and shameless, deliberate eavesdropping. I discovered I was shameless, as big a spy as Mama.

"'Bout time," I heard my father say.

"He's Jewish. He'll never marry her."

Daddy said nothing. He turned a page. I could see him through the little space in the lock.

I was free to knock, and then let myself into their bedroom for an ordinary day's recap. I did neither.

Once upon a time, my mother would not have worn hair curlers to bed, nor all this greasy face cream. I could see her through the keyhole now, matronly in her pink gown and bunny slippers. Once upon a time, my mother had dressed for romance when she got ready for bed. I had gotten the impression, during the early days of our mother-and-daughter chats, that she had never really cared for sex. She had seemed to put a premium on cuddling and kissing and being held. I knew that my father still held her and kissed her these days, and sometimes still danced with her to a radio tune, if an oldie they especially liked ever got played.

But my dad was a diabetic now, and I had read enough to know that sex, for male diabetics, could become rather iffy with age. I also was well-read enough to understand that sex eventually became iffy with practically all married couples. Iffy and stale. I felt very wise tonight as I diagnosed my parents through the keyhole.

"Jews get married," he spoke up after a while.

"Not to Catholic girls."

"Seems like a nice enough kid to me."

"Yeah, she likes him because she knows that *I* don't," said my mother. "Look at all that ugly long hair he has, little draft-dodging smartass."

My father C. Ray read his book. He was reading even more *National Geographic* magazines and nonfiction these days, since his diabetes had put an end to his customary evening beers. C. Ray Buchanan, beerless. Bless his heart.

Light glinted off of his reading glasses now. The blue smoke of his cigarette curled itself around his head in the stillness of the room like something alive.

"You hear Larry lecturing me about Vietnam?" my mother Velma turned around to look at him. "Like I was some dumb bunny. The other night. Him advising Rocky about how to get out of going to Vietnam. Beat the draft."

C. Ray read a small book with a plaid cover. His white hands overlay Royal Stewart tartan, its brilliant reds. The soft light from the bedside table lamp glinted off of his bald spot. There was gray among the fading rust of his hair. Hidden like this, I could see how my father was aging. Face to face with him, I couldn't see it. His personality did not age.

"You aren't listening," said Velma.

"Sure I am," he said. He stubbed out his smoke.

C. Ray Buchanan had not given one hoot in hell about the clans of Scotland, or the Scotch-Irish emigration to the Carolinas, or Flora MacDonald or William Wallace or the Covenanters, or any of his other current Celtic passions, as long as his parents had been living. But as soon as my stern and wry old grandparents were laid to their rest in the rocky soil of a rural Associate Reformed Presbyterian churchyard, C. Ray had taken to his ancestral past like a salmon swimming upstream to its hatching waters.

Maybe it takes the place of beer, I realized. Maybe beer and his teetotalling roots can't coexist.

He ran up big phone bills these days, speaking long distance with his bachelor brother Wallace about family names and family trees, who had married who, who had fought in the Civil War, who had fallen in which Scottish or American lost cause.

Velma lit a cigarette and watched herself in the mirror while she did it. Her eyes squinted against the smoke. She must have seen the way her cheeks became distorted when she inhaled. She touched the corner of her left eye.

"Jay-jay's got a right to have a boyfriend, I reckon," said my father.

"Well, she's gonna get hurt. That Jew won't marry her."

I'm going to set a trap for her, I realized at that moment as I watched my mother watching herself. She's snooping in my private life, and it's going to get worse. Listen to how ugly and bigoted she sounds. I'm embarrassed that she's my mother, and I'm going to have to put a stop to this. She's definitely reading my diary. And I'm going to have to prove she's doing it, in order to get her to stop.

"Hell, Vel," my father looked up, "*everybody* gets hurt, sooner or later. You can't get off this planet without getting hurt, unless you die in infancy."

"I'm talking to somebody who doesn't know what he's talking about. I give up." She stubbed out a cigarette.

"Uh-huh." He read his book.

"I'm talking to somebody who doesn't understand how girls are at the mercy of everything."

"Seems to me," said C. Ray, "a smart girl can grab the reins, anytime she wants to. Level-headed girl like Jay."

My eyes teared up at the special pet name he had for me. My father's mouth could not properly enunciate French sounds. My father either could not or would not call me "Zhonn." The best he could do came out plain "John," which neither of us particularly cared for.

I love you, Daddy, I thought now.

"A girl's at the mercy of whatever creep she marries, C. Ray, if she settles for the first creep who winks at her," said Velma.

"A smart and strong girl might not want to *settle* for anybody, honey," he said. "Like Eleanor Roosevelt. She didn't remarry."

"For Chrissake, C. Ray Buchanan, you want your daughter to be *Eleanor Roosevelt?*"

I heard him laugh.

"*Who the hell would've married a mutt like Eleanor Roosevelt?*"

His laughter was loud and ironic. There had been sassy humor in my mother's outburst, and I didn't want him to respond to her this way, but he did. He was such a sucker for her brass.

I couldn't see either of them now. I was standing, leaning against the wall by their door, the muscles of my back complaining from the prolonged stooping. My heart went out to Eleanor Roosevelt, her weak chin and crooked teeth.

"I just wish Jeanne had been able to hook up with that Frank Campo," said Velma after a while, lighting another smoke. "Nice Catholic boy, we know his family, fine people. Got a scholarship to LSU, good-looking boy on his way up in the world. Jeanne used to be crazy about him."

"No, she wasn't."

"Yes, she was."

"News to me," said C. Ray.

"Mothers know things," said Velma. And she did not tell him that she knew it for a fact because she had read it in my diary. Velma kept her red lips shut.

I saw red.

She opened my diary again the next morning, I know, because she broke its guardian hair.

chapter 9

One
Single
Long
Red
Hair

"I really don't know what you're talking about," said Velma.

"Oh yes, you *do* know what I'm talking about, Mama!"

"I didn't even know you kept a diary, punkin."

"How could you *not know* I kept a diary?" I felt sweat gushing out of the pores of my hot face. My bangs were on fire. "You've seen me writing in it! You've certainly snooped through my dresser drawer for years!"

"I put your things away for you when I do your laundry, yes." Her stance was guarded but mild. Her shapely forearms hugged each other. "I put away your nice slips. This morning."

"Bullshit. You do this all the time." Water began to leak out of my nose. I don't know what I had expected, but she was so composed. Like we were discussing the weather, or something as neutral. I watched her preparing our supper. I took in the sure movements of her beautiful hands, red nails. "Bullshit. What utter bullshit. What, exactly, are my rights in this house?"

"Such pretty language."

"My language is not the issue. I'm talking privacy."

She didn't look at me. "If you did your own laundry and pulled your own weight around here, nobody would be in your stuff except yourself. I'm just a coolie. I don't know anything."

She had a point. My sudden, small guilt made my eyes prickle with the threat of furious tears. "I guess I should've made up some scandalous fiction for you to read. I guess you've found me pretty tame. Sorry I'm so boring. And lazy."

"Are you calling me a liar?"

"I should've made up something about orgies with priests. Incest with Daddy."

Quick as a striking snake, she slapped me. I had not known her arm was that long. "Call me a liar if you want to. But you keep your filthy mouth off of C. Ray Buchanan."

I was paralyzed with disbelief. She had spanked me and Rocky sometimes when we were little, and most of the time we had deserved it. But she had never hit me like this, in this woman-to-woman way, with her back stiffened and all of her anger in her opened palm. She didn't shout. Her voice had not been raised. It was such a cinematic act, slapping me. I wondered if it was another of those elements of style she had learned from the movies. Or had slapping and getting slapped been an integral part of that Irish Channel upbringing that she never talked about?

"Get down the dishes and make yourself useful around here," she told me. Her voice was quiet and dismissive. "Get the table set."

I had no intention of being brushed off. "I don't *believe* this! You're making *me* out to be the bad guy here!"

"There are no bad guys. There are no good guys. Go call Rocky and tell him to get washed up."

"You don't trust me, Mama! You say you trust me, but you're reading my diary! *You don't trust me!*"

"I'm tired of being shouted at, young lady."

"How can I ever again trust *you*, now, Mama? Huh?"

"Hey!" My father materialized in the doorway, reading glasses down on the end of his nose, index finger keeping his place in the magazine he was holding. "Take it down a notch, Jay-jay! I can hear you clean out there on the front porch!"

"You know what's going on here, Daddy?"

"None of my business what's going on." He looked owlish. He wasn't happy. "None of the neighbors' business, either."

"I'm getting *screwed* here, Daddy!"

"Let's just drop this, Jay. Just drop it."

"Mama read my diary, my *private diary,* and she won't admit it! And she won't even say she's sorry! And she slapped me!"

I saw him watch my mother as she carried a hot dish of snap beans to the table, with her smooth and gliding movements. Her face was pinker than usual. The steam from the snap beans left a tiny vapor trail in the air.

Daddy's lips twitched in half-amusement. "Hell, Velma might slap the daylights out of an old nun, if she looked at her the wrong way, but she'd never infringe upon anybody's privacy. No way."

Mama became pinker. "I don't want to hear any more about this. Acting like a bunch of common trash. Somebody go call Rocky, and I do not want to hear one more word about this."

"Daddy." I looked to him. "She read it."

"Jay, if your mother says she didn't read the diary, then she did not read the damned diary. Now let's just drop it."

"But she *did!* She *did!* I can prove it!" I was crying freely and noisily now, my cheeks slick with tears, my hands literally itching with fury. If C. Ray had not been present, I might have actually acted upon my urge to grab Velma Connolly by the shoulders and shake her until her neck got loose, until she *looked* at me, until her hard blonde bouffant hairdo split open like a cracked egg. Until I shocked her and hurt her as much as her slap and her lie had hurt me.

But she *was* looking at me now, I saw. She was. And I saw no real anger in her now. I detected a mild plea. She opened her mouth to say something. To recant? To apologize?

"You don't ever call my wife a liar, young lady!" my father said. "You hear me?"

Velma herself began to weep, and she stopped looking at me.

"*Nobody* calls my wife a liar!" C. Ray had to shout above the sounds of both me and Velma sobbing. The act of shouting made the veins on his temples uncoil. "*Nobody! My wife's no liar, and I want you to apologize to her! Right now!*"

Whether or not she was comforted to be backed into a very real corner like this by Daddy, where admitting the truth had suddenly become much harder, Mama allowed him to put his arm around her. They went into the old C. Ray-and-Velma routine. She cried very quietly and with dignity, her hands over her face. Daddy looked at me like I was a poisonous centipede.

"I expect my kids to show some respect for their parents," he said, "while they're under my roof."

I could not fight them both, Velma and C. Ray. When they were wrong, like now, each fed the other's wrongheadedness. They became a monolith of bullheaded righteous error.

I fled to my room and had a long cry, over poor ugly Eleanor Roosevelt and misunderstood kids like me.

My self-pity, after about thirty minutes, slowly transformed itself into an urge to phone Larry Roth.

We talked of J.R.R. Tolkien, as we always did, and of how much Larry would have liked to have been a professional stand-up comedian in another life, as we always did. We talked of politics and classes and philosophy. We speculated about quasars and black holes in space, the songs of the humpback whales, pheromones, palmistry.

When I told Larry that I loved him, he didn't hang up.

chapter 10

Conrad
Aragorn

Larry and I and our baby Conrad lived with Larry's parents out on Long Island those first few months. Larry took the train into Manhattan every day in search of work and an affordable apartment for us. The work search didn't go too well, since Larry had not finished college. As a matter of fact, nothing about our life together was turning out real great. We had been evicted from the first place we had rented, before Rad was born, for our inability to pay for it. We didn't seem to know how to do anything, except philosophize.

The Roths lived in Port Washington, the last stop on the LIRR. So sometimes Larry didn't make it back home until after seven in the evening. Some days he skipped the job search, tempted by open call auditions for off-Broadway comedies. I breastfed Conrad in the relative privacy of Larry's old childhood room, with its Yankees and Jets pennants curling up in age on the blue walls, so that I would not have to make small talk with his mother, Nancy, while I waited for him.

Nancy Roth herself waited on these evenings for her own husband's arrival, and she usually did it with vodka sours. Each of us waited separately.

"Can I get you a drink, Jeanne?" she would ask, rapping on my closed door with the knuckles of one hand.

"No thanks. I'm nursing, you know."

"Okay," she'd say.

And then she would move away, finally padding back up the long hallway in her stocking feet, their twin perplexed rhythms cushioned by her own thick carpeting.

"I don't think Jeanne likes me very much," she told Larry. Or, at least, that's what Larry told me that she'd said.

And I felt kind of bad, because I didn't dislike her at all. I was just uncomfortable around her. Nancy was such an accomplished woman, used to being well-liked. She played the piano, and sang. She was the daughter of a noted Broadway orchestra conductor, now deceased, who had done several of the Rodgers and Hammerstein productions. Truth was, I felt like a complete and total moron around her.

"She likes you okay, Ma," Larry said that he told her. "Just stop bugging her, willya?"

"Oh great," I told him. "Now I sound demanding. Like some kind of dragon lady. Now she'll think I'm a prima donna, Larry."

"What's with this 'Conrad' name?" his father Sidney kept asking us. "This is a name for my grandson? It sounds German: Conrad Aragorn!"

So we'd try to laugh because Sid was laughing. But he spoke just partly in jest, and partly in something else.

I had always been partial to the name Conrad. I had never given its ethnicity much thought. I didn't know what to say to Sid.

"So what the hell kind of name is *Aragorn?*" he'd go on.

"It means like 'Royal Tree'," Larry told him. "In Elvish."

"Always a joker."

"I'm serious, Pop."

"You kids." Sidney would shake his head, laughing, but looking mostly at me. "Never serious for a moment. Larry the comedian."

I wanted to feel at home here, but I couldn't remember exactly what home should feel like. The actual physical details of my childhood home back on Napoleon Avenue, like the dents Rocky's horse had made in the linoleum of the kitchen floor, my dad with his beer and radio out on the front porch on warm spring nights, and my mother's long curtain of bright hair, were very clear in my memory.

I still knew what the black shade underneath the live oaks out front looked like. I recalled how my ballerina doll Nina danced in the beveled mirror of the dresser in my parents' bedroom. But the memories shook no emotions loose. They made me feel nothing.

I've become disconnected, I realized, feeling small comfort in the sophistication of my alienation.

The Roth house was gracious, totally carpeted in pale green deep pile, modern and insulated. Larry had always joked to me about the suburban Jewish housewives he had grown up among, with their taste for covering every item of formal brocaded living room furniture in clear protective plastic slipcovers, their gilded lamps, and smoked glass mirrored walls. Nancy's furniture sported no transparent slipcovers, and her lamps were imports from Bali. African tribal masks hung over the sofa. But she did have a mirrored wall. I was comforted by that, for some reason. Maybe I needed to have one expectation fulfilled. My expectations were maps to uncharted waters, clues to mysteries like marriage and motherhood. I was disturbed by their inaccuracies.

This was a very quiet house, for one so close to New York City. I lay awake at night to listen for Conrad's breathing so that I'd know he wasn't dead yet from crib death, and all I could hear would be Conrad's baby sighs, and Larry snoring beside me, and the hiss of heat through an air duct.

I am someone's wife, and I don't know how to feel about that, I would realize in sweaty silent panic. I am someone's *mother*, for God's sake, and I don't know what I'm supposed to be feeling. This is like a dream. I keep expecting to wake up. This is all so *not-me*, it's ridiculous. I'm flunking this. Or faking it. I'm flunking faking it.

Sitting in Nancy's formal living room with Conrad when nobody else was home, facing my own darkened reflection in the wall of smoked mirrors, I nursed my baby and wanted to feel something. I let down my hair, seeing the way it tumbled in disorder over the pink infant in my arms, and I tried to look like the Virgin Mary.

And I became so absolutely conflicted, so viscerally pleased by the sensations of the baby's mouth on my nipple, and yet so unsure that it was proper and natural for me to feel this way. I looked down at innocent little Rad, the way he rolled his eyes with effort as I pressed my breast away from his blunt nose with two fingers so that he could breathe, and I wondered if I was perverted, enjoying what felt to me like eroticism. Was I somehow molesting my own child, enjoying our closeness this way? Would he grow up all warped and strange, the son of a mother who didn't feel real love for him yet, who felt only astonishment, disbelief, and really kind of trapped?

In my gut, in my innermost heart, I knew that my own mother Velma had not felt any ambivalence at all about my birth. I knew without being told, I knew for a fact, that Velma Connolly had loved and cherished me from the get-go, from first slimy sight, because I was C. Ray Buchanan's flesh and blood. Velma Connolly had been rehearsing for wife- and motherhood her whole life, waiting for Mr. Right to show up. She had had a religious faith in the eventual advent of Mr. Right. No doubts at all about his existence, no sir. And when he had finally approached the cosmetics counter at D. H. Holmes' department store where she was working as a sales clerk in 1946, showing up right on time in his guise as a redheaded Carolinian sailor, using his polite "ma'am" to her and revealing excellent taste in the bath powder he picked out to send his mother, Velma could not have been very surprised. Thrilled, yes, the way the Magi were thrilled to see the star, maybe, but no more *surprised* than they had been. It had all been foretold.

But what had been foretold for me? What had I been rehearsing for, my whole life up to now? What expectations did I have left? Where was my faith, and in *what*, exactly?

I could only take comfort in the knowledge that Velma had never breastfed me or Rocky. She had not wanted to ruin her figure for C. Ray Buchanan.

"But I didn't breastfeed, either," Nancy Roth told me, over a cup of breakfast coffee at the dinette table near her kitchen. "Us gals in the Fifties were sold bottle feeding and formula as modern improvements. And we bought it, the entire line. This was *science*."

"Unbelievable."

"Jeanne, dear, this was back when *smoking* was recommended for the digestion."

"Yeah, and now we know how essential to a baby's health some of these breast milk components really are," I said. "Like a boost to his immune system. This should have all been self-evident, shouldn't it? I mean, this is the way humanity evolved."

"We did do pretty well on the tit," she agreed. "Einstein was breastfed."

"George Washington, Dickens, Homer."

"And Moses."

I smiled. It did not yet occur to me to think of some notable women to add to our list. I was trying to get through another morning. It wasn't so bad to be trapped this way with Nancy over coffee and danish, with Rad down for his mid-morning snooze, and my feet toasty in my fuzzy bunny slippers.

"See," said Nancy, "women of my generation, your mother's generation, believed whatever the medical community told us. They knew more than we did. It was impossible for them to be wrong. American technology had won the war. They had to know."

"Formula was enriched," I conceded, "yeah."

"Formula," she leaned forward to flick the ashes of her cigarette into the tray in the middle of the table, "was a bitch. To heat up in the middle of the night."

"What was Larry like as a baby?"

She raised her brows and smiled with long but perfect teeth. I admired the precision of her layered haircut. She was a very slim brunette with frown lines and a good nose job. Blue smoke drifted out of her opened mouth. "You want me to say he was adorable."

I laughed.

"Okay, he was adorable. Both he and Kenneth, adorable. Kenneth was quiet. Larry cried all the time."

I bit into my danish.

"You could not shut Larry up, ever, ever. Started talking, never stopped. He was a sweet kid, let me tell you. A very sweet child, but always the funnyman."

"Yeah," I said, and I wondered which of us owned Larry the most.

Her brown eyes looked right at me. "You've married a very good boy, Jeanne."

"I know," I said. "Yeah."

"I mean, Larry's a very, *very* good person. And I'm not just saying that. Because."

I smoothed the quilted robe around my thighs. Something seemed to be called for here from me, an apology of some kind, perhaps. Maybe just an acknowledgment. But I was no good at this either. Flop sweat began to roll through my long bangs. "He married me, I know how good he is. Because he could've done like some guys do, and he didn't. He could've . . . You know."

"'Wham, bam, thank you, ma'am?'" she supplied.

I stirred my coffee. "Thank *you*, ma'am," I told her, too grateful for her levity to show my gratitude any more forcefully than this.

"We raised our boys to be responsible."

"I can see that."

"We also sort of hoped that Larry would become a doctor."

"I know."

"What he's always wanted to be is Milton Berle." She poured herself another cup of coffee. I put a hand over the top of my cup when she held the percolator out to me. I was afraid of transmitting caffeine in my breast milk to Conrad, who tended to be rather naturally wired.

Nancy put the pot down and lit another smoke. "Sid and I used to take the boys to the Catskills every summer. With Sid's mother, just yesterday, it seems like. How can that have been that long ago? Larry was practically a newborn. The *routines* he used to do, on the drive back into the city! We lived in the East Twenties then, same building as Sid's mother. Shecky Green, Mort Sahl—such a memory Larry had, and such timing. Sid Caesar? Larry's favorite television show."

"I'm sorry."

She looked up. "For what?"

"That he didn't become a doctor. That he dropped out of college to marry me. I feel bad about that." And, of course, I was lying. I did not feel bad. I was too young to know what college was for. I was too young, or too naive, or too sheltered by Velma and C. Ray, to know what *any* damned thing was for. I was too Legolas.

Love conquers all. That's what I thought I knew. I concluded that I just didn't know enough about love yet.

If I was deficient in any area of human experience, I thought, I was deficient in love:

Capital-L *Love,* the Beatles' Love-Love-Love ("All you need is—"), the passion I thought I felt for my husband and should soon be feeling for my son. My baby son. My baby husband. We were babies, all three of us. We thought that we could live on *Love.*

That's what I thought I had absorbed from a childhood around Velma and C. Ray Buchanan. Love was the supreme emotion. The ultimate noun.

I did not yet know that love is really a verb.

Forgive me, Larry Roth. Forgive me for a lot of things. If I had known, or even been able to imagine, what things looked like from your viewpoint then, we might have had a better life together. I don't know if we could have made it past the Bimbo Shoals, but we might've had a better voyage in those early, calmer waters.

So forgive me for imagining now, decades too late, an interview with your mother. I heard doors slamming in those days, and your raised voice, and bits of conversations that I was not supposed to hear. But I was a practiced eavesdropper, and so I can't be too far off the mark.

"Jeanne likes you, Ma," you probably told Nancy at some point. "You're totally wrong about her not liking you."

"I know. I'm noticing."

"She actually gets a kick out of you, I think."

A shrug. "I'm outspoken."

"So what's the story?" you ask her.

"You tell me, Larry."

You just stand there, her son the comic, with your hands open and swinging at your sides. You wear one of those wide leather hippie watch bands, and it goes flickety-flickety as the strap flaps against the seam of your jeans.

"Oh, Larry," Nancy sighs. "Larry, Larry. How did this happen?"

"I don't get it," you say, but a wariness in your eyes says that you do get it, a little. You don't sit down. Sitting down might give her the impression that you want to talk, and you most definitely do not want to talk.

"You've just turned twenty-one, you've already got a wife and child, the only job you care about is show business, when you should be trying to attend night school and get your degree. Your father worries, Larry."

"You know why you're not supporting Ken?" you ask about your older brother, the firstborn whom you still faintly resent, the heir-apparent to the family business. You'd rather spear litter on the shoulders of the New Jersey Turnpike than work in the family business. You'd rather be a doctor. But it pisses you off that Kenneth also treats it so casually. Kenneth has run off to Vail, after graduating from Harvard, to become a ski instructor. "You'll be supporting Ken, too, after global warming kicks in," you say.

"This isn't about Ken," says Nancy. "This is about Larry, who went to Tulane for pre-med, who made good grades and made his father proud, and who dropped out to get *married.*"

"To a Catholic girl. You can say it, Ma. I know you're thinking it."

"One day, Larry, there won't be any Jewish people left! Your son, my infant grandson, is not Jewish. This is a *grief* to us. There must've been Jewish girls at Tulane."

"There's nothing to keep Conrad from eventually converting, Ma. Jeanne won't mind."

"But why Jeanne? And why so *soon* with everything? There's such a thing as birth control. She's quite tall. She's taller than you are." Your mother is looking at you and she is deciding that she hates that absurdly wide watch band; It will leave a big white stripe around your wrist, whenever you take it off. It will look terrible with a suit.

But she does like your little face. For you do have a little face, cleanly planed and very neat, nothing misplaced, straight heavy eyebrows. Your curly dark hair gives you a soft aura of puppyhood. Your father is desperate for you to get it cut. But Nancy secretly likes it. It is childish and winning, sweet.

"Jeanne's just really cool, I don't know. She reads palms," you finally offer. You'd like to go into the full range of the subjects you share with Jeanne, the companionship, the conversation, Tolkien.

But you're afraid that your mother will say that nobody can build a marriage on Tolkien. "She's a really deep person. I love her. What exactly do you want me to say here, Ma? That I'd be happier with some shallow princess who lives to *shop?*"

"Jeanne is a rather cold young woman."

"Not to me," you say. "Jeanne makes me less lonely," you say, and mean it. "She's my best friend, Ma. It's just that simple."

"She seems very ambivalent about motherhood, I hate to say it. She doesn't seem very enthusiastic about the baby."

"Ever hear of post-natal depression?"

"She nurses Rad constantly, at all hours of the day and night, whether he cries for her or not. He's going to develop a weight problem, if somebody doesn't do something. He's going to be a very fat child, Larry."

You move closer to the door. "I don't have to listen to this shit."

"She isn't even looking for a good pediatrician! Was she orphaned at birth, or something? Raised by wolves?"

You're not satisfied with the slamming noise the door makes as you go out of it. You open it again, you step back across the threshold, and then you tense your shoulder muscles so that you can slam it *really* significantly, this time.

This is a great slam. Pictures on the wall jump askew. Uncle Frank and Aunt Esther on Miami Beach underneath the palm trees are in an earthquake.

chapter 11

Saturday
Night
Live

J eanne was the one who did not sleep well at night.

I worried enough for both of us in those early days. And I became very concerned about Larry, because he was serious now about trying to make it in show business. Larry was funny. But I wasn't sure that he was funny enough to get people to pay decent money to watch him be funny.

Conrad thought he was funny. But then Conrad thought that dog doo on the sidewalk was funny.

We were living in an okay apartment in Manhattan now, not too far from the subway stop on Fourteenth. It was also close to the Madison Avenue bus stop, where I could catch the bus to my own full time job in the East Fifties. Rad was in daycare now, and did not seem to be psychotic from the experience yet, and I had found work in a gallery.

Larry had finally taken a position with his father's business in the garment industry. As the son of the boss, he was making good money through unenthusiastic effort, but he hated it.

"We make muu-muus for fat women," he'd grouse. "We furnish two-hundred-pound housewives with nylon tricot *tents*, printed in colors I defy you to find in nature."

"Here. Sit." I'd help him out of his overcoat. "You want a beer?"

"Put lace on 'em, you know what happens? They look like a fucking *daybed.* Like fucking *furniture.*"

"I don't know if we want to expand Rad's vocabulary in this precise way just yet, honey."

"Sid-Nan Lingerie: eye pollution. Crimes against nylon." He'd sit. "Jeanne, I think I've finally met somebody who knows somebody, and there's been some early talk—early, yeah, okay—but *talk,* about getting me an audition with (fill in the blank here with any one you want, because the names of the agents kept changing. But the story was always the same.)"

Conrad would bring Larry his stuffed dolphin toy to hug. I would watch my husband get all jacked up with hope one more time, and I would wonder if Larry was really that naive, to believe that jumping from the tiny downtown clubs he was currently playing, to something like Johnny Carson, was actually possible. Did anybody ever get a lucky break of that magnitude, or was that mostly just showbiz legend? Did Larry personally know anybody who had made that jump, besides Bette Midler? And he really didn't know Bette all that well.

Or was I the fool, in being such a secret naysayer, broadcasting these negative vibes, when all it might take to insure Larry Roth's popular immortality would be my total and clear-eyed faith?

I stood at the bus stop on frigid days after getting Conrad to daycare, when the temperature was just above single digits, and I would feel almost dizzy with disorientation.

Why doesn't this feel like my authentic life yet? I'd wonder. This *is* the American Dream, non-Velma version. We have almost enough money. Our kid is normal. Our marriage is okay. I have a job I can tolerate.

I refused to admit it, but I missed the familiar seasonal rhythms of home. The long and intolerable summers with their consolation of Junior Atomic Snow-Bliz snowballs in piña colada and creme de menthe flavors. The mild, rainy winters. Up here, late winter was just late winter. More dirty sleet. Back home, late winter meant the sequins and feathers and cheap glass beads of Mardi Gras, the camaraderie of neighbors around Daddy's beer kegs on sunny warmish days. Daddy had held me or Rocky on his shoulders for the parades, so that we could see and catch the throws. Mama had made our costumes. Rocky had always wanted to be a cowboy, but Mama had stitched many a pretty pink tutu or fairy princess dress for me, during the years of my childhood.

Now, on New York mornings, I stood at the bus stop and had nothing to look forward to. Fresh from my morning shower, my hair would still be wet, and I would ponder its stiff, frozen spikiness with my fingers. I could snap the little haircicles in half with an audible popping, uncovering bright red strands and liberating them for a second from their sheathing of ice before they refroze.

Where was I? What was this icy place I was in?

"Your father just won't stop smoking," my mother called from New Orleans. "Doctors all say he's got to quit, diabetes affects the circulation. Rocky tries to talk some sense into him, but I swear, you know these hardheaded Buchanans. That hard head up under all that red hair."

And I could hear her own obvious puff of cigarette smoke coming over the phone line to me, that telltale pause in conversation, the sharp inhaling. "How can he quit, Mama, if you keep spewing it in his face all the time?"

"He's a grown man, he could quit if he wanted to."

"Well, so could you. It might help him quit, if both of you tried to quit together. You do everything else together."

"He's always got his face shut up in some book these days, you know how he is," she said. "Won't listen to anybody."

"You need your own hobby, Mama."

"My hobby is your daddy."

"Well, you need to give Daddy his space, Mama, and just find yourself something else to fuss with. I don't imagine it's so easy for him, his body slowing down on him this way, without having to be reminded of it every single second. He'll quit smoking when he's ready."

"Yeah. Sure." She exhaled what I was sure was blue smoke.

"He gave up beer."

"Only because I kept telling him I was way too young to be a widow."

"Why don't *you* get a job, Mama?" I said, fed up.

But I was sorry as soon as I had said it because it was unfair. Velma was no longer job material. She had been out of the work force for too long. She had once been very clever, and beautiful. And she was still goodlooking, even if her tastes ran to frilly whimsies that were much too tight and too young for her now. She had an unfortunate weakness for sleeveless outfits, and her upper arms were developing flabby wings. But Velma had lost faith in her own cleverness.

C. Ray now balanced the checkbook.

I used to fret that they loved each other too much, I remembered, and didn't have enough left over for me and Rocky. Now I worry that they love each other too little. Or have lost faith in each other.

Maybe they're just losing faith, in general. In everything. Mama never goes to Mass anymore. Maybe that's what getting older really means. Losing faith.

I can analyze my own subtle loss of faith these days, but I don't know what to do about it. I can see Larry's losses mounting. They are obvious, and very public. And I don't know how to help him.

"So why do we call 'em *Billy*goats and *Nanny*goats, anyway?" went part of his comedy routine. "Were Billy and Nanny the trendy upscale baby names among Old English goatherds? Modern take: Jasongoats and Jennifergoats. Brandongoats and Kimberlygoats, why not? You see where I'm going with this. What is your name, sir?" he'd lean into the audience with the microphone held out to some old guy he hoped would be named Irving.

Larry wasn't bad onstage. He had confidence in his own appeal, and took advantage of his own naturally rapid speech pattern. He improvised a lot, and much of what he said wasn't flat-out hilarious, but he did have great timing. He never gave the audience a chance to notice if something he said wasn't particularly funny, because he immediately went on to something else. His body language and facial expressions were instinctive and terrific. He was a gifted mimic, a fine observer of people, and unpredictable.

"This is my impersonation of the late great Clark Gable," he might say, and then lie down flat on his back on the stage floor with a white lily clutched over his rib cage.

But the larger clubs did not call. The good agents said that they already represented too many clients to take on another one.

"A Rockette attack!" he'd suddenly yell, mid-monologue, and then yank up the legs of his flared jeans to his knees and do two or three manic hairylegged high kicks. "A Rockette attack, ladies and gentlemen!"

Then the microphone might go into the audience again: "Pardon me, sir, can you rhumba?"

But Larry's big break finally did come. Just like he'd always hoped, it showed up when least expected. And it came on the worst day of my life.

Or the worst one I'd had, up until then.

He was working that Saturday at his father's office. So when I got the phone call for him at noon, I just gave the caller his work number at Sid-Nan Lingerie. It was an ordinary Saturday afternoon. Conrad, captivated by Muppets these days, was twisting the television dial in a Muppet search. I was deep in a book about adult-onset diabetes. After answering the call for Larry, I remember that I made myself a cup of herbal tea and sat beside the dirty radiator to sip it. Sleet fell outside. Rad couldn't find any Muppets, and got cranky about it.

Larry, up to his ears in next fall's nightwear, thought that the caller was kidding.

"You're kidding," he said into the phone. "Who is this?"

"Please hold for Mr. Michaels' office," said the female voice, and then Larry found himself connected with a production assistant at *Saturday Night Live.*

Larry had been courting the show ever since its debut back in the autumn, and his various club dates had been cruised by NBC scouts. One staffer very much liked him, or claimed to. She did come to several of his shows. I got to meet her. I even read her palms for her. But Larry didn't get a call.

He'd sit up with me late, long after Conrad was bedded down with his plush stuffed dolphin, and we'd catch the show on Saturdays, if Larry had no club date himself. The show used a nucleus of unknown comic actors who performed most of the sketches and special material. But once in a while, a totally new face would pop up for five minutes of fill-in, like a guy we saw doing a macho lumberjack number in a brassiere. "I'm funnier than that, aren't I?" Larry would slip a perplexed arm around my shoulders. "Aren't I funnier than that? Maybe I should try *musical* schtick like that. I'm tone deaf, my father's side of the family. Maybe that'd be funny, actually."

"No," I'd say. "The audience would feel sorry for you."

So Larry had just about given up on *SNL,* when this phone call came out of nowhere. He was alone at Sid-Nan, working overtime on an ordinary Saturday. He looked at his watch. It was five after two, here in the Twilight Zone.

"Jeanne, listen," he called me, hyperventilating, pulling on his overcoat while he babbled, "LaBelle has canceled for tonight's show, they need somebody else on extremely short notice. I've gotta go audition for the producer, some other people, I can't even remember my own name. I need your magic, honey. Chant something, light some candles. Invoke the Elvish pantheon."

"I don't understand why you need to audition. Jean's seen your act. She likes you."

"She's not the head honcho. Look, I've gotta go. Shit, I don't know if I can boil down what I do into a strong three minutes. Should I interrupt with the Rockette thing? I don't know how physical they want this. Is the Rockette thing too physical?"

"Their cast is pretty physical. The Samurai thing is physical..."

"Shit, I don't want to get *too* physical, if all their people are physical already. What have I got that's cerebral? Do I do anything cerebral?"

"Clark Gable is cerebral."

"Yeah, but I have to physically lie down on the floor!"

Behind me, Conrad began to whine, because he couldn't find anything on television but nature documentaries and college football.

"I've gotta go," said Larry. "Kiss, kiss."

"Break a leg," I told him. "I love you."

Well, I thought, plopping down into my rocking chair after hanging up the phone. Well, well, well. *Elbereth Gilthoniel.* Send him some good vibes, Lady Elbereth and all you Elvish gods. Jesus. Saint Joan. Whoever's listening. He really needs to ace this, guys.

My tea cup rattled in its saucer with my nerves.

Larry was rehearsing his act on the subway at that same instant, doing it mentally because he didn't want people to think he was disturbed. He couldn't get into a flow situation. The Puerto Rican kids near him looked like criminals. One of them cleaned underneath his nails with a sharpened screwdriver.

Screwed, thought Larry. My middle name.

He kept hoping that time was really on his side, and since tonight's performance was mere hours away, *SNL* would be willing to take whatever it could get on such short notice. But there were a number of other people waiting outside the production offices when he got there. Larry recognized a face or two, from clubs and from flyers.

A female voice came from behind a closed door in a parody of the Queen of England as a game show contestant. Nobody laughed audibly in there, but the unseen comedienne was distressingly good.

The producer and Jean and several writers made up Larry's audience when it came his turn to go inside. They were all gracious, and they smiled, and Jean gave him her hand and told him how good it was to see him again. But there were so few of them, and they kept looking down and scribbling things onto legal pads. The lighting was very bright, not like at a club. Nobody laughed out loud at Larry. This was very serious business with them.

This is like performing in Pop's office, thought Larry, despairing. To six accountants. To six *deaf* accountants at an audit.

"I didn't get it," he finally called me from a pay phone, after he'd walked almost thirty blocks downtown towards home in the cold. He had not wanted to call me until he could stop sounding like he'd been crying. He still sounded like it. "Some woman got it. Some British woman. From the cast of a Noel Coward thing off-Broadway. She's really good."

"It's okay, honey, there'll be other times. Jean won't forget you," I bullshat, feeling really bad and sad. "Come on home. Maybe we can do something tonight, get a babysitter. Go to Chinatown. Take in a show or something."

"No Noel Coward," he said.

"No to Noel. Right on."

"You need anything from Gristede's, while I'm out? We out of coffee or anything?" He sounded too normal to be normal.

"Milk. Rad's low on milk."

"Right. Okay."

But he forgot to stop by Gristede's, and he was milkless and oblivious to that milklessness when he got home. Sleet melted in his hair. His brown eyes were hyper bright and intensely calm. He was the definition of nonchalance as he shrugged out of his overcoat. I hugged him and hung up the wet coat near the radiator.

"Daddy! Daddy!" roared Conrad. "Find me the Muppets!"

I decided to go out for the milk, because I didn't want to be around Larry's controlled misery and bright eyes just yet. He stooped to fiddle with the television antenna while I went off to find my galoshes, mumbling about milk and sleet and where my purse might be.

Larry, noticing, remembered. "Honey, I'll go! Honey, I'm sorry."

"No," I said, "Rad's waited all day to see you, and I could use some exercise. And I can't bring in Channel Four with those stupid rabbit ears the way you can."

So it all boiled down to rabbit ears and milk, the reason I went out that evening. Rabbit ears and milk and *Saturday Night Live*.

I looked back and smiled at my guys, but they were head-to-head at the TV screen. "Don't sit so close to the television, Rad," I said, sounding like my own mother. "It can ruin your eyes."

Neither of them looked up.

I went down the stairs.

chapter 12

The Worst Day of My Life, So Far

I really didn't mind going back out for the milk, because I knew that the cold air would bring me around and wake me from this sad stupor.

It had been a very unattractive day, even before Larry's *SNL* disaster had capped it off. Conrad was coming down with another cold. I hated it whenever Rad was sick, the anxiety, the sitting up with him, the constant temperature checks. I hated the whining, bellicose moods fevers put him into. And I especially hated how guilty I felt, mashing a pillow over my head whenever I heard him crying or heard the alarm clock go off, reminding me to get up and check him or give him more medication. I hated myself for wanting more sleep in my life.

I dawdled at Gristede's now, shuffling down the aisles of the supermarket in my galoshes, looking at smoked oysters in tins on the canned meat shelf. I thought about New Orleans, about the way fresh oysters sat in ice in that seafood shop on Magazine Street. I felt myself at Mama's hem again, Rocky alongside in his stroller, shiny baby slobber oozing down over his multiple chins. I could smell Mama's perfume even over the stink of fish. I could hear her overly modulated actressy voice telling the man behind the counter how many pounds of shrimp she wanted.

Let Larry watch Conrad for a while, I told myself as I went over to the paperback aisle and read cover blurbs. Do him good. Do both of them good. If Larry's got to cry some more, Rad can cry right along with him, poor little feverish guy. I don't know what to do for either of them right now. What I need right now is a good, involving novel.

But after a while, what I felt as I lingered over the books began to seem more like guilt than freedom. I bought a promising mystery and a quart of whole milk. I let myself through the black glare of the glass front door, back out into the noisy frigid night.

The sleet was turning to snow.

I loved snow, with all of the impossible ardor of a Louisiana child singing "I'm Dreaming Of A White Christmas" right along with Bing Crosby on the radio, and yet knowing that the chances for snow were just about as good as the chances of a Martian invasion. We saw snow only twice, Rocky and I, growing up. The second time had come in the dark, and Velma and C. Ray had turned on all the porch lights and had let us run out into the small front yard at eleven o'clock at night so that we could try to build a snow man before it all melted.

I felt something now as I remembered. I felt something unexpectedly tender as I thought about Mama dressing me in warm clothes in the middle of the night, so that I could experience one modest little snowfall before it was too late.

I smiled now in the Manhattan darkness, snowflakes messing with my eyelashes. I remembered the way C. Ray and Velma stood silhouetted in the yellow rectangles of light from the house windows, arm in arm, laughing at Rocky and me as we frolicked and hollered, laughing just to be laughing.

I do love you, I thought at the memory of my parents in the snow, you ridiculous pair of old lovebirds. I guess I ought to remember that more.

I hoped that Larry would be feeling better by the time I got back. I didn't know how to comfort Larry. Velma had let C. Ray handle his own comforting, back when men weren't supposed to need it. I didn't know if my father had, in fact, needed it much. Whenever Daddy had come home glum, like when the Falstaff Brewery had closed and he had needed to sign on with someplace else, a few cans of cold beer had soon put him to rights. Beer, and *National Geographic,* and that old white plastic radio. Daddy had always been able to find some sort of ball game on that radio, whatever the season. He'd take it out there on the front porch, and twirl the dial, and move the whole thing up or down or right or left, until he could get a clear signal from somewhere. He could pick up other places after sundown, other states. He never minded listening to baseball from Fort Wayne, Indiana, or a college football game from someplace in Florida. He would chug his beer and listen until the signal faded out, or until Mama called us all inside for supper.

But Larry was different. Larry couldn't be distracted by sports or magazines. And Larry was not a beer person. Larry believed that drinking alone was unhealthy.

His disappointment frightened me now, a little, because I had never before been close to a person who had wanted something this badly and then lost it. I didn't know how to help. C. Ray and Velma had never seemed to want or to need anything besides what they already had.

And all I ever really wanted for myself was just to put a little distance between me and the two of them, I realized now. To *breathe,* I guess. And I got that. I got it so easily. Larry did bring that to me.

Thinking about Larry made me tired. I dragged my galoshes over the dirty wet sidewalk. It's so *tiring* to love somebody, I thought. Mama and Daddy made it look effortless. But it takes so much out of me. Am I the anomaly, or are they?

I was thinking these things as I pushed open the front door and stepped into the tiny foyer of our apartment building. A young man with a brown ponytail stood near the mailboxes. I juggled my belongings and paid him no attention at all, until he threw a leather belt over my head and began to strangle me.

chapter 13   My
                              Turn
                              with
                              Crime

H e was not trying to kill me. He was trying to get me to do something.

"You got keys?" he grunted, lifting me off my feet, pushing my knees and the toes of my galoshes against the painted white wood of the locked inner front door. *"Keys!"*

So now it comes, I realized with mild surprise. My turn with crime. My turn as victim.

My assailant jerked at the belt again. *"Keys,* Red. You think I'm kidding? You think I won't kill you?"

My ordinary personality, the one which had been pissing and moaning about life with Larry awhile ago, was ready to swoon away in panic, the way it expected to. It had been conditioned by movies and books to believe in panic and the inevitability of it.

Imagine this personality's astonishment, then, when another layer of consciousness elbowed it aside like a rubbernecking bystander. The newcomer was as businesslike and cold as an assembly line robot. And when it looked out of my eyes now, my vision cleared to eagle levels. Time slowed, almost stopping altogether. I felt my brain switching into a much higher gear than I had known it possessed.

Circuit breakers were tripped. Emotions were turned off. Fear disappeared. Fear was *not*.

The state of being, for me, went under a cosmic microscope. I could see every flake of debris on the dirty tiled floor between the dangling toes of my galoshes, and every flake had meaning.

"Keys!"

I held the clump of my keys in my palm. The brown paper sack with the milk and paperback in it had been dropped. I saw the white liquid puddling on the floor, mixing in spiral swirls with the black sooty melted sleet. There was logic to what was happening.

I held up the keys so that my attacker could see them.

"Good." Tobacco breath was at my ear. "Open the door."

Go along with him, counseled my new inner robot. You can't see what he has back there, could be a knife or a gun. You don't know how sane he is. Play along. Collect data.

It was hard to get the keys into the lock and twist them while being garroted like this. Am I getting enough oxygen? I consulted my atomically clear mind.

You're breathing, aren't you? it answered. Don't antagonize him into cutting off more of it, though. Stay calm. Collect data.

So this is how they do it, soldiers in combat, people trapped in fires or stewardesses landing airliners, I marveled. People don't actually go to pieces in panic, not if you can get beyond panic. There is another level of consciousness beyond it. Books don't tell you that. Maybe the authors who write the books have never experienced it.

Wow.

I heard the door slam behind me, behind both me and my attacker, as he dangled me ahead of him and maneuvered me onto the stained deep blue carpeting of the heated first floor hallway. Tall as I am, I must have been very hard to dangle.

The closed doors of the two apartments on this level presented themselves, their tarnished brass numbers glittering above their fish eye peepholes. The radiator clanked. What now? I wondered. I've let him inside the building. I've actually let a robber inside the safety of this locked building. That isn't very neighborly of me.

Be quiet! my mind warned me.

Conrad is upstairs, I remembered. Larry and Conrad are right upstairs, unarmed. Little Rad with his blotchy, feverish face and his stuffed plush dolphin and his tender baby eyelids is up there with his sad pacifist daddy, neither of them with so much as a decent steak knife. There is not one single thing between Rad and Larry and this criminal now, except four flights of stairs and a flimsy locked door. And I'm holding the keys.

Quiet! shouted my mind. Let me handle this.

What if—?

Shut up! One thing at a time. Don't anticipate. Don't get rattled. Take one second at a time. Evaluate it. Collect data. Wait for your chance.

I was stopped in front of a door under the staircase, at a door that wasn't an apartment door. It had an old faceted glass knob, and a painted-over lock. It stood an inch or so ajar. I felt the heaving of my attacker's breath against my back. His chest was at my shoulder blades. He was tiring from lifting me off my feet this way. His elbows dug into my back as he sought leverage against my height.

Is this my chance? I wondered, realizing.

Not yet, came the answer. Take it easy. He might have a weapon. And since he is male, his upper body strength is greater than yours, whatever your relative heights. Wait.

"What's here?" he grunted at my ear. His breath stank like an ash tray. "What's this door?"

"Boiler room."

"Open it."

I pulled the door open. Light fell onto an unpainted planked landing. Rickety wooden steps led down into the basement. I had an impression of blackened brick walls. I had been down here a time or two, changing fuses, but had never paid much attention to details. The wooden steps were tricky, I did remember, narrow and uneven. The cement floor was a long way down.

"Go," said my attacker.

Somebody had mercifully left the light on down there, a bare low-watt bulb swinging over the staircase from a utilitarian cord, its bead chain dangling. The light was very dim.

"*Go,* I said!"

I went.

This is either a robbery or a rape, I thought. Probably both, since he doesn't need to take me down to the basement just to snatch my purse. But why would anybody want to rape *me?* I'm Jeanne, ugly duckling. Poster child for the hopelessly homely. Maybe he thinks he's doing me a favor.

"You don't have to do this," I heard my inner robot say to him with my mouth. "If we'd met some other way, like at a bar or party or something, we might've hit it off, who knows? You're not a bad-looking guy, why do you think you have to do this?"

"Shut up." He jerked the belt and forced me down the first two steps.

Your talk is making him nervous, my robot told me. Keep it up. Say what I tell you to say.

This is dissociation! realized my ordinary personality, recalling what I had read about psychology. This is how multiple personalities get started, one splitting off from another during a trauma!

Yeah, said my robot, and we're both going to have to survive this evening if we want to live long enough to become *Sibyl,* honey. Focus on the main danger here. Forget going psycho. Concentrate upon living.

"I betcha you've never done anything like this before," my voice complied in a grotesque rasp, the pressure upon my larynx making me sound like a stranger to myself. "This is ridiculous, risking your future like this, when we might've just hit it off in the ordinary way and just had a magical thing going, you know? Buy me dinner, go back to your place—"

The guy cut off more of my air supply. "Shut up!"

Where's the next stair step? I wondered. If I trip myself in these fucking galoshes and miss it, I'll get my neck broken.

I tried to assess his strength. I had not gotten a very good look at him as I'd come in from outside, and that had been a mistake. I had let down my guard, had turned my back on him. But he hadn't given off criminal vibes, and he wasn't hispanic or black or doped-up or a biker type. He'd had a long brown ponytail and a mellow little hippie beard on his chin, deceptively all peace and love and flowers. He was a fairly young guy, too, no older than me, maybe twenty-four, and skinny.

But he could be armed, I reminded myself. You don't know what he's carrying. What kind of hopeless amateur goes a-raping with nothing but a leather belt?

"You seem like a real mellow guy," my mouth continued its chitchat, on automatic pilot, while I felt for each uncertain step down and forced air in and out of myself. The belt interfered more with my voice than it did with my breathing. "I'm slightly psychic, I read palms and all that shit, I figure you for an amateur. Don't turn pro here, man. It's not too late."

"Shut up! Shut up!" he said. "No talking!"

Good, I thought. He's the one who's getting rattled now, losing concentration. Don't get him too rattled, though, or he'll kill you by mistake. A crushed larynx is not your goal. A fall down these stairs could be fatal.

"I don't think you're used to this shit," I croaked, reaching the concrete floor. "You're above this kind of behavior, I can tell. You seem like an okay guy. But this is crazy."

"Yeah," he panted, "I'm crazy, and you're crazy, and this whole fucking city is crazy. Take off your clothes."

Yes, go ahead, said my robot self. Take them off. Rad and Larry are safe upstairs, as long as you can keep this nut from wanting to go upstairs. What've you got to lose? They're only clothes, they're not worth dying for. Take them off.

"I can't get my turtleneck sweater off, with this belt around my neck," I said out loud. "You want me to just leave it on?"

He hesitated, and then loosened the noose and slipped it off over my head. "No. Take everything off."

I wanted to turn my head, to get a look at him and see if he had a knife or a gun. I made a tiny movement of my head as I pulled the sweater over it.

"Don't turn around!" he warned. "I'll kill you."

Yeah, he might, I thought. He's an amateur. He's too rattled now to be efficient. He could screw up.

So I did not turn my head. I stood carefully on one leg and then the other, like a flamingo, removing my galoshes and then my jeans. My black shadow made a long dim stirring on the dusty concrete floor. His shadow stood alongside it. He was still near. He breathed very loudly.

Something popped, his knuckles or the leather belt. He made soft, nervous poppings. I could hear him over the noise of the boiler.

Be as unerotic as you can, my robot self coached me. Remove your clothes like Conrad. Like a five-year-old boy. Scratch. Burp. Kick your underwear into a heap.

I stood naked now in the half-light, a splash of white skin atop the feet of my own long black shadow.

"Caress yourself," ordered my attacker.

Yeah, caress yourself like a truck driver, said my robot. Pretend you're old Mr. DiBenedetto, searching yourself for malignant melanoma. Pretend you're Larry in the shower. Sing. Something inappropriate. Roy Rogers and Dale Evans: "Happy Trails To You."

"Stop singing! Christ!"

I pinched and prodded at myself, like a teenager squeezing acne eruptions.

"This isn't working," muttered the guy. "Stop."

I stopped.

"Come over here. Don't look at me."

I crept across the cold concrete floor on my bare feet, head down, until I could see high-topped basketball sneakers. It was snowing outside, but he was shod in canvas shoes. That might mean something.

"Come closer," he said.

I came closer, until the knees of his jeans and then his unzipped fly came into view. He wore dark green bikini briefs. I couldn't see his hands, what weapon he was holding.

He put a palm on the top of my head and pushed me down, urging me to kneel. He slipped the noose of the belt back over my head, but did not tighten it this time.

There is no knife visible, I noticed. Both of his hands are accounted for now. I wish his palms were open, so that I could see what kind of Head Line and what kind of Heart he has, what relationship they have, whether the Line of Head joins the Line of Life or not. At what angle. I'll bet they're not joined at all. I'll bet this moron has impulsive palms, probably a Fire type, with a simian line, fingertip loops opening towards the thumb on, like, Jupiter and Saturn. Everything chained and indistinct. A real mess.

But both of his palms are closed. He holds the belt buckle in one hand, his limp penis in the other.

"I can't get hard," he complained. "Suck it."

I took his floppy little penis into my mouth, and I felt the unknown power of *Woman,* of the witch.

It's just a penis, for heaven's sake, I realized. You could bite it right off at the roots. You have the power to resurrect it, or you can bite it right off. Here it lies in your mouth like a big dead slug. Some rapist.

"Suck it," he ordered.

So I did. I sucked it exactly like I would have sucked a big dead slug.

Nothing happened. It shriveled further.

For God's sake! I thought, don't sex offenders normally get it up *before* assaulting a victim? What if he blames me for this, and decides to kill me for it? Maybe I should pay more attention to what I'm supposed to be doing here, and do it right.

No, my inner robot disagreed. You're doing fine. This is not a beauty contest. Be as unexciting and disgusting as you can be. Too bad you can't pick your nose in this position. See if you can manage a fart.

"I can't fuck you," mumbled the guy, half to me and half to himself. "I can't get hard."

I took my mouth away from him, noticing that he no longer had a determined grip on the belt noose. He wasn't doing anything now, as a matter of fact. Just standing there like that, literally at loose ends, limp all over, with his free hand dangling at his side and his fly still open. I even felt a little bit sorry for him.

No! objected my robot self. Do not let your guard down! This asshole has threatened your life and perpetrated violence. This asshole is your enemy.

"May I stop now?" I asked him, my voice soft, using my mother's correct and ladylike locution.

"Don't look up at me!"

I kept my head down and my eyes on his sneakers. "May I stop? I don't want to hurt you. My teeth are kind of serrated and sharp."

"Might as well," he muttered after a long pause.

His sneakered feet shifted. I did not look up, but I could definitely hear him zipping himself back up, neatening his clothing. He took his belt from around my neck again, finally, and I sensed him snaking it back through the belt loops of his jeans, where it belonged.

"I've never done anything like this before," he said.

No kidding, I thought.

"You gonna call the cops?" he asked me.

And that's when I realized that I had won. He wasn't going to kill me now. He could have. All it would have taken would have been that belt and my neck, and his greater upper body strength. He could have even just pushed me down the stairs, if he was in too much of a hurry to throttle me. But I could detect defeat and befuddlement in his voice, and I knew that he was no longer capable of it. Whatever devils or furies that had possessed him five minutes ago were gone. Sucked right out of him.

Am I going to call the cops?

"I don't know," I answered truthfully. "Maybe."

Sure you are! countered my inner robot. You are going to do whatever it takes to nail this motherfucker's amateur ass to the Attica Prison wall!

"Just give me about five minutes head start," he said. "Don't look at me."

I stared at my clothes piled on the floor, eight feet away. "I don't know what makes you think I'm going to run up these unheated stairs stark naked in January and locate a telephone in under five minutes."

He came very close to me. I flinched, eyes still on my clothes.

He leaned over and kissed my cheek. I smelled his cigarette breath again. "You're sweet, Red."

I stood there not looking at him as he went up the stairs, aware of feeling very cold now, goose bumps popping out on my thighs and upper arms. His feet pounded the steps above me.

The door creaked open at the top of the stairs. The hallway light swept the floor with its opening. The door closed again and the light vanished.

I looked up.

The heavy outside door to the street crashed shut, vibrating the building.

The boiler made ordinary noises.

I stood motionless for another five minutes, making sure that he wasn't coming back. Then I gathered up my clothes from the dirty chilled floor and tugged them back on.

Larry's probably called all over, looking for me, I realized. He's probably called Gristede's, called the cops, called Nancy and Sid. He can't go out looking for me because Conrad has a sore throat, he probably wonders if I have just left him or something, gone to a bar; he's probably mentally replayed every exchange, every conversation, every interaction that he and I have shared in the last four days, looking for clues and hidden meanings, calling my co-workers from the gallery, biting his nails and searching his soul, listening for sirens in the street . . .

I mounted the steps now with brio, but my knees were weakening as I climbed. Well, this is what I expected, I told myself: weak knees, like in books or movies. It's that other thing that I didn't expect. That *strong*-kneed thing.

Maybe I'm in some kind of shock, but I feel wonderful, actually. I feel like hugging Conrad until he giggles, and baking a chocolate cake, and making a big pot of coffee and staying up all night dancing to Motown records with Larry, and pouring brandy into my coffee, and going out into the street to build myself a snow man.

No, make that a snow *woman*, a big, fearless figure with her head up and her mouth open, ready to outtalk and outwit any nut burger stupid enough to pick on her.

Look at me. I'm actually sort of a heroine now, I guess. I've met my enemy, and I psyched him out, grossed him out, and verbally castrated the poor bastard. He'll be impotent for the rest of his life. Someday he'll visit a shrink and tell him all about the time the tall redhead fucked him over and left him a shell of his former self. I'll live forever as a demon in his psyche.

I began to laugh out loud as I went up the stairs, identifying with the warrior maidens and battle queens of history, shaking my head over my assailant's ineptitude. I thought about Tolkien's valiant females, Luthien and Éowyn and especially Galadriel, who had played mind games with the Dark Lord himself and won.

I wonder if she wanted to bake *lembas* afterwards, I grinned to myself. Dance all night with her husband.

I let myself into my own apartment four flights up, flushed hot with my triumph, knowing that my face was as red now as my hair. I rattled the key in the lock longer than I needed to.

Larry sat dozing on the sofa, mouth gaping in a snore. Rad lay sprawled on the shag carpet, asleep, in front of the unwatched television set. The radiator hissed in the peace of the place. The air of the apartment was warm and ordinary.

"Larry?" I touched his shoulder, incredulous. How could he be *napping*? His wife was missing! How could he be asleep?

"Wha?"

"Larry?"

He blinked up at me, no longer bright eyed, and he was neither overjoyed nor astonished to see me. "Still sleeting?" he asked me, saying the first thing that came to his waking mind.

And I realized that I had not been gone long at all. I hadn't been absent long enough to cause anybody the slightest worry. My ineffectual attacker had slunk off early, had given up on this particular crime very early, and my husband had waited up here in this comfortable warmth until it had put him to sleep. Larry had not been worrying about me. He had been eating his own heart out over *Saturday Night Live*. This real-life movie was still about Larry Roth. Larry was the star of this Saturday night movie.

"I dropped the milk," I said finally, having nothing else at all to say.

But I could see the pupils of Larry's eyes contract as they focused upon my disordered clothing. My turtleneck sweater, inside out. The reddened and abraded skin under my jaw.

"Rad'll just have to make do in the morning with apple juice, if he finishes off the milk tonight." I tugged at the neck of my sweater to cover the marks on my neck. I didn't feel like playing heroine any-more. The moment had passed.

"What the hell—?"

I tried to cut my losses, because I realized that I was not going to get battle cries or praise here. It wasn't just Larry Roth. No man in the world was going to shriek his woman's triumph to the skies and toss his sword into the air, under these circumstances. No, husbands would bemoan a wife's oral violation—any damned husband would—and then call the police.

"Jeanne? What the hell—?"

I smoothed back my red bangs and marched to the telephone table in a fury, fury at both my innocent husband and my attacker, both of them. And let me say here how much I hate calling that inept criminal weenie "my attacker," as if he belongs to me, the way we mean it when we say "my date" or "my admirer." But I don't know what else to call him, and God knows I hope he's ten years dead now with some wasting and painful disease like pancreatic cancer. If I am indeed somehow voodooish, he definitely is. He was *wrong* about me. I am not sweet.

I grabbed the phone now and called the cops myself, before Larry could think about it and do it for me and then lull me into a stupor of victimhood with chicken soup while we waited for the police to drop by. I foresaw the hugs, the handholding. My unwilling tears.

Do I sound unreasonably angry here? I was.

It had also begun to occur to me in a very faint way that grossing out a rapist was not necessarily a positive thing for my own already shaky body image.

Was Larry totally innocent? He was.

Do I sound like a complete witch here?

chapter 14

How
to
Scare
off
Men

T hat rapist wasn't the only man I've scared off in my time.

Since Larry Roth, the terrain of my life has been somewhat flat and sere, dotted with gal pals from the gallery where I worked in New York, my ex-mother-in-law, some casual men friends, my son Conrad, my parents and Rocky. And the main point of this chapter: those several brief love affairs that never quite got off the ground.

In fact, through personal experience as well as observation, I've now become an expert in guaranteed and time-tested methods to scare off a man. It will become perfectly clear why I was still unattached at the time of my mother's diagnosis, if I share some of these methods here, in no order of importance.

One can talk a lot about one's kid, for instance. Make sure that Mr. Not-Quite-Right-But-Hey-He's-Breathing knows that you have a kid. Be especially sure to emphasize how moody and fucked up your kid is.

Utter the word "relationship" as much as you can. Encourage him to "talk things out," and criticize him when he doesn't confide in you like your girlfriends do.

Cry during the love scenes in movies.

Dwell upon that cute anecdote about how your mom met your dad, and stress the notion of romantic *fate*.

Supply him with your ring size.

Don't forget to tell all your girlfriends how big/small his penis is, so that they can give him those giggly embarrassed looks the next time they see him. If he tends to be naturally paranoid, this can work wonders.

Buy his Christmas presents in September, *and make sure he knows it*.

Send him lots of pastel greeting cards upon every possible occasion, with soft focus photos of couples holding hands in the rain. Between official occasions, send him the ones which begin, "Just Thinking About You . . ."

Speak in baby talk when you introduce him to your teddy bears. I haven't actually tried this one. I am not fluent in that language. But I hear it's effective.

Place a framed photo of him on your desk at work, and kiss it whenever you wear lipstick.

Make sure he knows that he is absolutely the only thing in the entire universe which gives your lonely life any meaning whatsoever.

Lock yourself in the bathroom whenever he seems distant, and threaten to swallow the contents of the medicine cabinet.

Telephone his mother frequently for long, warm, family-style chats.

Insist upon handing him the receiver, whenever your parents call you long distance, and wear a coy smile. Tell him how much they *love* him and want to meet him as soon as possible, in case they don't get around to telling him this themselves.

Then prepare to spend the rest of your life singly, living with your mother in some dead-end insular one horse town, watching old *Love Boat* reruns on television every night. Until one of you goes nuts enough to be locked away.

Which one? It's a toss-up.

chapter 15

St.
Rocky
of
Napoleon
Avenue

"They have wonderful daycare programs here now," Nancy Roth told me that summer that I cut all of my hair off in Auletta, "for people in Velma's situation. I would imagine that someone down there, the Alzheimer's Association or somebody, is running something similar in your general area, Jeanne."

"But this is a very rural place out here, Nance," I'd dodge. "I'd have to drive a very long way to find any kind of competent adult daycare. All the way to Covington or Mandeville, probably. Slidell is probably not sophisticated enough, I don't know. People in Slidell keep proudly telling me about how they kept Grandpa at home, until he got run over flashing his privates out on Highway Eleven."

What I was sidestepping, actually, was my mother's fright now at seeing people. Or, to be more precise, at having them see her, even old friends like Dolores Bordelon from Napoleon Avenue. Each new day was already a scary adventure for Velma. She already felt like a new kid at school, even in her own home, where you don't know if you'll be able to locate your classroom, remember the teacher's name, or if the other kids will laugh at you if you make a mistake. And, horror of horrors, what if you can't find the bathroom, and you wet your pants? My mother became extremely upset at the mention of daycare. She made terrible toileting errors whenever she became upset.

What kind, you ask?

Have you ever had a parent bring you a human turd in the palm of her hand at two o'clock in the morning, to ask you what it is?

"I do love you, Jeanne. I'm thinking about you," Nancy reminded me now, her voice coming over the telephone line like blessed October coolness amid all this killing heat.

And I wanted to see Nancy, to be close to Nancy. I needed some mothering and felt ridiculous to acknowledge that need to myself, me in my forties like this, gray in my faded hair. My hair mostly chopped off. I wished that I could go have a calming lunch with Nancy Roth. Just share a cup of coffee or a vodka sour with Nancy, like in the old days.

"You're not a martyr, dear," she said. "You do have a choice. You made a choice. Just remember that. Remember that you've acted of your own volition, Jeanne, and you'll be empowered."

But here is where I've always been stumped:

Choices?

Volition?

I'd pitch myself into a tatty armchair after one of our telephone conversations, and I'd ponder choices and volition. And I'd do something like study my own bare feet. I'd have never known that I was aging at all, if all I had to go on was my feet. I had great feet—us tall women spend lots of time in flat heels, and unwittingly avoid the deformities like bunions and hammer toes that higher heels can cause—and my own feet looked pretty much the way they'd looked in college, only slightly longer now. Still bony. Toes no crookeder.

Am I already middle aged? I'd wonder. Because I don't feel middle aged. How is middle age supposed to feel? These are the same shins I've always had. Same legs, same feet. I can even point my toes like my old ballerina doll, Nina. I've still got a child's dirty feet, with toenails that cry out for a clipping. Big feet, for a tall girl.

"I've never seen such big feet on such skinny little legs in all my life!" the beautiful Velma used to marvel, back when I was ten or eleven. "Looks like two toothpicks stuck in marshmallows!"

Do I have a choice, Nancy? I'd wonder, looking at my feet. I've had a problem with Mary Velma Connolly all my life, and I do not know what caused it, and I don't know whose fault it is. But I've got this problem with my mother. And it's always been there, off in the background somewhere. But there.

And if I give in now, and put her away in some nursing home like I so desperately want, I'll eat myself up with guilt, Nancy. It'll seem like something that I've *always* wanted to do, even before she was sick. It'll feel too much to me like a dream come true, an evil dream that I had no business dreaming. It'll feel like some kind of revenge.

And what's left of my own life will be poisoned. I'll no longer be able to think of myself as even a halfway decent person, because I know how lost and sad Mama will be. I'll watch myself through my father's eyes, and I'll see me shut away his beautiful Velma like she's some convicted felon, like I don't care one nickel about her. I'll know how much he wouldn't understand. He'd remember the diary business, and a hundred other disputes down through the years, and Daddy would think how mean I was, no pearl at all. Just a mean old witch with no hair and these damned big healthy feet.

And Velma Connolly will have *won.* Mean old Jeanne will have proven herself to be the thoughtless and ungrateful and selfish daughter that Velma always thought she was.

"I don't see how Larry put up with that coldhearted mood of yours as long as he did!" Velma told me in a pet about a month after I had moved in with her, when I'd gotten on her wrong side by making her take a bath. "Don't care about anybody but yourself, and poor ol' C. Ray in the ground."

See?

"You do too much for her, Jeanne," was my brother Rocky's input these later days. "Don't take away what little independence she has left. You're making her more dependent than she needs to be, this early in the illness. She really isn't all that much off the beam yet, from what I can see."

Yeah. Right.

"And Mama's actually looking pretty great these days, you know? Barbara keeps saying how she hopes *she* looks half that good, when she's Mama's age. Mama's still got some things going for her, Jeanne. Barbara and I are concerned about both of you, if you want to know the truth. You need to let go and let Mama have a little more independence, for both of your sakes, promise? You don't have to work so hard."

Now how in God's name could I set any store by what Barbara thought? My sister-in-law probably believed in a flat earth, and she'd make Judy Garland look stable. Barbara had had an affair and had actually run off with the man for a while some years ago, abandoning Rocky and their two little kids, both of them under the age of six. My brother's heartbroken phone calls to me up in New York had been appalling, the unbearable wounded sobs of a man with no pride left. I had almost gone nuts myself, having to listen to Rocky this way and suffering for him and his kids, wanting to physically be with him, to hold his hands. To hunt down Barbara Trahan and shoot her like the rabid bitch she was.

And then, once me and Larry and Mama and Daddy had gotten all whipped up into a permanent frenzy of outrage and pity, Rocky just upped and took Barbara back. Just like that. She'd grown tired of her boyfriend, after he had spent all of her money, and she'd come back home to Napoleon Avenue. To the house that Rocky and I had grown up in. And Rocky and the kids had welcomed her with open arms, all is forgiven, no questions asked.

And now I was supposed to love her again.

It bothered me that my brother would let her pass judgment upon me and my dealings with Mama this way, because Barbara wasn't exactly an expert on successful parent/child relationships. When Barbara gets old, I fumed privately, her kids'll throw her into a ditch.

But she certainly is correct about Mama looking great. Yeah.

Barbara's damn right about Mama looking good. Mama looks good because I make her look good. I do her hair, while she fusses and squirms. I dress her. She no longer knows how to button clothing. Brassieres are deep mysteries. She'll put her two feet through the sleeves of blouses, if not coached and helped. And *boy!* does she ever hate the coaching. She balls up her fists and threatens to put my lights out, to knock my teeth down my throat. I have no idea why she is so threatened by the act of getting dressed, but she is. Mornings are not my favorite time. I would love to be able to take

Barbara's and Rocky's advice, and sit back in the mornings with the newspaper, enjoying a second cup of coffee, while Mama got herself together. Sounds like a dream come true.

But expecting Velma to dress herself is kind of like expecting her to diagram the molecular structure of polyurethane. I could wait two hours. I could wait all week. But it won't happen. What eventually happens is the same filthy bathrobe gets worn day after day until it rots off, or a naked elderly lady angrily paces the bedroom with underpants stuck around her neck.

The only thing that she can still do for herself these days is to put on that thick, dark red lipstick of hers. I read that the earliest skills an individual learned in childhood are the last to go in Alzheimer's. If so, Velma has probably been wearing this goo since the age of three.

These are the big red lips of the World War II generation, lips that said things like "hubba hubba" and "victory garden" and "war bonds." Mama's generation had seemed so indestructible once, these kids on black-and-white archival newsreel film, doing the Jitterbug and smoking unfiltered cigarettes and beating the shit out of Hitler. If the Great Depression, Mussolini, Tojo, and Adolf-fucking-Hitler couldn't get them down for long, what could?

I grew up watching them on *The Valiant Years* and *Victory at Sea* on television, bursting with pride over my parents being part of this remarkable cohort of brash and heroic kids. Rocky and I watched the war movies, and read *Sergeant Rock* comics, and chewed our nails over the weekly episodes of *Combat!*, but we knew our side would eventually win out, no matter how many guest stars had to die in action that particular week. The girls had such dark lips and big shoulders, and talked tough like Lauren Bacall. The guys were irreverent and skinny and humorous, even in the face of enemy machine gun fire, but they never forgot to write their moms and dads and kid brothers back home a long letter once the shooting stopped.

How can old age do what Hitler couldn't? How can a mere notion like Time, a concept that may not hold true everywhere in the universe, shrivel those big shoulders and quiet those brash mouths?

I would think these thoughts as I passed my parents' old bedroom in Auletta, and see my Daddy's pathetic junk piled in dusty heaps around the walls. I would watch Mama put on her red lipstick with a gnarled hand, and I would think these thoughts. I glanced at old photographs of Velma and C. Ray over my late night bourbon sometimes, and I'd cry some. But only when Mama was definitely asleep. And in another room.

I couldn't cry for her when I was face-to-face with her. In her presence, I felt nothing but exhaustion and impatience.

"You don't have to ruin your life, Jeanne," was what Rocky kept telling me, "you know that. You know I'm here for you. Barbara and I have that extra bedroom, and you know how Brooke and Adam would love having their Mam-maw here."

And I wish that Rocky would just think through everything he's saying before *tempting* me this way, I'd say to myself, depressed. If he and Barbara would just consider the specifics for two or three days, discuss the details and what caregiving could involve, then I might actually listen to him with more attention. But bless his heart, he's clueless. If he and Barbara would maybe arrange to take Mama for a week while I went up to visit Conrad, and try to bathe her and get up with her in the middle of the night to take her to the bathroom, then I'd probably let them take her in permanently. Gladly. With no guilt. Not feeling like a bad person. If they still wanted to do it.

And then?

Oh Christ, and then. You don't have to be a voodoo fortuneteller to see this one coming. I say: "Yes, Rocky, you're *right about everything*, take her!", and in two weeks he'd hate me forever. He works six days a week, Adam and Brooke are already one handful, and Mama hates Barbara. Mama's memory may be going south, but she hasn't forgotten how Barbara ran off with that sales rep. Barbara used to do that to Rocky back before they were married, too, leaving him for somebody else. And Mama and Daddy had to listen to poor Rocky crying his guts out, night after night.

So would having Velma Connolly in his house *enrich* Rocky's home life now in any conceivable way, even in an alternate universe, on another planet and in a parallel dimension?

It is to laugh.

How fast would dear Barbara hit the singles bars, bags packed?

That little red cowboy hat that my brother used to wear as a kid must have cut off all circulation to his brain.

I do know a thing or two about an iffy marriage.

chapter 16   Taking
                                               My
                                              Mind
                                               off
                                              Larry

Larry Roth gave up on comedy right about the same time he gave up on me.

"Marriage is supposed to be a pleasure and a convenience, honey, not an unsolved equation!" he'd fend off my complaints of inattention. "It's not supposed to be hard. It's not supposed to be something you've gotta work at. You don't see Russian peasants working at marriage."

"I don't see Russian peasants at all, Larry."

"My great-grandfather, a Russian peasant—working at *marriage?* The very idea would've been absurd! He worked at *work.* Marriage was what you came home to."

"Larry, it's just that—"

"Honey, I'm up to my ears in back orders, there's the shipping strike, we've apparently got undocumented seamstresses on our payroll—I don't know if it's kinder to just terminate them, or let the immigration people bust us and ship them back off to Santo Domingo or wherever—!"

"Okay."

"I mean, you see where I'm coming from?"

"Yeah. Whatever."

"Jeanne? Can't we discuss this some other time, honey?"

But there was never any good time to discuss what was happening to us, because shit kept happening. Sid-Nan's autumn problems and goals had to be addressed retroactively, in the preceding spring. Similarly, the spring agendas and product lines of the garment industry were attended to during the previous autumns.

We're always one season ahead of ourselves, I thought. Our divorce will be finalized six months before we even separate.

"Gotta work late, gotta work late," was Larry's mantra. "Gotta work late again, sorry, don't hold dinner."

Such an unoriginal excuse for such a creative man, I thought, unless he's become so estranged from my mental processes now that he figures I'll swallow anything. Or maybe he just doesn't care. Just doesn't fucking care.

My hair was a duller auburn now. I had gained a few pounds.

Conrad and I spent our evenings together watching TV, eating takeout Chinese or pizza, and not talking about much of anything, until Larry would finally come dragging home, long after Conrad was in bed. I didn't know if Rad was doing his homework or not. His teachers told me that he was a very smart kid, but seemed to be unmotivated. I had to go to most of these parent-teacher conferences without Larry.

Larry would speak of nightwear and daywear, and would rub his thinning hair in convincing, harried worry. And I would appear to be listening, but I wasn't.

"Don't tell Mama," I told my father, not planning to, just hearing it come out, when he telephoned me long distance one evening, "but I'm pretty sure that Larry's having an affair."

Daddy didn't say anything for a minute, because he was a careful person who would rather not say anything at all than risk saying the wrong thing. "I'm sorry, Jeanne," he said finally. "I'm real sorry to hear that." And he didn't tell me that I might be mistaken, or quiz me about just how sure my *pretty sure* was, or act the way most other people in his place would have acted. I had subconsciously known that Daddy would behave this way. I was comforted by it. I had been needing to tell him, I understood now, for weeks.

"Not that it's exactly a surprise," I went on. "I've sort of pushed him to it, I guess. I know I can be cold. Act indifferent. And when Larry acts indifferent himself, it's like I get all whiny and naggy to him, I don't know. I don't think I always used to be this way. I don't like myself like this."

"You've never been a whiner, Jay-jay."

"You're my father, not my husband. You don't know."

"I like Larry," he said. "I've always liked ol' Larry."

"He's changed, Daddy. He's not funny anymore. He doesn't even seem to want to be funny anymore, and that bothers me, because it was always such a part of who he was and what he wanted to be. He takes himself so seriously these days. Maybe this is just a mid-life crisis. Maybe I'm making a mountain out of a molehill."

My father made a chuckling noise in sympathy.

"Did you and Mama have mid-life crises?"

"Nope," he said. "Not unless this here is one Velma's having right now. A late one."

"What's up?"

"You know Velma, worries about the least little thing. Worries herself sick over every little detail. Rocky and Barbara."

"Yeah."

"Now she's starting to say somebody's embezzling from us. We get all this trash in the mail from sweepstakes people and whatnot, Velma's worrying where our money is. You know, all that trash saying 'You may already have won five million dollars,' stuff like that. Phony checks made out in your name. The fine print says it's phony, you got to win the sweepstakes first. But Velma don't read the fine print."

"You're kidding."

He sighed. "She says we've won five million dollars, so where's our money? That's our name printed on the check all right, where's our money?"

"She never tries to understand anything," I commiserated. "To listen to somebody."

"It's all done with *computers*, I tell her. The name is printed on there with a *computer*, it doesn't mean anything. They make it look official, trying to tempt gullible suckers to subscribe to *Modern Bride* and *Motorcycle Digest,* that's the only reason why it looks so official, I tell her. Read the fine print, I tell her, we ain't won nothin'."

"She doesn't believe you?"

"She's skeptical, you know Velma. The way she was brought up, that was kind of a rough neighborhood. Nobody pulls the wool over her eyes."

"Yeah, and she runs her mouth before her brain can catch up with it sometimes, Daddy," I said. "She doesn't think things through before she jumps to a conclusion. So how *are* Rocky and Barbara doing?"

"Still cozy, you'd never know anything had ever been wrong between them. Velma's worried that it's all a front, though. That Barbara's just putting up this good front before she gives Rocky the old heave-ho again."

"Don't breathe a word to Mama about me and Larry, Daddy, okay?" My blood literally ran cold now at the vision of Velma in high mouth mode, turning her ditsy attention to me and Larry and mouthing off, not caring about the fine print. Unconcerned with anything like objective truth, just being Velma—armed with her own brand of maternal love, a neutron bomb on a hair trigger. "I don't know for sure, anyway. About the affair, I mean. Maybe the women in this family are just ungodly suspicious. Maybe I'm just being my mama's daughter."

"I'll keep my mouth shut," he assured me. "There's a lot of things I don't tell Velma, Jay."

He sounded cheerful, but weary and kind of slowed down. I was dismayed to hear him beginning to speak with an old man's voice these days. My father was undergoing whatever precise physical changes that were responsible for making an elderly man's voice reedy, even as they also made his body reedy and flabby.

Does the testosterone diminish? I wondered, distancing myself emotionally. Do the vocal cords thin out, is that it, opposite of the way they bulked up during adolescence? I ought to look into it. Go to the library.

"So how's Rad holding up during all of this?" C. Ray spoke again, as I mentally stood at the "Gerontology" heading in the library card catalog.

"Well, it's not a matter of 'during all this' yet, Daddy, since I don't think he suspects that anything's going on. Larry and I don't disagree in front of him, or anything like that."

"Good."

"I mean, Larry is just never here. But when he *is* here, I'm not accusatory or anything. In front of Rad. I've asked Larry if he's having an affair. He tells me what a lunatic I am. But gently. In a very quiet, very loving, very gentle voice: 'Jeanne, you must be out of your mind, this must be early menopause, but it just makes me love you even more, honey, you poor thing.' Ugh. *Barf.*"

"Good."

"Larry and I are quiet. We're just growing apart," I said, and felt a tiny pain at the back of my throat, at the root of my tongue. Not an emotion I could identify, just a small and transient contraction of some sort that came and then went. "It's a very quiet process. We don't even like the same books anymore, and I've only just begun to notice that. He's into this macho right-wing war stuff like Tom Clancy. Spy thrillers. They're all too derivative and formulaic for me, Big Boys with Big Killer Toys. What's on my own night table are biographies, Eleanor Roosevelt, Louisa May Alcott. No more fairy tales for either of us."

"Well—"

"Daddy, I do know how hard Rocky's and Barbara's troubles have been on their kids. But Barbara is a screamer and a cryer. She can't control herself. She's given in to every single impulse she's ever had. That's the whole trouble in that marriage, in a nutshell."

"Yeah, you're right."

"Conrad, on the other hand," I tried to picture my son's face in my mind, trying to read his expression to see if he was happy or sad, "is older. Wrapped up in his own milieu, friends, films, trying to decide which colleges to apply to. He has things to fall back on."

"Any chance he might apply to Tulane here, maybe?"

"His compadres are all up here, Daddy, so I don't know how far south he'd want to be. He's very happy up here," I said, wanting to believe that Rad was happy. "He's gone all the time, out of the house. Out in Port Washington with Nancy and Sid, off to visit some pal . . . He's working at McDonald's part time to augment his allowance, that McDonald's we took you and Mama to that time, in the Village. Rad knows the Village like the back of his hand."

"I might just try to talk him into Tulane," said Daddy. "Be right nice to have him so close. Take him fishing. Me and Skeets Bordelon used to try to go out once in a while, take his boat, put in near the Highway Eleven bridge. Don't seem to get out there much anymore."

Daddy sounds kind of lonely, I realized now. But how can Daddy be *lonely*, with Mama always hovering around so close?

Mama's mission in life has always been C. Ray. And Mama never fails in her missions. She makes sure he gets his medications on time. She keeps him away from beer, cooks his food, jollies him up, loves him to distraction.

Mama refuses to let anybody get lonely or depressed.

That way she'd sit there at the supper table, back in my college days, when I'd try to puzzle out depressing things like the Watts Riots or Vietnam: "Don't give us a whole lecture, punkin," she'd interrupt me, her pretty nose wrinkled up, one winged brow in an arch as she performed precise surgery upon her roast beef. "Give somebody else the floor. I don't want to hear anything depressing."

"The whole world is *depressing*, Mama," Rocky would say. Good ol' Rock.

"Not *my* world."

"This isn't the Planet Velma, Mama!" I'd protest, wanting to mash those big red lips of hers right into the creamed corn. "This is *reality!*"

"I'm a homemaker," she'd put down her knife and fork and blot her lips, "and my job is to make a home for you kids and your daddy. And the home I choose to make is a *happy* one."

"Daddy?" I'd say, looking to him in silent appeal, but knowing that I would get no backup there.

No, he'd chew his food, and make eye contact with Mama across the table, and crinkles of amusement would show at his freckled temples. He wasn't interested in what I thought about Watts or Vietnam or the War On Poverty, not here at the supper table with Mama seated across from him, her blonde hair shining under the bright lights of their happy home while I stewed, dismissed, marginalized.

You saw the way C. Ray and Velma existed to amuse each other, to reinforce each other. To keep each other company in a way that Larry Roth and I would never be able to manage. Rocky and Barbara could never manage it, either.

So how can Daddy be lonely, I wondered with him on the other end of the telephone line now, how can he be lonely in retirement in a comfortable country home not too far from the lake, where he can go fishing, surrounded in his house by his magazines and radios and swords and prints of Highlanders; pampered and mollycoddled by the beautiful Velma, the incomparable ultimate wife and helpmeet Velma; the almost supernatural Mary Velma Connolly, who I will never resemble and who can succor her man in ways that I can't even identify? Who is able to satisfy masculine needs that I don't even know exist?

"How long has it been since you've come down here for a little visit, Jay-jay?" my father asked me now, while I was still wondering about his loneliness and beginning to feel vaguely guilty for not keeping in closer contact with him and Mama.

I was faintly startled by the parallel tracks of our thoughts. "I don't know. A while."

"Well," he said. "Little visit down here might do you good. Change of scene. Take your mind off Larry."

"Daddy, I don't know. I'm still at the gallery. Full time."

"Maybe somebody else might want to swap days off and fill in for you. Give Larry a chance to miss you."

I wasn't sure that I needed any sort of vacation right now. What it would give Larry would be the opportunity to carry on unhampered for a week or two, if he was really carrying on. It'd give Conrad the chance to run wild in the streets at all hours.

And it'll give Mama the chance to get caught up with what all I'm doing wrong with my life, I thought. If I were to benefit at all from a change of scene right now, it definitely should not be Auletta, Louisiana.

Why doesn't somebody think of maybe sending poor troubled Jeanne to the Caribbean? Let's buy poor Jeanne a ticket for "The Love Boat," why don't we?

My father spoke. "Jay, I do need to see you. I need you to come down here. We need to involve you in our retirement plans, your mother and me. It's kind of hard to do it over the phone, baby. I'll send you the plane fare."

My blood congealed. "Are you ill? Are you okay?"

He laughed. "Got the same incurable illness everybody else has got, old age."

I was only slightly mollified. I tried not to frown, to create more wrinkles in my face.

"You pack your bathing suit, and we'll ask Skeets Bordelon for the use of his boat, and we'll have a ball, you and me and your mama," Daddy went on in a fake-hearty voice that scared me to death. "But I've got some things I need to talk over with you, financial planning. Family concerns. And Rocky's too busy, I can't bother Rocky with any more concerns than he already has."

I am not now nor have I ever been a genuine psychic. But you didn't have to be a psychic to start pulling your hair out, literally, at the bad vibes coming over that phone line. I plucked out four of my hairs, one after another, one of them kinky and gray. I looked stupidly at it, letting it fall to the carpet with the others, while my father raved on about the wonderful vacation we would share.

A key, Conrad's, rattled in the lock. I turned, receiver still to my ear, and he came inside the apartment in his school clothes, neat jeans and preppy golf shirt. He was already a head taller than Larry, darkhaired, so clean that he sparkled. He threw two notebooks at the sofa and headed for his bedroom.

"I'm going out," he said to my glance.

I mimed feeding myself.

"I've eaten, thanks." The door of his room closed and hid him.

It would be a toss-up, which one would get home first that night, Rad or Larry. I wondered why I bothered to ask anybody about food anymore. I put my bare foot over the place on the carpet where I imagined that my plucked hairs had landed. I was becoming fatter, rounder, with more physical bulk than I had ever had. How could I be so invisible?

"Well, I guess I can work things out with the gallery, if I can give them enough advance notice, Daddy," I said into the telephone receiver, remembering who had called who. "But if it's really urgent . . ."

"Oh, no hurry, no hurry," he immediately began to back off "Jay, baby, I didn't mean to make this sound *urgent*. I know you got things to take care of. Hell, it's not that important. If you can't come at all, it's not important."

He had just finished telling me that it was. "Well," I said again, "I can come. Later."

"We'd just love to see you, you know that," he laughed low. "Kill two birds with one stone, I thought. You can get your mind off your troubles and get in a little vacation, and I can get some minor little financial matters talked over with you."

"Well, okay. Let me check the schedule at the gallery."

"And if you can't come at all, Jay, no big deal."

"I can come. I'll work it out, Daddy. I'll call you when my plans are set."

"You don't have to," he said.

I wanted to scream. "Gas up that boat!" I told him, leavening my tone with laughter, and he joined in and we eventually said good night to each other.

But the laughter didn't fool me. All the bad vibes I had gotten from him merged into the slight bad vibes I got from Conrad now. And the constant bad vibes that came from Larry on a daily basis flowed into them, and they all became one Big Bad Vibe that sent me into the kitchen to pour myself a double.

chapter 17

Rocky
and
Barbara

"Mama was tricked out in something that looked like a Sid-Nan housecoat, when they met me at the airport," I told Rocky over dinner at Manale's a month later. "But she had on that lipstick, man, lemme tell you. Her hair's still real blonde, I see."

"It's toner," said Barbara.

"Mama's fine." Rocky went at his barbecued shrimp.

"She's pretty whiteheaded underneath all that toner," said Barbara.

Rocky looked across the table at me. "It's Daddy that's real peculiar."

"Him and all that historical stuff and swords and junk," said Barbara. "You can't even hardly walk around."

"There was a time," I gobbled my shrimp and wine, "when Mama wouldn't even think about leaving the house unless she was in high heels and full drag."

"It matters when you're young," Barbara explained, all dooded up in eyeliner and mascara and a linen blazer with padded shoulders, as if I were my own grandmother.

"How are Brooke and Adam these days?" I asked her, unable to ask her all the things I wanted, like: "Ever hear from the boyfriend who spent all your money?" and "How does it feel to be an unfit mother?"

"They gettin' big. You'll get to see them while you're here, I promise. But I got us a sitter for tonight, they're a little too rowdy for a place like this. We want you to really enjoy your dinner, Jeanne."

"I am," I said. And I was.

"Can't get anything like this up in New York," Rocky chewed and pontificated about my hometown of choice, as if he knew.

Barbara smiled with slick coral lips.

"Adam looks kinda like Daddy now." Rocky's meal made him thoughtful. "He's not redheaded, but he's built like him. Long legged. Got real long arms."

"How's your practice?" I asked him.

"Shots and fleas. Never run out of fleas down here," he said. "I've hired a dental technician."

"My husband makes money off of *fleas*," Barbara chirped like the twerp she was, and laid a lush and mascara-clotted, besotted gaze upon my brother. She twirled her wineglass in her hand. Her fake nails were half an inch long.

I looked at him. "You still putting in days at the zoo?"

"Cleaned the teeth of a Bengal tiger day before yesterday."

"You put them to sleep first, right?"

"No, Jeanne," he said. "I just tell 'em to open wide."

I blotted my lips. "I didn't realize animals' teeth ever needed cleaning."

He nodded and swallowed his wine. "Gum disease. Tooth loss. Tigers in the wild frequently die of infections from broken teeth."

"I didn't realize that."

"What else can I get for you, Dr. Buchanan?" asked the approaching waitress, an older woman in black slacks and waistcoat. "Y'all care for dessert?"

"Coffee for me." Rocky looked at us women. "Barbara? Jeanne?"

"That bread pudding souffle," I decided. "And decaf, please."

"You've put on a little weight, Jeanne," said Barbara. "I can see it in your face." The waitress left us through swinging doors, admitting the clatter, hiss, and voices of a busy restaurant kitchen for a second. The doors swung again and shut away the noise. "Looks good," Barbara told me.

Like hell, I thought in fury. I've got a butt like a dufflebag now.

Loud conversations assaulted my ears from every side. Every table was full. The place was packed.

I took in the yawp and honk of local accents, comforted and yet annoyed by the tasteless hurlyburly and naked gluttony of my native city. Maybe Conrad would find it exotic. Conrad hadn't been down here for a visit since he was ten or twelve. Conrad found Mama exotic.

Maybe I can bring Rad down with me on a visit sometime soon, I thought. Rad might enjoy the contrast between the wispy Hollywood depictions of New Orleans and the real raucous, full-throated article. Conrad might prefer the real thing.

"Folks still take their time over food here, I see," I said now. "In New York, it's all hurry-up, hurry-up, eat in a hurry, demand the check in a hurry, so you can grab a taxi in a hurry and get to your movie or the theatre on time."

Rocky's eyes pocketed underneath, his smile beginning higher than his mouth. "Ain't no movie to get to tonight," he said like Daddy, with the deliberate use of the word *ain't*, his voice even sounding like Daddy's. "This here's the main event, I'm afraid."

His face was so *us*. I was so glad to see him, to be in his presence.

I raised my wine glass in tribute. "Dr. Buchanan. A *splendid* main event it is, too, sir."

"Y'all two are getting sloshed," said Barbara.

Rocky was holding his wine glass with a scabbed hand, the claw marks of frightened cats on his freckled fingers. My brother had a very kind, a very fearless hand. I didn't need to see its palm. This was a strong and benign hand. This hand had held terminally ill old dogs and had comforted them while they were euthanized.

"They think you're a real doctor here," Barbara giggled at him. "Y'all don't embarrass me, okay?"

I was almost sloshed enough to throttle her.

"The maître d's rottweiler is a patient of mine," said Rocky. "My cover is blown."

Barbara leaned over and kissed him on the tip of his nose. "You're so *cute.*"

Silly twat, I thought. *They think you're a real doctor,* what ignorant bullshit. Yeah, you're pretty, Barbara, you're a social climber, I used to think that Rocky had been looking for Mama when he married you. But hell, you're no Velma Connolly, not even in your most extravagant dreams, you worthless bimbo. Rocky might be subconsciously drawn to the Velma type, yeah, but he sure has gotten shortchanged.

Think what you will, Barbara, but Velma Connolly would've never teased her husband about being brewmaster instead of brewery owner or whatever, not even for a cheap laugh.

Rising to the rank of brewmaster was a pretty big deal in our circle, and C. Ray was making very good money by the time he retired, but nobody would've ever asked him to join Rex. Nobody would've mistaken him for a neurosurgeon. Yet if brewmaster was what C. Ray became, then brew-fucking-master was right up there with President of the United States, as far as Velma was concerned, think what you will.

And what is this *real doctor* shit, as if a person who has studied internal medicine, gynecology, obstetrics, ophthalmology, orthopedic medicine, dentistry, surgery, neurology, the circulatory system, and I-don't-know-what-all of several different species, who *specializes* in *all* of them, and who can accurately diagnose *mute* patients, isn't worthy to be called a doctor? Human beings suck so thoroughly, and so many doctors for humans are so greedy and shallow, that I believe a goodhearted veterinarian to be clearly superior—ethically, intellectually, and morally. The good man who saves a sweet ol' kitty is doing the planet a far greater service than the medical weasel curing the CEO of an industrial polluter.

I'm bigger than Barbara is, I thought, sizing up the small brunette across the table from me. I could stomp her flat. With only one of my feet.

"I haven't been out to see Mama and Daddy in a while now," Rocky was saying, oblivious to my rage. "Don't get but one day off. Sunday."

"Yes." I bit back everything else.

"But Daddy seemed pretty okay the last time I saw him, except I don't much like those nitroglycerin pills."

"I'm kinda alarmed at that prescription, myself," I said, not too wild about digging into the bread pudding souffle being set before me now. It smelled wonderful, but my preoccupations had shifted away from food. I stirred my decaf. "Nobody told me that he was having angina."

Rocky reached for the sugar. "He downplays everything."

"Diabetics are prone to circulatory problems. Men his age. What about a bypass?"

"He said anything to you about a bypass?"

"No."

"I doubt he's a bypass candidate, Jeanne. Blood vessels in his legs can't be in any shape for transplant. That's diabetes for you."

"What about angioplasty?" I asked, getting seriously bothered.

"I wish you two'd speak *English*," said Barbara.

Rocky paid her the tiny attention of a peripheral smile, but then came right back to me, full bore. "Daddy elaborated on any of this to you yet?"

"All he tells me, since I've been down here, is how he's worried about Mama. She's afraid to drive the car anymore. She won't even go get her hair done anymore now, unless he drives her."

"Toner." Barbara shook her head. "I can teach her to do her own toner, won't need no peroxide, as gray as she is."

Rocky's elbows lay themselves down onto the tabletop. "So what does Mama say?"

"She's worried to death about Daddy. All she does is fret. I don't think the man can even get a decent night's sleep, without her waking him up to make sure he's all right," I said.

"She met your plane in a *housecoat?*"

"No time to get dressed. All she does, to hear her tell it, is wait on Daddy hand and foot. I think she kind of likes being all stewed up, if you want to know the truth, Rock. She's always made sure that all of us know how much she contributes to the family unit. Heroine kind of mingles with martyr in Mama, you know that."

"Daddy had his 'big talk' with you yet?"

"This is all it's turned out to be, Mama driving him crazy with her worry, that kind of thing." I pushed away my dessert. "What he'd like is for me and you to come up with a way of getting her out of the house more. To make some friends out there. He can't even go fishing anymore, I take it, without feeling guilty for having left her all by herself. You know Mama's never made a whole lot of friends over there in Auletta."

"I hated Auletta," said Barbara. "El Barfo. Yuckamundo."

"All Mama's friends are back here in Orleans Parish."

"Or dead," said Barbara.

"Maybe we can come up with something," said Rocky.

What I didn't tell my brother was that Daddy and I had just begun to really get into the meaty issues that were bothering him the most these days. And I think he's extremely concerned about *you*, Rock, I thought at him now, if you want to know the truth.

You're a big part of what's bothering Daddy, through no fault of your own. But I think you are one of the main reasons I'm down here.

I watched Barbara simper through dessert, but I no longer minded as much. The bread pudding souffle I was reconsidering was mingling its sugar very nobly with all the wine inside me.

Barbara took a corner of her napkin and wiped invisible barbecue sauce from Rocky's chin, and both of them beamed batty little looks at each other that led to a quick kiss.

She *is* sort of winning, I decided, in a dopey Barbara way, if you're a man and you want big tits and a pretty face. Her little Cajun accent is cute. She means no harm to anyone, actually, and there's no malice in her. She does cause harm because she's greedy and selfish, and always looks out for Barbara before she looks out for anyone else. Barbara comes first. Before husband. Before her children, even. Barbara pursues Barbara's own happiness, above all else.

But isn't that what Thomas Jefferson said that we're all supposed to be doing? I'm confused.

I'm drunk, actually.

I'm also a permanently unhappy person, and is this why: because I don't *pursue* happiness enough? But how can I pursue it, when I don't admire the Barbaras who do? Because I admire the selfless Hobbits of the world—the Frodos and Sams—am I unable to ever rise above the passive-aggressive approach of which I've become an expert and put myself first, without apology, even when it becomes a moral and correct thing to do in certain cases?

Like in this case, this me and Larry case. What would Barbara Trahan do, if she were in my place? Well, first of all, Barbara would never be in my place, because she leaves 'em before she can get left. But let's say she was. Let's say it was Rocky who was messing around now with somebody, and it was Barbara who was home waiting, drinking coffee and Kahlua until 3:00 A.M. What would Barbara inflict, besides guilt?

Shit, you know the answer. Barbara would find herself another man just as fast as she could, and take out newspaper ads and put up billboards to make damn sure that Rocky knew about him; and she'd rub Rock's nose into it every day and in every way, and she'd live out a grand passion with her new squeeze in as public a way as she could manage, even if it meant leaving her beauty parlor career and her kids and the good opinion of anybody who had ever known her. She'd reduce Rocky to an insecure blob of emasculated protoplasm. Just like she's already actually done. And he'd be begging to come back, if she still wanted him. But she wouldn't want him now.

Me, I hint around that I know what Larry's up to. I confront him, yes, but in a very nonconfrontational way. I make very sure that he knows I'm sad, but I don't get Anna Karenina about it. I try to make him feel guilty, but in such a subtle way that I can't be accused of it. I know that if he knows I am deliberately trying to make him feel guilty, he'll leave me even faster. I'm sneaky.

Ol' Barbara makes no bones about anything. Ol' Barbara sees what she wants, and goes right after it, damn the torpedos and full steam ahead.

Is that knavery or bravery? Is Barbara Trahan somehow a better woman than I am?

I'm confused. I have a headache. I want to lie down.

But I didn't lie down, once I got to Rocky's house with my overnight case in my hand. The kids were already asleep. Rocky paid the babysitter. Barbara gave me a goodnight hug and went off to bed. An antique clock ticked in the front room, on the mantel between two ficus trees. Brass and polished wood gleamed in the dimness.

Rocky wanted to make coffee and sit up a while.

I followed him into the kitchen of the house I had grown up in, mildly excited at the novelty of having my brother to myself for a little bit, surprised at the feeling. It had been a very long time since just the two of us had been alone together, the way we had been as children. It made me feel young now. Conspiratorial.

"You drank that Clorox right there where you're standing," I told him, and it was the truth. He was at the sink, rinsing out two mugs, over the spot where our mother Velma had once crouched and tried to comfort him.

"Yeah, I've told Brooke and Adam that story a bunch of times." He turned and swept out a hand. "Like what I've done with the floors?"

The linoleum was gone and the hardwood floors were perfect and polyurethaned, even here in the kitchen. There were no signs of dents made by a toy riding horse. I regarded the white walls, the butcherblock counter tops. Rocky did most of the really serious cooking in this family, I knew. He was an able chef, and enjoyed it as his major hobby. So this was Rocky's own taste on display in here. Rocky's domain. The coffee was brewing from freshly ground gourmet beans.

"Yeah," I said. "Looks great."

He brought me the coffee to a breakfast bar that had not existed when we had been kids. We pulled out stools and sat. "Well, you know, Auletta drove Barbara nuts. Look at how far she had to drive to work, for one thing."

"Yeah."

"You and I, we grew up listening to Daddy talk about growing up in the country, and I always thought there's a lot of country boy in me, but it's not like I had a huge practice over there. What they've got over there, around Auletta, is cattle inoculations. Heartworm and rabies. Very basic stuff. The pet population runs wild. Nobody spends any money on spaying and neutering."

"They don't take their kids to doctors, either."

"It's easier here in the city, I guess. Adam and Brooke seem to like it. I wanted to give them the bucolic country childhood I'd always heard about, but I guess it's more fantasy than anything else. They had to ride a school bus four miles. There's crime out there, too. Somebody stole Barbara's antique milking cans from right off our front porch."

I leaned onto my elbows. The butcher block was cool and hard. "So how are Adam and Brooke? Really?"

"Oh," he said, and seemed deflated, "about as good as it gets, under the circumstances. Adam's ten now, still having a few behavioral problems at school. Attention-deficit disorder. But that's just him. I mean, even without Barbara's breakdown, even if that had never happened, Adam would probably still be antsy. Attention-deficit disorder isn't caused by environment. I mean, I was an antsy kid. Brooke's okay, but maybe girls are easier."

So what Barbara had had was officially a *breakdown* now, not just some trashy affair. I wondered when I could expect to see her on a tell-all afternoon talk show.

"Where're they in school?" I asked.

"He's at Newman, she's beginning third grade at Sacred Heart."

I whistled. "No wonder you work all the time."

"You do what you can for your kids. How's Rad?"

The ball bounced back into my court, and I wasn't ready for it. I felt suddenly defensive. "I don't know, really. His grades are okay, although he doesn't seem to ever reach what I'm told is his potential. We don't talk much. They're so independent when they're this age. And he's always been so self-contained."

"It's that good Jewish blood," said Rocky. "Intellectual gene pool. Do Jewish people ever have out-of-control, hard-to-handle kids? Really bad, unruly, disruptive students? You hardly ever hear about a violent Jewish criminal."

"Mama and Daddy used to think Rad would grow up to be a jail-bird."

"I don't think they were talking about *violence.*"

"Well, I'm not talking about violence, Rocky. I don't know. Rad keeps to himself. He keeps his own counsel. He seems happy enough, but I just don't know."

Rocky finished his coffee.

"Larry and I are having problems," I said finally.

"I know. Daddy's told me a little bit about it, I hope you don't mind," said Rocky, and took me off the hook of having to explain. "Look, it happens. This shit happens. Never thought it'd happen to me, but it did. And we got past it."

"Yeah."

"You want to talk about it?"

"Not particularly." I went to the pot for more coffee. "I told Daddy everything I knew. I don't know what else to say. I don't know exactly what's wrong, except that something's wrong. I keep feeling like it's me. Like I've failed to hold up my end, and so Larry's had to look somewhere else. Maybe it is me. I feel like it is."

"I thought it must've been me, too, Jeanne. I felt that way."

I slapped my thighs. "I'm getting *fat*. I've let myself go. There is no court of appeals for wives who 'let themselves go.'"

"Maybe I put too much of myself into the practice. Maybe I didn't reassure Barbara enough about how much I needed her, shit like that."

I smiled. "You're getting real good at girl talk, pardner."

He shrugged. "When some marriage therapist keeps hammering at you about how women need to talk, that they need to verbalize their feelings, they'll leave your ass if you won't verbalize in turn. In their own mother tongue. So what d'you expect? I'm a literate guy. I'm a well-read guy, I'm not a caveman."

"Daddy and Mama never seemed to have to talk stuff out, though. Did they have to work as hard at their marriage as we've had to work at our own?"

"That generation," Rocky put down his handmade ceramic mug, "was on a whole other wavelength."

"So are they good role models for us? Or bad role models?"

"C. Ray and Velma aren't *realistic* role models, that's what's wrong. Not in marriage, I mean. You've really got to hand it to them, Jeanne. They've taken the simple institution of marriage, and raised it to an art form. If marriage were the Olympics, they'd get a perfect ten. Even by the standards of their contemporaries, they get a ten.

They leave everybody else in the fucking dirt. They're not average, and they don't even realize that they're not average, and that's what you and I are cursed with, Jeanne. Our role model is *perfection*. We grew up living with perfection, thinking that perfection is normal."

"Yeah. I've always been a sucker for fairytales."

"Daddy, you know, he settled down here and just left home permanently, because of her. How could somebody *mean* that much to somebody? Are we deficient in feeling?"

"Isn't that what you've essentially done for Barbara, though?" I asked him. "Wasn't Auletta your home of choice?"

"I don't know, it was a fantasy. I don't know—kindly Dr. Buchanan, Country Vet." He leaned back on his stool, like he used to do as a twelve-year-old, and I was still afraid that he would overturn. "Mama and Daddy swapping houses with us, that was Mama's idea. She knew how crazy Auletta made Barbara. 'C. Ray's a country boy,' she said, 'and we're getting too old for the noise and the traffic and the crime uptown here now, and we could maybe swap houses with you for a while, Rocky, if that'd help you out any.'"

"Yeah, and what're you going to do when she wants to swap back?"

He shook his head. "I've bought this place from them now, and they've bought mine from me. Daddy wanted to put it on a business footing, so that's what we did."

"I thought swapping houses was his idea."

"Mama, Daddy, they're a unit, Jeanne. They speak with one voice. But it was Mama's idea, originally. She's quite a gal. When the chips are down. You never give her credit for anything."

"I give her credit," I said, my voice soft with guilt and displeasure.

"Maybe it's because you're both women, I don't know. Competitive. I just wish you knew her the way I know her, Jeanne."

"Human medicine, Dr. Buchanan, lost a fine shrink when it lost you," my mouth said, but my brain was remembering the million innocent insults, the *Sit up straights* and *I told you so's*, the diary, Larry, the arched and perfect brow, that curtain of long and blonde and unattainable hair, the lies, the manipulation, the sense that I was somehow falling short of Velma's expectations and was letting her down in some fundamental way. "I wish you knew her, Rocky, the way *I* know her. She's not a saint."

"Well, she's some kinda gal, that's all I can say. Daddy grew up in the country. She didn't. I hope she's happy out there, because I don't know what I would've done without this move."

"Maybe you could've rented out the Auletta property and bought something in Covington, if you weren't ready to come back to the city."

"Dammit, Jeanne! Do you have to be this way?" Rocky's face was reddening.

I stirred my second cup of coffee, almost angry. "Mama's happy, wherever Daddy is happy."

"I sure hope so." His fervor was real, and the flush in his face was related to it. His faded freckles were yellow dots that floated upon pink skin. He wasn't angry, he was fervent. He was worried about Mama, the same way I had come to worry about Daddy.

My drift towards anger corrected itself. "She has her flowers out there, Rock. That huge yard, landscaped to a tee. All her stuff in the house, all fussed over and decorated and spread out. More room than this place, her beautiful things on display like that oak dresser we used to play saloon with. She's the queen out there, Rock."

"I just hope so."

"Daddy always wanted to retire to the country, remember how he used to talk about that when we were little?"

"No. He used to talk about brewing the ultimate beer."

"Mama and Daddy *love* it out there, Rocky, honestly. You know that if C. Ray is happy, then Velma is happy. You know how they are."

"Jeanne, tonight at dinner, you said that Daddy's afraid she's lonely. That she needs to get out more."

Well, yes, I had said that. "I didn't mean for you to feel guilty about it though. You didn't cause it. She was that way here too, here on Napoleon Avenue. You remember her spending much time with anybody but us, and maybe Dolores Bordelon next door? She never went to see her sister much, and she still has old aunts and uncles and cousins all over the city here. And even when her daddy was still alive, she never spent much time with any of 'em. Her husband, and the children of that husband, were all she ever needed or wanted."

"That's not normal."

"And isn't that what you've been telling me?"

He smiled and rubbed the short sandy hair at the back of his neck, and I saw again that he was handsome. The years that lay on him had merely given him dignity.

Uptown women bring their yorkies and dalmatians and Persian cats to him because he's a hunk, I realized. He could have any woman he wanted. And all he wants is Barbara Trahan.

Doctor Calvin Ray Buchanan Junior, son of his father. As warped in his own way by the absurd love saga of C. Ray and Velma as I am. Doomed to accept the abnormal as normal, and doomed to seek it.

"I thought I loved Larry," I said out loud. "I kept waiting to feel *more*. To really feel it. Passion, not just love. Real passion, the forever category. The real cinematic article."

My brother laughed, and I laughed, and then I actually began to guffaw at myself, because what I had just said was so naive and idiotic and so true, and I had meant it, and I wanted to know how to not mean it.

"Let me look at your hand," I said on impulse. And Rocky reached his hand out, and I examined his palm. He sat very quietly and nonjudgmentally as I registered the long and clean and uncomplicated Heart Line on his dominant right hand, the idealistic upward swoop of it towards Jupiter, the well-balanced Line of Head fairly united with Life for a considerable distance, the healthy Mounts of Venus and the Moon. "Am I okay?" he asked me, smiling.

"You're very okay. You're not impulsive. Or stupid. Or insane. Or weak."

We sat over the place where we both knew Rocky's toy horse's vanished dents still existed on some molecular level.

"Can you see the future?" he asked me.

"A little," I said, and realized that it was true. I didn't need his palm to see it. And it didn't look all that great.

"I love you, Rocky," I said.

chapter 18

My
Promises

Campo/Judge. I saw the blue and white campaign signs posted in front yards as I drove past the houses of Auletta—*Campo/Judge*. People here in Louisiana were not secretive about their voting choices, I remembered.

"Campo," I muttered to my mother, who sat beside me up front in my father's large car. "Campo is everywhere."

"You remember Frank Campo?" Daddy called out from the back seat. "The DiBenedettos' grandson?"

"Yeah. Dimly."

"That's him. Lives in Slidell now. Running for judge. We're thinking about putting up a sign for him ourselves, neighborhood kid."

I recalled a shirtless and tall boy mowing the grass down on the corner of Napoleon and Claiborne, back in my adolescence. I remembered the startling mystery of his outie navel and black armpits, his sleek skin, the insolence with which he flicked cigarette butts into the uncut portions of the lawn. I smiled now. "Yeah. Frank. He married Cathy Noel."

"You were crazy about him," said Mama.

"Well, sorta." The phantom of my old invaded diary stirred and opened itself for a second, and hung in the air, flapping its pages in an invitation to unpleasantness. But I refused to bite. It wasn't worth the effort anymore. It didn't matter anymore.

This woman sitting in the car here beside me, this small old woman with her red lips and new eyeglasses, her faded and thin hair, just wasn't the same deceitful harpie who had once caused me so much angst. She wasn't, and yet she was.

And I'm not that same Jeanne, I thought. I'm not, and yet I am. And here we three go again—all that's missing is Rocky—riding down the highway in Daddy's big old-guy luxury Chrysler. A mama and a daddy and a daughter, chatting away about mama-daddy-daughter subjects of no import, relating to each other in the same old comfortable ways of my pre-adolescence, speaking our lines as if they were roles actually written for us.

All we need is Rocky in his red cowboy hat.

This is really not so bad.

Okay, so Mama and Daddy are old now, I was thinking. And me, I'm fat and tired and about to give up on my marriage. I have a son in high school, my hair shows some gray. But it's all okay. Right now. We're still us. We're still here. We'll always be us to each other. I can relax. I am relaxed.

The sky is blue and the gas tank is full, here in the Buchanan Eternal Present. What extraordinarily lucky people we are, when you come right down to it.

"Turn right up here at that sign," my mother said suddenly.

"Turn *right?*" I put my right blinker on.

"No, wait, go straight," Daddy said at my ear, leaning over from the back seat. "We got about another three-quarters of a mile to go yet. This ain't it."

"Oh, yeah," said Mama. "I have it all mixed up with that other sign back there. It's a big Ryan's Steakhouse sign. That's where you want to turn, punkin."

"I'll tell you when to turn," said Daddy.

"You're really going to like Ryan's," Mama told me, sunlight glinting off the lenses of her unfamiliar glasses. She wore golden clip-on button earrings that bothered me with the way they pinched at her dangling lobes. Her polyester blouse and slacks did not match. "They've got this big salad bar where you can get all the dessert you want. All kinds of dessert. Cake and ice cream, hot fudge sauce. All you can eat."

"Velma always knows where all the sweets are," said Daddy.

I laughed. "Hey, I really don't need anything like dessert these days, y'all. Too fat as it is."

Daddy made a pshawing noise. "Hell, you're just right, Jay. You look fine. Doesn't she look fine, Vel?"

Mama looked at me and I looked at her, briefly, and I did warm to the honest and loving smile that began underneath her glasses, just up under her eyes. She reached over and patted my knee. "Jeanne looks *beautiful*. All filled out."

"*Fat*," I corrected, unable to let her compliment stand. "And I've been eating too much junk since I've been down here, you two. I'm going to have to stick to salad today."

All you guys have fed me since I've been here are high-fat frozen microwave dinners, I did not say. All Daddy lives on are high-fat convenience foods, stacked in your freezer like shelved books. Can that be good for his heart? There's got to be a lot of ingredients in that junk that a diabetic isn't supposed to have, either. Like sugar. Tons of sodium.

What good is his blood pressure medication, if he's loading up on salt at every meal?

What's the matter with you guys? Doesn't Mama believe in cooking anymore?

I'm going to have to talk to Rocky about this. Changes are going to have to be made, y'all.

"Frank Campo mows our grass for us," Mama said now. "That big yard we've got. Too big for us to do it ourselves, these days. Too *hot*."

"Velma used to love her riding lawnmower," said Daddy. "Got her suntan on her mower, like she'd been to the Riviera."

"Not since it almost overturned with me that time," she looked back at him, "down at the ditch. You won't catch me on that thing anymore."

The notion of my mother driving a large lawnmower with whirling blades was a very alarming one to me now. I was glad to hear that she'd stopped.

"Frank Campo doesn't mow our grass *personally*," Daddy clarified before I could conjure up the image of a middle-aged candidate for public office sweating atop a lawn mower out off Highway Twelve. "But it's Frank who has it done. He sends 'round some kid that works for him."

"For free?"

"Oh, no. We pay him," said Daddy. "We pay the kid. Nice kid, too."

"Frank finished law school about the same year that Rocky finished his first year at vet school at LSU, didn't he?" I asked. "I remember he married Cathy No—"

"*Watch out!*" Mama flinched loudly at a semi-tractor trailer truck merging innocently into traffic on my right, and scared me shitless for a second. Panicked, I looked to see what else she saw, what imminent catastrophe, since the semi had already been noted and accounted for. My blood pressure spiked. There was nothing else over there in the right hand lane, though. The semi was waltzing into traffic harmlessly behind me now.

"I see him, Mama!" I felt a flash of my old Velma resentment. Her sudden interference here had caused me to lose my driving flow for a second. It was dangerous.

"He doesn't see *you!*"

"Yes he does, Mama!"

"It's okay, Vel," said C. Ray from the back seat, reaching out to pat her on the shoulder. "Jay-jay's a good driver."

"How is she a good driver, living up in New York City where she doesn't even have a car?"

"You want to do the driving here, Mama?" I asked her.

She pushed out her lips. "No."

"Okay, then."

"I just don't want to get killed."

I sighed. "I promise not to get you killed, Mama."

"Jay," C. Ray touched my own shoulder from behind. His hand

was reassuring. It urged me towards calm. "Get in your right lane up here, baby. You're gonna be turning up here."

"At that sign," said Velma. "That big sign."

"We probably ort not to've moved way out here," Daddy told me that night, while Mama did the dishes in the kitchen.

"Go in there and keep your daddy company," she had said upon my offer to help. "He's so glad to have you here, punkin, and it isn't going to take me more than a minute to get washed up here, God bless TV dinners."

It irritated me now a little to hear the clanking and clanging of Mama scrubbing tableware in the stainless steel sink, when Larry and I had given her a brand new dishwasher two years ago. Mama had never seemed interested in learning how to use it. Barbara kept trying to show her how it worked.

"We're pretty far from everything out here, I guess." Daddy pressed the television channel remote, and images flickered by on the large screen. "It's real pretty out here, though. Peaceful. We got a yard full of birds. This is a bigger place here than what we had in the city. House is a whole lot newer."

"I thought you'd found a doctor in Slidell."

"Yeah, good doctors in Slidell. I just wish Velma had herself more friends over here, though."

"Daddy, y'all have been in this house for—what? Five years now, almost? This *is* home to Mama now, as much as anyplace is going to be. The old neighborhood is changing. The DiBenedettos are long gone. Dolores Bordelon is thinking about selling her house eventually, moving to Houston to live with Margaret."

"Seems like just yesterday, Barbara was leaving Rocky, all that sadness. Us moving out here. I planted that little rain tree in the back yard."

"But they seemed fine, last night at dinner," I said. "So lovey-dovey, you'd want to puke. It does look as if time is on their side now, Daddy. So you and Mama don't need to stay stuck out here, if you feel stuck. I've talked to Rocky. He'll help with whatever you need. Sell this place, you can move back to Napoleon Avenue, maybe even buy the Bordelon house next door. See Adam and Brooke all you want, get your regular grandchild fix." It sounded like a fabulous idea to me, as I sold myself on it. It left me entirely out of the picture.

"Too much crime in Orleans Parish now. Bad crime. Murders. So much meanness on television, Velma made me put in all these lacy burglar bars, even way out here."

"Well." I looked at the television show he had settled on. Another nature documentary.

"I *love* the country," he said in a faintly argumentative way, as if he wanted to challenge me. I had no idea what he wanted from me. "I grew up in the country."

"I know you did."

"I didn't know the country was a bad place to grow *old* in."

"Daddy, I do think Mama loves it here. She's got her flowers. She's got this place decorated to within an inch of its life. She's so proud of this beautiful yard. This is the kind of dream house she used to only dream about, looking at *Better Homes and Gardens* back on Napoleon Avenue, all modern and brick and spread out. Daddy, she's the queen of this place."

"Hell," he said, "we're four miles from the nearest supermarket. She don't drive anymore."

"But Rocky says it was Mama's idea to move out here in the first place."

It was a while before he spoke again. His faded green eyes watched the television screen where lions roared. I saw how deeply lined his face was. His brows were colorless, long and wild. There was no red in his hair anymore. His freckles had become ill-defined liver spots at his high hairline. "Jay, I just don't know if Velma can live way out here *alone,* baby."

My mood lowered. My emotional temperature went down into cooler readings. "So how are you feeling these days?"

"Not bad." He watched the lions. "And I'm being totally honest with you. My blood sugar's pretty good. Blood pressure pretty good."

But I could feel my inner self descend into winter. A herd of zebras grazed on the screen. Three lionesses lay in wait in the tall grass. They weren't going to just pack up and go away.

"We've got one of those pre-need funeral plans," Daddy went on, "both of us. Already paid for, plots and all."

Maybe this is where I get that quality from, the one that Larry and his family call *cold*, I thought. Daddy speaks as if he's discussing somebody else's cemetery plots.

C. Ray Buchanan shot a Japanese kamikaze Zero out of the sky when he was twenty years old, before it could crash into the flight deck of his aircraft carrier, I remembered. C. Ray Buchanan keeps a very cool head. I can't understand anybody who'd see that as an emotional defect. I admire it.

"Okay," I said to him, chilled down to hibernation. I actually felt sleepy.

"Frank Campo's our lawyer," he continued. "Law offices in Slidell. Even if he wins the election, our files'll still be there. Ol' Frank'll make sure we're well looked after. So anything you need to know, you and Rocky, just ask Frank."

"Okay." I had to replace the image of my golden lawnmowing god with the substantial attorney he probably now was. Frank would be even older than me. Probably fat again.

"I've named you as my executor, Jay."

I wondered how cold I could go before I lost consciousness. "Okay."

The lionesses moved in for the kill. An old zebra went down with fangs in his throat, kicking at tawny bodies. I closed my eyes. I opened them. There was nothing wrong with what the lions were doing. This was nature. Nature made way for younger zebras. Lion cubs had to be fed.

"It'd be easier on you if Rocky could do it," Daddy said, "him living so much closer. *But.*"

"Barbara."

"I've learned to just stay out of it. I've tried to keep Velma out of it. You know."

"Yeah."

"She'd be in it all the time, if I didn't keep a whole lake between them and us. She used to be in it more," he said.

"We all were. Rocky involved all of us."

"Does more harm than good. Once you get a person like Velma to think certain things about somebody, you can't just turn around later and expect her to *un*think 'em. Can't be done."

We both broke into fond laughter, Daddy shaking his head. The televised lion cubs had reddened faces. They romped while their mothers tried to clean them up with rough tongues.

"Well, I'll see that Mama's taken care of, Daddy, when the time comes," I said finally, leaning back into my recliner and cracking my finger joints. "And I won't bother Rocky with any of it."

"That boy works mighty hard for his family, Jay-jay."

"I know he does."

"I'm going to sleep a whole lot better tonight, knowing that you and me have kinda gotten things settled here. Makes me feel real good to hear you're in my corner."

"I'm in your corner, Daddy."

We sat there side by side in twin recliners, watching hyenas carry off the bones of the lions' kill. The cute lion cubs were gone. Hyenas weren't photogenic.

Mama noisily put things away in the kitchen, opening and shutting cabinets.

"Jay," Daddy said after a long moment, "Velma's going to require a lot of looking after, baby. She's never been on her own."

"I know."

"A *whole lot* of looking after. She can't live by herself, Jay. Not now."

My inner thermometer went below thirty-two degrees Fahrenheit. I understood what my father was asking of me. Deep inside my brain, I had long known what he would ask of me, long before I had even gotten on the plane to come down.

"I promise," I said, and I knew what I was saying.

But I began to hope with every cell of my body and mind that it would never come to that, that C. Ray Buchanan would live on another ten years, or maybe even an unlikely fifteen. That maybe he'd outlive Velma. Better yet, that perhaps both of them would even get to die a romantic death together in some very far off future, hand-in-hand in some sudden and painless auto accident that would bring neither fear nor grief to either of them. I began to hope so hard that my neurons overheated. My emotional temperature climbed.

I can't live with Mama, said my frantic brain, showing me literally hundreds of brief visions of blonde hair and disagreements and tears from the past. Out of the question. Absolutely out of the fucking question.

"I promise, Daddy," my mouth said again.

"Well," he reached across the space between us and touched my arm, "we don't know what the future holds, baby."

"But I do promise to look after Mama. Royally. She might like New York. I might not even be in New York then, who knows? So don't you worry about it. Don't stress yourself." I was addressing myself here as much as I was addressing him, trying to win back the evenness of the day. We were talking about the far off future, one that might not even take place. The sounds of Mama puttering about in the kitchen seemed eternal, thank God. "You've got to take care of yourself, Daddy."

"You know," he said, "my brother Wallace stayed on at the old place and looked out for our folks, after I settled in New Orleans. I don't know what all he did. He farmed for 'em, after Daddy got too old to farm. He made it possible for me to live over here with Velma and raise you kids, I do know that much. I've never thought a lot about it. Just took it for granted. Maybe it wasn't something that Wallace particularly wanted to do, I don't know."

"Maybe not." I desperately wanted to change the subject and change the television channel. I had had enough of hyenas. Lions definitely lurked, hidden in the shade.

"I don't know if I've ever thanked Wallace for what he did."

"Daddy, nobody can see the future," I echoed his own words right back at him. I mentally reviewed hurricanes and tornados and influenza and cancer, car wrecks, random crimes, the deaths of children, and other possible outcomes to our lives that would be worse than my living with Mama. There were many things so much worse.

Any of them could happen. All of them suddenly unnerved me. The inevitability of bad outcomes loomed on my personal horizon like a tidal wave.

We were so vulnerable, so mortal, not at all like those Elves that Larry and I had once theorized over. How had Tolkien ever imagined such a race of blessed people, him stuck like all the rest of us in these absurd, fragile, and decaying bodies? At what age had he begun to really get into his creation, imagining beautiful people who were free of Time? A young author might create them, in the strength and confidence of his own youth. But I thought now that it would take an older author to appreciate them and flesh them out. To discover the perpetual loss at the bottom of their existence in a mortal world, their sadness as they outlived everything dear to them, even their own homes.

"Daddy," I said, "you'll probably outlive us all. You'll probably have to be *my* executor."

"I'd do it."

I reached across the divide between our recliners, and I took his hand. "I know you would."

"Wallace didn't even ever get married," said C. Ray. And he cried.

chapter 19

Denial
Aboard
the
Titanic

I've already expounded upon depression, so let me now go into what I've learned about denial. I have a Ph.D. in the subject.

Denial is the cockroach of attitudes. It stays alive. And you stay in it, in spite of all your good sense and clear vision. I guess that you can't undergo upheavals like divorce, problems with your unhappy son always mouthing off about something, and the scariness of having to date again, without denying that your old parents are falling completely to pieces many miles away.

So you chalk up your father's weakness and breathlessness to low blood sugar. And you rag him about getting back to regular usage of his glucometer. You nag him about seeing his doctor to get his medication dosages adjusted. And you even feel self-congratulatory and self-important for getting on his case this way, because it's for his own good.

You attribute your mother's weird lapses in personal care and housekeeping to anything but Alzheimer's disease, because you simply cannot deal with the notion that it might be that. It *can't* be that. Anything is better than that, so you'll put it down to anything but that. You invent alibis, such as vision problems and stress. Alzheimer's is unthinkable, quite literally, so you don't think she's got Alzheimer's. How simple.

Here we are at the very heart of denial, whistling in the boiler room of the *Titanic*, convinced that all this cold water rushing around our feet is from a backed-up toilet.

But Mama's memory seems normal, doesn't it? Yes, indeed. Velma can still tell you what she ate for breakfast, and what *you* ate for breakfast. She knows the names of every single character on all the soap operas, and she can tell you every detail of their indiscretions, whether you care to hear them or not. She, too, nags C. Ray about his medication, and knows when he is due for each insulin shot.

But she can't locate her cigarettes after supper, not even when they're on the table right in front of her. She mistakes a lipstick tube for her disposable lighter, and keeps trying to light her cigarette with it, even when her thumb finds no little wheel to flick. She asks you if the dirty white sock on the bathroom floor is a fried egg. And you notice that it *does* look like a fried egg from certain angles. But you try not to wonder what could make a person think that the bathroom floor is a normal place for specific foods to turn up.

She stops shampooing her hair. She never goes to the beauty shop anymore. She also seems to have stopped bathing. Good thing that the elderly don't perspire much, and stink.

But all older people get a trifle spacy now and then, don't they? Sure they do. Like when they're under stress. And Mama's under constant stress, worrying about Daddy. She doesn't have time for her own personal care.

Rocky keeps calling you long distance and warning you that this might be Alzheimer's, but you don't believe him. This isn't Rocky's problem. You've made your promises to Daddy, and so it's *your* problem. And it can't be Alzheimer's, because you simply cannot deal with that. So Rocky doesn't know what he's talking about.

Yet your digestive system can pick it up on radar, like an incoming missile aimed right at your sternum. Your digestive system never falls for any of this denial bullshit, and it can be counted upon to put you right into the john with diarrhea, whenever you take some days off from work and fly down to Louisiana to see how the folks are doing. Your digestive system demands chocolate and bourbon. Your digestive system *knows*.

You have this big ol' cruise missile targeted directly at you now, and there is no way to dodge it. You can take no refuge in the fact of your own motherhood, since you've already finished fucking up Conrad. He's in college now. He's majoring in journalism, but he writes you few letters, none of them eloquent. You feel bad.

You can no longer plead duty to a spouse, and you don't even like Larry all that much anymore, not since he told the family court that you were a voodoo practitioner. Maybe Larry should have been awarded custody after all, you think sometimes. That way, if Rad needs one of us to eternally blame, Larry would get the nod.

Even your job at the gallery is expendable, no real career, it's not like you're a curator or something. What you are is a glorified sales clerk, selling overpriced and very bad art. This is no noble pursuit to which you might have been able to claim pained allegiance. You are not curing cancer.

No, there's nothing standing in the way of you keeping your promises. You keep looking for something. Some new man, some new circumstance, something that will get you off the hook with honor intact. Something incredibly important that your parents and your brother would respect, that would make them *plead* for you to just ride off into the sunset and sacrifice all but the most trifling contact with them for forever. Nothing turns up.

Nope, you're on the *Titanic,* honey, and your goose is pretty well cooked. In fact, you're on the *Titanic,* and the iceberg has already ripped open its hull, and you are personally tied to the bulkheads below the water line. And you can't swim. And you're wearing seven pounds of mink.

But that cold salty water that's creeping up around your ankles is merely overflow from a backed-up toilet, you keep telling yourself. You summon aid: "Oh, steward? Somebody go call a plumber, please? It's just a teensy bit damp down here, nothing to worry about."

And good thing you're somehow tied to a bulkhead like this, because the floor is beginning to tilt. And you're wearing bright red teetery high heels.

"Gimme another glass of champagne!" you sing out. "The night is young, and all is peachy!"

Doesn't the orchestra sound *divine?*

chapter 20

Semper
Fidelis

"I'm still sorry, Nancy," I told my ex-mother-in-law on the afternoon of the first anniversary of my divorce.

"Whatever for?"

"I don't know. I did something."

"It was Larry who had the affair, Jeanne."

"Yeah, but because I did something wrong." I sat on the arm of my own plush stuffed chair, a hideous thing I had paid too much money for in a whole other life. It was chunky and post-modern, and nothing else in the apartment went with its violent blue.

I pressed the cordless phone against the colorless hair of my temple. I kicked off my gallery work shoes, Swedish clogs. "I think I sort of gave up too easily, Nancy, you know? Long before Larry actually began to stray, or whatever he did. Before he even began to want to, maybe. I just sort of began to doubt everything, I don't know."

"Nobody blames you, Jeanne, darling. Larry never blamed you."

"Conrad blames me."

"Kids'll do that, yes. They don't have all the facts."

I let my skirted buttocks slide over the chair arm and into the soft cushion of the seat.

The damned ugly thing was comfortable. My large calves flattened where the arm mashed them. My whole body was mashed and cradled, and there was so dismayingly much of it. I weighed more now than I had ever weighed before, even during late pregnancy.

I'm just big-boned, I kept telling myself, as if *tall* were a license for *fat*. It might have been okay if I had been happy, but I was miserable. I had no energy.

"Kids're so goddam *right* when they're nineteen," I grunted into the phone, "all full of righteousness."

"That's why they're called sophomores, darling."

"So sure that they know just exactly where their elders have screwed up, and angry about it, and absolutely convinced that they themselves will never make the same mistakes. *Ha!*"

Nancy's own sigh came as a soft echo.

"I'm going to go for a walk," I decided suddenly. "I'm going to go put on my sneaks, and put a Sousa tape into my Walkman, and see if I can't lose a few of these pounds of flab, as soon as we're done with our conversation. That's what I'm going to do."

"What a fine idea. I wish I could come with you."

"It looks like it might rain, though." I saw gray buildings across the street as I turned my head towards the window now. Gray air. Higher up, above the tall Manhattan structures, the sky was gray. I left my soft cradle and went to the window where I could look down. There were pedestrians on the street, yes, but then there were always people on the streets here. "I didn't used to mind the rain. Autumn was always my favorite time of year."

"A few more weeks, and Daylight Savings Time will be gone. It'll start getting dark at lunchtime, it always seems that way, doesn't it?"

"Maybe I ought to stay put. Stay inside. Maybe it's not worth the effort, if I'm gonna get soaked," I said.

"Well," said Nancy, "Sid's calling me. I guess I'd better go."

"How's he feeling these days?"

"Some men should *never* retire. Driving me *frantic*." She exhaled. "He can't let it go, keeps calling Larry at the office, driving Larry frantic—Sorry. I know you don't want to hear that. Things about Larry."

"But it's okay," I said, and it was. I rarely saw Larry Roth these days, now that Rad was at Georgetown and away from both of us. I rarely thought about Larry. Nancy Roth existed completely apart from her son Larry in my mind. She was Conrad's grandmother. She was someone I often met for lunch, whenever she was in the city for shopping or appointments. She was my friend.

"So how are your parents?" she asked me now.

"Crazy. Mama, at least."

"But I keep telling you, darling, that deficiencies of certain B-complex vitamins can cause mild dementia in older people, remember. Our stomach linings no longer absorb nutrients the way they used to. There are blood tests for this."

"Nancy, they're *gentiles*. Southern gentiles are people who don't go see a doctor until they've had a fucking near-death experience."

"And she could be having small strokes. TIA's."

"She could be having *kittens*, for all we know. Nobody knows. She says she's fine. Won't go see a doctor. My dad hints around to me that things aren't so hunky-dory. I've told you how Daddy is: confides his worries to me, hints around that they're deeper and darker than he lets on, but then winds up by saying, 'I just want you to be happy, Jay. We don't want to be a burden on anybody. Don't worry about us.'"

Nancy laughed. "Sid and his triple bypass. Sid to Larry and Kenneth: 'Don't you boys worry about me, I've never felt better. Just enjoy your memories of Sid-Nan Lingerie, the business I built from nothing for you boys and your children, which it would break my heart to see diminished or unappreciated in any way. Which it took the best years of my life to build from nothing, all for you. Don't mind me. Go live your own lives.'"

"Ken seems impervious," I mentioned Larry's older brother, whom I had never really gotten to know. "He does live his own life."

"Yes, but at what cost, Jeanne? He breaks out in hives whenever Sid gets heartburn. Even in a place as far away as Vail. Even surrounded by celebrities."

I watched my fat legs kick the air. "So where does it end? Who gets to live his own life? Is Conrad getting to live his own life?"

"Is he?"

"I doubt it. He thinks I'm a flake. He says he worries about me. He'll probably put me in a home before I'm fifty."

"Are you okay, Jeanne? Really?"

"You mean right now? Yeah, I'm pretty okay. That guy that my friend Sallie fixed me up with—that buyer for Bloomingdale's—he never called me back. That's okay. Fine by me. He had a toupee like roadkill. His first wife committed suicide."

Nancy made a noise like she didn't know whether or not to laugh. But I laughed, and I wanted us both to laugh. What I had said was the truth. About the toupee—how could a man who made such great money settle for such a bad hairpiece? Was it bad taste, bad vision, relatives in the hair replacement industry, *what?* And what I had said about his wife's suicide was also the truth. Poor unknown woman. Why were we laughing?

"It's just so *gray,* Nancy," I told her when we stopped. "Everything. My hair. My life. No color to anything. There were these intensely vivid colors in my childhood, I remember: my mother's lipstick, her hair. The blue skies of October. My brother's cowboy hat. They were more than just colors." I leaned on the windowsill of my apartment window. The streets weren't wet yet, but people hurried. Bright nylon team starter jackets and warmup suits were grayed over by the somber topcoats and tweeds of the older or more businesslike. Where is everybody hurrying to? I wondered. Why hurry? What's the point? We're all going to die. Life is short. We get fat, we get gray, we get old, we get crazy. And we die.

I watched two young Hispanics, male and female, go laughing down the sidewalk with a linking of hands and bumping of hips, obliviously dying. On the road straight to death, with no pit stops for even pregnancies. Pregnancy doesn't slow it down at all, kids, I told them mentally. The day your kid is born, it starts to die. Watch how fast your tits sag, honey. Watch those varicose veins pop out on your legs.

"It's all this *grayness,*" I said out loud to the phone. "Living in all this grayness. What's the point?"

"You won't always feel like this, darling, remember," said Nancy. "Someday soon, you're going to meet someone very nice, and your future will just open up for you, Jeanne. Just think about it. Rad's in college, you'll have your freedom, you'll be able to live anywhere you like with anybody you love. Life will be purple and red and yellow."

"All the marriageable men will be dead."

"Trust me, Jeanne. You're young. You have no idea how young you still are."

"What am I supposed to do with my parents when I move to Tahiti?"

"Sid and I are making plans. Looking into retirement communities in Florida. Actually looking forward to it, in a way. We have so many friends in Florida now."

"Well, Velma and C. Ray don't do Florida. Velma and C. Ray do Auletta, Louisiana. Velma and C. Ray hunker down in their country home and don't make plan one."

"When the time comes," said Nancy, "you and Rocky will know what to do for them. There are so many nice options now, darling. So many facilities that are caring and homelike, with real chefs in the kitchens, and contemporary paintings on the walls. Sunlit atria, filled with green flowering plants."

A mental image of my parents amid contemporary paintings gave me sudden indigestion. I pictured my father trying to make himself at home with white linen tablecloths and hothouse orchids. "I've made my daddy sound like a manipulative ogre, but he's not. He's a lovely person. He's a *country* person, and that means self-reliant and self-effacing. He's a scared old man who can't admit he's scared. He's a strong and kind person who won't ask for help outright. Who hates to impose."

"I've always found both your father and mother to be very kind and gracious people, Jeanne, what little I've seen of them over the years."

"They are. I need to remember that more often."

"Perhaps you ought to try your walk now," she said. "The sky out here where I am is some lighter, maybe your weather is also improving. You'll feel better."

"I need my parents to level with me," I said, "and be specific. No more vague hints. I need concrete diagnoses, because Rocky and I need to make concrete plans. We need to know how sick? How long? Who is willing to relocate where, and when? Are Velma and C. Ray willing to move up here with me? Because my father has all but told me that Rocky is not an option, Rocky's marriage would collapse. God forbid Rocky's marriage should collapse again, his kids are still so young. Ol' crazy Barbara might take them way off somewhere on her search for a new man because Barbara *always* has to have a spare man in her hip pocket. God forbid Barbara should go manless for like even six months. So Rocky wouldn't get to parent his own kids. Unless she like dumps them on him, like she did the last time. Dumps them like baggage. It could happen. God forbid the Buchanan family should upset Barbara Trahan's delicate marital equilibrium in any way, because her kids would pay for it.

"I haven't spent a whole lot of time with Brooke and Adam, Nancy, but I know that they're still little enough to benefit from solid parenting. So they have to be considered. Now me, Conrad and me, Larry and Conrad and me, we've already had our shot at it. We screwed up a little, Conrad is a sullen person, but maybe he isn't sullen when he's around his literally dozens of friends. People who aren't Larry or me. Conrad does seem to run with a whole troop of people, who seem to really like him. So maybe we did all right, comparatively. I mean, he's not in jail."

"Rad's a terrific young man. You know that. Mannerly and affectionate, clean cut. I know I must bore him dreadfully when he's out here, I drag out all of Papa's old Broadway scores and play some of them, and he turns the pages and never complains."

"I wonder if families aren't somehow toxic, Nancy. *Nuclear* family. Doesn't that sound radioactive?"

She laughed. "Don't expect agreement from a card-carrying Jewish mother, darling."

"Well," I said, "I'm going to stop bitching and fix myself a drink, I think."

"You might be better off with the walk."

"Maybe this is menopause, this mood. Maybe I'm going into early menopause."

"Well, possibly, but you're very young. And there are other symptoms. But you do need to consider hormone replacement, I guess it's not too early to be thinking about that. I can give you the name of a very good gynecologist, if you'd like a second opinion."

"My mother never went to a gynecologist in her life," I said. "Just our family GP. And that was only when she had a kidney stone."

"You got something to write with?"

"You'd have thought it was the end of the world when Velma Buchanan began to have hot flashes. You'd have thought that Velma Buchanan *discovered* menopause."

"If you don't drop the phone this very instant and go take that walk of yours, and get your serotonin levels raised, Jeanne, I'm going to tell you in detail about how my worries over you are raising my blood pressure and possibly shortening my life. Is that what you want? More guilt?"

I laughed. "No."

"So go walk. Throw on a jacket and go walk, before it gets too dark. There's such a thing as an umbrella."

"Okay," I said, and I told her goodbye. And I hung up.

And I went into the kitchen and poured myself two fingers of bourbon.

Thirty minutes or so later, I also took the walk.

What the hell, I thought, stepping carefully down each stair step in my sneakers, knowing that most people did not exercise while intoxicated. I had changed into the sort of matching sweatshirt-and-sweatpants ensemble I so hated on other middle-aged women. Nobody but a middle-aged uncool plump lady would wear this crap. Young women did not wear baggy sweats, where the top matched the bottoms. Young women did not make a pant suit out of workout togs.

What the hell, I thought, I'm no spring chicken. And my jeans are all too tight, and it's too cold to wear shorts. So sue me. Call the fashion police.

I started west towards Sixth Avenue, the same route I had taken that night many years ago in my quest for milk for Conrad. But the memory was archival now for me, nothing more. I felt no unease or dismay, remembering that night and the sleet and the kid with the leather belt who had tried to rape me. Too much time had passed. I was somebody else now. I had too many memories now for any single one of them to really stand out.

And that kid had been so young, I recalled without emotion. Not much older than my Rad is now. Who was his mother? Had she worried about him?

It wasn't cold enough to sleet or snow on this Saturday afternoon, and it still looked as if it might begin to rain before I could get back home, but the possibility didn't bother me. The bourbon had warmed me up. Made me impervious to trivia like weather.

I walked pretty well for a drunk lady, light on my feet and quick to dodge pedestrians. My own nimbleness amused me.

The brown leaves of skinny trees flapped just above me as I passed. Some breed of exotic dog pooped in the gutter in front of a large apartment building where a doorman stood guard, and its mistress waited ready with pooper-scooper and plastic bag in hand to clean up after it. You don't have to walk cats, maybe I should get a cat to keep me company, I thought now, having some vague idea that I liked cats. I wondered as I passed what kind of dog this sweatered little hothouse flower might be. It looked as expensive as a Rolex. Rocky would know what it was.

I nodded to the dog as I hurried by, and turned up the volume of my John Philip Sousa. Loud band music came through my earphones. I stepped off the curb and swung smartly across Sixth Avenue in a secret march.

I had discovered the benefits of Sousa purely by accident a few months after my divorce, when I was feeling like queen of the losers. Conrad had just begun college and I was rattling around the apartment alone, and I wanted the radio to keep me company. Most popular music, however, was love music. Love songs. Even rock lyrics were about meeting the girl, meeting the boy, making love, breaking up and making up, crying alone. I certainly did not want to listen to any love music. I didn't need to hear anything about sex, good sex, bad sex, good love, bad boys, bad love, love gone wrong, love so right, *none* of that shit. Popular music made me feel worse.

The classical music station was an improvement. Mahler could make me want to crawl into the bathtub and slash my wrists, but Mozart was an upper. Debussy was okay, as long as I was in the mood for introspection and not suicide. Wagner was good music to vacuum to. Bach called for somber reflections and hard liquor.

But I lucked into Sousa on the night before the Fourth of July, and found my ideal powerwalking music. It had a great tempo for exercise. No lyrics. Marvelous barbaric trombones that got your attention and then dove straight down underneath pretty melodies. Softer passages that grew loud, and then louder. And just when you knew that it could not get any louder, it got *really loud* like a child would want it, with serious drum booms and cymbal crashes. You had to smile like a child, because it did not disappoint. Sousa music had no irony in it. It didn't set you up for a crescendo and then refuse to deliver. You got what you expected, and then some.

You could walk to it, but you couldn't think to it. It didn't make you think of anything. It didn't remind you of anything at all, except happy brainless memories of football games and parades. Sousa rarely evoked any sort of non-memory-associated visual imagery, unless it was the sea in the march *Manhattan Beach,* or a bunch of Marines in *Semper Fidelis.* Sousa's march music seemed to be mostly about itself, and that was fine with me. The composer might have had specifics in mind sometimes, like cavalry horses or crusaders, or gladiators, or commemorative statues, or world's fairs. But mostly, his music was just what it was, absolutely *great* exuberant noise, with unselfconsciously pretty melodies coupled to smashing downbeats you could feel in your solar plexus.

My own favorites were the less universally well-known marches like *Foshay Tower* and *Who's Who in Navy Blue,* really noisy pieces with ter-rific jagged places where the music just shattered the eardrums in fire-works of sound. Sousa marches were aural fireworks. They exhilarated me for no good reason the way fireworks always did. The way snow did. The way a truly spectacular thunderstorm could.

This is *really great stuff!* I would realize over and over, whenever I took my walks, whenever I was unwilling to tune into the deadly love lyrics of popular music. I had read somewhere that Sousa had actually written lyrics to many of his marches, but I didn't want to know what they were. Even if it was a pretty safe bet that none of them concerned divorce, losing your husband, disappointing your son, getting fat and ugly, standing by your man, love will keep us together, it had to be you, you're nobody 'til somebody loves you, sexual healing, he's so fine, my romance, get on yo pony and ride.

I crossed Seventh Avenue and headed towards Eighth now, swinging down Twenty-Third Street past newly trendy coffee houses and pubs and clubs, the bourbon in me saying "so what?" to the lowering leaden sky. I felt really pretty good.

The headset played another of my favorites now, *The Fairest of The Fair*. One way to interpret its title was in reference to the long ago World's Exposition that had inspired it. But there was another way to take its title, and that's what I did now. I always tried to make it be about me: Jeanne Buchanan Roth, fairest of the fair, with some downright gawky passages in my melody, but also with whistling brio, and a towering foundation of sound near the end that made me want to stand up and do the Wave, or go to war, or ride the space shuttle. Or walk down Twenty-Third Street slightly drunk, bumping into only two pedestrians, with my hair blown and my cheeks palpably flushed with the cold and with trombones. I was my own parade.

I remember taking this walk that Saturday after my chat with Nancy, because it was the last power walk I ever took in Manhattan like that, with my headset on, in my sneakers, brainless in my march music. I remember it very well.

Two nights later, my daddy died.

chapter 21

Lemonade

You want me to say that my telephone call to Frank Campo, upon the death of my father, finally supplied the necessary spark to a destined relationship. That in losing my father, and assuming the care of my mother, I found the love of my life. That my long-ago crush upon Frank had finally come to fruition in the bittersweet ending of a made-for-TV movie.

Get real. Welcome to planet Earth.

Welcome to planet Auletta. Welcome to Alzheimer's planet.

I was self-aware enough, that initial year of caregiving, to realize that I could use some serious counseling. But I couldn't leave Mama long enough to get any.

By that first spring, before I cut all my hair off, Mama no longer knew how to dial or even answer a telephone. I had to stop leaving her by herself on the day Daddy's car broke down with me at the supermarket, and I couldn't get her to answer my phone call home from the repair shop. All kinds of things go through your mind, when you're stuck at Auletta Auto Repair for umpteen hours, envisioning your mama turning on the stove or wandering away from the house or drinking bleach. My mind was getting a real daily workout anyway, with these kinds of things going through it day and night, running in and out of it, chinning themselves on it.

I knew that I'd probably feel better if I could see a psychologist or some kind of social worker, but I didn't know how to get away long enough to visit one. My restraint was still pretty good. I never laid a hand on Mama, and I was not yet screaming at her. But I would lie awake in bed at night, trying to sleep while I could, and I would know that something was deeply wrong with me. I didn't feel the things I should have been feeling.

I couldn't feel grief for my father. I couldn't feel compassion for my mother. Emotionally, I was pretty much pared down to anger and fatigue these days. Anger and fatigue, and sometimes hatred.

God help me, I hated my mother on those nights. I hated others of my loved ones, like Nancy Roth, with her useless and inapplicable advice. I hated my brother Rocky. I even hated my son. Rad would sit way up there at Georgetown, safe in his apartment, and would tell me over the phone what I was doing wrong: "You're too *overwrought*, Mom! Lighten up! I don't see where Mam-maw's even all that sick, she seems pretty okay to me, if you want to know the truth, I mean, she knows who I am on the phone and everything!"

Yeah, son. And I'm the one who hands her the phone when it rings. I put it to her ear.

"You know what I think, Mom?" Conrad would go on. "I think you need to just get out more. See a movie. Take like a vacation. Go on a cruise, why don't you? Just stop trying to make a martyr out of yourself. It's not good for Mam-maw's sense of independence, and I know it can't be good for you to shoulder all the burdens this way, Mom. I worry about you."

So I would lie awake nights, in the insomnia of perplexity, and wonder if I were imagining all this. Had I lost all sense of proportion? Was I insane? Had I somehow mistaken a speed bump for Mount Everest? I certainly didn't want to be the family martyr. Martyrs had a very negative image these days. And a sea cruise sounded absolutely wonderful to me. Even Joan of Arc might've given up on sainthood, if somebody had offered to send her to Jamaica in a first class stateroom.

I would begin, on those nights, to entertain the notion that Mama might still know how to use a telephone, if I wasn't around to do it for her. Maybe she could still cook breakfast, even. Maybe I could find affordable domestic help way out here, like maybe a teenage girl who babysat. Who wouldn't mind changing the diaper of an elderly lady, cook for her, and help her eat. Who would be willing to sleep over. Was I just being too dramatic these days? Was I crucifying myself for no good reason, making everybody who knew me sick to death of me in the process?

I didn't want to make Conrad sick of me. I didn't want to alienate him, or Rocky, or Nancy, with my whining. I hated whining from anybody. So why was I whining?

So I'll stop, I resolved. I'll exercise, and get my body into shape, and use my time here in Auletta constructively. Enjoy the country atmosphere, and let its peace come into my soul. Take up meditation. Live off my savings and Daddy's estate, since nursing care costs more per hour than I could earn if I found a job out here, and allow myself to be glad that I no longer have to go to work every day now. I can glory in my joblessness, without guilt. How many people get to do that? Think of all the poor slobs who'd love to trade places with me.

If I look at this thing right, this situation here, I have it made.

So smile, Jeanne. You have it made. "If life hands you a lemon, Jay," Daddy used to say, "then just make yourself some lemonade." Now I get it. I really do get it, now. This is lemonade. This situation is all lemonade. I resolve to believe that. I believe that. Why has it taken me so damned long to see it? From this night on, I'm concentrating upon lemonade. I'm thinking positive.

I'm going to find a sitter, and I'm going to take that cruise, Rad. I'm going to lose more weight first, so that I'll look okay in a swimsuit. Maybe I'll even dye my hair, back to its original brightness. Or maybe go blonde. How would I look as a champagne blonde? Thinner, and blonde? In a new swimsuit, on a Caribbean cruise, with maybe some self-tanning lotion that would let my redhead skin cheat a little?

Let's see if I can get a little sleep going here now, with that nice image in my mind. Let's think happy thoughts and drift off. Turn over and find a comfy position. Dream positive dreams. Let's see if I can imagine the sound of the sea.

And then I'd hear it, that uncoordinated shuffling, the uncertainty in my mother's voice as she sought me out in the middle of yet another night: "Jeanne? Is anything wrong? Where are the babies?"

I wouldn't know what babies she meant. And I didn't care. "The babies are asleep, Mama. Go on back to bed. Everything's all right."

"Where's Wallace?"

"Uncle Wallace is in South Carolina, Mama. He called Rocky a few days ago to see how we were, that's what you're thinking of. But he's all right. Everything's all right. Go on back to bed, now."

I could hear her breathing. "Wallace is at Rocky's?"

"Wallace is in *South Carolina! Go to bed!*" No doubt Rocky or Conrad could have told me that I handled these midnight conversations badly, introducing elements that confused Velma even more. But it was two o'clock in the morning, and I was doing the best I could. And the thought of Conrad or Rocky pontificating on a situation they knew absolutely nothing about made me furious.

"Well, who's at Rocky's, then?" Mama sounded both hurt and miffed. I could make out her silhouette at my open door. "You never tell me anything, C. Ray! You've got to tell me these things! I've got to plan, if we're going to have company!"

There she'd be, looking at me with that pissed-off look that I could imagine but not make out without my contact lenses. All kinds of really mean things go through your mind at two in the morning, when you're dead for sleep that you can't get, and a brain-damaged person castigates you for not telling her things. You are not at your best.

"Nobody's at Rocky's, Mama," I'd say, just barely keeping my patience alive on a mental heart-lung machine. "Just Rocky and Barbara and the kids, and they're all *okay*. Everybody's *okay*. Everything is fine. You'd better go on back to bed, now. It's late. You need any help, getting back under the covers?"

But she'd shuffle on up the hall without answering me. I'd hear her fumbling with the latch and then the lock at the front door. I'd hear the door squeak open.

"Mama?" I'd call, then listen.

"Are the babies out here?" she'd say, stepping out into the dangerous darkness of the front porch with its low concrete planter and steep steps. "I don't know where the babies are. Rocky's got that thing at his house, and Wallace wants the babies..."

God help me, I'd entertain the notion of just letting her wander on off, for about the four or five seconds it took me to kick off the sheets and get to my feet. I'd run to the door, wishing that I owned a tape recorder so that Conrad or Rocky or Nancy could hear the same things I heard at two o'clock in the morning. They could interpret them any way they liked. Or shove them up their asses.

The fact that what Velma meant by "the babies" was probably Rocky and me caused me no feeling whatsoever. I'd show her back to her own bed with no feeling at all.

I cut all my hair off that summer. I did it with no particular feeling.

When Conrad called me, my second spring in Auletta, to remind me of his upcoming graduation from Georgetown, I heard him with no feeling.

chapter 22

Sundowning

"Conrad's graduating from college, Mama," I told her two weeks before the event, on an evening when she was tranquil and fairly lucid. "Can you believe that? How 'bout that?" Our evenings together were our best times, in front of the TV after supper, with the dishwasher sloshing in the kitchen and the air conditioning at a comfortable level. Mama would sit in her recliner next to Daddy's, her arms crossed over her abdomen, drowsy with digestion and the familiar noises of the television set, while I read the paper or sewed buttons back onto our clothing. My evening bourbon sat on the lamp table, ten inches from my elbow.

"I'm tremendously proud of Rad," I went on. "He's never let anything stop him. Larry and me? He's let our divorce be like water off a duck's back. I know we've been a problem for him. But on he goes. What a kid, huh?"

To an outsider, it might seem rather futile to make conversation this way with a dementia sufferer. But it's the most natural thing in the world to do. Especially when there are just the two of you, and it's a peaceful evening, and another difficult day is behind you. I knew that I should limit myself to short, declarative, positive sentences. I had read all the literature. But Mama was the only human being I had seen all week. Except for Mama, I was in solitary confinement. You don't speak in short and positive sentences when you've been in solitary, and I could never tell exactly what she got out of TV these days at all. Maybe it was the comfort of familiarity, the uninterrupted evening routine she had shared with C. Ray.

His unoccupied recliner sat between us. His reading glasses still lay on the lower shelf of the lamp table, folded away and dusty.

"I'd like to find some way to go to Rad's graduation," I said.

"You *should* graduate," Mama affirmed.

"What about you, though? You can't stay here by yourself. You want to come with me? It might be fun."

She shook her head No. "I don't want anybody saying that Velma Buchanan has lost her mind."

She could be astonishingly articulate at times. I never knew what triggered this ability, what made these lucid periods so much better than her bad moments. I kept looking for clues, so that I could manage her behavior. But I hadn't discovered any.

"Not even Conrad?" I prompted. "Wouldn't you like to see Conrad?"

"Is he outside?"

"He's up at school. Let's go see him. Surprise him."

"I don't want *anybody* to see me until I get well, punkin." Her eyes, behind her glasses, were unclouded and very blue. Seated this way across from me, tidy and dressed and tranquil, she looked healthy and competent. She sounded rational. I almost believed for a minute that it *was* possible for her to get well.

I shook the paper to settle its pages. Dear Abby sometimes addressed Alzheimer's disease, but not today. I always looked, though. I always searched for clues that there were other people in the world who lived like this, enjoying trivial conversations like normal people one moment, living in Salvador Dali paintings the next. I had yet to get Mama into her nightgown, which risked bringing on a morning-style reaction and a threat to knock my teeth out. I considered just letting her sleep in her clothes tonight, something that I was allowing more and more lately.

If I neglect her personal hygiene, I'll get sent to jail, I reflected now. But if I accidentally bruise her, wrestling her clothes off, I'll get sent to jail.

Maybe if I get sent to jail, at least I'll get a good night's sleep.

I laughed at the mental image of myself snoring peacefully in a Velmaless cell block, and took a sip of my blessed drink.

Mama looked at me. "What's so funny?"

I got up, and went over to her, and patted her spotted hand. "I love you," I said.

She regarded the drink in my hand. "So when do you pass out?"

I laughed out loud this time, and sat down on the edge of Daddy's recliner. Neither of us ever used Daddy's recliner on a regular basis, maybe because he still seemed to be in it in some way. The light always shone brightest on Daddy's empty chair, but I was more comfortable reading in the sofa, letting his lamp light warm me from a distance like a small hearth. I had my own nearby lamp over there, and it was bright enough. "I don't plan to pass out, Mama. It's just one teeny little drink. See?"

She didn't look at it.

I never drank more than one drink before she was in bed, since I never knew what I might have to cope with while she was up. I had to be able to think clearly while Mama was afoot, ready to drive her somewhere in an emergency. The only time I felt it was safe enough to indulge was right after she had been tucked away, sometime after ten P.M. That was my private time, a small chunk of freedom I could use any way I liked, two precious hours carved out of the day for reading or writing letters, or watching rented movies. I felt a little guilty every night from ten to twelve, knowing that an objective observer would advise me to use this time for sleep. I wondered sometimes, over a novel and chocolate and another drink, if I was doing the right thing for myself. But this certainly felt like the right thing, this sundowning behavior of mine. This was my Jeanne time, my time of being Jeanne and not C. Ray. This was the time of day when I could stop living my father's life. This was all I looked forward to.

Dear Abby never touched on this, the quiet consolation of a caregiver's solitude in the late dark. Sometimes I opened my windows and just sat in the darkness with my drink, and listened to night birds and faraway train whistles, and felt vaguely religious. I had no real religion and I could not have prayed, even if I had had one, because my only true prayer would have been for my freedom, not for strength. For my *deliverance*, whatever that might mean for Velma. What would my deliverance mean for my mother? Her death? Consignment to a nursing home? How can somebody pray for such things?

Maybe it was better that I had no religion, then. Maybe it was better for me to have bourbon and darkness, and night birds, and good books; and two blessed hours a day in which to think my own thoughts and live.

There'll come a time, I thought now, sitting in my father's bright den with my mother nearby and a country singer wailing away on television about bad love, when I'll no longer have even two hours to myself. What will I do when I can no longer declare a victory over the day, when a day no longer has an end?

"You're not supposed to have any beer, C. Ray," Mama admonished me now.

"I'm Jeanne," I said, "and it won't hurt me. It's my little reward for getting through another day. For victory over another day. You want a drink?"

"No," she said.

"Okay." I patted her hand and went back to my place.

"I want a cigarette," she said.

It seemed wise to pretend that I hadn't heard her. I turned up the volume on the TV.

Mama checked the lamp table by her chair, patting its shelves, searching the crevices between the arms of the recliner and her thighs. "You seen my cigarettes anywhere, C. Ray?" she asked, struggling to push herself out of her seat as if she no longer knew how.

"Don't get up, Mama," I said. "I forgot to buy any cigarettes. We're out of cigarettes."

She looked at me without expression for two beats or so, and then succeeded in getting to her feet anyway. She began to shuffle to the kitchen in her awkward gait, arms held slightly away from her body, heavy on her feet for such an unheavy woman.

You have to go to the bathroom?" I watched her.

Her voice was deep, sarcastic now. *"No!"*

"What's the matter?"

She stuck out her red lips and kept going, on through the doorway and into the kitchen. I stayed seated for a while, trying to find something worth reading while the damned country singer wouldn't shut up, but I could hear Mama rooting through kitchen cabinets now, dropping breakable things. I threw down the paper and stood.

She was tearing the place up in small ways, spilling canned goods and cellophaned packages of dried beans from the lower shelves onto the counter tops. I went to her and tried to hold her hands, afraid that she would bring a big can of ravioli down onto her head if she began to reach higher. "Mama," I spoke calmly, holding her hands in feigned affection and not in restraint, although restraint was really what I was going for. "What are you looking for, Mama? Can I help you?"

She tried to pull her hands away. Her face was a mask of distaste now, for me, for what was happening.

"What are you looking for?" I asked her again.

"I don't know."

"Do you have to go to the bathroom?"

"Yes!" she shouted, angry that I hadn't gotten the message yet.

We went off to the bathroom, arm in arm, but she started to flail and fight me off when I tried to get her slacks down. She was furious now. I didn't see how I would get her pants down without making her more furious. Well, maybe it doesn't matter, I told myself, knowing that she was diapered. Maybe we can deal with this later. I could smell the whiff of intestinal gas, though, and knew that I might have a lot to deal with later.

"I could just knock your mouth out!" she told me, making fists.

My own anger rose like a thermometer. Her elbows were bony, and one of them hit my temple.

I yanked her slacks back up. This wasn't the first time I had not known what to do. "For God's sake!" I said as I took her hand and led her back into the hallway, jerking her along as she pulled in the opposite direction and tried to get away. I had no idea where she wanted to go. There was nothing behind us but the bathroom, which hadn't appealed to her. I let her go. "I'm just trying to help you, you old crazy thing!"

She went back to the bathroom, now dark. She went inside.

I watched. She didn't come out.

"Mama?" I padded back down the hall in my bare feet, teeth gritted.

She stood just inside the doorway of the bathroom in the darkness, facing the commode and the window with its pretty frilled curtains that she had sewed herself. She was immobile.

I didn't touch her. I was angry, and the urge to touch her roughly, to jerk her around and punish her like a child, was too strong in me. I stood still, too, and listened to her breathe.

We did nothing but breathe for a moment.

"Do you have to use the bathroom?" I finally asked her, when I was able to make my voice soft and neutral. It was like starting over, turning a page, beginning the whole bathroom episode again from scratch, throwing out the previous abortive version and rewriting real life.

Her tone was likewise neutral. "No thank you."

"Are you lost?"

"Yes."

I reached out and touched her fingers. "Would you like some ice cream?"

"Yes." She let me turn her around.

I took her hand and we went back to the disordered kitchen. The sight of the spilled shelves meant nothing to her. They didn't register. I pulled out a chair and helped her to get seated at the dinette table, and she watched me like an owl as I went to the freezer.

The opened freezer froze my anger. There was good sugary stuff in here. My mood could be repaired. I inhaled the arctic air.

"How about strawberry?" I turned half around.

"That just sounds wonderful. Will you have some?"

"Sure."

We sat and ate our ice cream in a fairly amicable silence.

But she began to search the tabletop with both hands. "Where are my cigarettes?"

Not again. "I thought you wanted ice cream," I said.

"Yeah."

"You want some more?"

"Yeah," she said.

I stood to get it, and brought the carton of chocolate to the table. Chocolate contained caffeine, I knew, and it might interfere with our sleep. But then, Alzheimer's already interfered with our sleep, and it wasn't nearly as endearing as chocolate ice cream, what the hell.

"Splendish!" said Velma when I set it before her. "Thank 'em!"

I sat down, and watched her spill it onto her blouse. Country music yowled unheeded from the den, and I could feel its high nasality scrubbing my last few nerves raw with simplistic lyrics about family values and the good ol' days. If I live through this, I promised myself, I'll never listen to country music again. Not even on a dare.

My eyes itched. My throat began to hurt at the base of my tongue.

This is one of our *good* evenings, Mama and me, I thought, and I'm about two seconds away from a major crying fit, for some reason. Or possibly a nervous breakdown. What are the precise symptoms of a nervous breakdown, anyway? Maybe I've already had one, and just haven't noticed. Seriously.

I'm parenting my own mother, when I should be parenting my son. My mother has another child. But Conrad has only one mother. What kind of mother have I been to Rad?

I picked up the phone, while my mama tried to feed herself ice cream with her spoon upside down, and I called my brother Rocky. Over the televised whine of some overpaid moron in a cowboy hat atonally mourning the demise of family sanctity, I told Rocky in no uncertain terms that life was short, that I was losing my mind, and that I wanted to attend Rad's graduation and spend some time with him while I still had wits enough to do it.

Rocky was Rocky. He didn't get it. His cheery input boiled down to "What's the problem?"

chapter 23

Flying

I stepped into one of those food nooks clustered at all concourse intersections inside the Atlanta airport. Shivering in air conditioning so cold that it seemed intergalactic, I bought an overpriced salad plate and a mini bottle of white wine, while waiting for my connecting flight north.

I was scattered. My carry-on bag was a hindrance, and I worried about setting it down somewhere and then forgetting it. My high heels hurt my feet. My clothes did not fit.

The wine didn't help much. I ate two or three forkfuls of my chicken salad and then abandoned most of it on its lettuce leaf. I went back to the self-serve line for more wine. Drank it, trying to sip it like a lady and not some weird old lush, and then got up to wander around.

Checking myself out in the full length mirror of the ladies' room proved to be a bad idea. I had lost a lot of weight and was almost gaunt now, but the muscles sagged, untoned, at my neck and belly and thighs. My turquoise suit was a joke. This Joan-of-Arc hairdo I had given myself did not make me look young or hip or even French. My hair was colorless, graying all over. The lipstick and blush I had so carefully applied back in Auletta looked positively Barnum and Bailey. A space alien could've tricked out herself more attractively.

My watch reminded me that my next flight would not leave for another hour, so I took a seat among my fellow travelers to Washington, D.C., taking care to wrap the shoulder strap of my carryon bag around one wrist so that I couldn't forget it upon boarding.

There were television monitors suspended above each passenger seating area, all tuned to a CNN signal broadcast exclusively at airline travelers. I watched the captive audience watching the homegrown network monopoly. Many passengers, especially the briefcase types, consulted newspapers. Other passengers conversed. Some people dozed, or fretted into telephones. A hefty lady, much plumper than I used to be, read a romance novel with a purple cover full of cleavage and pectorals.

I let my own paperback, a biography of Princess Grace of Monaco, stay inside my purse. I couldn't work up much interest or empathy now for wealthy blonde actresses who married into royalty, especially after that sight of myself in the bathroom mirror.

At least three men here wore cowboy boots. One wore a Stetson, too. I wondered if he was under the mistaken impression that it made him look sexy, instead of like the blowhard redneck he no doubt was. Then I felt kind of sorry for him, realizing that he was probably balding. Maybe that's what *I* needed: a hat.

Are these the losers I'm fated to die in a plane crash with? I had the same thought many people have before a flight, especially if they're out of flying practice, generally apprehensive, and have a little wine buzz going. Yeah, I'll fit right in, my own loser carcass'll be found roasted in the same smoking rubble as all of these other losers. In my suit that doesn't fit.

The toilet is where my body will be discovered, no doubt: an unidentified middle-aged corpse with a haircut like a squirrel, pantyhose down around her ankles, struck down in the middle of a nervous bowel movement brought on by her fear of attending her son's graduation. Killed without dignity this way, through the fear of her son and his judgment.

The strap wrapped around my wrist had cut off enough of my circulation to make my hand tingle now, and I made edgy movements to reassure myself that I was fully awake and not hallucinating. I didn't feel like myself. I had not been out in the world this way in a year and a half, I calculated, counting the months on my fingers. So how was *myself* supposed to feel?

I didn't feel bad, exactly, but I did not feel good. I felt odd.

But then you always feel odd, Jeanne, I reminded myself. And it was the truth.

I wondered what Mama could be up to at this very minute, whether she missed me at all. I wondered if she was able to miss me.

This last week had seen me blowing my top in a major new way, screaming alone in the car on the very rare occasions that Rocky could mind Mama while I shopped for things I'd need on my trip. I'd be driving down the highway, running late or experiencing some other very minor frustration, and suddenly I'd find myself just *screaming* at the limits of my larynx. The car windows would be up, and I'd be screaming like a madwoman, maybe because I needed to do it and the interstate was the only place where nobody would hear me. But the wild sound of my own trapped voice would finally frighten me, making my eyes water, scaring me with its absolute sincerity.

Hey! Get a grip here! I'd lecture myself, trying to shut my mouth and cap my mood like an oil well fire, Calm down! This is nuts!

Turn on the radio. See what's on the radio.

If it's country music, you might start screaming again, be careful.

What we need is an all-Sousa, all-the-time station. WSOU, high octane marches for crazy people, disco Sousa, loud trombones. No lyrics. Too bad this old car has no tape player.

Hey, you're only a couple of days away from seeing Conrad. Hang in there. Be happy! Is screaming making you happy? Is it therapeutic?

Yeah, maybe the car screaming is a healthy thing, a mere safety valve, I lied to myself. An indulgence, a harmless way of keeping me from *house screaming*. A good thing, definitely. As long as I'm not pulled over by the state troopers.

Because my house screaming, while never as loud or inarticulate, did have the potential to get so much worse. Off and on now, for the last six months, I'd been yelling at home. In the laundry room. In the kitchen, when I burned my hand on the stove or spilled flour on the floor, I'd begin to cuss and just wouldn't be able to stop. My brain would say, Okay, that's enough, Jeanne! but my mouth would just keep on yelling and swearing and carrying on, until I became a little scared at being so out-of-control.

And poor Mama would sit there and listen and watch me with no expression. And when I'd finally blow myself out like a thunderstorm and shut up because I had more-or-less yelled myself hoarse and had no more left in me, Mama would softly ask me, "What's the matter, punkin?"

My given name Jeanne might no longer come to her, but at such moments she could distinguish me from my father. She could recognize me. I'd see her sitting there on the sofa, looking at me with as much concern as a person no longer capable of much facial expression can muster, and I wanted so much to bond with her. What I needed so much was my *mother,* somebody who could witness me behaving so abominably and hatefully, and still love me. And sometimes this mysterious old stranger could channel the Velma Buchanan of Napoleon Avenue like a spirit medium, and I could see my mother looking out of these eyes. These droopy red lips would shape my mother's words: "You okay, punkin? What's the matter?"

How can you tell your mother that what's the matter is *her?* That *she's* the matter with you? Sometimes, in my fury, I *would* tell her that, I'd yell it out at her. I'd scream that she was ruining what inconsequential little life I had left. That she was making me crazy. That a good mother always put her child first, that a good mother would never put a child through what Velma was putting me through now. That good mothers did not suck up their children's souls like fucking vacuum cleaners. I was pissed that Velma did not offer to fling herself onto her sword for me, begging to go to a nursing home. I was furious that she was unable to put me first. I demanded that she mother me, and she no longer knew how. I'd yell vile things until I just ran out of yells.

"What's the matter, punkin'?" Her voice would be soft and loving. She'd sit there on the sofa, hands folded, not understanding or remembering a word I had said. "Are you all right?"

I'd go over to the sofa and sit down next to her, all blown out like a storm, and I'd take up her perspiry hand and just hold it.

chapter 24

Conrad's
Palm

"The fact that I'm here at all is a damned miracle," I muttered over dinner. Nobody heard me. I wasn't real sure that I wanted anybody to hear me.

"This magazine thing throws me," Larry was saying to Conrad. "I thought you were going to grad school."

"Mark's family is willing to invest. Mark knows people, Dad."

"There're already too many entertainment magazines, though, Rad, from where I sit. Isn't that market already pretty well saturated, son?"

"Not online."

"It's a miracle I got to come," I couldn't keep myself from saying again. "I didn't see how I was going to get to come. If it weren't for Rocky—"

"Oh," Conrad interrupted genially, patting my hand, "I forgot! This is *Mom's* movie! My graduation from college is really all about *Mom!* Sorry."

Larry reached across the white tablecloth and took my other hand, out of compassion or old habit. "So how is Velma now? How was she when you left?"

I drained my second glass of red wine and made meaningful eye contact with our waiter. "Out of her mind."

"Well, people do grow old and get a little spacy," said Conrad, watching the waiter's hand as it resupplied me with a really nice pinot noir. "It's sad, but it's natural, just a part of life, no big deal. Mam-maw is still Mam-maw."

"No, she's not."

"I like your haircut," he told me after a moment, and his brown eyes softened with the change of subject. "It's kind of Jean Sebergish. Sort of a fifties pixie thing."

"Thanks." I touched his sleeve. Smiled, finally.

"*So.*" Larry placed both elbows on the table and steepled his fingers, and I wondered if he was so-ing Rad or so-ing me. He wore no wedding ring, and the tiny white stripe on his tanned finger had filled in with melanin now, after his second divorce. Larry had a very young son by his second wife. I sipped at my wine and tried to compute the toddler's age. The marriage had been brief. I had never met Larry's second ex-family.

Maybe they don't actually exist, I thought now, wined up. Rad says he's seen him, his little half-brother. Met him. Watched *Sesame Street* with him. Rad says he likes him, and likes his mother. Rad could be lying. Or they could be space aliens. Conrad included. This could all be an alien conspiracy. Explains a lot.

I giggled.

"Maybe you'd better take it easy on the *grappa,* Mom." Conrad was embarrassed for me. He was laughing, but looking at me as if I had just crawled up out of some gutter clutching a bagged and opened bottle of Mad Dog Twenty-Twenty.

"I'm over twenty-one, son," I said. "Get used to it."

"I don't know much about how business is done on the Internet," Larry followed up on his *so,* leaning back in his chair and stretching, a somewhat gauche thing to do in a ritzy place like this. It made me feel better. "But it's a tough world out there, Rad. You can't just say, "I want to do this, and then go do it.""

"Why not?"

"Because it doesn't work that way. It's not that simple."

Conrad resembled Larry, dark brown eyes and hair. He had the wide Buchanan mouth. He no doubt would have had the crooked Buchanan teeth, too, had Sid and Nancy not intervened with an orthodontia grant years ago. Rad had Larry's nose. I watched him watching Larry. I wondered if girls found Conrad sexy. "Dad, it's not my problem that you don't understand the Web. Literally, that just isn't my problem. Mark and I already have a website where we're testing this thing, and the interest out there is just unbelievable. I'm trained in journalism, I can write, I've always been interested in the entertainment industry, and *many* people are really psyched about this. This is no less than the *Vanity Fair* for the young and wired, Dad, a complete website guide to movies, music, gossip and fashion. Mark has amazing connections, too, Dad. I mean, he really does know all the right people."

"I knew the right people, too."

"His dad is a *television* producer, Dad. His older brother works for Miuccia Prada, in Italy. They know *everybody,* in movies and TV and *haute couture,* and I'm not talking Sid-Nan Lingerie."

"You think *I* actually think that Sid-Nan is high fashion? Is that what you think?"

I tuned them both out. I didn't need to listen, I could write this conversation in my sleep. This was the same argument Larry had once had with his own father.

"Families are toxic," I muttered. Although my table companions and myself made up nothing like a traditional family now, toxic or not. We were fragments, prions, pieces of a virus; unable to self-replicate, able only to irritate.

Conrad looked at me. "Huh?"

"Eat!" said Larry. "Eat! We've got to meet your grandparents back at the hotel by ten."

Rad ate. But he spoke. "What was that again, Mom?"

I took up my wineglass, what the hell. "I said that I think that families are *toxic.* That's what I said. Even the Kennedys. I think that all this family-togetherness crap is total bullshit. Because nobody can pull it off. It's an ideal nobody can pull off, and it makes people crazy."

"Jeanne." Larry called my name with reproach.

"Mom, you're so incredibly weird," said Conrad, "that's why I love you."

"Well, look." I put down my glass. "Think about it. Look at how much has changed in society, since World War II. The original function of the family, as I see it, was to insure the legitimacy of children and supply an in-house labor force. It was all economics. Survival. You have kids, they work your farm or carry on your trade, and you pass those goodies along to them when you die. Who gets what, who does what, it's clear cut. Marriage wasn't based upon some ephemeral bullshit like sexual attraction, too much was at stake. Husbands and wives were literally business partners. But we don't live like that anymore. Women work. Earn their own money. This is no longer a frontier society. This is not the Third World. The family no longer functions as an economic unit."

"Jeanne is such an incurable romantic, that's why I married her," Larry gulped at his coffee.

"Look at it objectively, guys," I insisted. "Look at it biologically. Look at what we so superciliously call the Animal Kingdom." Images from the nature documentaries I had once watched with my father flashed on my mental movie screen. "The function of the female is to give birth and then to nurture, once the male has slunk off in search of new females. Because that's what his nature is, to sire offspring. Period. With anybody. With everybody. That's what he does. To insure the survival of his species.

"What the female does, she nurtures. But only so long as her offspring requires that nurturing for its survival. Once she's done that, she's done her job. She's available for the use of the next male that comes her way. Once that baby lion cub or baby dolphin or whatever can make it on its own, the animal family ceases to exist."

"Yeah," said Rad. "Okay."

"But it's all this human invention, this marriage shit, that we no longer pay anything more than lip service to, that gets people all fucked up," I went on. "We don't know when to call it quits. It's all this post-nurturing interaction, this endless meddling in each other's business, this constant interference and encroachment that humans do in the name of family that makes us all lunatics. Families aren't permanent among other animals, they aren't *meant* to be permanent. But we insist that ours be, and we maintain this lifelong stranglehold on each other, this deadly *ownership* that we call 'family,' and that we say we value but we don't. It's become just a useless fucking effort. Hypocritical. Unnatural.

"A mother sea turtle leaving her eggs on the beach to hatch and then fend for themselves, that's natural. Daddy sea turtle, hell, he's just a distant memory. So mama just swims off into the sea, wishing her eggs well, unable to understand what they want. Maybe she loves them very much, but how can she live their lives for them? Notice, guys, that there are no maladjusted sea turtles. No turtle babies on drugs. No turtle mothers on Valium."

"Jeanne," said Larry.

"You're just a distant memory, you swam off a long time ago," I told him without rancor, "so you have no right to speak up, honey. And you keep doing it, bless your heart. I rest my case."

"This is all about Mam-maw again, isn't it." Conrad didn't phrase it as a question. "Christ, you're a one-note samba, Mom."

"I don't like your tone, son," said Larry.

"Yep," I answered, "it's about Mam-maw. It's about your Uncle Rocky, who damn well ought to swim off but can't seem to. It's about me. I'm a sucker for all the bullshit. I bought it. I still buy it, I guess. I don't seem to know where the waterline is, Rad."

Larry raised a hand to the passing waiter, index finger up for the check.

"I desperately wanted to leave the nest," I told Rad. "I thought that was the whole point of growing up. I've just never seemed to be able to get away. The waves have thrown me right back up onto the beach, seems like. Here I am again, high and dry. Listen and learn, son. Go to Malibu. Start your magazine. Swim on off."

His immediate smile at me was uncertain but very sweet, and I realized that I had finally said something that my son wanted to hear. But I had also said something else that he wasn't sure he wanted to hear, and I thought back to when I had been his age, trying to get away from Velma and C. Ray and get my marriage off the ground. Would I have liked to hear an explicit invitation to break cleanly away without guilt? Would I have wanted to be shooed away?

Just what had I wanted to hear from my parents, when I had been Rad's age?

Lord, I can't let Conrad think that I'm just dismissing him, like he's too much trouble or something, I thought now. Like I don't want him.

"Do you still read palms, Mom?" He changed the subject.

His sweet face was turned to me, open to me, three feet from my own. I looked at that innocent face and did not know how to keep it from hurt or worry or despair, and felt my chest congest with futile love. Had Legolas's unknown Elf mother, in that Tolkien book that had been such an important part of my youth, ever looked at the beautiful face of her son this way? Had she ever suspected that not death, but *life*, would be the real danger to him? Was she still alive at the end of the book? What was in her heart? When Legolas who had outlived all his mortal friends but Gimli, builds himself a ship to convey both of them forever to the Arthurian Avallone in the Uttermost West, because he can't bear to *lose* anymore? How many irrelevant Elf rules had Legolas broken in the act of taking a Dwarf with him and setting sail in his own homemade ship, long after all the Elvish ports in the mortal world had been closed down and forsaken?

How many rules was my Conrad going to have to break?

"I love you, Rad," I said out of nowhere, meaning it.

He gave me his sweet baby smile again. "I know you do."

"I mean, I *really* do. And don't you ever doubt it."

"I don't. I won't."

"I wouldn't be here right now if I didn't think the world of you, Conrad Aragorn."

"Waiter?" called Larry again.

"Have you ever tried to read Mam-maw's palm?" Conrad blotted his mouth on his napkin, and then stood.

"Yeah."

"And?"

"I know too much about what's happening to her to see it in her hands," I said. Larry pulled out my chair for me and helped me to my feet. My high heels did not wobble as much as I'd feared they might.

My dignity was still intact. "I've always read better for strangers than for people that I'm real close to, because I expect to see certain known characteristics in people I'm close to, and it blinds me to what I might *not* be expecting to see. You follow me?"

"Sort of," he said.

"You think of your Mam-maw as a sloppy but personable older lady, who used to tell you you might go to hell because you hadn't been baptized, stuff like that."

"She can't help the way she is, Mom."

I took Larry's proffered arm. "You've missed the point, Rad. What I'm saying is, if you could read palms, and you read Mam-maw's, this is what you'd expect to see."

We reached the front of the restaurant, the reservations desk near the beveled and sparkling glass door. "What do you expect to see, Mom?" Rad asked. "What blinds you?"

"I remember her when she was young. I remember what she was like."

"She was pretty."

"She was *splendid*." My tongue was thick. "A child's goddess. A movie star. A warrior queen. Eternal, like a fortress. Like the Statue of Liberty, only with a cigarette."

Larry touched the tops of my fingers. His hand was warm. "Where are you staying?"

"Sheraton," I said, and we stepped out through the dancing lights of the glass doors onto the bricked streets of Georgetown. Maple leaves hissed over our heads, gray-green in the night light, disturbed by the damp wind on the steep hill. The air was warm and muggy. The clouds were very low, glowing white on their undersides over the city. Students and dog-walking residents passed us on the bricks, in short sleeves and summer cotton skirts.

Conrad fished through his pockets for his car keys, and then stuck the palm of his free hand underneath my nose in a studied afterthought.

"I'm old!" I protested. "I can't see out here in the dark!"

He pulled me ten feet down the sidewalk, into the window light of the Mexican crafts boutique next door, and I laughed. The palm of his right hand waved insistently before my eyes again, and I took it to steady it. I pushed it far from my face to focus. Cars passed us, the white lights of their fronts and the red lights of their rears. I saw the sheen of perspiration upon the fine and ordered lines of my son's hand. We were both laughing like drunks.

"Jeanne?" said Larry. "Will you join us for coffee at my parents' hotel, if you don't have any other plans? My mother, particularly, is anxious to see you, you know."

Coffee. My pal Nancy Roth. Sounded good to me.

"Okay?" Larry waited.

But Rad began to jerk on his hand now, pulling it away from me just as I had started to zero in on it, and I knew that he no longer wanted to be known.

"Yeah," he wiped the sweat of his palm onto the seam of his khakis, "come with us, Mom, why don't you?"

"I see you have a secret," I heard myself say to him, nevertheless, that intrusive nevertheless self of mine who could not shut up. The same self who screamed at Velma.

"No," he said wiping his hand again.

"Yes," I insisted, and then stopped, because his face was telling me more than his palm had.

"Are you coming, Jeanne?" Larry got right to the point.

"Sure. Okay."

"Remind Mom to stick to coffee," said Rad, but teasing me, deflecting me, as he led us down M Street to his parked Nissan. "Remind Mom that this isn't a *keg party*."

"You might not believe this," I told both men as Conrad drove us away from the curb, "but I had already planned to order decaf, thank you very much."

"You're welcome, Mom."

"Yeah, and then I plan to go back to the Sheraton and have myself a nice, long, uninterrupted bubblebath."

"Life in the fast lane," said Rad, "go for it."

"And then I plan to sleep, guys. And sleep some more. And then sleep some *more*. Sleep is the most underrated free pleasure on this planet, and you can quote me on that."

We rode amicably on, and I looked forward to a face-to-face session with my dear friend Nancy, and ultimately to my bubblebath and my hotel bed. As much as I loved and had missed Nancy these last few years, and as much as I wanted to see her and Sid, the images of scented white bubbles and clean peaceful pillows were momentarily more powerful. I craved the silence and solitude of the hotel room in an almost childlike way, hugging myself now in the front seat of Rad's Nissan with the same sort of shivery anticipation I had once felt for parades.

Conrad popped a tape of *Les Misérables* into his audio system. Larry cleared his throat and then began to hum along in the back seat.

I thought about Mama, and wondered what she was doing, and how she was feeling.

We pulled up out front of the Roths' hotel and a valet stepped up to help me out of the car. I was confused for a second, not used to having doors opened for me this way, and my skirt hiked up to my knees as I awkwardly scrambled out of my seat. I'm probably not going to get as much sleep tonight as I want or need, I realized, rubbing my elbows while Rad gave the valet his car keys. All these newnesses are hopping me up, these vast changes to my daily schedule, and there's probably going to be just too much adrenaline in me to get me deeply under.

"Jeanne darling!" Nancy Roth came out of nowhere, arms opened. And the way she stood smaller than I remembered, and the way her dark dyed head sank more deeply into her pearl necklace, were two more things that required adjustment from me. I was unnerved by her wattles. It hadn't been all that long since I had last seen her, had it? When had she found the time to become so old?

If my own appearance dismayed her, she didn't let on.

Conrad stood near the front desk, almost militarily straight, waiting for his grandmother to suggest a plan of action, to lead us to Sidney, while we cooed and gabbed and did nothing. Conrad waited, dark-haired and beautiful, not looking at us, his eyes on middle space in the large busy lobby. There was a field of silence around him. His shined black loafers sank into the wine colored carpet like he had taken root there.

Conrad waited to be noticed by the rest of us, to be *known*.

I let Nancy take my hand and begin to lead me down the silent carpet, past elevator banks and gilded telephone stations, and Larry bought *USA Today* from the clerk just inside the gift shop. Conrad fell into step behind us and I could feel his silence and his isolation like an aura touching my back.

No, I'm not going to sleep much at all tonight, I thought again. Decaf isn't going to do the trick. There is my mother in my brain, and there is my son and his quiet apartness. I'm not going to be able to shut my brain off. I might as well be back in Auletta. I no longer know where my off switch is, there or here. Because time is running out, time is *pouring* like sand in a cracked hourglass, and I want it to go even faster, to save me, to bring me to the end of my Auletta prison sentence. But I also, in complete contradiction, am frightened by its passage and the way it is taking us away from each other, and I want it to *stop*.

Maybe I do need another drink.

chapter 25

Knowing
Conrad

Questions to ask yourself, absolutely *guaranteed* to keep you awake, field-tested in a hotel room in Washington, D.C., when I should have been dead to the world:

Is Alzheimer's really this huge tragedy I keep on thinking it is, if Mama's not actually suffering? In fact, she'd probably suffer a lot more over losing Daddy, if she didn't have Alzheimer's. Have I got it all wrong?

What kind of weenie am I, that I can't take caregiving in my stride? Hell, I hear all the time about other women who are nursing demented parents, sometimes *both* parents, while raising a houseful of kids *and* holding down a job, all at the same time. What's the matter with me?

Mama won't live forever. Alzheimer's typically runs its course in— what? About ten years? She obviously had it for some time before diagnosis, some years. Daddy knew. He knew that something was wrong, and he was in denial himself, but he tried to warn me in as explicit a way as he could manage. So the meter is running. This is a terminal illness. Doing the right thing by Mama now is the right thing to do, just that simple. I owe her. She once diapered me, now it's my turn to diaper her. Turnabout's fair play.

(What the hell exactly does that mean, *turnabout's fair play?* Am I saying, "Turnabout *is* fair play?" What the hell do some of these old saws mean? *Fair* play? What is fair here? Where's the fairness in any of this? For Mama or for me?)

I can't keep on top of the dirt Mama creates now, the crumbs. The snotty tissues dropped onto the floor. The feces smeared on the seat of the toilet, on the towels, on the bathroom mirror. It just keeps coming. Other caregivers manage beautifully. Why am I not Supergirl?

(Is Conrad gay?)

I've never had very much of a life, and that's pretty much my own fault. I didn't know how to make things work with Larry. I've never known how to really connect with Rad. I don't know exactly just what I have to show for my life. And now it's over. Dead and buried in Auletta, Louisiana, Official Rectum of The Western World.

(*Of course* Conrad is gay, and you've probably known it all along, if you're honest with yourself, Jeanne. He has millions of friends, but his women friends have always been just pals. He's never brought one significant girl home to meet you or Larry. He wants to start up an entertainment magazine with somebody named Mark. He talks about Mark all the time. He keeps his distance from you and Larry, not out of hostility, but out of a need for privacy. He has never been rowdy or hostile. Only moody, and distant, and self-contained.)

I wonder how Rocky and Barbara are coping with Mama? I wonder if Barbara's found somebody else to run off with? I wonder if it'd kill ol' Barbara or throw her hormones out of whack, if she had to go cold turkey men-wise, just once in her maladjusted little life? Jeez, you'd think she would've discovered masturbation by now.

Rocky says that it's *romance* that Barbara craves, that she's a romance junkie, not a slut. But just what the fuck *is* that anyway, "romance"? It's a fiction, something propagated by hack women novelists with lavish invented names, like Elisa Devonshire or Raven St. Claire. It's a movie conceit. It has nothing to do with washing a man's dirty socks, or kissing him even when he has morning breath, or trying to remember why you married him, now when he's become boring and predictable, and soft around his middle, and tells the same jokes over and over, and isn't as smart as you once thought he was.

(What does Rad need from me? If he's gay? Besides my implicit support, what can I offer him, if he continues to wuss out on coming out to me? Larry and I can't very well make the first move here. I could be wrong, I'm not that great a palmist. Larry and I can't just say, "You and Mark go have a nice life, we're so glad you've found a congenial partner, remember to practice safe sex, we love you just the way you are, son," unless Conrad *tells* us the way he is.)

Does Mama dream? Does she dream about *her* romance, does she dream about Daddy? Are her dreams as incoherent as her daily existence, or do they make sense to her? Does her soul retain clarity, even as her mind loses it?

(Oh my God, I'm frightened now that Rad really *is* gay. I'm frightened that he's gay, and I'm frightened that being gay isn't really the wonderful condition I keep telling myself that it is. I'm scared that gay is really not the best way for my dear child to be, and that it's *me* who has somehow caused him to become this way. I'm terrified that he'll get sick. Be beaten up in alleys by bigots. Be discriminated against, harassed and unhappy.)

Jesus, I wish I could get some sleep here, now that I've finally got this golden opportunity. What time is it?—Nope, mustn't look at my watch, I'll get completely bummed out if it's after four. And I'm already bummed out enough by everything else here.

(I wish I had some real clue, besides vague hints and Rad's palm to glance at. What I really need is his diary.)

What am I saying?

(*What am I saying?*)

chapter 26

Meanwhile and Far Away

"Either she goes, or *I* go," Barbara was probably laying down the law to my brother back in New Orleans right about now, during this absence of mine, pointing at our mother Velma. Velma, who would be wandering through the Napoleon Avenue house on yet another agitated tour. "I've had it up to here with her! *Up to here!*"

"Come over here and sit down by me, Mama," Rocky could be beckoning.

I knew Velma. Velma would've been at it for at least an hour now, this relentless pacing, her arms held out from her sides at an unnatural and weird angle, feet splayed and shuffling, her dark red lips in a pouty frown.

"Mama?"

Velma would be ignoring him. It was like something that Rocky had seen on television about the autism of a child.

"Come on over here and let's sit down for a minute, Mama." He might stand and wrap his fingers around his mother's cool, thin wrist. Her skin would feel slick and unpleasant. He would try to remember what it had been like to want to touch her, back in his childhood. What her healthy skin had once felt like, young and taut and warm. Perfumed and safe.

She shook him off now. "Go have another beer," she grumbled, "I know that's what you want. You never take me anyplace anymore, C. Ray."

Rocky looked back at Barbara. "Get on back to what you were doing, babe. I'll watch her."

"You have *any idea* what time it is?"

"Go on to bed, then."

"The damn kids're still up, nobody listens to me. Nobody cares about me and what *I* need." She stood there in her satin robe on the hardwood floor, weight on the balls of her feet like a prizefighter. She was short and didn't weigh much, and what she did weigh was mostly concentrated in her tits. The lace at her neckline rose and fell. Rocky waited for her blackeyed death stare.

"Jeanne'll be home day after tomorrow," he reminded her.

"Your mama's wet all over that sofa bed in yonder."

"You never pay any attention to me," Velma said to Rocky, big red lips all droopy in what might have been an attempt at a sexy pout. It gave Rocky the creeps, like his own mother was flirting with him. "Nobody pays any attention to me, C. Ray."

"*All we fuckin' do,*" Barbara shrieked at her, "*is pay you attention, Mama!*"

Velma's fingers dug into Rocky's biceps. "Some girl is being mean to somebody."

"Don't holler at her, Barb," said Rocky, helpless.

"Oh *Christ.*"

"Jeanne'll be right back, just a matter of some hours, baby. Come *on.*"

"Jeanne's probably screwing her brains out with Larry or somebody right now, if she's got good sense. She's not going to come back, if she's got any sense at all."

"Jeanne'll be back."

"I don't know what kinda husband Larry was, but as long as he's breathing, he beats this all to hell. That's what *I* know." Her bosoms heaved. She stood there and waited for something, for Rocky to do or say something unknown and unguessable. Barbara's big puff of dark hair was lionine, the color in her face was high. Passions became her.

"Go on to bed, baby," Rocky told her. His voice became softer. Barbara looked like her feet might be hurting her. "Forget about the kids, I'll deal with 'em. You go on."

Loud thuds and treble yelling came from the back den: Brooke and Adam fighting over the computer, probably a game.

"I'm gonna kill those damn kids." Barbara didn't move. "Don't do nothing but fight and holler. I'm going to rip out that computer and throw it right out the window in a minute."

"*I didn't do it, I didn't do it,*" Velma broke into sudden wheedling singsong, twisting her body in some kind of weird flirty dance like a six-year-old girl possessed by Jayne Mansfield. "*I didn't do it, I didn't do it, I—*"

"Nobody says you did it, Mama!" said Rocky. "Sit down!"

He steered her to an armchair, but she didn't seem to understand how to settle herself in it. He tried to keep from stepping on her feet. She was stepping on his.

When he looked back around, Barbara was wiping at gushing tears.

"Aw, hey." He was encumbered, he had his hands full. "Hey, Barb? Come on, baby. Hey."

Velma was still considering how to sit. She was oblivious to Barbara's fury, absorbed in the mysteries of the chair. Rocky held her by an elbow, watching her prod at the chair's stuffed arm with her free hand, tentative, as if it were some species of sleeping animal.

"You and Jeanne better not dump all this off on me, is what I'm saying," Barbara was pink and mad. "I've already done my time, up to my fuckin' eyeballs in old folks and little brothers back in Thibodaux!— So don't try to dump this off on me, feeding my grandmama with a soup spoon like a baby, every damn morning before high school! I've done my time. It's somebody else's turn now."

"This isn't your problem, baby. Nobody said it was."

"Damn right it's not my problem."

The fighting between the unseen kids grew louder. One of them was bawling, and Rocky knew it was Adam. He was the elder, but he just couldn't take things in stride. Rocky felt a sort of muffled panic sometimes for his twelve-year-old son. What if Adam never learned to roll with the punches? What if he continued to cry at frustration, on into puberty? What if he turned out to be gay? A nerd? A sociopath?

Velma pulled at Rocky's arm, giving up on the armchair. "Let's go to that cottage in yonder, C. Ray."

"You kids want me to come back there and kill you?" Barbara roared, the veins on her neck in bas relief.

"There's something the matter with that girl," said Velma.

Barbara had abandoned Adam and Brooke and Rocky once already, and Rocky watched the strain of her neck muscles now and knew that her very deep anger was not feigned.

"Something's wrong with that girl," Velma had muttered after Barbara's departure, not all that many years ago. "You might be better off without her, son, I know you don't believe that. But what kind of person leaves her own children? Something's really wrong with her, Rocky. Nobody'll ever be able to depend on her for anything. Look how many times she broke up with you, while you were in vet school. How many times?"

Barbara *moves* me, Rocky had thought but couldn't explain it to his mother and father, as he cried and waited. It's more than sex, yeah, Barbara's sexy, but it's more than that. Barbara had it real hard, growing up. She's like a forgotten passenger at some bus stop, waiting for somebody to come get her and take her home, but she just doesn't trust anybody to really go to the trouble. She doesn't trust me to do it. Right now, she trusts that guy she's run off with, but that won't last. I could do it, I've been doing it, I'm here for her. Her sadness moves me. What can I say?

I'm pretty much a one-woman man, raised by a one-woman daddy, and our popular culture tells me that both me and my daddy are wimps. So I feel like a fool, an emasculated fool. Even my parents tell me what a fool I am, and they ought to be able to empathize with me more than anybody.

"Barbara Trahan is trash," Velma had told him, her blonde bouffant hairdo nodding in sympathy, a cigarette held to her lacquered lips while her husband C. Ray lit it for her.

"I've got to go see that white car." Her tug at the bottom of his tee shirt now brought him back from the past, her frail fingers like claws where they knotted into the white cotton. "Let's go over to the thing."

Barbara folded her arms. "She wants to go to the bathroom."

He had no idea how Barbara had deciphered that, but he looked down at his mother and thought that Barb was probably right. Velma was like a cocker spaniel with a full bladder, barking to be let outside.

Barbara did not unfold her arms. "You'd better do something *quick*, Rock."

"I should take her?"

Barbara snorted. Her arms unfurled.

"I mean," said Rocky, "it doesn't seem like the proper thing. For *me* to take her. Wouldn't it embarrass her, sort of?"

"You changed Brooke's diapers. When she was a baby."

"Yeah. But."

"This is why wives set their husbands' beds afire. While the fuckers are asleep." But true rage had left Barbara's voice now. She sounded only tired and resigned. Rocky stopped feeling vaguely turned on by her passions. His own fatigue hit him. The back of his neck ached from stooping over a microscope and a canine bacterial infection earlier, performing a spaying operation on a Siamese cat, examining many mute patients and one parrot with mites.

Barbara had lost her angry dazzle. Rocky heard her deep sigh as she crossed the floor to take Velma by the arm. "Come on then, Mom. Let's take us a stroll."

"We're going to the streetcar, aren't we?"

"For real."

Velma obediently allowed Barbara to steer her around and get her going in the right direction. She was muttering something, but Rocky couldn't hear her well enough to make it out. Whatever it was, it didn't elicit any reaction from Barbara, who led Velma away with a patting of the older woman's back and soft meaningless syllables of her own.

Two peas in a pod, he thought, there they go. Two peas in a pod, that's what Daddy used to say to me in private. Two spitfires. Too much alike to ever get along. Daddy always thought that Barb was a lot like Mama, deep down. Before Barbara ran off this last time, and Daddy stopped knowing what to think.

Hell, maybe it's true. I don't really see it, but maybe it's true, Daddy was right about a lot of things in his life.

I'm sort of glad you're not alive to see Mama this way now, Daddy. But I miss you. I wish Adam and Brooke were growing up with you close by, and you could tell Adam all about your boyhood on a real farm, and about the Highlanders and the Civil War, and about shooting down that Kamikaze. The kids could watch those nature shows with you, and discuss their science projects with you, and get some kind of continuity and healthy pattern going in their disjointed lives that I just don't know how to establish now. Here it is, after midnight, and they're in the den wide awake with no intention of going to bed, unless I go in and be the bad guy and make them get mad at me and cry. How did you get me to obey you, Daddy, without being a bad guy? How can parents *parent* their children, without making the kids resent them?

Rocky sat down in the armchair he had tried to interest his mother in, and he pinched at the corners of his eyes with—

(Wait. Stop. Hold everything. Put that image of Rocky Buchanan on hold. Freeze-frame his eye pinching. Render him motionless.)

Because I can't imagine this any longer. I'm losing my brother's signal here. I have absolutely no idea what Rocky would think about beyond this point, beyond his collapse into the chair and his pinching of his eyes. I am familiar with that eye pinching, a nervous habit of his. But afterwards? Does he get right to his feet afterwards, and go shout at his children, and order them to bed? Does he go to the refrigerator for a beer? Does he seek Barbara in their bedroom and make ambivalent love to her? Turn on the TV and catch the last few minutes of *Saturday Night Live?* Study family photographs, himself and Barbara, on the walls, and let them make him sad? Does he go to Mama's bedside and just look at her?

I have no earthly idea what Rocky was doing that night while I was at the Sheraton. If he'd had any sense, he would've already gone to bed. Rocky had no way of knowing just how little sleep Velma would let him get. He and Barbara had had Velma Buchanan under their roof for only one night so far, not nearly long enough for them to taste the full flavor of chronic sleep deprivation. Not anywhere near long enough for Rocky to realize that Velma's wanderings and midnight confusion weren't isolated events brought on by unfamiliar surroundings, but instead were a constant and ever-escalating way of being that would continue to get worse and worse by increments. Irreversible. A carrousel spinning ever faster, its mad centrifugal force throwing off wooden thoroughbreds and Arabians, clearing its decks of all who would stand upon them, its speed and the sheer volume of its amplified music threatening inevitable crashing ruin.

Whew. Could Rocky have mixed metaphors like that, on that particular Saturday night? Could Rocky have waxed that rhetorical in even his wildest, sleep-deprived dreams? Was he yet intimate with the dull fear that tonight would be as good as it would ever get again, Mama-wise?

I don't know. I do know that Mama's condition dismayed him, and I know that he thought about Daddy. I'm certain that he did a lot of thinking about Barbara, but not in the way I was assuming he still did. Rocky was wrestling with himself, even then, turning Barbara over in his mind like a lab specimen. He studied the situation from all possible viewpoints.

But did he think at all about me, Jeanne, before he went to bed? Did he wonder how I had kept my sanity so long, what was left of it? Or did he find me silly, finally? Prone to over-exaggeration?

Poor immature Jeanne, maybe he was thinking, *Jeanne blows everything totally out of proportion, bless her heart! Mama's being an angel. She's not nearly as bad off as Jeanne would have you think. Hell, I've never seen Mama sharper, as a matter of fact. Tomorrow after Mass, I'm taking her to that anthropology lecture at Tulane that she's asked to attend. And next week, we're enrolling her in night classes. For a degree in chaos theory.*

Okay, so I sound too nasty here. I don't mean to sound nasty. I loved and admired my brother. I have no idea what he was thinking. Maybe the thought of me never crossed his mind that night, beyond some vague hope that I might be having a good time on my week-end away. That would have been like Rocky, to wish me well.

So this is finally all beyond me, any ability to put myself into anybody's shoes except my own, as far as what was going on with me and my mother was concerned. My mother and I had become a closed circle of two. I tried to enlarge the circumference of her world, even as she caused mine to constrict. I no longer knew anybody else, not my brother, not my son, not my ex-husband, not my friend Nancy. Other people were becoming a cipher to me, especially Conrad, whom I lay awake and puzzled over that same night. I could no longer read body language; nuances of voice; nonverbal warnings that I had gone too far in my own behavior.

All that was left of me was Velma, cipher of ciphers. If Velma had a good day, then Jeanne had a good day. If Velma, for some inexplicable reason, was moved to throw a tantrum, then Jeanne's day went downhill from there. She had nothing to re-build a good mood upon, no anticipation of upcoming pleasant events, no hope of the situation improving, no ability to pray, no escape in sight—except for the remote possibility of abduction by aliens. Jeanne wondered how to flag down a UFO.

My son Rad was right. Jeanne Roth had become a one-note samba.

I was a crashing bore. A whiner. A melodramatic martyr.

chapter 27

An
Imaginary
Look
inside
Mama's
Head

And what of my mother, Velma? What was she up to, while I
was stewing in my own juices up in Georgetown, witnessing Conrad's
graduation, meeting his best friend Mark and trying not to let the
kid's platinum hair lead me to any conclusions?

In Mama's presence, Barbara and Rocky and the kids were probably speaking about her and reacting around her as if she were deaf,
or in another room. It would've been very hard for them to behave
otherwise. Mama's self wasn't always present in her body. She did
things for literally no reason, prompted by nothing more than the
misfiring of damaged neurons. Cause and effect were largely missing
from her days and nights. She seemed oblivious to so much. How
regrettably easy it was to objectify her, to discuss her condition
within her own hearing, as if she were an infant or a puppy.

But she was still an adult human, even with this diseased brain. And
she exhibited moods, fears, desires, rages, and occasional moments of
contentment. She had needs to satisfy, yet could not articulate them. I
knew that she was still capable of feeling embarrassed. It must have
been very hard to be Velma Buchanan, especially that particular week.

Maybe she understood at rare moments that she herself had once
lived in this same Napoleon Avenue house, but I doubt it. Rocky
and Barbara had made many changes. The front porch, where C.

Ray had once listened to his ball games over that old white radio, had been restyled and repainted. There were no metal chairs out there anymore, just large potted plants and a park bench. New colors, new furniture, new fixtures had transformed the house's interior.

This was a strange place. This was Rocky's house, and Rocky's wife's house. Even at her most lucid times, Velma no longer had any name for Rocky's wife. When she wanted to use one, nothing would come. Sometimes, maybe, she thought it might have been *Bullwinkle*. Rocky and Bullwinkle sounded right. But Velma couldn't say Bullwinkle. Her tongue and mouth were slow to shape those syllables. By the time she got them ready, the name had vanished from her memory.

This was how conversation went for Velma. Right words would not come, and wrong ones would just pop up to take their places. She was embarrassed by this, and terribly frustrated. She pounded her forehead with both fists one night when she heard herself say "automobile" for "refrigerator" twice, and tears came to her eyes. Fifteen minutes later, she had forgotten what she'd wanted from Rocky's refrigerator, and then forgot her frustration. Even the memory of punching herself in the head was gone, but she did notice that she had a headache now. She tried to ask Barbara for an aspirin, but couldn't remember the word for it. What came out of her mouth was, "May I have a dime?"

"Here, Mam-maw," said the boy Adam from the sofa, digging into the pockets of his jeans and getting up to hand her a quarter. "Keep the change."

And when Velma hesitantly put the coin to her mouth, and then began to place it inside her mouth to cure her headache, and Barbara shouted at her, Velma had no idea why. She studied the quarter in her fingers, shiny with saliva, and did not know what it was.

That girl is going to tell everybody in the neighborhood that her wife has lost her mind, Velma might've thought, deeply upset and embarrassed. Barbara and Adam all fussed around her and spoke loudly to one another.

Dammit, Velma corrected herself, I *know* that didn't come out right. I'm not *her* wife. I'm Mrs. Calvin Ray Buchanan. She's somebody else.

Velma held her quarter in her right hand until Adam pried it out gently and took it from her, and then replaced it with a piece of chocolate candy. Barbara began to cry when brown smears of chocolate somehow transferred themselves to the ivory upholstery of the sofa.

Barbara cried often, Velma did notice a time or two. Velma wept frequently herself, not knowing why. She just knew that she had lost something. Maybe Bullwinkle, too, had lost something.

Velma knew most of the time that C. Ray was lost, but not always. Sometimes he was still there, in the next room, reading a book. It seemed to Velma sometimes that she was also missing several children. She didn't notice that they were missing whenever Adam and his sister Brooke were around, being as much children as anybody could want or deal with. But when everybody was gone and the house was dark and quiet, and when Velma couldn't find anybody, she thought that she might have lost two babies. The boy wore a red hat. The girl had red hair and white eyeglasses. They were not in any of these strange and empty rooms that Velma passed through.

"Oh, *Christ*, she's up again!" a woman's voice would moan from some bedroom somewhere, from some bed, some automobile, some refrigerator. "Rocky, you hear her? She's in the hallway! I can hear her coming up the hallway, she's already up *again!*"

Velma searched the house for something else, too, but wasn't sure what she was looking for there. It was always a pleasant surprise whenever Rocky showed up and lit a cigarette for her, because this was one of the things she had been looking for without knowing it. The man called Rocky would light her cigarette just the way C. Ray used to, and Velma would lean back to shake out her long bright hair. This man Rocky would become C. Ray, as a matter of fact, and all was well again whenever that happened.

C. Ray was letting Velma smoke again, and what a wonderful man he was.

chapter 28

Larry,
Again

On the morning of my departure for Louisiana, Larry Roth was lying on the bed in my hotel room and watching me pack.

Okay, Barbara had been right about me and Larry, yeah. But not for the exact reasons she had come up with. I had no idea why Larry had wanted to sleep with me, except that maybe it was just because he was at loose ends now and I was there.

As for me, I had done it mostly to see if I still could. And because it might be a very long time before I got propositioned again, unless I eventually became one of those old-bag barflies in some far off post-Velma existence, with too much smeary makeup and no minimum standards. Where Barbara is headed, I decided now as I folded my extra slip. Someday even Barbara is going to lose her looks, and she'll just have to learn to stick with the husband who'll have her, or settle for whatever blob of semi-employed and drunked-up male smegma she can fasten onto down at the Bridge Lounge.

But isn't that what she already did with that office furniture sales rep who spent all of her money? If Barbara has already trolled the bottom, where does she go from here?

I've got to stop comparing myself to Barbara. Barbara is certainly not the norm. But maybe I ought not compare myself with anybody anymore, because I'm not the norm, either. I can't be the norm. I'm unable to live a normal life right now.

Which is not to say that I'd be living anywhere close to normal these days, even if I didn't have Mama on my hands. I'm not real sure that I could hack it, or that I even know what it means. Where is the road map for the typical divorcee of a certain age? How should she dress, act, decorate her apartment? What career should she be pursuing? What sort of relationship should she enjoy with her grown son? Do I measure up?

What *is* normal?

I tried to think of something normal to say to Larry. I really had to reach. "You know," I attempted to relax and let the Sixties speak for me, "you still have a cute little bod, Mr. Roth."

"Too fat."

I slapped my own left thigh and let it jiggle, "I've lost weight, but can't seem to get back any muscle tone."

He smiled. "And what did you mean by a 'little' bod?"

"I didn't mean *that*." I was slightly embarrassed by my gaffe, and by all the busted blue veins on the backs of my legs. Larry had a great view of my blotched thighs from where he lay. "You know what I mean."

"What do you do for sex, Jeanne, down there in Auletta?"

"What should I have said? 'Big' bod? 'Enormous, studly' bod?"

"*God* bod."

"You've got your feet on my good silk blouse there, Zeus."

He laughed. It was rather pleasant to spend time like this again with Larry Roth, both of us dismayingly older and sort of banged up, like two used sedans which nobody expects to go from zero to sixty at a green light. No Porsches. Nothing to prove. This was a very low pressure situation here. Comfortably low key. If I said something stupid and made an ass of myself, there was nobody to witness it but plain old Larry Roth.

It took too much effort now for me to remember hating him. Anyway, I was a different person now. And so was he. I did take smug satisfaction from the knowledge that his ex-wife Ruth had been the one who wanted the divorce. Larry's mother Nancy had kept me well informed over the years. Young Ruth, pretty and accomplished, an entertainment lawyer who made great money and had now fulfilled her urge to give birth, no longer needed the flabby and disappointed father of her child for anything. Showbiz had once again flipped Larry the big cosmic finger.

I pressed my flannel nightgown into the top of the pile of folded garments in my suitcase. "Look," I said. "Flannel. No lace, nothing red or black. It quietly screams, 'My wearer has no sex life.'"

"If I ever try marriage again," yawned Larry, "I'm going for a woman my own age this time."

I closed the suitcase.

"You're not the only one with no sex life, Jeanne."

The old suitcase's clasps snapped into place. I remembered packing this same suitcase with Sid-Nan tap panties and camisoles two years ago up in New York when my father died. I tried to feel something now besides oppressed.

"I think that Conrad might be gay," I said finally.

I could hear Larry breathing behind me. From the corner of my eye, I saw his white tee shirt rise and fall. "Yeah," he said.

"Yeah what? You know for sure?" I turned.

"I don't know for sure. But yeah, I've wondered about it."

"So what do we do?" I pulled on my traveling outfit, a rayon dress that would wrinkle badly in the heat. Larry hauled himself off the side of the bed to zip it up the back for me. Except there was no zipper. Fake buttons went down the front of it to the hem.

He stood there behind me, useless, until I turned around. "Nothing appropriate for us to do," he said, "not until he asks us for something. Or tells us something."

"I guess."

"All we can do is just what we're already doing. The love and support thing."

"Yes."

"At least he's obviously healthy, Jeanne. Presumably, he knows how to stay healthy. If he's gay, I mean. Well, you know what I mean."

"It's a toxic world for everybody, straight or gay."

"Well," he said, "no argument there."

"Maybe I should've let you raise him." I located my hair brush and lashed my Saint Joan cowlicks into place with frizz tamer. Larry sought his pants and shirt and sports jacket. "I should've said, Yeah, I'm a voodoo queen. Unfit mother."

He made a rude sound with his mouth. "God, I was such an asshole."

I said nothing.

"I can't believe I actually *paid* a lawyer to encourage me to be an even bigger asshole than I already was."

I recalled our long college communions on the Quad or over coffee, philosophy and politics and Tolkien rehashed with a hashish pipe in Larry's apartment. "We seemed to like each other so much once, didn't we? Or was that just an illusion? I can remember liking the hell out of you."

"Jeanne, I wish I could go back and re-do the last ten years or so, I really do. I made some wrong choices. Fucked up. In just about every way a human being can fuck up. I wish I hadn't treated you so badly. I don't remember what got into me."

"Sex. Ruth. Mid-life crisis. Fear of getting old."

"I wish you didn't have to fly out of here so soon, Jeanne. That's the truth."

It sounded like it might be the truth. It was the kind of truth men felt comfortable divulging when it couldn't possibly get them into any entanglements or commitments. The kind of truth that could be told only when a woman was in a hurry to catch a plane and fly far away.

But I felt how comfortable Larry was with me. How he didn't have to keep his belly sucked in for me, or avoid overhead lighting that might reflect off his bald spot.

"Maybe you could come up to New York sometime, Jeanne," he continued. "You know, nothing high pressure, no high pressure situation. Just friends. We could, like, take in some Broadway shows. Museums."

"The opportunities for me to travel are going to be few and far between, from here on out."

"Any idea about the time frame of 'on out'?" He watched me do my makeup.

"None whatsoever." I decided to skip the eyeliner. It was hard to draw on that fine little line while somebody was watching you do it. And his oblique reference to my Auletta situation had given me the tiniest tremor of remembering, of facing again exactly what it was that I was getting aboard a plane to go back to.

"You look like hell, Jeanne," he said.

"Thank you *so much*."

"I mean, it looks like you've been through hell."

"When are you going to ask me how much I drink? Are we about to discuss my incipient drinking problem now?"

"You have one?"

"I don't know," I answered. I told him my own truth. "I don't think so, but I don't know."

"How much do you drink?"

"As much as I need to."

He didn't comment, and I looked at myself in the mirror with dismay. I imagined the conversation among the various Roths on that first night of reunion, after I had gone back to my own hotel for my bubblebath. I knew what Nancy had probably said about my wretched hair: "It looks as if poor Jeanne cuts it *herself!* Are there no talented hairdressers in Auletta?"

Larry had probably answered something like, "Her sister-in-law Barbara is some sort of beautician, Ma."

"Notice that I said *talented*."

"I think she just doesn't care," Conrad would've said. "Like it's all part of her drudge routine. Like, 'Look at me: I'm the Little Match Girl.'"

"This is getting unattractive, son, all these cute putdowns of your mother."

"But I mean it as constructive criticism, Dad! Does she have to act out this way? I mean, doesn't it bother you guys to see her acting out, and looking so strange? It bothers the hell out of *me*, let me tell ya! I *love* Mom, Dad. And I don't want to see her get all weird."

"Jeanne isn't capable of weirdness. She's about the most level-headed person I've ever met. She's almost unimaginative, in some ways, even though she tries not to be."

"But she's really kind of psychic, though. I mean, she's not pretending when she reads palms, Dad. She really does read them. It's no act."

"And how weird is she about it? Does she call herself Reverend Mother Jeanne? Does she wear a bunch of crystals around her neck?"

"Yeah, well. But *Mam-maw* got all weird, remember. Before she became obviously sick. She stopped bathing. Her clothes didn't match."

"At what age," Larry's father Sidney would have spoken up at Larry's elbow, his elderly voice like an idling truck motor, "did Mrs. Buchanan begin to exhibit symptoms?"

"I don't know, Pop. She's always seemed kind of flighty to me, although I understand that there was a time when she wasn't flighty at all. But I don't know how long ago that was."

"Are there no nursing homes in Louisiana?"

"How would *you* like to be locked up in a nursing home, Pop, while you've still got brains enough to be homesick? Is this something that you want me and Ken to do to you anytime soon?"

Sidney might grunt, and his jowls might shake. He was looking alarmingly old these days, large brown spots sprinkling the shiny bared scalp at his vanished hairline. He needed cataract surgery, but dreaded it.—Irrationally, thought Larry now. Hearing his father speak bullshit about nursing homes and recalling his irrational evasions of necessary cataract surgery made Larry feel angry impatience with the older man.

Even the quiet way his mother Nancy was chewing her strawberry cheesecake bothered Larry. Her lips were parched and wrinkled. The pink of her lipstick bled into the tiny creases and was channeled onto her chin in an unappealingly mortal manner.

"Can't you people give Jeanne just a little credit for simply doing *the right thing*?" Larry hated this feeling, these subtle reminders that his own parents were disintegrating, right here, right now. It felt like they were betraying him in some way, falling apart on him like this, and it made him childish and petulant. He experienced vague panic.

My God, all of you keep reading between the lines with Jeanne, looking for hidden subtexts! What if there aren't any?"

"She still gets to play a heroine," said Rad.

"So? What's the definition of 'hero', son?"

Conrad's exasperation was audible. "I've no idea. I've never read *The Lord of The Rings.*"

"Well, someone wise—I forget who, but it wasn't Tolkien—someone once said that a hero is simply a person who does something important for another person who is unable to do it for himself. I wish I could remember who said that, because it's so basic a definition, so easy to grasp."

Nancy was smiling as she blotted her runny lipstick.

Larry looked around the table. "So isn't Jeanne permitted that basic piece of self-knowledge, that she's doing something for Velma that Velma is unable to do for herself? Isn't Jeanne permitted that tiny degree of satisfaction? Will *I* be permitted it, when Ken and I have to make the choices about what to do for you two, Ma and Pop, when the time comes? When I have to learn if I have what it takes to keep you out of a nursing home for as long as possible? And what about *you,* Rad?" He stared over at his silent son. "If you decide to lift a finger to keep me out of a home, at considerable cost to your own happiness as well as to your bank balance, are you going to let yourself feel good about it?"

Conrad would probably have not answered him here.

And maybe I've gone way off the track here in my reconstruction of this family session. Maybe nobody ever spoke a word about my motives, my martyrdom, all the neurotic items on the agenda that Conrad and Rocky and Barbara suspected me of having. The same things that I suspected in myself. Maybe all they talked about that night was Rad's graduation and his Internet plans with Mark. Maybe nobody even mentioned my bad hair.

"You matter to me, Jeanne," Larry told me now, lifting my suitcase for me from the hotel bed and setting it onto the floor. I watched his shoulders work. There were still muscles beneath the fabric of his shirtsleeves. "I hope you know that."

"I do."

The clear brown of his eyes made an appeal. "Stay a few more days. Let's check out the Smithsonian. Sample all the tony restaurants."

"Can't," I said. "Rocky needs me."

"Rocky's a very competent individual."

"You know what I mean. *Mama* needs me."

"You're tough," he said, a hand on my shoulder. "Always in armor."

I leaned into the warmth of his palm. I let him rub my back in soothing circles. "Maybe that's the only way to be."

"Let's make a date to go out to dinner sometime, at least," he told me after a long and silent moment. "After all this is over. I'll hop on a plane, and you hop on a plane, and we meet each other halfway. Where's halfway?"

"I don't know."

"Tennessee? Does Tennessee sound about right?"

I thought about Auletta, and my stomach gave a warning gurgle. "I don't know when that'll be. When I can do that. It might be years from now."

"I'm proud of you, Jeanne."

I didn't risk saying anything. I just went on letting him rub my back a little, and then I checked my purse for my ticket.

"—for what it's worth," he added.

"It's worth a lot, Larry." I closed my purse, putting a paperback novel inside the zippered exterior pocket of my carryon bag. "I'm not used to hearing those words much."

"I *understand*, Jeanne. I think. I hope."

"Well, then that makes one of us. Because I sure as hell do not understand myself. I do not understand one damn thing about all this. I feel like a phony. I feel like I'm out of my body."

"What you're doing is the right thing. I admire you."

I laughed, because I had been wanting to hear those words from somebody for a long time. But actually having them spoken out loud to me now made me also want to scream. I felt like I had been fishing for them. I felt like I had manipulated Larry into saying them, and hence was not entitled to them. It was possible that Larry didn't mean them, I knew. "Oh hell, I don't know if I'm doing the right thing or not, Larry. I'm just *doing*, for whatever reasons. Just doing. Until I can't do it anymore, I guess. And then I don't know what will happen. I want to be *free*."

He wrapped me in his arms like a pal or a brother. "When you're free, come see me."

"I want her to die, I think." I laughed again, low and fake. "Real admirable of me, huh? Do I still get the Mother Teresa award?"

"Maybe there's other ways to get free." He didn't sound shocked. Maybe he hadn't heard the degree of truth in my statement.

"How? Either death or a nursing home, or ruining Rocky's marriage: those seem to be my options. Mama becoming either dead or miserable, Rocky bottoming out. I hate myself for what my freedom will cost somebody."

"God is wise, Jeanne."

"Where is God?" I put my hands on my hips. "I keep looking for him, but I can't find him. He just fails to show up."

"The Universe, then. It changes, and it evolves. It will evolve. Something will evolve."

"I've never heard you sound so rabbinical."

"I'm still not observant," he said, "just your everyday old hippie semi-mystic. But it can do a person some good, I think, getting out of themselves and into the Universe. Bonding with it. Contemplating its mystery. Puts your troubles into perspective."

"Learn to love black holes."

"You're catching on," he said. "We still doing okay on time?"

I glanced at my watch. I had hours to spare before my flight, but then I had always been an early starter. "You know me. We're fine."

"You ever read any of the new physics? It's almost like a synthesis of science and metaphysics, at least to me." He looked at his reflection in the dresser mirror. "I read a whole lot of interesting stuff, when Ruth left me. Stephen Hawking. The dancing Wu-Li Masters. I stayed up a lot of nights, reading."

I detected remembered pain in his voice. Funny, it had never occurred to me that Ruth's leaving had actually hurt Larry. I had always thought of Larry as the hurter.

"I read," he went on, touching the wrinkles at the corner of an eye with a fingertip, "Zen. I read about alien abductions. UFO's. The debate about that face on Mars."

"I'm sorry. About you and Ruth," I told him. "I'm sorry that it didn't work out."

"Yeah. Well." He finished with whatever he was getting out from looking in the mirror, and turned and sat down on the edge of the unmade bed. "Let's just say I now know something about big fuck-ups. Bad times."

But I realized that Larry had always known about lost opportunities and bad times, long before Ruth. I remembered *Saturday Night Live*. The young comedian I had married, who didn't want to give up show business for a career in ladies' lingerie. I felt bad. I said nothing.

"Jeanne," he said, "you really need to push open your existence, because it's closing down around you. You need to push back. Make it expand. I'm not saying you gotta get religion, but you've got to expand beyond that house in Auletta before it squeezes you dry, honey."

My insides froze at this confirmation of my own personal truth. It was gratifying to be taken seriously like this, but it also shook me that my need was so obvious to him. I still wanted to be invited to *tell* my sob story. I didn't want people to be able to read it in my face and body language.

"Stand outside some night," he went on, "and just look at the stars."

"I've tried. I do."

"You always trusted your dad. If you can't pray to God, maybe you should try C. Ray Buchanan."

The sound of the name caused a tiny pain at the back of my throat. My eyes suddenly watered. "I don't see what good living in a dream world is going to do me."

He knew better than to touch me now, but his voice was like a touch. "Jeanne, when I first met you, Dream World was your home address, honey. You remember? We discussed fantasy characters as if they were real. You remember?"

I remembered. "I was young and stupid."

"You read my palms. You even *thought* in fairytale vernacular. We named our kid after a fictional warrior prince. This was the truest part of you."

I was tired. I looked at my watch. "My mother's brain is shorting out, Larry. It hurts me to watch this happen to her, maybe more than I can acknowledge even to myself. Part of me hates her and resents her, for sucking up my life this way. Part of me loves her and grieves for her, and just wants to climb into her lap where she can kiss my hurt and make it all better, and this is the part of me that hates her most: because she can't do that. I'm in such conflict with myself, Larry, I can't even think straight. But I've got to keep a clear head. And a grip on reality. Because Mama's mind isn't there anymore. I can't go all looney-tunes and New Age gooey here."

"Where is Velma's *soul*, Jeanne? That's what you should be asking yourself. Is it here? There? In transition?" He saw me studying my watch, and he stood to tug on his sports jacket. He smoothed the lapels and flattened the pockets over his thighs. "This is what you should be asking, because Velma Buchanan, brain-damaged or not, is still more than just a defective piece of meat. *You* wouldn't be down there caring for her, if you, too, were just animated brisket."

I smiled. This was the first humorous Larryism I had heard out of him in quite some time.

"We walk and live and breathe," his arm took in the hotel room and me and the view of Washington from the window, the birds and sky, the automobiles and buildings and pedestrians, "in profound *mystery*. Here. Let me get your suitcase."

I locked the door behind both of us and he carried my luggage to the elevator that would take us down to the lobby.

"You know, dolphins have souls," he said, punching the down button. "They have funerals. The Cousteau people once witnessed a dolphin funeral."

I recalled my father watching his nature documentaries and telling me the same thing. Larry held the elevator door open for me. His hand, at my eye level, was white and kind and deceptively strong; more than just a piece, yes, of human beefsteak. The fine black hairs on its back glimmered under the overhead light, as it pushed back at the door mechanism and guarded my entrance. My voice became too thick to use.

I stood with my face to the closing door, my carryon bag held at knee level.

Larry touched my back.

"I don't want to cry," I said. "Please don't make me, Larry."

I had a couple of whiskey sours on the flight back, but couldn't get involved in the paperback novel I had brought along. The cloud formations outside the window looked like peaks of whipped cream and made me vaguely hungry. I thought about Larry's term "animated brisket." I thought about Mama. Something came to me then about Mama and whipped cream, Mama sipping Irish coffee through whipped cream, somewhere before I was born. How had that story gone?

Leaning back in my seat and letting the whiskey sours relax me, I looked at the fluffy white cloud blobs until my Aunt Irene's voice came back to me from across the years, Aunt Irene, my mama's sister, the one who had married a drunk and lived in a trailer park in Mississippi until she died. I remembered Aunt Irene telling an anecdote to my father and the Bordelons on a warm summer night, out front on our porch on Napoleon Avenue, with me and Margaret Bordelon and Rocky playing in the dark of the tiny yard. "Velma!" Irene was shrieking and slapping her own knee, sloshing beer in her mirth, while Rocky and I caught lightning bugs. "You remember, Vel? You remember that?"

"I remember," my mother had laughed, her hair like a curtain of light while she held onto my father's arm, her hair like the aurora borealis, her cigarette tip a spark.

"Velma and me was at the bar at the Roosevelt Hotel, I'll never forget," Aunt Irene wheezed, "and we was sipping Irish coffee through some of those little straws so that we wouldn't mess up our lipstick. You remember this, Vel?"

"I remember," said my mother.

"It was war time, C. Ray," Aunt Irene went on, "and there was a whole lotta soldiers and sailors around. There was a real hot band playing there that night, and we'd just come to hear the music. 'Cause Velma was saving herself for you, even though she hadn't met you yet."

Some listeners would giggle at this, and my dad would slip an arm around my mother's shoulders and tease her about whether he had been worth waiting for.

"'Course, *I* wasn't saving myself for nobody, since I didn't know what kinda shelf life I had," said Aunt Irene. "I'd got myself all dolled up, making eyes at all those cute men. But I tell you what, dawlin': those soldiers and sailors just about fell over themselves, watching my baby sister suck that whipped cream up through that straw like that!"

All the grownups whooped with laughter, but I hadn't found it very funny. What was so funny about a lady with a straw?

"You remember, Vel? You remember that Marine Corps officer?"

"I remember, Irene,"

"C. Ray, this Marine Corps officer, like a captain or something, he keeps watching us and finally he comes up behind Velma, and he excuses himself, just as polite as he could be. And he says 'Doll, you're just about the prettiest thing I have ever laid eyes on!' And Velma, she gives him the once-over, but she don't say nothing. She sees what I see, he's got a little groove worn into the skin of his ring finger. And he's real old, maybe thirty."

Grownups would dependably laugh again at that.

"But he don't go away. He says, 'Can I buy you a drink?' And Velma, she says, 'I've already got a drink, thank you.' And then he says, 'I'm staying here at this hotel. Room number seven-eleven, easiest number in the world to remember. If you've got nothing to do tonight, why don't you come up and see the view of the river from way up there?'

"Now Velma, she's as cool as a cucumber, she just says, 'No thank you,' she don't insult him or call him names or anything like that. But he takes a key out of his pocket, and lays it on the bar in front of us, and he says, 'If you change your mind, here's my room key. I'll be up there after eleven tonight, waiting on you, baby.'

"'What if you wait forever?' Velma kinda teases him. 'Would you be mad?'

"'You wouldn't disappoint a man who's facing death, about to ship out overseas, now would you?' he says, real serious, voice like a movie star. He ain't bad looking. 'Take the key. Just come up at eleven, and let yourself in. I'll be waiting. We'll just talk, if you want.'

"'You're awful sure of yourself,' says Vel. 'And I ain't that kind of girl.'

"But he just winks, and off he goes. And as soon as he's out of earshot, we both start to giggle. Shit, *I* woulda probably gone upstairs with him," Irene slapped her knee and her laugh was like a box full of rocks, "but he don't ax *me!* All them guys looked good in uniform, you know, ordinary guys seemed handsome. Those were some fast times."

"You snagged yourself a couple or three, Irene," my mother said playfully, "now tell the truth."

"Yeah, you're right, I got my share of dates, but not that night. They only had eyes for my kid sister, that night. Not a half-hour later, some other guy comes up to us and taps Velma on the shoulder. Well, lots of guys've been axing us to dance, but this one has more than dancing on his mind. He was in the Navy. Right, Vel?"

"Right."

"He's younger than the first guy, and pretty cute. You know, I can't imagine what gave these guys the idea that they could just proposition a lady like that, without even an introduction, unless it was the war and the uncertainty of everybody's future, and so on. But anyway, this guy comes on strong, and he just won't go away. He just won't take 'No' for an answer, he keeps sweet-talking Velma, telling her what a dish she is and everything. And I'm kinda fed up, because nobody can get close in enough now to pay *me* any attention.

"And this sailor, he buys Vel another Irish coffee, and he buys me one, too, as if getting me on his side is going to help him any. And he's monopolizing us so bad, that if any other guy might want to ax us to dance, he'd have to make an issue out of butting in here.

"So finally, Velma says to him, 'If I make a date with you, will you be sweet and let us have some private girl talk? I'm from out of town, all the way from Hollywood, and I won't get to see my sister again for three whole years, 'cause she's going overseas with the USO.'

"'Well, sure,' he says, 'but how do I know you'll keep the date, gorgeous?'

"Velma reaches for the key to room seven-eleven, and hands it right to him, with a cute little pat. 'Come upstairs at eleven sharp, big boy,' she bats her eyelashes at him, whipped cream on her red lips like they were cherries, 'and just let yourself in. I'll be waiting.'"

A big howl went up from all the grownups on the porch, and Aunt Irene got a coughing fit from laughter and cigarette smoke, and Daddy playfully yanked at a strand of Mama's light hair. He handed everybody another round of beer. Mama sat in the dim light and fanned herself with her open palm, and held my Daddy's hand with the other, and I looked up at them from the driveway and they both seemed like laughing movie stars. My mother's lipstick had left a heartshaped kiss mark on my father's face, at that place between cheek and chin that has no name.

"You remember, Vel?" Aunt Irene shrilled again in my memory. "You remember how you were?"

"I remember," said my happy mother.

I remember, said the beautiful Velma, destined to lose her memory and herself. To lose everything she had over there on Napoleon Avenue, including me.

When I woke up, the plane was still in the air.

But all the whipped cream had gone from the windows. The clouds below us were smooth now, still white in the slanting light, but losing brilliance as the sun got lower. They reminded me of a snow field now, but my experience with fields of snow was limited. No more specific memories were summoned, just vague and sour ones of Larry and me and Conrad in Washington Square, with the snow coming down and the three of us coming apart.

I wanted another drink, but didn't think that they'd serve me a third. I didn't want to ask, anyway. I didn't want anybody to think I was a lush. There was a complimentary set of earphones tucked into the seat pocket in front of me, and I tore the clear plastic wrapper off of them and stuck them onto my head.

The audio jack was in the armrest at my elbow. I plugged in the headset and leaned back.

Maybe it was because the Fourth of July was getting near, that peak vacation time that airlines wanted to grab a chunk of, I don't know. But I didn't even have to spin the audio dial to find this Grand Sousa Concert. It came loudly over the headset as the plug went into the jack, and by the third note, I had recognized *The Fairest of The Fair.*

I wanted it to be about me. But I knew that it was really about my mother.

chapter 29

The
Twilight
Zone

Frank Campo, family attorney and my long-ago adolescent love object, was waiting for me at the New Orleans airport when I came back down to earth and got off the plane.

"Your mama's about the same," he told me in response to my mild surprise over Rocky not showing up here to meet me. "Rocky's going to bring her to Auletta and meet us there, that's the plan now. 'Cause Barbara can't get off work to do it."

"Well, I'm sorry we've had to put you out this way, Frank," I said, as he helped me and my luggage get settled into his Acura. And I wondered if we were indeed imposing, or if Frank, more likely, would be paid by Rocky for his trouble. "Looks like it would've been easier for Rocky and Mama to just meet me here, and then the three of us drive out, instead of having to involve you."

"Well, it didn't seem like such a good idea to make your mama wait too long here, if your plane was going to be late or anything."

I pictured my mother, stuck at an airport or stuck in a car for a long wait. I pictured Rocky stuck with her. "Yeah."

"I had to come out to Kenner anyway," said Frank, "on business."

He drove on, and was polite but fundamentally uninterested in what I had to relate about Conrad's graduation. And I really didn't have that much to say. I watched the dilapidated scenery of old auto paint shops and the backs of strip malls whiz past the windows, comfortable enough with Frank these days to say nothing.

Frank Campo had become human for me. As a matter of fact, Frank was even *hyper* human now, having been so thoroughly robbed of the golden godhood of his youth by age and circumstance that he had almost come out on the other side of evolution. He was chiefly Basic Primate now, a large and nondescript hulk in a damp suit.

"Cool up there?" he asked me, turning the air conditioner to a chillier setting.

I wondered just what latitude he thought Georgetown was on. It was possible that Frank had never traveled any further than Houston or Destin, Florida. "No," I said. "Cooler at night than here, maybe. But D.C.'s really pretty humid."

"The Hoyas," he said, naming Georgetown's basketball team without enthusiasm. "What's the origin of that name? You know?"

"Nope."

"Is it like, maybe, 'Hot On Your Asses', or something?"

It seemed like a pretty good guess, once I thought about it. Frank was actually kind of smart. Or maybe he had just read something somewhere, half-remembered. "Beats me," I shrugged.

If I had been male, Frank might've found a conversational topic here in college sports. But he cleared his throat, and said nothing more, and just drove the car.

I felt sort of sorry for Frank Campo these days. He had not won his election for judge. He had run for office an additional time since, but had lost that one, too. His body had reverted to the fat of his childhood. His hair was graying and mostly gone. He also suffered from a very annoying smoker's cough, full of phlegm and mucus and mock death rattle, which seemed to irritate Frank as much as it did me. But he was hopelessly addicted to tobacco. He smelled of stale smoke and expensive aftershave.

His three kids were rumored to be big disappointments, especially for a lawyer with political ambitions. One daughter was a defiantly unwed mother, living with her architect girlfriend in uptown New Orleans and active in what passed in Catholic Louisiana as a pro-choice movement. The younger girl was lower-profile, tattooed and pierced, an art student at Newcomb. Frank's son had been in drug rehab a time or two. Frank would mention one or another of his children from time to time, without self-consciousness or apology, with fondness.

All in all, I liked ol' Frank a lot these days. I rode beside him now and recalled his brief glamour, the arrogance that had rubbed Rocky the wrong way all those years ago. He was no longer an arrogant sort, exactly. He was a good lawyer, though—at least good enough for my family—and he genuinely felt that he had something to offer to the voting public. His marriage to Cathy Noel was still intact. There was still a cockiness in the way he strode across a parking lot and unlocked a car door. He liked to keep clients waiting for a return phone call that might never come.

"Mind if I smoke?" he asked me now.

"Not at all," I lied. I didn't mind his second-hand smoke all that much, but his wet cough was a real gross-out. Well, what the hell, I thought. Frank coughs all the time anyway, whether or not he actually has a cigarette in his mouth. You can't ask the man not to smoke in his own car.

He pressed the power window button to open a crack of ventilation on the driver's side, glancing at my hair to make sure that the wind wasn't disturbing my coiffure.

"Haven't got enough hair here left to blow," I said, appreciating his thoughtfulness. He didn't tell me he liked my haircut, but he smiled as he lit a smoke. What touched me about Frank Campo, finally, was that he did not yet suspect that his best days were behind him. I was pretty sure that my own were already in the past, and Larry's, and possibly even my brother Rocky's. But Frank didn't know this about himself. He didn't understand that his ridiculously short career as high school quarterback, LSU football prospect, and handsome boyfriend of the most popular girl at Ursuline was as good as it would ever get. Well, all of us had had very short careers as up-and-comers. Look at Larry and show business. Look at Rocky and his Auletta stint as "Kindly Country Vet." Look at the romance of Rocky and Barbara. Look at me. It was as plain as my plain face that our best days were behind us.

But not to Frank. Frank would keep on running for judge or assessor or tax commissioner or even dogcatcher, and he'd probably keep on losing. He didn't have the big money or the power base, not to mention the standard political family rectitude, of his opponents—scary husband-and-wife teams of big-haired north shore Evangelical Protestants waving from the after-dinner podiums of countless right wing fundraisers, surrounded by children so vacuous and well-scrubbed that you feared for their sanity. But Frank would keep on running, I knew. Part of Frank insisted upon living in an imagined future.

And he's probably a very happy man, I realized now, watching him drive and smoke and sweat.

"Rocky'll already be there when we get there," he told me, "with your mama. Get her settled back in and everything. I called him from the airport, once they told me your flight would be on time."

"Good," I said, but didn't think it was so good. I would've preferred arriving first, me and Frank, so that I could get myself unpacked and rested and psyched before Mama came back. But nobody had asked me. People were very busy with their lives down here. People had places to be and things to do.

Frank turned off of I-10 at the Auletta exit. My stomach began to slosh and rumble.

Rocky had arrived at the house about thirty minutes before we got there, just long enough to turn the air conditioner on and make the temperature comfortable. The kitchen's atmosphere still held that sourish closed-up odor of a garbage disposal that could stand to be cleaner, left unused too long in weather too hot. Rocky had left Mama's luggage in the hallway, and something about the shallow way he breathed spoke of haste. He'd made her a ham sandwich. He was seated at the kitchen table, showing her how to eat it, when I let myself in through the back door.

"There she is!" he announced my entry, standing to give me a fast kiss on the cheek, wiping his hands on a paper napkin. "Hello, stranger!"

"Hey." I hugged him.

Mama's eyes were uncertain and vague.

"Hey, Mama," I bent and kissed her. There was red lipstick smeared above her upper lip and well below her lower one. The wheat bread of her sandwich was stained with it. "You miss me?"

Her little shoulders were very bony and delicate underneath my palms. She felt thinner to me, older, even though I hadn't been gone long enough for that to be really the case. "Where's that thing?" she asked me.

"Welcome back." Rocky touched my biceps with two fingers. "Gotta run, surgery at two. I'll call you tonight."

He moved away from me. I couldn't think of anything to say.

Frank was carrying in my suitcase and setting it on the floor in the hallway when Rocky passed him, catching his hand in a brief shake. "Hey, Frank? Thanks. Settle up with you. Call me."

"Where's that jar?" said Mama.

"Rocky?" I called.

"Got to spay a cat at two," he jingled car keys in his hand. "No time right now. But I'll catch up with you. Tonight."

"Okay." There were things I wanted to ask my brother, things I wanted to tell him. I needed to touch some kind of base through him. Sunlight fell on his sandy hair and I saw gray in it. He was going too fast for me, walking away too fast. "Okay," I said again, as if he needed my agreement to leave.

But here was Frank, leaving too, now, waving from the front door where Rocky had opened it to the daylight. "Bye, Miz Buchanan!" he called to Mama for no reason except courtesy, because she was no longer in sight of the doorway. "Bye, Jeanne. Sure glad you had a nice time up there. Y'all be in touch. Take care of yourselves."

I tried. "Want some coffee or something before you go?"

He shook his head. "Got to get back to the office, you know how it is."

"Thanks for the ride." I stepped out onto the porch with both men, taking Frank by an elbow. "Give my regards to Cathy and the kids."

Rocky had already stepped down the front steps and onto the cement walkway, lined with the dead stems and tangled weeds of what had once been my mother's showplace flowerbeds. The white sneakers he wore for comfort at work made no sound. I watched the white shoes silently walk away from me. I did not see his mouth: "Jeanne? I'll call you tonight, okay? Hear all about the graduation and everything. Okay?"

"Okay."

Frank made a sweep with his arm at the tall, wild grass of the yard. "I'll get somebody out here to cut this for y'all, remind me."

I nodded.

Both men got into separate shiny automobiles, and waved separately at me, and drove off. Just like that. Hot white sun spilled off of the glass of their rear windows and side mirrors, lasering into my eyes, making me close them. White road dust smoked into the air. And these men had every right in the world to drive off just like that, in that much of a hurry, with no further chat or socializing. They had places to be, after all. Schedules to meet. Each had already performed amazing kindnesses for me. Their obligations here had been more than met, duty done.

I found my sense of abandonment unworthy, and I sat on it as I went back to the kitchen. I was going to have to do something about the stale odors in here, air the place out or something, pour coffee grounds down the sink or whatever the hell it was that they'd used to do in the old days. There wasn't anybody left from the old days now to tell me.

Mama met me in the hallway with no acknowledgment of my presence, just shuffling along with her sandwich in one fist and a wad of kleenex in the other. She was taking bites out of the kleenex.

Like the actual crashing *clang* of an enormous prison door, I felt the lockdown of my daily life resume at that very moment. My breath became shallow and fast. The audio from old movies and television shows reverberated stupidly inside me, the clichéd close-ups of the faces of hopeless convicts were visualized in black-and-white as I crossed my arms over my stomach and held onto my elbows and thought about how silly I was, and how glad I was that nobody could ever read my mind.

My suitcase there in the hallway testified that Georgetown had not been just a short dreamlet during a daytime nap, but that's what it suddenly felt like. Even that melodramatic clang in my mind no longer echoed, with lockdown having resumed so seamlessly now, so immediately, that it seemed as if the routine of my daily life couldn't have possibly suffered any interruption. I had just dreamed Rad. I had dreamed Larry. So much for the therapeutic benefits of a vacation.

Mama wandered down the hall carpet as if she'd been pacing it since last Thursday.

"Get a grip," I muttered to myself, feeling silly and invisible, as insubstantial as a silver screen image from a very bad movie.

My soul, though, became leaden as I watched my mother in her aimlessness and heard the clock tick from her bedroom. All gods, all Elves had fled my imagination. There remained only this moment of entrapment for me, and the next moment which would be exactly like this moment, and the coming evening, which would be exactly like this afternoon. Tonight, too, would turn out exactly like this same moment. Tomorrow would be an exact copy of today. Next week would be exactly today, too. I was trapped in an eternal *now*, with no promise of deliverance. I was in *The Twilight Zone*. I half-expected to hear Rod Serling's voiceover beginning any minute: *For your consideration: Jeanne Roth, menopausally unstable, about to realize that the hands of her own personal clock have stopped forever: stuck eternally on this precise hour in an ordinary day when her mother has begun to wipe her own nose with food.*

"Stop eating that kleenex!" I screamed at Mama, who did not register this as even a blip on her personal radar. I had the urge to rip the tissue out of her fist, not to save her from a hazardous meal, but rather to deprive her of something.

It's roughage, it won't hurt her, said Rod Serling. *Non-toxic. High fiber. What the hell.*

I sat down on the nearest piece of furniture, and it turned out to be a side table and not a chair, but I didn't have it in me to stand back up. My face collapsed. I became blinded by water. And I bawled like a starving baby, keening in a peculiar high pitch that began to make me kind of nervous when I found that I couldn't stop it. I cried helplessly, humbly, like I was alone. And I more-or-less was.

Here's another of those lessons I learned in Auletta: If you've been hanging by your thumbs for a while, a brief break makes going back to it all the harder. I'm not saying to skip the vacations, because respite is necessary. But be prepared for a certain brutal rebound effect, pals and gals. Be prepared to hear Rod Serling.

I also learned something else, something *extremely* important, which is to always examine the contents of your impaired mother's purse after she returns home from a stay somewhere. Forget her right to privacy. Because you never can tell what she's got in there.

I'd like to compare Mama's purse with my teenage diary, and say something profound here about the right to privacy versus the right to safety. But making that comparison now feels too facile, too self-serving. I really don't know how to put it all into perspective except to say that such a search was not made, and it should have been.

And I don't know if I've ever really forgiven my mother for lying about reading my diary, and it's incredibly silly of me not to. It's a very childish thing, to hold onto that trespass like a credit card, waiting for it to be somehow honored in some cosmic department store of Poetic Justice, where Velma is again a (surly) salesclerk whom I am determined to complain to the manager about, and get fired.

But a search is something that I just failed to do. Not out of a consideration for her privacy or anything like that, but only because it never occurred to me to do it. I unpacked my own sad suitcase later that night, and put my things away. I opened Mama's luggage and was touched and grateful to see that Barbara had laundered even yesterday's underwear, leaving me no dirty clothes to cope with, except the ones that were on Mama's back. I had no stomach now to try to get her out of them. She was lying across her bed in them, snoring, one sneaker off and one on. I didn't dare risk waking her by messing with her feet. She would be awake again, soon enough.

It crossed my mind—an unworthy thought—that perhaps Mama's suitcase of clean clothes was less a testimony to Barbara's thoughtfulness, and more likely actual evidence that Rocky and Barbara had been allowing Mama to sleep in the same set of duds for days.

The smirk on my lips got busted, since I was doing the same thing here. As I stored Mama's suitcase away in the hall closet, I tried to figure out if knowing that Rocky and Barbara had coped in this same way made me feel worse towards them, or better. Heaps of Daddy's junk, tax records going back ten years, Scottish family trees, folded acrylic sweaters, threatened to topple over from their high closet shelves onto my head. I shoved the suitcase as far against the back wall as it would go.

But Mama's large purse never once crossed my mind.

chapter 30

The
Beauty
Lady

As good as his word, Frank Campo did find us a kid to mow our lawn that next week.

Conrad wrote fitfully. He and Mark had found an apartment in San Francisco.

And my sister-in-law Barbara started driving out on her Tuesdays off for reasons I could not begin to imagine, sharing morning coffee with me while Mama explored the house and talked to herself. After our verbal visiting was done—chat about Rocky and the kids, tricks of the beautician's trade, famous hair mistakes of Hollywood stars— sometimes Barbara seemed unaccountably near tears—she would reliably offer to stay and look after Mama so that I could go into Slidell for a movie and a restaurant meal, or just go to my own room and close the door for a long nap.

It was an amazing turnabout, Barbara's gifts of time. "I don't have to be home tonight until way after six," she'd say, feeding Mama cold cereal with a soup spoon. "Kids're out of school for the summer, Rocky'll pick 'em up after day camp. So you just go have yourself a good time, Jeanne, for a change. We'll be fine. Won't we, Mom?" she'd ask my mother, wiping her chin.

"Maddle purfie winky," Mama would try to answer. "Blue munny?"

"Baryshnikov," Barbara would fondly affirm.

My God, I would think, they speak the same language. What can this possibly mean?

"Mama'll try to get out of the house on you, if you're not looking," I briefed my sister-in-law. "And she hates to have her diaper panties changed, but you might have to do it. *God,* I hate to ask you to do that. Just wait until I can get home, unless it's a really bad situation."

"Baby, I took care of my grandmama," Barbara would wave me away. "Seen one old lady, seen 'em all."

In fact, Barbara's new solicitude so puzzled me that I forgot to scream in the car these days on my way back to Auletta after a silly romantic comedy. What's in this for Barbara? I kept wondering, because I couldn't imagine Barbara relieving me for duty like this unless she had some hidden agenda. It wasn't just my longtime suspicions of the woman that asserted themselves here. Because *nobody* in their right mind, Barbara or not, would offer to do this for free, I realized. Barbara or not, you'd have to be crazy to take on a chore like this on your one weekday off, unless you were either handsomely paid, or up to something.

Never look a gift horse in the mouth, my father reminded me in my memory.

Is she stealing? I wondered. But Barbara is a slut, not a thief. What is there in that house that she'd want to steal? Hell, she used to live in that house. That house used to be hers.

Is that it, that she's seeing somebody, having a romantic rendezvous with an old Auletta flame? While I'm driving down the highway on the way to a fluffy comedy and a big Cobb salad at Applebee's, is she screwing somebody in Mama's bedroom? While Mama's yelling at the walls, is Barbara yelling in ecstasy? Is that it?

Rocky was no help. "Barbara wanted to do it," was his reaction to my indirect questioning these days. "It was her idea. She wants to help out. Family means a lot to Barbara. That's the way she was brought up, you know how those country people are."

"She's *Barbara.*"

"Yeah, and she's Mama's daughter-in-law. She's your sister-in-law. Both of you mean a lot to Barbara, don't criticize her for pitching in, for God's sake! What do you want from me?"

"I don't know," I said, and it was the truth.

"Hell, you've been moping around and hinting around for months that you'd stick your fucking head in the oven if you didn't get some help here! So here's some help! Barbara and I talked it over, kind of did that division of labor thing to see what we could do to help out. You want us to *quit?*"

"No."

"Then don't look a gift horse in the mouth," he said, his father's son. "Let her take a swing at it, hell. She's trying to make up for everything, I guess."

And I suddenly saw myself as Queen of The Hypocrites. Because after all my bitching about how nobody was willing to take my caregiving to Mama at face value, here I was, doing the same thing to Barbara. Looking for subtexts, unsavory motives, whatever. I wanted to be credited as simply doing the right thing, but I was unwilling to give that same credit to somebody else.

But this isn't just somebody else, I reminded myself. This is *Barbara.*

Occasionally, I got the definite feeling that she was pumping me for information about Rocky, but I couldn't imagine why. After all, she was the one who was married to him. If she didn't know what made him tick, maritally speaking, how was his big sister to help out? "Don't cheat on him," was all I would've been able to contribute, but our conversations never got that explicit. I felt like her unwitting patsy, set up to play some obscure game.

Still, she was a godsend. As the weather grew hotter, and the day camp that Brooke and Adam had been attending neared its end, I anticipated the cessation of Barbara's visits with dismay.

She brought Mama and me ice cream, fashion magazines, and good cheer. She'd come laden with curling irons and hair brushes and mousse and perfume to do Mama's hair. "Here's the 'Beauty Lady!'" she would be trilling as she crawled out of her little white Miata on blistering mornings, ice cream in one hand and a sackful of

Vogues in the other, her tanned trim thighs in pressed pastel shorts, the thong piece of gold-studded leather sandals between her painted toenails. Her hairdo was even bigger these days, her mascara thicker, and I wondered who she was trying to impress. "The 'Beauty Lady' has arrived!"

"Come on in and have some coffee, 'B.L.'," I greeted her, genuinely glad to see her. I had begun planning my Tuesdays several days ahead now, reading the newspaper ads for movies and comparing cinema reviews, deciding which restaurant to eat at, which clothes to wear. I was becoming afraid of my anticipation, as I waited at the window on Tuesday mornings for that small white sports car to pull into the driveway.

You're being set up for something, I warned myself. Barbara won't keep this up forever. We all know Barbara. What'll you do when she gives it up?

"What'd you say, Jeanne?" she called out to me as she neared the back door now.

"*B.L.*: Beauty Lady."

"Ohhh." And the dumb white smile encircled by pink pearl lips would be so candid and disarming that you just had to love her. "I didn't know what you were saying. I couldn't make it out."

Mama did, in fact, love her. Mama had forgotten who she was.

"Thought you were saying 'bail,' or something," Barbara shouldered her heavy cosmetics bag.

Barbara probably had more first-hand experience with bail than I did. I helped her juggle the goodies she had brought for us. I stashed away the ice cream and set the cosmetics bag and magazines on the dinette table while she went to Mama's flounced rocking chair, but I saw my mother's face light up when Barbara came near and leaned down to take her hands and kiss her cheek. I did have some mixed feelings about that.

Well, you know that they never prefer the primary caregiver, I compared my mother with my son, Conrad. Maybe they get tired of the same old face telling them what to do and how to behave, over and over. That's just human nature, it doesn't mean anything. Children of divorce always want to hang out with dad, if they're being raised by mom. Or vice versa. Doesn't mean they don't love you. It just means that everybody's always hoping that somebody fresh will cut 'em a better deal. Grass always seems greener on the other side of the fence.

But I'd drive away on my Tuesday adventure with the image of my mother serenely allowing Barbara Trahan to brush and arrange her hair, after having suffered screaming fits and actually trying to bite me on the mornings that poor ol' me tried to do it for her.

Poor ol' me, I thought, stopping at a red light and not really wanting to see another frothy romantic comedy. I stayed in the stopped position too long, noticing that the light had turned green only when the driver behind me began to lean on his horn and call me names. Poor ol' me. What's to become of poor ol' me?

Exactly what is Velma keeping me from doing? If it wasn't for Velma, would I be living a frothy romance, taking cruises, becoming engaged to some cute guy I met at the gym? Would I be working out? Getting a tummy tuck and an eye job? Would I be going back to college, getting my degree, learning how to let go and unleash my inner beauty? Would I become the fairest of the fair, a late-blooming femme fatale like Sarah Bernhardt or Lillie Langtry, the object of desire and unattainable erotic prize of every young man who met my smouldering gaze?

I began to laugh at myself. I didn't know what I was capable of, nor exactly what it was that I wanted. Except my freedom.

Oh, I'll be free again someday, all right, I acknowledged as I turned off at the public library, having lost all taste for the movies that were currently playing in the Slidell multiplex. If I outlive the beautiful Velma, and chances are that I will, I'll certainly be free, yeah. But will I be too old to enjoy my freedom? Will I have cancer? Will my own life be over?

Goddammit! I began to seethe as I looked for a parking space, and those lifetime images of Velma and C. Ray Buchanan rose up again from behind my eyes. I saw Velma and C. Ray holding hands again, dancing out on the front porch to radio music, meeting Hollywood cute at D. H. Holmes' department store, living their own frothy romance. *Goddammit, god damn their heedless ways, their lack of plan-*

ning! God damn all that beer and serenity and faith in each other, all that love-conquers-all bullshit, all that shortsightedness that kept them from facing their own mortality! God damn whatever kept them adolescent, and left me and Rocky this big adult mess to cope with!

I pulled to the curb and saw that my knuckles were about to burst open. I was making fingerprints in the steering wheel. My teeth pressed together so hard that my ears roared.

God DAMN them! I shrieked in my mind, furious at them both, those entwined hands, those private looks at each other, that cinematic romance. *Mama and Daddy got to live their lives! Nobody dared make a claim on C. Ray or Velma, no parent or sibling, or even one of us kids, because everybody knew that that grand holy love of theirs had to come first! Mama got to live her life, and it was a very happy one! All I want is a chance to finish living mine!*

Maybe I had been making noises or faces, because a small girl with big glasses and many library books under her arm was on the sidewalk now in front of my car, staring at me. I tried to smile back at her when she registered in my vision, and I noticed that she did not have red hair. Nor was she especially tall. But I wondered who her parents were as she gave me one last look and then walked away into the shade of the library portico. I hoped that they weren't like C. Ray and Velma. And then I thought about all of the child molesters and abusers and schizophrenogenics and dope users and me-firsters that passed for parents these days, and I hoped that they were.

I waved at the child. Savvy kid that she was, she did not wave back. I thoroughly approved. I wouldnt've wanted a kid of mine to get too friendly with somebody as weird as me, either. *Beware of big women with no hair,* I might have told her. *Especially the ones who scream bad words at their steering wheels.*

I finally went inside the large air-conditioned brick building, and obtained a library card, and checked out a biography of J.R.R. Tolkien and two books on the history of palmistry. I decided to read Barbara's palm for her, one of these days, if she would let me. I decided to just give everybody in my life, dead or alive, the benefit of the doubt.

"She keeps trying to get out of the house, when I'm not looking," Barbara reported on Mama when I got back to Auletta that evening.

"If I'm watching TV or something, not paying her any attention, she'll get up and try to open the doors."

"She's begun to do that a lot at night, lately," I said, throwing my books onto the sofa. I threw myself down after them. Kicked my shoes off. "I'm not sure that she still knows how to turn a doorknob, though. Or turn a key in a lock."

"I didn't know," said Barbara in a very low voice, gathering her things. "I took the keys out of the doors, and put 'em in this fruit bowl here on the table."

"I leave at least one key in a door—in the front door—in case we have to get out of here in a hurry."

"Well," said Barbara, "it's in this bowl here. Now. You want me to go put it back?"

"Who's vem bargle finnifee?" called my mother from the hallway.

"Nothing, Mama."

"*Who?*" Her stance, rickety as it was, was combative.

"We've had a kinda bad day," Barbara apologized, stowing away the curling iron in her large bag. "She didn't sit still long enough for me to get her hair done."

"Where're the keys again?"

Barbara pointed with one long pearled nail at the silver bowl full of fake fruit that sat in the middle of the dinette table. I reached for the front door key and padded down the hallway carpet to replace it in the brass lock, my mother watching me in demented and demanding fury.

"*Who?*" she roared again.

"Stella Dallas, Mama," I said the first name that came into my mind. "The President of The United States."

"Oh. Kay!" she answered in two widely separated syllables, but triumphant.

Barbara lay a hand on my arm as I came back to the kitchen area. "She might be constipated, maybe that's it. I fed her some peanut butter for lunch, that's all she'd eat."

I found myself hugging my sister-in-law without forethought, just turning around and folding her small tanned tidy self into my arms. "Oh, Barbara, honey, thank you."

Her reaction was muffled by my clavicle. "For what?"

"For everything. For everything you've been doing for us. For this one day."

"I didn't mean to make her constipated."

Poor little Barbara was so dumb, one dose of peanut butter at noon was probably not going to cement up somebody's innards by six. But I didn't stretch this out. I was too tired for a long explanation. Next Tuesday, the day I would be living for, was too godawful far off. "You didn't make her constipated, Barb. You didn't do anything wrong. It's this fucking *illness* of hers. It's this unfair, this unholy brain damage she suffers from. How unfair. God should be spanked."

Barbara's brown eyes became golf balls at my blasphemy. I thought she was about to cross herself, until I sensed some sort of agreement from her.

"Thank you, *so much*," I hugged her again. "Be careful driving home, now."

"I will."

"Tell ol' Rocky and the kids how grateful I am, for them doing without you today like this."

Her eyes were opaque. Tiny black blobs of mascara hung from her lashes like plant fungus. Sudden moisture made a sheen over her brown irises.

She drove away from us, like everybody else we knew. Nobody stayed here with us for any longer than necessary. I closed the door.

"*Who ranza melga?*" Mama demanded from the hallway, her wild gray hair half-moussed, nothing but complete madness in the watery blue eyes behind her smudged glasses.

"John Wayne," I said.

"*Who?*"

"Barbra Streisand."

"Oh."

Mama tried to get out of the house again that night, after I was in bed and mostly asleep. She was having a hard time turning the door knob when I busted her, but she had done astonishingly well with the key.

Barbara's idea about the keys was practical, as good as any. I locked the door and tossed the key into the fruit bowl on the table, and went back to bed, and put the extra pillow over my head while my mother roamed the empty house and called out, "*Who? Who? Who?*"

chapter 31

That
Auletta
Fifteen
Percent

Another thing I learned in Auletta was about worry. The reason it's so hard to stop worrying is because worrying feels a whole lot like *planning*.

Yep, you just plan and plan until you can't think straight. You can't carry on a linear conversation anymore, you plan so much. And all of your concerned loved ones begin to harass you about how much you plan: *Relax, Jeanne. Stop worrying so much, you're going to give yourself an ulcer. Be cool. Chill out. Just leave it all in God's hands.* And my own personal all-time favorites: *Things will all work out. Things will all fall into place.* Yeah. Just like the jigsaw puzzle pieces from that big box magically assembled themselves in mid-air into a photograph of Mount Rushmore the time Mama got into a snit and tossed them.

Hell, yeah. Good advice, well meant. But there you are with a great big hellacious mess on your hands which threatens to metastasize into an even bigger horrific hellacious mess of epic proportions, unless *you* come up with a foolproof plan to keep things under control. Anybody with the brains of a tree frog will try to plan here. Even for the unplannable. To control what my friend Nancy Roth once pointed out was the uncontrollable.

But when you've tried to mentally tame the untameable for a long enough time, you just don't realize anymore the futility of what you're trying to do. You can no longer tell what's controllable and what's not, what's plannable and what's not. No, you certainly don't want to be a *worrier,* that soggy incarnation of womanhood, a second version of what your own mother was once accused of being.

No, what occupies your own mind, morning, noon, and night, are *plans,* not worries. Plans are sensible and actually sort of masculine, when worries are silly and half-imagined, and lurk in the fuzziest shadows of femininity. What you're doing is *planning.* Any rational person would be trying for proactivity here, to come up with a solution to the problem of how to get to happily ever after: What will I do, if Mama gets into some kind of trouble in the middle of the night, and I don't wake up? How long would it take paramedics to get out here? What are the symptoms of a nervous breakdown? Have I had one? What if Mama has cancer and is in pain, and can't tell me about it? What will happen if Barbara leaves Rocky again? She's so unhappy, I worry. —No, I don't worry, I *plan.* Sleepless, I try to plan:

How to tell when the time has come to take the dreaded nursing home step. How to face the realization that you will be abandoning your own mother to total strangers, who might neglect or mistreat her, when she is begging you to take her home. How to face the related fact that you will eventually despise yourself, and probably will never be proud of your behavior during these last few years of her life, no matter what you do. How to accept that there are no easy nor painless ways out, for either one of you.

To paraphrase the disappeared Jimmy Hoffa, who certainly didn't go down in history for his foolish worries: *Eighty-five percent of what you worry about won't ever come to pass. And you can always deal with that other fifteen percent.*

Of course, look what happened to Jimmy Hoffa.

chapter 32

Conrad's
News

My son Conrad called me on a hot Tuesday morning in August, right before Barbara the Beauty Lady was due for her last visit. I was really bummed out by the prospect of losing Barbara's assistance, but had known for a long time that it was inevitable. School was scheduled to start soon, and Barbara's last few days off would be devoted to securing new clothes and notebooks and backpacks for Brooke and Adam. It was a given down here that dads, even one as conscientious as Rocky, did not do the back-to-school sales thing. Besides, how would a workaholic like Rocky ever find the time?

Time, I thought, waiting at the window for Barbara's white Miata to pull up and temporarily save me, is the one thing none of us has enough of. Except for Mama. She has oceans of it, and no way to spend it. Who was it who once said that Alzheimer's looks a lot like actual death by boredom?

Mama was folding towels at the sofa behind me, or trying to. She could not line up the corners. Her lips puckered, in frustration or waning interest or beginning rage: "Damn fick thapper," she muttered. "Floo thing!"

"You're doing fine, Mama. Thanks for helping me." I made myself sound as supportive and brainlessly enthusiastic as a caffeinated camp counselor. "I *really* appreciate it."

I was trying.

Two of my recent summer Tuesdays off had been spent at a monthly Alzheimer's support group meeting in Slidell, and I had discovered a surprising comfort in the companionship of other people in the same pickle I was in. It did me no good now to wish that I had been able to attend these meetings earlier in my caregiving service, but I did wish it. And how I dreaded the upcoming loss of Barbara, when I would no longer be able to go. We commiserated and shared coping tips, those plucky support group members and I. I was learning that there were people who had it worse than I did.

One elderly man, sole caregiver for his afflicted wife, routinely tied aluminum pie plates around his wife's side of the bed, so that their clatter would wake him whenever she got the crazy-lady roaming urge, several times each night. I would look at this unhappy but courageous old guy and wonder how on earth he kept going, living the way he did. And I would consider my own situation with Velma, and realize that I at least had my relative youth and good health to fall back on. This old man suffered from the heart disease and aches and pains of his generation. He was losing the sleep that his body desperately needed for his very survival. And that water in his reddening eyes, as he'd relate his wife's steady decline, also told me that he suffered acutely from the grief that I didn't really feel. What I felt at these meetings, me the youngest participant, was mostly unworthy and profoundly *lucky*. I would someday outlive my mother's disease. I had a future. Many of these older people, certainly married ones who were caring for ill spouses, were facing their own parallel destruction as they had to watch their respective beloveds slowly lose their minds. Yes indeedy, here were those wonderful golden years that vitamin ads and pop culture had promised them: Whoopee: One long retirement pleasure cruise right straight into hell. My hair literally stood on end sometimes, listening to the understated horror in these quavery voices, hearing what it was like to be shrieked at and called a thief, and to be actually *bitten* by the only love of one's life. This was a level of grief that I would not experience with Velma, I saw.

Good thing you died when you did, Daddy, I thought and meant it. If there really is a God, he sure took you at a merciful time. All I suffer with Mama is the loss of my freedom, and restlessness. Hers and mine.

One thoughtful support group member, a quiet lady, caregiver to an older sister, shared with the rest of us that folding laundry seemed to be a good way to keep her sister busy. Maybe it also made her feel useful. "She folds and unfolds the same washcloth a dozen times, she don't know the difference," the lady told us. "But it keeps her occupied for a while. 'Here,' I say, 'help me out some, Mae.' And she does what she can. And you always gotta remember to thank her, y'all know what I'm talking about."

And yes, we all did.

"*Shit!*" said Velma now, and wadded up the small stack of towels, and threw them like garbage onto the carpet behind my feet. "We can't muvvle farvel this shit!"

So much for laundry therapy, I thought, as the telephone rang.

I pulled up the antenna on Daddy's old cordless. "Hello?"

Mama shuffled through the terrycloth disorder, one of the towels momentarily tangling around an ankle, and I moved to keep her from falling. She shook me off, stomped free of the laundry, and headed for the hallway. "*Shit!*"

"Mom?" said the telephone.

"Rad?"

"Yeah, it's me. You okay? You sound out of breath."

I held the phone to my ear as I followed Velma at a discreet distance. "Mam-maw's getting ready to have a little tantrum, looks like. I'm tracking her to keep her out of trouble until your aunt gets here."

Mama went for the back door, but could find no keys to turn. The knob wouldn't turn without a key. She kept trying to turn it. The back of her neck and the side of her face were flushed. Her big red lips stuck out like a puckered scar.

"Is this a bad time to call?" Conrad asked.

"I am glad to hear your dear voice," I told him truthfully, monitoring my mother like a video camera as she gave up on the door and went for the kitchen to mess with the cabinets. My Crazy-Cam followed. "And there are no really good times for calls. What's up?"

"Well, could you and Mam-maw stand some company?"

I heard Barbara's key turn in the back door lock, and I hurried to help her with her hair stuff and burdens. I saw her notice the phone held to my ear. *Conrad,* I mouthed to her, and she nodded in an exaggerated way, her poufy dark hair bobbing and shining, her made-up eyes red and swollen. Sometimes, lately, Barbara looked worse than I did.

Conrad's question finally sank in. "*Company? Anybody we know?*" I asked, becoming a little excited.

"Well, just me and Mark."

Where's Mom? Barbara's pearled lips shaped the words.

I shrugged and pointed to the kitchen, and Barbara hitched up her designer jeans and squared her small shoulders. I heard her soft murmured greetings as she stepped into the lion's den, somewhere off camera. Crazy-Cam had ceased to track Velma. Fag-Cam had turned its attention now to the unseen Mark, as I pulled out a chair and sat down at the dinette table. "Rad," I began, dying to see him again, to have him under the same roof with me, to sit up late over coffee with him and talk to him until I ran out of things to say, but not wanting to share him with anybody else—certainly not with the platinum-haired Mark—"Son, I'm just not sure ... Um, your grandmother is kind of a handful these days, and I can't keep the house clean enough for company. I mean, *you're* not company, you know what a slob I am, I raised you. But I'd be kind of embarrassed—"

"We won't have to actually *stay* out there in Auletta, since Mark wants to mostly see the French Quarter ..."

Yes, Mark would certainly be drawn to all those tight little swishy asses in the Quarter. "Well, no, I didn't mean that you couldn't stay here, son, that isn't what I meant. You're always welcome, Rad. And any friend of yours is welcome, too." I understood what I had to say, and I said it. And I knew that I'd have to find a way to eventually mean it. Conrad was a grown man. He was capable of coming all the way to Louisiana, staying in New Orleans with Mark, sampling its night life, and never once driving out to see me, if he thought that that's what I wanted. "When are y'all planning on coming?"

"Well, Mark begins grad school at Berkeley in September, so I guess it'd have to be around the end of this month."

"Fine!" I heard myself say, over the sounds of muted crashes and Barbara's cajoling voice coming from the kitchen. Mama made argumentative babble, and something unseen fell quite loudly into the stainless steel sink and broke. But when I heard no resultant screams, nor sudden pleas from anybody to drop what I was doing and call 911, I turned my attention back to my son. Barbara, off-stage, was coping.

What will I do when she has to quit coming? I couldn't make myself stop rubbing that particular sore spot now. I felt a tiny rise of panic. How can I get this place ready for these boys? How can I keep Mama in line? How will I keep Mark from thinking that we're all nuts?

"Mom?" said Rad into my ear.

"Lost my train of thought for a moment, I'm sorry," I told him. Telephone calls were becoming increasingly difficult for me these days, even with a cordless phone to let me ride herd on Mama while I talked. My concentration was shot. Even those long, blessed calls I had once enjoyed from Rad's grandmother, my dear friend Nancy Roth, were becoming less frequent, briefer, disjointed. *I'm really afraid that I'm coming down with Alzheimer's, too, Nancy,* I had told her last week. *Nonsense, darling,* had been her answer. *What you have is sleep deprivation, and the drive to be proactive. You keep trying to control the uncontrollable, Jeanne. That takes a lot out of a person. It's time to let that sister-in-law of yours take on more of this burden, darling.*

But she's got a family of her own to look out for, Nancy. When school starts, and the kids begin to come home earlier, she's gotta be there. She has to drive all the way across the lake to even get here, almost an hour's drive.

Doesn't she work, Jeanne? What becomes of the children on the days that she's working?

I don't know. But Barbara is entitled to her day off, that's all I know. I'm just so grateful to her for giving me what time she already has, this summer. I don't know what I would've done without her.

Aren't you entitled, too, to something, Jeanne? Here you are, making excuses for this girl, when all you've ever told me is about how selfish and thoughtless she is.

Yes, I thought now, that's about all I have ever had to say for ol' Barbara Trahan. And, yes, I am making excuses for her. I'm defending her. I have no idea why.

"Mom?" said Conrad into my ear, and I realized that I had been doing it again, letting my mind wander off in half a dozen different directions at once. I felt pins and needles in my upper leg when I uncrossed it now. I had been sitting in rigidity. My ear hurt where I was pushing the phone against it.

"Sorry," I said.

"So is it okay? If we come?"

My hungry Springsteen heart reached out to him with both of its selfish little hands. "*Please* do," I said, trying to allow real emotion into my voice, but unable to summon it. How odd, when it was all backed up inside me like a dammed lake, keeping me awake nights. How dysfunctional, to display only rigidity and actual locked muscles, and hear only feigned warmth in my voice, when the real thing, inaccessible, was burning in my chest like angina. "I'd like to really get to know Mark. I can't wait to see you, son."

"How's Mam-maw doing?"

"Like the entire zoo monkey house."

"How're Aunt Barbara and Uncle Rocky?"

"Rocky's just like always, working himself to death," I said. "Barbara seems to be about one boo-hoo shy of a crying fit, most days."

"Why?"

I shrugged. "That's just Barbara. Barbara just gets like that, sometimes. She lives in her own soap opera."

"You know, Mark is a very dramatic personality himself, when you get to know him. But, I mean, he's not like a diva or anything. Just interesting. He's a very interesting guy, Mom."

I can't wait, I thought. "How's that Internet magazine coming?"

"We'll tell you all about it when we get there."

"Mark's going to graduate school? Then why can't *you* go to graduate school, Rad? I thought the whole idea was to pour all of your energies, the two of you, into getting your magazine up and coming."

"We'll cover all of that when we see you," he said again, and dodged: "By the way, Dad says hello."

I let Rad get away with the non sequitur. I visualized Larry Roth and I smiled. "So how's he doing these days? How's life at Sid-Nan?"

"He's fine, he has a new phone number. He wanted me to give it to you, I can't believe I'm actually remembering to do it. You have a pencil or something handy to take it down?"

I noticed my mother's large battered purse on a nearby chair, and I stuck my hand down among the fuzzy tissues and lipsticks and rumpled papers to fish out a ballpoint. I was too preoccupied to notice anything else in there. I took out a pen and clicked it, and then took up the telephone bill from the stack of mail in the middle of the table to write on. "Okay," I said. "Gimme."

Rad gave me the new Manhattan number. I read it back to him in a pleasant, slowed mood. The unruly sounds from the kitchen had stopped. Barbara's soothing murmurs came from the TV room now, where the routine theatrics of daytime television played themselves out. "So Larry's moved? Did he get a nice place?"

"Dad's, um, dating again," said my son. "They, like, got a new apartment together. I understand it's really nice, I haven't seen it. I haven't met her yet."

I stopped smiling.

chapter 33

A
Fairly
Good
Day

If Conrad was dismayed by Mama's worsening condition, he had too much class to show it.

He hopped out of his rental car while I watched and waited at the window, and he came tanned and hallooing to the front door, where I intercepted him in a bear hug. He was a breath of cologne and soap, and his dark hair was soft at my cheek. What I had not remembered was his poise. The arms that hugged me back were those of a strong and thoughtful man, assured in the way they graciously grabbed me, no puppy awkwardness or hesitation.

"Hi, Mam-maw!" he said to the old woman who stood behind me, and he disengaged himself from my embrace to embrace my mother. It couldn't have been a pleasant thing to do, since Mama had dribbled milk onto her good blouse at breakfast, and had not held still enough afterward for me to get it all blotted up. Mama's vacant eyes and the total lack of recognition she gave Conrad couldn't have been very welcoming, either. But his capable arms encircled her without shyness. She didn't smile—Mama was forgetting how to smile these days—yet Rad's closeness brought some of her old reflexes back and her thin hand made an attempt to pat his shoulder.

Barbara and I had done what we could to make Mama pretty this morning, double-teaming her as we got her bathed and dressed.

Barbara had taken the morning off from her job for this, and waded right in with me to face the scratching fingernails and sullen resistance that Velma put up—doing Velma's hair while I worked at getting a little makeup on her face. I went easy on the lipstick, choosing a light coral that I thought flattering, while Barbara fluffed and teased at the limp gray hair. We had done our best.

"Thank you, Barb," I breathed when we were done, and Mama, freed, took to her feet like a released wild animal. "I wish you could stay until Rad gets here. He'd love to see you."

She'd shaken her head. "Wish I could, too, but I gotta get back to work."

"You're a treasure." I hugged her goodbye.

"Tell that to Rocky."

"Yeah, I've told Rocky how much your help has meant to us this summer," I said, watching her pack up her brushes and curlers. "I keep telling him."

"I love you, Jeanne," she said, and sighed, and left.

I watched my son as he kissed his grandmother now, and told her that she was beautiful. And I was so proud of him, of his sensitivity and kindness, that my breath became short. My heart was speeding. My mother was smiling.

"I need to get a few things out of the car," said Rad.

"Where's Mark?"

"He wants to hook up with a friend of ours in the Quarter today, do a little shopping and so forth, before it rains. Weather report is calling for rain this afternoon." Rad walked rapidly to the shiny hot automobile parked under a pine tree, me tagging along, and unlocked it to take a camera and a cell phone from the front passenger seat, "I'll bring him out here tomorrow."

I hid my pleasure at having my son all to myself. "So you'll be coming back out tomorrow, then."

"I want to see as much of Mam-maw as I can, while I'm here."

She hadn't noticed that we had stepped outside. And she wasn't waiting for us when we came back indoors into the relief of the air conditioning. We found her in the dining room, doing nothing, just wandering in her splay-footed way. Rad gently took her hand, and the three of us meandered willy-nilly through the hall and the rooms of the house, Rad and I catching each other up on family news and the doings of Nancy and Sid up in New York, as if the only way a family should do a reunion was on foot.

"Bwoo baby here," said Mama.

"Yes," Rad patted her hand. "And I can't get over how pretty you look. And what a nice house this is. And Mom looks pretty good, too. Don't you think so?"

I wanted to instruct him in the approved communications methods for talking to Alzheimer's patients, but I never could remember what they were.

"Yes," my mother answered him, and I realized that Conrad was doing very well on his own. He continued to speak to us in low and positive tones, and we continued to listen and comment. He told us of San Francisco, his new job as a production assistant at the local NPR station, and how he spent as much time as he could these days at the beach.

He didn't mention his father Larry's new love interest, but I did, eventually. I didn't want my son to think that the subject was taboo, that I thought I had some prior claim on Larry which had been violated. Because I knew very well that I did not. No matter how I felt.

"Her name is Suyuan," Conrad told me. "I finally got to meet her last week. She's mid-thirtyish, maybe. Divorced. Teaches at CCNY. Really friendly. I like her."

"Doesn't sound Jewish," I teased, but the shadow of this update covered me like an overcast sky.

"Chinese-American." Rad stopped our slow pacing. All three of us came to a full stop. "But guess who *is* Jewish."

"Dinah Shore."

"I'm supposed to be too young to know who Dinah Shore is, Mom. Guess again."

"I don't know." But I suspected.

"Me," he said. "I'm officially converted."

"That's wonderful!" I told him, and meant it, envying Rad's urge towards spirituality. Of course, maybe this step had not been taken out of any kind of religious impulse. Maybe Rad had wanted to do it because Mark was Jewish. Was Mark Jewish? Or because perhaps they lived next door to a liberal congregation of Reformed gays, or something like that. "I know that your grandparents must be pleased."

"I haven't gotten around to telling them yet."

"Well, tell them, son. Life is short. There are certain things that older people need to hear before they die."

"Where'd I put my camera? I want to get a picture of you and Mam-maw while I'm here."

"On the hall table," I told him, and he started for that location.

"Vrooo! Brooo! Brooo!" roared my mother suddenly, her lower teeth bared when we turned to look at her, veins standing out on her stringy neck.

"Mam-maw?" Rad held out a hand to her. "You okay?"

"*Brooo!*" She backed away from his touch, her body language communicating distilled fury of a purity rarely seen in anybody above the age of two.

"Maybe she didn't like that part about older eeple-pay eyeing-day," he muttered out of the side of his mouth.

"Maybe she thinks she's at a Bruce Springsteen concert," I said, becoming angry. The day had been going so well, up until now. "Come on, Mama. We'll walk some more."

"*VROOO! Mecklin barson!*" Saliva sprayed from the coral mouth.

"I'm sorry, Mom," said Rad.

"Honey, you didn't do anything. This just happens, sometimes. I'm sure there are reasons, but I'll never know what they are." I took my mother's hand and pulled her into the beginnings of another tour around the house, making her feet jerk. "You want some ice cream. Mama? I bet we have chocolate."

Her lips stuck out and she said nothing, but she was shuffling alongside me compliantly.

"Maybe she just wanted us to keep walking," said Rad, "and we stopped."

"Maybe. I know she gets restless."

"You want to take a ride, Mam-maw?" he asked her. "Go for a Sunday drive? Even if it's not Sunday?"

When she didn't pitch a fit at this suggestion, either, we took them both as mandates. First we had ice cream, and then we all three got into Conrad's spiffy newish rental car and headed out to see the sights of Auletta, Louisiana, U.S.A.

"Maybe your lot in life, Mom, is to counterbalance Dad's and my impulsive life choices," said Conrad, as he drove us down Highway Eleven. "Maybe the Roth men are too quick to fall in love with dramatic people, and you're meant to remind us of the virtues of having one's feet on the ground."

He couldn't see my face, nor I his, buckled up in the back seat like I was. But with that simple throwaway observation, he had come *out*. He knew it, and I knew it.

"You ever think about that, Mom?" he prompted.

"Something like that has occurred to me a time or two," I said, and released a deep breath, as if I had been holding it for months. My mother's head nodded, up front there beside Rad, the mobile monotony and motion of the car having put her to sleep. I looked at the passing scenery of water and boats and flotsam as we turned off the highway near the bridge, and felt an obscure sense of relief. Whatever suspense I had been in was over now, at least. The lake seemed calm and metallic, stainless steel, in this cloudy sunlight. We would go on from here. I wondered how many times my child had rehearsed his bit of news to get it just this right, this understated. "Looks like it might be raining in the city," I spoke my own casual piece. "Hope Mark's not getting too wet."

"He won't melt," said Rad, sounding extremely happy.

"Is Larry's Chinese girl dramatic?"

"Well, she's pretty low-key, the times I've seen her. But her divorce was very ugly and emotional, I understand. So there's definitely some drama there."

Mama snored.

"Mam-maw'll be up all night," Rad commented, half-turning to me. "You want me to try to wake her up?"

"There's no way to keep her awake," I said, pondering his little coming-out speech and thinking about how prosaic and cloddish he and Larry must think me. I was apparently not dramatic enough for either of them. I had my feet on the ground. I embodied sensible virtues. I stopped looking out of the windows and looked at the back of the front seat. "She's up all night, anyway. All the time. It's okay."

"Dad would really like for you to get to know Suyuan. Have you called him yet?"

"No."

"Well, he really wants you to. Whenever it's convenient. He wants to know if you can read Suyuan's palms from a Xerox copy. If she Xeroxes her palms, I mean."

This was too much. I wanted to say something about Larry's having made me out to be *very* dramatic, once, when the situation suited him, calling me a voodoo practitioner. I looked at the sky with a sort of generalized malevolence and hoped that it was raining hard in Orleans Parish, right up Mark's nose. I also hoped that it was coming down in bucketfuls way up in Manhattan.

"Can you do that, Mom?" Rad asked. "Read a palm off a Xerox? Could you read Mark's?"

"I'm a fake," I said. "No witch. I can't do anything witchy."

"You've seemed genuine enough to me."

No, I'm an undramatic nobody, I thought, feeling sorry for myself, feeling old and marginalized and left out of things, and damned with the proverbial faint praise. When do I get to be dramatic? Fickle and fascinating, giggly, deep and mysterious, all of the above? When do I get to be my mother's daughter?

"This is really kind of an interesting area," said Conrad, taking random side streets near the lakefront. "There are some really impressive houses out here, this near the water."

"Yeah," I said, tired of the small talk. "Don't get us lost."

But having once worked himself up to get his say said, my always-private son retreated into banality now. All I got was small talk, of the tiniest variety. He drove us back towards Slidell, pointing at signs and buildings, quizzing me about what crawfish tasted like and how deep Lake Pontchartrain was, what was the difference between Creole and Cajun food?

What I wanted to hear from him was about how well I was evidently coping. Now that he had seen for himself what Alzheimer's disease had done to both Mama and me, what I expected to hear and needed to hear was ratification. Admiration, even. Where was the *God, Mom, I just don't see how you do it!* and the *How on earth have you kept going this long?* Where were the words I thought I had a right to expect?

Here was Mama, blessedly asleep, giving us the opportunity for a very rare heart-to-heart exchange. And what I was getting from Rad was questions about cuisine.

I thought about just bringing him up short with something shocking like, "Which of you pitches and which catches, you and Mark?", and realized simultaneously that I never would. That line of conversation was beyond me, even for jokey shock value. I could never say such a thing to my child. Maybe there were likewise things that he could never say to me, for whatever reason. Maybe there were some gifts of language that he just couldn't give me.

I tried to visualize his palms and remember what a sensitive person he was, how guarded and introverted. I understood that he still liked to keep his distance, and that he did love me, but small talk was about the only level of communication he would entertain.

He's *cold*, I realized, with a flash of self-recognition. Just like Nancy Roth had once found me. Rad's not thoughtless nor unkind, he's just *cold*.

I looked at the back of his head and saw myself.

chapter 34

One
Last
Auletta
Lesson

The final insight that came to me during those days, while I was hearing all about Suyuan, waiting to get to know Mark, and wondering what my sister-in-law Barbara was about to do to her life, was maybe the most important lesson of them all. It even approaches genuine wisdom, and I cannot stress it strongly enough. As a matter of fact, let me even italicize it. You might want to cut it out and stick it onto the door of your refrigerator, so crucial is it to human relationships.

Here goes:

Let beloved idiots ruin their own lives, if that's what they're dead set on doing, with no attempt whatsoever at control or behavior modification from you.

I know, I know. But just think about it for a minute here. They'll definitely resent your advice, if you're stupid enough to try to give them any of the honest sort. And you know that they'll just go ahead and fuck up their lives anyway, no matter what you say.

Yep, when some beloved of-age idiot of yours asks you what you think about a certain moronic and foreseeably catastrophic course of action they plan on taking, they don't want to hear your real opinion. They only want approval of what they're about to do. And if you want to keep these adult sons and daughters, brothers and sisters, friends and whatever else in your life, then you had damn well better give it to them.

But what if your sister, say, calls you up one night to tell you that she's running off to get married to a Mexican dope dealer, and they plan to finance their dreams by routinely smuggling narcotics back across the U.S. border in a 1968 Volkswagen bus with peace symbols painted all over it? What's the correct answer, if you just can't bring yourself to congratulate her upon the total wonderfulness of her marital plans?

No, you *don't* suggest that she check herself in somewhere for some serious counseling. You don't use any four-letter words, not even for the bridegroom. Don't tell her she's crazy, not if you love her. Because I guarantee that you'll never hear from her again, if you do. These beloved idiots need support from us feet-on-the-ground types, even if they've just shacked up with a platinum-haired, pierced-nose glamour boy who has somehow manipulated them out of all notions of going to graduate school. If you can't say something supportive, then keep your big mouth shut, and mind your own business.

It is very easy to get excommunicated from a loved one's heart over something like your secretly reading their damned diary, even if you're behaving out of a genuine and commendable desire to keep your idiot out of trouble. Even if you're operating out of maternal love. It takes guts to risk that excommunication, and I haven't got them.

So what is the proper reaction to all idiotic news?

What, after all, is the only thing these idiots will let you say?

"Wonderful!" you lie, and cringe, and hope that you're wrong about this big, looming, utterly monstrous mistake they seem bent on making. "*Won*derful! I'm *sooo* glad!"

So.

Everybody who is of legal age has the fundamental right to fuck up his or her life in the way that he or she sees fit. Cut out this nugget of wisdom, fold it up, and keep it in your wallet, I'm telling you.

There's nothing you can do about any of it, anyway.

chapter 35

Beloved
Idiots
Run
Amok

On what would prove to be the last night I would spend in that Auletta house, I lay awake in bed, slightly drunk.

Rad, after much more chocolate ice cream with Mama, more tales of all the reported cute things that Mark had said or done since birth, and a glass of a fairly decent shiraz with me, had headed back across Lake Pontchartrain for a hotel room with his favorite person. He left me alone to cope with my chocolated mother, full of sugar and energy, who would probably not sleep tonight even three hours.

"Glessy," Mama had noticed Rad several times and had smiled, reaching out for him with a clawlike hand. "Baby noo noo."

And Rad would take up that hand and kiss it, and say, "My Mammaw," and it would move me more than I would let on. Maybe Mama did remember who he was. The two of them did seem to have something going on together here.

But Mama's the one we should be giving the wine to, I had thought, watching them, knowing how hard it would be to get her calmed down and settled for bed once Conrad had to leave. We should just pour the wine into Mam-maw and knock her out.

I invited Rad to spend the night with us, but he didn't want to. He offered excuses, all of which came down to the same reason.

I lay awake now and gnashed my teeth at the memory of how

many times that single syllable "Mark" had come up in the evening's conversation, and I deeply regretted all the nights I had once inflicted the name "Larry" upon my own parents and brother in that now-renovated Napoleon Avenue house. What is it that we get out of the mere utterance of the loved one's name? I wondered. Why do we take such pleasure in speaking it, even if our listeners are so sick of hearing it that they'd rather have an enema?

It's as if the very name "Mark" is an incantation, I told myself, woozy with red wine and fatigue. If Conrad can just *say* it enough, the magic of the universe will ensure that Mark will love Conrad forever. But it has to be said within the hearing of listeners. To speak it to a dog or a cat is no good. It has to be uttered in the presence of friends and family, preferably to friends and family who find Mark's charms rather obscure. In fact, the sicker we get of hearing the name, the more potent the incantation seems to be. Apparently, you get extra credit if you can work the name into a fairly inappropriate context:

Me: "I haven't read a good book in such a long time, and I miss them so much."

Mama: "Boogle ferthan fwah?"

Conrad: "Mark says that he was attracted to me because my middle name is 'Aragorn,' and *The Lord of The Rings* is one of his favorite books."

Will Rad tell his grandparents that he's gay, at the same time that he tells them he's Jewish? I wondered now, trying to find a comfortable position for my feet—it's bad to become aware of your feet in bed, when you realize that there's no comfortable position for them under covers. Or does Rad expect me or Larry to tell them? Maybe nobody tells grandparents, maybe that's not how it's done. Maybe grandparents are thought too old-fashioned to handle it. I can't see myself having a conversation with Nancy, though, and leaving out Mark's name, whenever we mention Rad. I guess you just officially say "roommate," and let it go at that. I imagine that's what Rad already does.

Hell, I don't want to have to solve all the sociological difficulties of the Western World, as they pertain to this family! I thought, punching my pillow. All I want is one good night's sleep. And *damn* if I know how to get it here.

Too much chocolate ice cream had left me real gassed up after he had left, insomniac, caffeinated. I kept plumping up my pillow and rolling over and over, with leftover conversation rattling about in my head and dinner rambling in my bowels.

Mama, similarly jacked up, had finally dropped in her tracks on the den sofa in front of the television set. And that's where I had left her, fully clothed and shod, at the other end of the house. From which I knew that she would soon issue forth like a hurricane or just a creeping street flood, to nevertheless drown me out of the sleep I wasn't getting, to wash me out of my lair.

My pillow was a sodden lump of rocks, misaligned with the shape of my anatomy. I feared to hear the noises of my mother's awakening, and yet couldn't stop monitoring all the night sounds for them. My brain was a flywheel that had no *off* switch.

Who will take care of me when I'm old? it wondered, driving me crazy, worrying at imponderables, making me physically dizzy as I rolled over and thrashed. Who will care for me this way, like I care for Mama, when I'm no longer able to care for myself? Will it be Rad? Will Rad care for me this way, like this, while I keep him awake with my noises and my dangers and my toileting difficulties?

Oh, *just shoot me now*. Just put me out of my misery with a big elephant gun, because I do not want to do this to my child.

And because, maybe, I doubt that my child is up to it. In a choice between serenity with Mark (or, more likely, one of Mark's successors), and craziness with me, I doubt very much that I will win out.

Do I want to win out?

No.

I will want to die. I would rather be dead than have my son Conrad do what I am doing now. No doubt about it.

The very thought of compelling my son to care for me in this way makes my blood congeal. It causes my stomach to liquefy, I thought. Hell, I can't sleep. I might as well get up and read the newspaper.

But I must have slept, or at least fallen into a hypnogogic state for a few minutes, because my mother came in to my bedroom at some point after this conclusion of mine, and agreed with me.

She came into my bedroom on light, trim feet, in shoes with high heels, and I opened my eyes when she sat on the edge of my mattress and took my hand. "Punkin?" she spoke my pet name to me, her brilliant hair dipping low and tickling the base of my neck, her red nails against the shiny skin at the back of my hand like jewels. Her perfume enveloped me, a scent like Easter lilies.

"Mama?" I said, too thoroughly taken in by the experience to be astonished.

One of her hands held a cigarette, and I could smell the tobacco smoke. But the other released my own hand, and lay itself across my brow like a cool cloth. "You okay, punkin?"

"Yeah," I said, comforted by her touch. "I'm fine, now."

She was so beautiful, and her beauty existed only for me. It concentrated itself upon me with a frowning of brows and shaded blue eyes, and I remembered now that those blue eyes, once upon a time, had been the first things that I had literally ever focused my infant gaze upon. This slim body in a cotton housedress had once been my first home. The first scent I had ever smelled in my life had been of her. The first sound I ever in my life had heard had been Velma's heartbeat.

I was overwhelmed with a love for her that almost choked me. She loomed over me like a goddess or a shelter, and I wanted to be taken into her arms for good.

"Jeanne, punkin," she said, using the first human voice I had ever heard, "I don't want to see my own child go through this, either, I completely agree with you. I'd definitely rather be dead, myself. But I'm still technically alive, looks like. And I can't kill myself now, punkin. I don't remember how to do it."

"But why would I want you to kill yourself, Mama?" I started to cry. Because her beauty hurt me so much. It was so fragile. "I do love you. Still. Always."

The goddam telephone started to ring. And it rang and it rang, while I looked into the eyes of my lovely mother and watched them fade out.

The phone won. I woke up for real, and no longer expected to see the young Velma sitting on my bed. And she wasn't. I leaned across an ordinary mountain of wet pillows to pluck the receiver out of its cradle, there on my night table. My contact lenses were out, and I couldn't see a clock from here, but I knew that it must be pretty late.

And then the big jolt of fear hit me, right before I could irritably bark, "Yeah?" into the phone at my caller—Rad was on the road, I remembered, driving back to New Orleans, vulnerable to accidents or foul play. . .

"What?" I said into the phone, sitting up and clicking on my bedside lamp.

"Jeanne?" I heard my brother Rocky's voice.

"Yeah? What is it?" I didn't hide my impatience.

But Rocky didn't sound like somebody we were related to had been in an accident, or was lying stiff in the morgue, or anything like that. When he spoke again, he sounded slightly drunk, as a matter of fact. "I've left Barbara," he said, in immediate answer to my demand.

Whatever I had been expecting, this was not it. "Say again?"

He said it again, more slowly this time. "I've left Barbara. I've moved out."

I couldn't come up with anything to say.

"I guess I just need to tell somebody," he went on all by himself, "and I guess that you're it. Sorry to be calling so late . . ."

"No, no," I said, looking blindly for the time without my contact lenses, as if that would help clear my foggy mind. "Rad left just a little while ago. I'm still up."

"Well," he said, after a longish pause, "I'm in an apartment in the Warehouse District. With no phone, no furniture. I'm calling from a bar."

"Oh, Rocky," I said. I waited for him to sound miserable.

"Well, Mama and Daddy always used to tell me that I should just forget about Barbara Trahan and go live my own life," he said, "and so, well, here goes. Better late than never, maybe. Maybe that's just a middle-aged guy talking, I dunno. More expensive than a Porsche."

"Oh, *Rocky.*"

"Well," he sounded intoxicated but cheerful, "I never thought it would end like this. But here I am. Waiting to see what happens next. I know you've always distrusted her, Jeanne. Maybe you and Mama and Daddy could see her for what she really was, all this time.

I had blinders on, looks like. But, well, maybe they're off now. We'll see. What's done is done."

"Oh, Rocky." I bled for him, his concealed sorrow. My anger blazed up on his account. "So who was it, this time? Who's our latest homewrecker?"

"Who was who?"

"The man," I said. "Who'd she run off with?"

"Who?"

The theme music from *The Twilight Zone* began to beep in the depths of my mind. I tried to grab firm hold of my consciousness, and coaxed Rocky to grab hold of his. "Who did Barbara leave you for?"

He sounded exasperated. "She didn't leave me for anybody. I left *her.*"

Well, yes, he had said that already. I thought about that now. I wasn't sure that I entirely endorsed it. "So why . . .?"

"Look, Jeanne. Me and Barb, we've gone to counseling, I've read those *I'm-Okey-You're-Dokey* self-help books until I'm blue in the face . . . I've been waiting for the other shoe to drop for so long that I can't remember what it's like to live with anybody any other way . . . I just couldn't live like that any longer . . ."

"Okay, fine," I said. "Wonderful."

"There's this girl in my clinic, she's my office manager . . ."

I didn't want to hear any more. It was very late and my mother was very crazy and I was very, very tired. And now somebody else was wanting to crow about his love life.

". . . we've been sort of attracted to each other for a long time, I think, without doing anything about it. Up until last April, that is . . ."

Long time, echoed my brain. How long a time? *How long ago* did you begin abetting in the total fuck-up of your marriage, Rocky, while I was doggedly concentrating upon keeping our mother off your hands so that your marriage could *survive?*

". . . name is Danielle, she's really mature for her age, I know you'll love her when you get to meet her, Jeanne . . ."

Why does everybody want me to meet these new loves of theirs? I wondered. Why do they expect me to love them? Am I supposed to go, "Ya-a-ayy! You've made my day! Even if I don't have someone of my own, you wonderful people have made it possible for me to vicariously share in your passion, thank you *sooo* much!"? Why don't I just tell everybody that I'm having an ongoing nervous breakdown, and hearing about anybody else's love life makes me psychotic? So if you don't want a big lady ax murderer hacking your brand new adorable little sweetie to itty bitty pieces, then just go away and get out of my face and *don't tell me that I've wasted the last two-and-a-half years here in HELL, trying to protect a marriage that you long ago decided wasn't worth your own slightest effort!*

And what about Barbara, I thought, who did me some honest kindnesses and who I've learned to really like? What becomes of Barbara's happiness now, and Brooke's, and Adam's? Are your kids as thrilled about Danielle as you are? Yeah, Barbara's already put them through this once, already. So they're prepared. Let's all call up Conrad and debrief him about the myriad delights of living through parental divorce. Right now. I'll even give you his hotel phone number.

But of course, what I said to my brother was, "Wonderful, wonderful! I'm sure she's wonderful. And I'm so happy for you, Rock."

"Well, it's what you guys always kept telling me I should do, forget about Barbara Trahan . . ."

Well, yeah. We had sort of implied that, many years ago. Some of us had even been more explicit. Silly, nosy us. I had been just as guilty as Mama.

". . . find somebody who I could really *trust* . . ."

"Wonderful," I said again. "I'm sooo glad! But it's kinda late right now, Rock, and I've really got to try and get some sleep. Conrad and his friend are coming back out here at about eleven A.M.—"

"Yeah, sorry. I'm sorry to have called so late. Guess I'm just *pumped.* Kind of excited."

"It's okay," I said. And it kind of was, actually. I was too tired and too burned out to let it be not-okay. I felt a big rise of hysterical laughter working its way up out of me. It trampolined on my guts now, reaching up to chin itself on my diaphragm, and I discovered its dangerous initial whoop just about to force itself past my tonsils. If something like this ever started coming out of me tonight now, I knew that it would never stop. "You jerk," I said to my brother, the laughter in my voice a mere choked-down ghost now of its real killer self. "An office romance. You wild romantic, you."

He really heard me then. "Are you drunk?"

"Not yet," I said, determined to find the rest of the wine, once this conversation was over, and knock myself on my ass. Insomnia could be sipped away.

"Are you okay, Jeanne?" he pursued; and I felt again the unbreakableness of whatever tied him to me, and me to him. What I heard was the voice of my own little brother. "You need help? You want me to come over, or anything?"

"*Now?*"

"No, Jeanne. In the year twenty-fifty. November."

"I love you, pardner," I told him. "You're swell."

"I love you, too. You let me know if you need help, now. I mean it."

I told him that I would be happy to meet Danielle eventually, and that I was behind him one-hundred per cent in any way he wanted to fuck up his life, but that I had to get about three hours of sleep first. We told each other good night, and then I hung up.

Mama was snoring like a bulldozer when I tiptoed into the kitchen for more shiraz. Rad and I had finished off one bottle, I saw. I opened another, a cheap California burgundy, not bothering to provide a clean glass for myself. There were paper cups in the bathroom.

I put away the corkscrew, made sure that the child-proof gizmos covered all of the knobs on the stove, checked the lock on the back door and reassured myself that the key had been removed, and then checked on Mama one last time.

She lay on her side, eyeglasses askew. They dug into her nose that way, and it bothered me, because it looked painful. I snuck in, risked waking her by removing them, and I folded them up and put them away inside the glasses case she kept in that big old purse of hers.

The table lamp near Daddy's recliner still burned. I left it on for her, because she would need to have light to be safe when she got up. And she would definitely, soon, get back up.

On impulse, I bent down again and kissed her cheek, for old times sake. "I love you, Mama," I whispered to the quiet lines of her face.

Then I took up my burgundy and my paper cup, and crept back to my refuge at the other end of the house, bent upon setting a world's record for rapidly induced sleep.

But not before crouching down for a moment to stick my head into the gas oven, just to see what it would be like. For future reference.

chapter 36

Catastrophe

The smoke detector went off sometime before daylight, and I sat right straight up in bed like I'd been electrocuted. It's amazing just how much noise one of those little gizmos can put out, and I had no idea what I was hearing at first. Air raid siren? Police car? What would a police car be doing inside the house, somewhere up near the ceiling in the hallway?

I groped for the lamp stand on my bedside table, and turned its switch with a click. But nothing happened.

"Oh, shit," I said out loud to myself, throwing off the sheet and feeling my way to the wall near the door. I found the switch plate and pushed the little lever upwards—nothing.

The smoke detector shrieked on, clanging around in my drunken brain, making the insides of my eyes hurt. "Yeah, yeah," I said to it, "I get the picture. You can shut up now."

There was a flashlight under my bed, kept there for just such emergencies. I groped my way to it in utter blackness, feeling smug and competent. It did work. Its sudden white beam stabbed right into my tender eyes. My knees popped as I stood up.

The smoke detector was shining a similar spot of light down onto the hall carpet to my left, as I exited my bedroom. Nothing moved in its frozen aura.

"Mama?" I started up the hallway, aiming the flashlight beam out ahead of me, seeing no sign of either her or smoke. The circle of light made me aware of my blurred vision, but I didn't bother to go back and put in my contact lenses. I knew my way around in here by now, anyway. This was probably just a false alarm, caused by heat lightning or an electrical glitch.

The goddam smoke detector was probably scaring Mama out of whatever was left when all her wits were already gone. I made for the sofa in the TV room, preparing for a really bad case of sundowning behavior.

My flashlight cast galloping black shadows into all the corners, as I padded towards the other end of the house. "Mama? It's okay, Mama. Everything's okay."

I didn't find my mother, but I found a fire. It was just blazing away in the TV room, going up the curtains behind my father's recliner, in a white-orange so voracious and bright that my eyes screamed. The stack of Daddy's old *National Geographics* underneath the window was lit up like a bonfire. On the carpet near the sofa lay my mother's opened purse, a squashed pack of cigarettes, and several wooden kitchen matches.

I took off for the nearby kitchen and the fire extinguisher, finally discovering it under the sink, yanking off its protective band and pulling its handle, praying that it would work. It worked, and I sprayed white foam all over the blazing magazines and curtains. But I could see through the collapsing ceiling into the attic, and brilliant orange flames were already up there. They had already shorted out the house's wiring.

The cell phone lay in the middle of the kitchen table. I lifted it, and watched my fingers dial 911 in the wavering firelight. I heard my voice giving the dispatcher the necessary information, while my abandoned flashlight rolled on its side to the edge of the table and then fell off.

Pick up your flashlight and go find your mother, coached my inner self, my emergency self, the clear-headed computerized "Me" whom I had not heard from since that long-ago rape incident in my New York days. *She's not back here, thank God.*

Hello, robot, I thought. Nice of you to drop by.

Yeah, and stupid of you to be drunk. I'm affected, too.

Sorry.

Don't aim the flashlight out in front of you that way, you're not able to take in a whole room at a time in the diameter of one small beam. Aim it at the ceiling, and the light will reflect all over.

I cast the light beam upwards, and the whole blurry hall became dimly visible. I could make out furniture in the living room behind me, and the glare of the burning wing of the house, but couldn't see my mother anywhere. I had to physically go up to each dark lump of furniture and closely inspect it, lest she be curled up beyond the scope of my terribly bad eyes.

When are you going to get yourself some eyeglasses? my robot asked, as I pawed at a big stuffed armchair.

I could smell a lot of smoke now, and wondered how much of my inability to see clearly was myopia, and how much was cloudy smoke. As I stood on the carpet in the hallway and circled to go check the bedrooms, it began to seem as if the air itself was getting whiter. Foggier. Hotter.

It is, said my inner self. *Go. Be quick about it, too.*

Shouldn't I go back into my bedroom and put in my contact lenses first?

Where is your mother? You haven't got the time to waste now to get your lenses put in by flashlight, you moron! This is serious smoke!

So it was. I jogged down the hallway to Mama's bedroom, but the bed was unoccupied. I checked the floor. The closets. Her private bathroom.

"*Mama? Mama?*" I shouted, beginning to panic, my robot coach notwithstanding. It couldn't help me with the unpredictabilities of a demented elderly woman here, who could have gone anyplace at all in this house after her recent cigarette break, hiding under sinks or in pantries for God-only-knew what reason. Velma wasn't somebody that we could outthink, like my long-ago attacker. Thinking was no help here.

I noticed that the smoke detector had knocked off. When had that happened?

"*Elbereth Gilthoniel,*" I muttered, not recalling what these words meant, just having some vague notion that they constituted a prayer, and that this was the only prayer that my subconscious remembered now.

Mama was sprawled in the white sofa in the formal parlor near the front door when I found her, arms folded across her stomach, sleeping peacefully, and inhaling white smoke with every calm breath. It did no good for me to wonder how she had ignored the smoke detector, so close by. If I had had the wits to look in here first, among the brass and glass and framed photographs, the polished dark woods of end tables and coffee table, I would have discovered her right off.

I stooped to shake her and pull her up, and she was a warm and limp weight. I shook her some more, jiggled her up and down, tried to get her awake and focused. "Mama! Mama!"

She opened her eyes and just looked at me.

I stepped to a window and undid the latch. *You'll be giving the fire more oxygen,* warned my robot, and I knew that it was correct about that. But the fire was still at the other end of the house for the moment, and we needed oxygen ourselves very much, right here and now. I opened the window with a creaking of my back, and warm night air was sucked into the room.

The reflected orange glow grew vastly brighter, several rooms away. I could hear it now, its crackling and chewing.

Big mistake, said my inner coach. *Get her up, and get out of here.*

But Mama, bless her heart, light sleeper that she was, had already gotten to her feet behind my back, and was shuffling, unconcerned, towards the doorway to the hall in the aura of the flashlight. Maybe she was going for another cigarette.

I didn't know whether to leave the window up or down. Its draft was sucking the smoke in the room on back towards the firelight, but making the blaze more ferocious. *Close it,* said my robot. So I did. *Grab your mother. Be calm. Don't get her upset.*

So I took up my flashlight and intercepted Velma and got her turned around, and we made our very serene and deliberate way to the nearby front door.

And that's when I remembered, even before I tried to turn the doorknob: *The keys were on the dinette table in a fucking dish full of fake fruit, at the kitchen end of the house.* And the kitchen was an inferno by now.

"Oh, *fuck!*" I shrieked out loud. I tried to turn the doorknob anyway, but it was as unyielding as if all its moving parts had been welded together. And the brass of it felt scorching to my hot hand. The air inside the house was hotter now than any Auletta August noon. Drops of perspiration rolled down my face and fell off my chin onto my wrist.

"Wha moons vic?" said Mama.

I let go of her and ran to the window, and swept it with my flashlight, and my disbelieving eyes took in the dull shine of burglar bars outside its pane. Impregnable steel burglar bars festooned the window from top to bottom, black and lacy like French Quarter balcony iron, bolted into its very frame. With a *really* serious oh-shit feeling rising in me now like gorge, I galloped from room to room, from the parlor to first one bedroom and then the others, to the living room and back, finding everywhere the same thing. My father had been so thorough, so foresighted, that there were even steel burglar bars on the tiny bathroom windows.

Finally, drained by my tour, I came again before the paneled wooden front door, and pounded futilely at its surface, furious at the fears and follies of old people, as my mother stood in the dimness of the flashlight spillover and watched. The door was thinnest at its inset rectangular panels. But even broken out of their frames, the panels would leave openings too small for us to crawl through.

Maybe.

Stymied, I leaned both hands against the hard wood and stood with my head down, thinking about the hammer in the kitchen utility drawer. It might as well be on the moon. I rubbed my fingers over the door's hinges and wondered if I could remove their screws in time, even if I could come up with a screwdriver substitute. How long would it take the Auletta Volunteer Fire Department to get out here to us? How far did they have to come?

"What I need is an ax," I thought out loud, speaking it. "*Damn!*"

"C. Ray's big sword is under my bed," my mother said very clearly, saving me.

I raised my head and stared at her, and very much wished that I had had my contacts in so that I could have seen her face in that one instant of clarity. But her face was a blur to me. I'll never know what expression she wore at that unlooked-for moment. In my memories of the fire now, I tend to picture her as she once had been, very long ago, during the hurricane blackouts of my childhood, because that's what her voice had sounded like. But I know that she was instead her stooped old self that night, gray hair all on end, her feet splayed, as she waited.

"So it is, Mama," I breathed finally, nodding, able to take a deep breath of what oxygen there was now. And I took her by the hand in case her clearheadedness was as temporary as I feared it would be—I couldn't have her wandering off again. Aiming the flashlight ahead of her feet, I guided her down the hall to the master bedroom, where I firmly held onto her with one hand, and stooped and groped under the bed with the other. I touched cool metal. The solid, gleaming weight of my father's claymore slid across the soft carpet, out into the light.

The thing was much heavier than I had remembered, longer than I had remembered. I held it tip-down, out before us, as we made our way back to the front door amid the thickening smoke. *Hurry,* warned my inner personality. *The fire is upon you.*

Yeah, orange light licked the ceiling, coming from the livingroom now. The flashlight was no longer necessary. I didn't know if that was bad or good.

Having no idea what suffocation would feel like, I expected both of us to be coughing our heads off, but we weren't doing all that much coughing. I wondered if I should risk another opened window. *No!* said my robot immediately. *The flames will explode all over.*

The metal hilt of the claymore was very hot now. I grasped it in both hands, stood before the front door, and took an experimental side swing.

Pussy move! taunted my robot, unimpressed, as the tip of the sword sank into the wood just far enough for me to have some difficulty jerking it free. *Don't do it sideways, like a girl.*

Get your back into it. Bring it over your head.

It'll catch on the ceiling that way! I objected. The ceiling's too low. I'm going to have to swing sideways.

Then think Babe Ruth. But hop to it. Quick. And remember Velma.

"Mama?" I turned, and saw to my alarm that she was five paces up the hall now, wandering off again. Did the fire mean nothing to her? Even an animal would run from fire, not towards it!

At my own wit's end, I ran for her and seized her roughly, turned her around again, and then just shoved her inside the door of the nearest bedroom. Her blurred, expressionless face disappeared from my sight as I slammed the door against it. Maybe it would be too dark in there for her to become oriented enough to find the doorknob and escape. Maybe the smoke would be thinner in there. At any rate, I needed both my hands for my job at the door, if either of us was going to get out of here. And I needed to be able to swing that very long and heavy weapon, without worrying about slashing her if she shuffled in too close.

My eyes watered. My breath came short.

Excuse me for a moment, time out, I told my robot, actually holding up one hand, palm out. I think I oughta first go into the bathroom and wet a towel or something, and wrap it around my nose and mouth like all the fire safety experts tell you to do.

No! It said. *No time! Strike!*

The smoke is thinner, near the floor. And I'm very tall. Shouldn't I be down on the floor, for more oxygen?

Can you swing a claymore from down on the floor?

The robot had a point. I felt no emotion as I obediently went back to the front door, planted my feet, and then positioned the sword slightly over my shoulder and to my right, like a baseball bat.

Are you waiting for dramatic soundtrack music here? Strike!

I released the tension in the muscles of my shoulders, my arms, my torso, and swung with all my weight. The blade hit the wood on its heavier crosspiece, and the shock of the impact astonished me with its violence. It had been like clubbing a cement bunker. Sudden pain flooded my wrists and arms and shoulders. I felt like I had been kicked.

Wake up, coached my inner self. *Do it again.*

Wood trapped the blade now, and I jerked with ferocity to free it. But I saw that it had bitten very deeply into the crosspiece, splintering a nearby rectangle of paneling. Tiny slivers of streetlight shone through the cracks.

Look at that! said my robot.

You liked that? Watch *this*:

The air whistled with the force of my next blow, and the big blade hacked right through the weakened paneling. I yelled like a battle queen when I saw the mercury vapor glow pouring now from the tall curb lights through the opening, and I used the hilt of the claymore to knock almost all of the wood out of the jagged rectangular hole.

The fresh night wind whooshed inside through it, feeding the fire.

You're too big to crawl through, my robot commented, but I already knew. And if I was going to get Mama out at all, I had to go for those crosspieces. I was a big girl, yes, but maybe a very big girl is what it would take to get this deed done. My back and shoulders were already primed. I was conscious of the the carpet under my bare feet, and willed both of my soles to stick right there.

"*Elbereth Gilthoniel!*" I screamed suddenly, thinking that I was hearing myself speaking Scots Gaelic in my madness. It wouldn't be until tomorrow that I would realize that I had actually been hollering in fictional Elvish. "*Clar Innis! Clar Innis!*"

. . . but that last bit *was* Scots, all right, the ancient battle cry of Clan Buchanan. And I swung that sucker for my mother and my father, for my brother and for my son, for all my hairy and tartaned ancestors, for the future I still wanted to see. Those considerable but overlooked laundry-toting muscles in my back and shoulders and arms drove the blade of my Daddy's claymore right through the wood of the crossbeams with a heaving crash, and I shrieked a wordless howl as I saw the wood grain separate. Screaming, I reared back for a second hack, and a third, and a fourth, until the door was a framed ruin. I positioned myself for a fifth, sweating, yelling, consumed, a complete Celtic savage. All I needed was the smears of blue woad on my body. My own strength had become a drug.

Hey! said my robot. *Take it easy. Don't have a heart attack. You're free.*

So I was.

I let the sword rest tip-down through the opening in the destroyed door, and blinked my streaming eyes against the incoming wind and the light of the streetlamps. Fire roared overhead and ate at the roof.

You're free, said my robot again, *just like you always wanted. Without lifting a finger to bring it about, even. Yay.*

Like I didn't have to lift this giant fucking sword?

You know what I mean. You can leave here, now. Move away from this place, in honor. Leave this town. You'll even have insurance money, you and Rocky. You're the sole inheritors.

I did know what this voice was driving at, in this slow-motioned moment. I did understand where it was going. But I had to ask: What about Mama?

The fire was her fault. An investigation will bear that out. You did all you could.

I'm not doing all I can, right now, I panted, turning around at the opened doorway, going all the way back inside. I know exactly where I left her. The fire isn't there yet. She'll still be in that bedroom, shuffling along, mumbling nonsense to herself, probably not the least bit frightened. She could die of smoke inhalation.

Easily.

You're not a very nice person, I told my inner self, and put down my claymore, and started back up the hot and smoky hallway to the room where I had left my mother. Are you my God? My own personal "voice," like Saint Joan heard all the time? I'm glad I don't hear you more, if you're going to behave like this. If I'm going to dissociate, I need to develop nicer multiple personalities.

Jeanne, it said, *you have one final FINAL lesson to learn here in Auletta: Be careful what you wish for . . .*

Because it might come true. I've heard that one. Trite.

Do you understand that you had a choice here?

Yes, I said, as I turned the burning doorknob to the bedroom.

Remember that.

I won't. I'll be just as fretful and complaining, just as evil-tempered and self-pitying as ever, in a few days, as soon as I find myself stuck with Mama again. In new surroundings, in a new prison somewhere, I will loudly resume bemoaning the miseries of my fate.

Remember.

I opened the door.

"C. Ray was here," Mama said in a little-girl voice to my sooty and scary self, when I came through the exit of her own roaring prison, and took her by the hand, and led her out. Unworried, unhurried, she accompanied me without struggle or argument, as we passed through the boiling hallway, through all of the windy white smoke that was my father's books going up in ashes, and stepped through the shattered front door.

The fire truck approached like a blurry red dragon, in noise and light. We two crept carefully down the front steps and stood watching in the garden, hand in hand, in silence, while our collected and tangible family memories disappeared in the crackle and the roar— photograph albums, baby books, my old high school yearbook; Daddy's Highlander lithographs, Mama's wedding dress, the oak dresser that Rocky and I had played "Saloon" with. Somewhere in the fire storm was my old ballerina doll, Nina. Somewhere was my wretched diary.

The firefighters galloped before us with shouts and hoses, in a choreographed dance of male purposefulness. But I saw that the house was beyond saving. The smoke that I had inhaled made me vomit, and I leaned over and puked into the clover where my father's claymore lay nearby. I saw, even without my contacts, how big and dirty my feet were. How unhandsome, how ordinary, my forearm and wrist.

I was supposed to remember something, but all of our memories were going. The night roared like a beast.

I wiped my mouth on my filthy biceps, and took my mother's liver-spotted hand, and squeezed it gently.

"C. Ray," she said.

Those were the last intelligible words my mother Velma ever spoke.

Acknowledgments

I get by with a little help from my friends.

I especially want to thank Phyllis Alltmont, Sallie Lowenstein, Joe Ory, and Tom Rayer Jr., for reading and commenting on the various drafts while this thing was taking shape. Their points of view have been invaluable, and the time and trouble they spent on it have made it a much better book. I just wish I had the talent to write up to their expectations and visions.

Thanks are due Marcia Hartwig, also, who suggested the idea; Marcel Wisznia, who gave me the computer and tech support; and Emory M. Thomas, who put me in touch with Hill Street Press.

Marie Thompson helped me find the time to begin the first draft, and the Alzheimer's Association chapter of Columbia, S.C., kept me from going crazy. Sheila Hyman shared her memories of New Orleans as it used to be. Ian Shoales (dude!) commiserated.

Finally, Judy Long, my patient editor, and Tom Payton, publisher, have taken up the project and are making it happen—elegantly.

But I can't sign off without mentioning my own mother and father, Gennette and William Harper, who lived out their own happy love affair, did their dead-level best to raise us right, and fought their own final illnesses with a bravery, grace, and good humor that will always have the power to choke me up. They loved us, and they weren't bashful about telling us and showing us how much they loved us, either. My sister Donna Thompson was on hand for all of that, just as she is on hand for all of this. And because her love and support is always there for me, all of my little stories, when you get right down to it, will always be for her.

Reading
Group
Guide

Reading Group Guide

1. Why do you think this novel was written from a single point of view? Is such close focus on Jeanne effective or claustrophobic? Is it valid for her to relate the experiences and states of mind of other characters—Larry, Rocky, Velma—even though she admits she can't know for sure what they are thinking?

2. How likely is it that the adolescent resentment she felt for her mother in the past colors everything she says about Velma now? Did that resentment stem only from envy? What other things has Jeanne held against her mother? What does she hold against her father?

3. Are Jeanne's ferocious witticisms a weapon against others, or a coping mechanism? Are anyone else's feelings ever hurt by them? How complicit does the reader become, reading her thoughts? Does she ever carry us across that line? What does this say about her mental health?

4. Can Jeanne be as ugly as she feels herself to be? Why is physical beauty such an issue with her? What other kinds

of beauty are touched on in this novel, and why are they relevant?

5. Despite the eventual failure of her marriage, is Larry a good match for Jeanne? Is the friendship that springs up between his mother and Jeanne genuine, or does it seem superficial? If her own parents' marriage had not been such a fairytale romance, would Jeanne be a better wife to Larry, or an even less suitable one?

6. What role does their father, C. Ray, play in this family? How accurate can Jeanne's perceptions of him be? Has he left his childhood home and family behind in South Carolina because he wanted to escape them, or rather because he was pursuing something?

7. In how objective a light is C. Ray able to see his daughter Jeanne? How clearly does Velma see her? Does Jeanne genuinely want to be understood?

8. What, besides Jeanne's diary, are symbols of memory in this novel? What significance is there in the repetition of color— Rocky's red cowboy hat, Velma's red lipstick and nail polish, C. Ray's red hair? How does color relate to memory? Are there correlations between the fading of both?

9. When is memory loss presented as a positive thing in Jeanne's narration? What similarities are there between memory loss and forgiveness? Is Jeanne capable of true forgiveness? Do you think she ever forgives the rapist?

10. Jeanne notes that her sister-in-law, Barbara, pursues her own happiness above all else, but has Barbara ever been happy? Who is the happiest character in the novel? Does the author

present happiness as something that can be consciously sought and won?

11. Who suffers the most from Velma's Alzheimer's disease during its earliest stages? Does C. Ray recognize it for what it is? Why can't he be more specific with his children about his fears? Is he protecting Rocky's marriage, or is he merely in denial? Does Jeanne attribute to C. Ray the same heroism she'd like to be able to claim for herself? How accurate is the narrative's definition of heroism?

12. How easy is it to empathize with Velma as her disease progresses, given that a later-stage Alzheimer's patient can't communicate? Jeanne tries to make it possible for us to "get inside" her mother's head, but how successful is she? Does she attempt to use any of that empathy in her own dealings with Velma? Is she truly giving the situation all she has, or is she holding something back?

13. Alzheimer's disease frequently touches off explosions of suspicion and resentment among members of the family members. Why hasn't that happened between Jeanne and Rocky? Knowing what we know about them, is their good relationship likely to be maintained after the events of the novel's final chapters, or will it suffer?

14. How does Jeanne's memory of the way she herself was parented influence the raising of her own son, Conrad? It appears to take her longer to understand Conrad than it takes for her to understand anybody else in her life. Is this an inability on her part, or denial? Is Conrad the only person she has failed to understand? What about Velma? Do you think Jeanne has ever really understood her mother, even by the novel's end?

15. When Jeanne says that love isn't always a noun, that sometimes it's really a verb, what does she mean? Jeanne describes herself as cold. Does this mean she's incapable of love in its emotional, "noun" sense?

16. What do you think happens to Jeanne and Velma immediately after the fire? What will happen to them in a week's time? In a month? A year? Does thinking about a likely ending make the beginning of the novel more significant or less so?

Discussion questions were prepared by the author.